Mulligan's Yard

www.**booksattransworld**.co.uk

MULLIGAN'S YARD

Ruth Hamilton

BANTAM PRESS

LONDON • NEW YORK • TORONTO • SYDNEY • AUCKLAND

TRANSWORLD PUBLISHERS
61–63 Uxbridge Road, London W5 5SA
a division of The Random House Group Ltd

RANDOM HOUSE AUSTRALIA (PTY) LTD
20 Alfred Street, Milsons Point, Sydney
New South Wales 2061, Australia

RANDOM HOUSE NEW ZEALAND (PTY) LTD
18 Poland Road, Glenfield, Auckland 10, New Zealand

RANDOM HOUSE SOUTH AFRICA (PTY) LTD
Endulini, 5a Jubilee Road, Parktown 2193, South Africa

Published 2000 by Bantam Press
a division of Transworld Publishers

A catalogue record for this book
is available from the British Library.

ISBN 0593 045858

Typeset in 11/12pt Times by Falcon Oast Graphic Art

Printed in Great Britain
by Mackays of Chatham plc, Chatham, Kent

1 3 5 7 9 10 8 6 4 2

For Diane Pearson, the best editor in the world . . .

. . . .

. . . . probably

(no apology to lager brewers, by the way)

I thank you, Diane, for nursing me through thirteen books, for teaching me so much, for your forbearance with this difficult woman. Most of all, I thank you for your friendship, your loyalty and your humour.
God bless you and yours.

Apologies

If there is a Makersfield in Texas, I am sorry that I used the name herein.

The crematorium in Bolton was built much later than 1921 – I beg licence.

Any religious community bearing a name similar to the one in this novel should be aware that I mean no disrespect to its founders and fellowship.

Acknowledgements

My family – Alice, David, Michael, Susan and Elizabeth.
Dorothy Ramsden, researcher, Bolton.
Members of America On Line who also helped with research.
Staff at Bolton Central Library.
Sweetens Books of Bolton, who provided me with
information.
The Rev. Geoff Garner and his wife, Elisabeth, for
investigating crematoria throughout Britain.
All my friends for sensing when to visit and when
to stay away!
Father Albert Shaw of St Helen's Church,
my friend and confessor.

I say goodbye to Jenny Byrne, who died in June 2000.

ONE

Diane Hewitt was as bright as a button. She could run like a racehorse, was light-fingered, crafty, and several shopkeepers in Bolton were on the look-out for her.

In her younger, slightly more innocent years, her gamine appearance had won hearts, but once belts tightened in the wake of the Great War, the charity in people's souls began to run dry. Many had their own families to worry about. Widows wept, mothers grieved, crippled soldiers begged on street corners.

So Diane went into the business of finding things. She found bread, milk, fruit, vegetables and, on good days, purses with an odd sixpence or two wedged into folds of worn leather beneath pennies and farthings. She could be in and out of a back kitchen or a scullery without the busy householder noticing any draught created by an opening door.

At the age of ten-going-on-eleven, Diane broadened her horizons. She picked carefully from a crowd of eager applicants, choosing children who, like herself, were thin and swift, boys and girls with lines of hunger and disappointment already etched into fine, undernourished skin. The rules were few and simple. Groups were formed, scenarios planned, babies, dogs and cats borrowed. A child crying over a lost pet could empty shops and houses in seconds, while a wailing baby was worth a fortune, especially on market days. Like a seasoned

11

choreographer, Diane Hewitt trained the members of her chorus line to slick perfection.

On a windy March Tuesday in 1921, Diane discovered the wash-house. It was situated in a square originally called Massey's Yort, now titled Mulligan's Yard. Rumour had it that an Irish card-sharp had won the yard and its buildings at the turn of an ace, but Diane could not have cared less about names and origins. Her attention was riveted firmly to the present day. She didn't care who owned what – as long as she got her unfair share.

She pressed an inquisitive nose against a steam-misted rear window and watched women doing battle with sheets, possers, scrubbers and mangles. Tilly and Mona Walsh were in charge of the huge laundry. Spinster sisters built like battleships, they were poor movers, not at all hasty off the mark. Diane knew the two women from the Temple of Eternal Light, a new faith that had started to burgeon in Bolton's Deane and Daubhill. Yes, she had seen this pair bobbing and scraping about in the congregation.

A woman brushed past Diane, turbaned head lumpy with steel curlers, workday clogs slapping the cobbles, a pramload of washing in front of a shapeless body clad in a bottle green coat. She entered the building, walked to a desk and handed money to Miss Tilly Walsh. After this transaction was complete, the customer passed her purse to Miss Tilly for safekeeping, then hobbled off to claim a place at one of the massive sinks.

Diane's gaze was glued to the older Miss Walsh. She was mountainous, a great deal fatter than Miss Mona, with several wobbly chins, a huge belly and legs like twin oak trees. Tilly Walsh took the purse and placed it under the counter. The child's blue eyes narrowed as she counted the laundry's occupants. About twelve, she reckoned, though there might have been a couple more behind the steam-heated drying cupboards. Easy pickings? How best to play this one? Lost dog, a sick baby, an accident in Mulligan's Yard?

Serious thinking set in. Wandering back on to Deansgate, Diane Hewitt sat herself on one of the steps leading into the Red Lion coaching house. The Red Lion was an unmentionable place in the Hewitt household. Diane's mother

12

used to borrow a room here, a place where she had taken men. Of course, once the landlord had cottoned on to Brenda Hewitt's doings, he had kicked her out and had sacked the member of staff who had made the arrangements. Shortly after that event, Diane's mother had packed a cardboard suitcase and had left the family slum in John Street for ever. A nearly-orphan with a frail brother, the daughter of Brenda Hewitt was now fighting for survival.

She sucked a thumb, chewed on the filthy, broken nail. Perhaps it wouldn't be for ever. Mam might come back with a load of money from all the men she was going with in London or some such place. Tuesday. The wash-house would be fuller on Mondays. Mam wasn't a nice woman, anyway. Gran was always going on about how horrible Mam was. A fuller wash-house would mean more purses, more money. But it would also mean more folk, more eyes, more chances of getting caught. The Misses Walsh were slow and fat, but many of Bolton's housewives were quick, thin, and used to defending their property in the face of young marauders.

She must not sit here for too long. The School Board had men on the look-out for children these days. There was even a rumour that those who truanted too frequently might be taken away and put in orphanages. As a breadwinner, Diane had responsibilities. If she went to school every day, she'd have fewer chances of getting her hands on food or money. But she had better start putting in the odd appearance: an orphanage place could mean that her younger brother and her grand-mother might starve.

A shadow fell across her body, so she shifted sideways to allow its owner into the hotel. In a way, an orphanage was almost attractive. Three square meals, clean clothes, no messing about and stealing . . . What about Joe and Gran, though? The shadow remained. When, after several further seconds, no one ascended the steps, she glanced upwards at a tall, dark-haired man dressed all in black.

'And what are you doing here, young lady?' he asked.

Diane made no reply. He was Irish. Gran had ordered Diane to stay away from Irish people. They were usually drunk or Catholic, sometimes both.

13

'Shouldn't you be at school?' the shadow asked.

She lifted a bony shoulder. 'Nits,' she replied, then added, 'and fleas,' for good measure.

He leaned on an ebony cane. 'Wouldn't it be a good idea to go home and clean yourself, in that case?'

Again, she shrugged listlessly.

'Well, you can't stay here. We don't want the hotel catching fleas, do we? You could infect the whole building.'

He didn't need that cane, mused Diane. He wasn't old. Idly, she wondered how much the silver-crowned item might bring if offered to a second-hand stall on the market. She stopped gnawing at her thumb. 'Fleas can't jump that far.' She jerked the chewed thumb over her shoulder in the direction of the foyer.

'But they might jump from you to me,' he argued reasonably.

She awarded him her full attention. No flea on God's earth could ever possess the temerity to light on such a man. From her present position in life, low down on the Red Lion's steps, he looked as big as the giant in *Jack and the Beanstalk*. 'You'll never have fleas.' Her tone was flat.

'Won't I, now?'

'You're too clean.' He owned the appearance of someone who took a bath every day.

'Nonsense.' He stooped over her slightly. 'A flea doesn't know the difference between dirty and clean. All it wants is a free ride and an ample supply of blood.'

'Eh?' Dark eyebrows raised themselves. 'Blood?'

'What else did you think they feed on, child? That's why they bite. They're blood-suckers.'

Diane Hewitt had never given a thought to the domestic and social arrangements of lower life forms. Fleas bit folk. Everybody recognized flea-bites. Like freckles, they appeared on the skin before disappearing or relocating from front to back, leg to arm, hand to foot. 'So . . . so fleas eat us?'

He nodded gravely. 'See, I'm standing here next to you, am I not?'

'Yes.'

'If fleas were athletes, they'd beat every human being into a cocked hat. They can jump so far – well – it would be like one of us leaping over a cloud.'

14

'Like the giant in *Jack and the Beanstalk*?' This fellow could clear the Town Hall clock if he set his mind to it. And his cane would clear half-a-crown and all. He talked a bit like a teacher, though he was a sight more interesting than most of the dried-up sticks in Diane's school.

'Exactly,' he said. 'So a few might leap from you to me, then from me to someone inside the inn. Why, there'd be murder done if the best hotel in Bolton became infested.'

She understood now. The creatures on her body were both threat and asset. 'I'll go away for sixpence,' she announced bravely. 'For a shilling, I'll stop away.' She spat on her hand, then pushed the wet palm against her chest. 'Promise. Hope to die if I don't keep my word.'

He smiled.

'It's not funny,' Diane insisted. 'I'm serious.'

'Are you, now?'

She didn't want to like him. In fact, she needed to hate him, because he was one of them, one of the folk who dressed well and hung on to money so that proper people couldn't eat or have a decent set of clothes. And he was Irish into the bargain. Mr Wilkinson down at the Temple of Light was always going on about Catholics and all that kind of stuff. 'Yes, I'm serious. I've got something you don't want, so you can pay me to keep it to myself.'

'Ah. A business arrangement, so.'

'That's right'. He was good-looking, she admitted grudgingly. Big broad shoulders, large brown eyes, some black curls peeping out beneath the brim of a tall hat. His voice was soft, fascinating, the sort of voice that might put you to sleep if he read a story out loud. 'It's business,' she snapped.

He looked at his watch. 'And if I don't pay?' What a bright child this was. Thin, straggly brown hair hung over her forehead, almost obscuring eyes that seemed to cut through to his core. The irises were dark blue, the cheekbones as fine as he had ever seen. 'What if I get the police?'

He would not do that. Diane stared into his face and saw something for which she could find no name. It wasn't pity or sympathy – she had the ability to recognize such expressions. No, it was as if he already knew her, as if he'd known her always.

15

'Or the School Board man? I could go and fetch him.'

'I told you – I've got fleas.'

He pulled a silver disc from a pocket. 'A florin,' he said. 'But don't push your luck, Miss ... What is your name?'

Her mouth watered. Two bob. But he held the money aloft while awaiting her answer.

He coughed impatiently.

'Mary Pickavance,' she replied, after a short spell of hesitation.

His head shook slowly. 'I don't think so. Give me your full name and address – don't worry, I won't visit as long as you behave yourself. It's just that I like to have some idea of my money's destination.'

She wavered. 'Diane Hewitt, number thirteen John Street,' she admitted eventually.

'And your parents?'

She sighed. They were all the same, this type. They either wanted to know everything, or they ignored you completely. Busybodies and Couldn't Care Lesses, Gran called them. 'My dad died in the war. My mam ... she went away. There's me, our Joe and my gran. Joe's got crooked legs and Gran's got no heart.'

Immobilized by this final piece of information, the man waited for further news.

'Rickets,' offered Diane. 'Our Joe caught rickets.'

'And your grandmother?'

'She went poorly when Dad got killed. Mrs Atherton next door told me my gran lost all heart after Dad died and ... and ...'

'And what?'

She took a deep breath. 'And after Mam went no good. She used to be no good in Bolton, but now she's no good somewhere else. Gran lives in the kitchen. Mr Atherton brought her bed down when she lost her heart.' Why was she telling him all this? The truth, the whole truth, nothing but the truth, all for a measly two bob?

He gave her the coin. Something was stirring in the region of his stomach, a feeling he recalled from childhood. But remembered hunger was one thing; hunger contained now

16

within this small scrap of flesh and bone was more urgent. 'Diane?'

'What?'

'How do you get by?' He noticed that the blue eyes were old, too knowledgeable for a person of such tender years.

'We get some off the welfare – Gran calls it parish pennies. Then the Temple folk send stuff on a Friday – bread and a bit of meat, like. Our Joe cleans fireplaces and does a bit of stepstoning for old folk, then I . . . well, I get what I can.'

'Stealing?'

Lying to such a person was strangely difficult. 'I look round the market at closing time. There's fruit and that on the floor, stuff nobody wants, gone a bit off, some of it. Leaves fall off cabbages. If you get enough leaves, you can cook them as if they're a real cabbage. I run errands and do bits of jobs.'

At last, he placed her. This was one of several who had been standing outside when Freddie Williams had lost over two pounds of sausage, a shank of ham and three rabbits. There had been a small gang, a member of which had fallen next to a tram outside the butchery. While much screaming and wailing had ensued, two ragamuffins had nipped into the unsupervised shop and relieved Freddie of a substantial amount of merchandise.

She squirmed under his steady gaze. 'We have to eat,' she said. 'For some of us, it's . . . well, it's steal or die.'

'I know.'

'Are you one of them Catholics?' she asked, seeking a change of subject. His eyes were boring into her, cutting through, seeing her as she really was.

'I am.'

Catholicism was one of Gran's pet hates. Catholics bred like mice, according to Ida Hewitt. When they weren't having babies, they went round sinning as often as they liked, because they could get away with murder. All they had to do was tell the priest, give him a few coppers, then they could just go and do whatever they wanted all over again. Mr Wilkinson said Catholics had never seen the Light and would not see the Light in a million years. They worshipped what he called icons and plaster statues, then drank themselves stupid as soon as they got paid. Their children were always dying, because there were

17

too many of them, and their fathers spent food money on Satan's liquor.

'What's on your mind?' the man enquired now.

'Eh? Oh, I were just thinking, like, about sins.' Her sins could never be forgiven until she could look into the Light and see the Almighty. She was a terrible sinner, too. 'Can a priest really get rid of your sins? Like if you pinched some things or killed somebody, would it not matter to a Mick?'

He shook his head. 'Not quite as easy as all that, Diane. If we steal, we have to return the property before being forgiven. As for murder, well, there is no forgiveness for that until the murderer gives himself up to the police.'

Diane's eyes were huge. 'But I thought, well, I—'

'A lot of people think, child. My religion is not the easy option.'

'Neither is mine,' she breathed. Her religion was becoming a pain in the neck, because she could never get away from it. There was thanksgiving for the Light every Wednesday, celebration of the Light on Sundays, bearing of the Light on Fridays, beauti-fication of the temple on a rota basis, then the bringing of the Light to 13 John Street whenever Mr Wilkinson felt like it. The beautification was the worst, since it involved brooms, shovels, mops and a lot of polishing. 'Have you heard of the Light?'

He had. 'Are you one of the Temple?'

She nodded. 'I'm a loud-it-ary.'

'Laudatory,' he corrected.

'That's what I said. I have to get cleansed soon. Then I might get made up to a bearer. Mind, you have to have a white frock. I don't think I'll be able to get one.' She didn't really want to be a bearer, anyway. Bearers got taken under Mr Wilkinson's wing. It was something to do with some foolish virgins in the Bible, and Mr Wilkinson made sure that his virgins didn't go daft like the ones in his Great Book.

The man reached out and touched her cheek. 'Well, Diane Hewitt of thirteen John Street, I'd better away and carry on with my business.'

Diane shook herself out of the reverie. 'What is your business?' she asked unexpectedly.

18

'This inn, the yard, a couple of farms, some shops, cottages – shall I go on?'

She jumped up. 'You're him, aren't you?'

'Yes, I suppose I must be.'

'The gambler.' There was an accusatory edge to her words.

'No. My father was the gambler.'

She swallowed hard. According to Mr Wilkinson, gambling was the greatest sin, and Catholics gambled all the time. They were forever having raffles and games of lotto, grand Christmas draws, Easter draws, tombolas, shove ha'penny stalls, guess your weight, how many raisins in a cake. 'Gambling's bad,' she mumbled.

'Perhaps.'

'And my gran says your dad would have put money on a dead horse.'

'True. It was his weakness.'

She considered that, deciding that she had done nearly enough thinking for one day. But her mental machinery seemed to have stuck in gear. 'Is a weakness the same as a sin?'

'Sometimes. Not always, though. A weakness has to be fought against, but occasionally it can overcome a person.' This young girl was of a cerebral disposition and, in spite of her reputation for thievery, Diane Hewitt displayed a strong sense of morality. 'Be off now,' he said.

She remained where she was. This was Mulligan. Mulligan was a miserable chap who would not get off his horse to save a blind man. He was tough on his tenants, never had a kind word for anybody, was not the sort to stop and give two shillings to a dirty, ill-dressed, nail-biting girl. 'Everybody hates you,' she advised him, her tone conversational.

'I know.'

'You've no friends.'

He laughed. 'Is that a fact, now?'

She nodded. 'So why are you being nice to me?' This was no Mr Wilkinson. She shivered suddenly. Some of the white-clad virgin bearers of the Light looked a bit shaky when emerging from the inner sanctum. Mr Wilkinson took them in there one at a time to cleanse them, and he often looked sweaty and afraid when he came out. The chief guardian of the Light was

19

oily, but there was no grease attached to this tall, dark man. So if Mr Wilkinson, who was supposed to be good, was not really good, and if James Mulligan, who was bad, was good, then—

'Diane?'

'Eh?'

'Give your brain a rest.' He patted her head and strode into the inn.

Diane tossed the coin, caught it deftly. Fish and chips all round soon. It had been an interesting sort of day. She'd almost forgotten about the wash-house, but she would give it some thought later on. Whistling in a fashion that would not have suited a bearer, she made off in the direction of food. Dismissing thoughts of Light versus Catholicism, she went about the business of filling Hewitt bellies.

As soon as she entered her house, Diane sensed the presence of the guardian. From the midst of a hundred household smells, she caught his sickly odour. It came, she thought, from the stuff he layered on his hair, a kind of gluey application that enabled him to wind thin strands back and forth across a fast-balding pate. Well, bugger him, she thought irreverently. Here she stood, fish and chips three times with salt, vinegar and batter-scraps all wrapped in newspaper, and the guardian had to choose today to bring the Light to Gran.

She entered the kitchen, walked past the end of Ida Hewitt's bed, then placed her bundle in the oven. She stoked the fire, added a bit of nutty slack from the bucket, sat in Dad's rocker.

'Diane,' said the guardian, 'come into the Light with us. Praise the Lord.'

She stared blankly at him. He had set a couple of night-lights on a low table by the bed. These he had lit from a glass-sided lantern which, earlier on, would have taken its life from the ever-lasting source in the temple. Mr Wilkinson was not just the Guardian of the Light, he was also an insurance man. He had two homes – one in Noble Street, with his sister, one in Pendleton, a village north of Bolton. Diane wished he would stay in Pendleton with his brother, then he wouldn't keep turning up here. She suspected that he moved about from one place to the other because no one wanted him, not even his family.

'Aren't thou going to pray with us?' he asked.

Diane was not in the mood for prayer. It was hard enough pretending to be a proper laudator three times a week. On top of all her attendances at temple, there was this business to contend with, Guardian Wilkinson on a mission to bring the Word and the Light to Gran at least once a week. What was it all about, anyway? Praising the Lord and telling herself that the Lord would provide? She was the one doing the providing, the stealing—

'Did you hear Mr Wilkinson?' asked Gran.

'Yes.' Fish and chips were never the same if you left them in the oven. The fish went soggy, while chips stuck to the paper and tasted musty.

Mr Wilkinson carried on chanting, thanking God for some burning bush that had appeared in the middle of a place called Texas in America. Diane fixed her eyes on him. He was short and round, and his belly hung over his trousers. He had little eyes like currants stuck in grey, uncooked pastry, while his hands moved a lot, stumpy fingers clinging to each other, then stretching out in front of him, above his head, at each side of his bloated body. He was, Diane thought, just about the ugliest person ever created.

'Pray,' mouthed Gran.

No, she wasn't going to pray.

The visitor glanced at the child. 'Praise and glory,' he said, the words forced between crooked, gappy teeth.

'Fish and chips,' muttered Diane, her stomach rumbling in agreement. Why had Gran joined this daft lot? she wondered. Just before losing heart, Ida had thrown herself into the Temple of Light, had screamed for her dead son, had taken comfort from a man who looked like something off the fair, one of the freaks in those green tents round the edges and away from the rides. A gnome, he was. He should have been an exhibit like the Fat Lady, the Smallest Woman in the World, the Two-Headed Baby.

He finished praying. 'How was school?' he asked.

'All right.'

'Hast thou learned thy Bible verses?'

21

'No.'

He tutted. 'She needs to spend more time with the Good Book, Mrs Hewitt.'

Ida looked at her granddaughter, so thin, so pale and tired. 'If only I could shape meself,' she moaned.

'Thou shalt,' said Peter Wilkinson. 'Just lie there and look into the Light.' He pointed towards the tiny candles. 'The Almighty is in there, Mrs Hewitt. Seek and ye shall find. When you've found Him, you'll be out of that bed in two shakes.' He pulled on an overcoat and picked up his lantern. 'Learn the verses,' he reminded Diane.

Diane waited until he had left the house, then she called her brother. Joe always ran upstairs when the guardian visited. She took the meal from the oven, then blew out the night-lights.

'Diane,' cried Ida.

Diane shrugged. 'No use setting the house on fire, Gran.'

'But . . . but that was the Light.'

'And this,' replied the ten-year-old, 'is food.' She dished out the portions, making sure that little Joe got plenty of fish. She didn't really want to upset Gran, but sometimes, after a hard day, Diane got a bit fed up with her grandmother. It was as if Gran was the younger of the two females in the house, because Diane had all to do and all to worry about. It wasn't right.

'Where did you get money for fish and chips?' asked Ida, her mouth full of cod.

'I did some errands for the doctor.' Lies and more lies.

'Nice,' said Ida.

'Lovely,' grinned Joe.

It was all for him, Diane told herself firmly. For him, she would look after Gran, because there had to be a grown-up with them. If anything happened to Gran, the two children would go into the orphanage. For Joe, she would steal, make do and mend. For herself, well, there were several things she wanted. And a white frock for cleansing was not on the list.

The food was too much for little Joe. He studied his leavings while they cooled, wished with all his heart that he could stoke up against an uncertain tomorrow. Force-feeding himself was not a good idea, since an overloaded stomach often led him down the yard where all would be lost in the lavatory shed.

22

Diane understood. 'One day, Joe,' she whispered.

'One day what?' asked the woman in the bed.

But Diane said no more. One day, there would be a glass bowl on a table, apples, oranges, pears for Joe to pick at. He wouldn't need to wait for mealtimes, because the food would be there all the time. White tablecloths, silver cutlery, thin cups and saucers. A garden, a dog, blue skies, sunshine. One day, she told herself. One day, life would begin.

18 March 1921

Took the Light to Mrs Hewitt. She still cannot get out of her bed. The child is so thin, her soul darkened by sin, yet still untouched, since she has not reached the age of reason and she knows no better. Time will heal. Praise the Lord.

Through the latch hole in the back gate, I saw the girl dragging a zinc bath, struggling as she took it inside the house. The copper must have boiled, because I saw Diane carrying water to the bath tub, a heavy jug in those frail little hands. The grandmother was hideous when unclothed, her flesh loosened by bedrest.

Then the child took her turn, lowering herself into water already sullied by Ida Hewitt. Her bones are thin and sharp, easy to bend, easy to break. Concave belly, no body hair, no secrets to hide.

One day, Diane, I shall cleanse thee not with water, but with the fire in my heart. Praise the Lord.

23

TWO

Louisa Burton-Massey flicked through the pages of her fashion magazine. Not too long ago, she could have afforded the Chanel crêpe-de-Chine suit with its squirrel trim, hip-length cape and narrow, ankle-skimming skirt. Making do was all very well for the younger generation, but Louisa had grown used to the best and was having great trouble settling for anything less.

She sighed heavily. Anything less? Everything was less, was sub-standard, third-rate. Five years she had spent here, at Caldwell Farm, with its smoking chimneys, draughty rooms, noisy and primitive plumbing. It was just as well that Pendleton Grange was not visible from here, because she might well have gone mad had she been forced to look upon all she had lost. No, she hadn't lost anything. Her whole life had been stolen from her, frittered away by the man she had loved so dearly. As far as she was concerned, the price of love had been immeasurably expensive.

'Damn the Irish upstart,' she muttered, in a hiss that fell short of ladylike. So magnanimous this morning, so charitable. He had offered to swap places. To exchange Pendleton for this hovel. She shivered. If only she could have taken him up on that, but—

'Oh, to hell with him,' she cried, throwing her magazine to the floor. Standards were indeed slipping. Why, a few years

24

ago, the words 'damn' and 'hell' had found no purchase in her vocabulary.

Amy dashed in, face flushed from riding, cavalry-twill jodhpurs stained from mucking out and, no doubt, as a result of tumbling from a mount that was far too large and frisky. 'Mother—'

'I do wish you wouldn't ride his horses, Amy, dear.' Margot, the youngest, was the tomboy of the family, though Amy did a fair imitation at times.

'Mother—'

'He is using you as a servant. Why, when we lived at the Grange, you never looked after your own tack, did you? What is going to happen to us?' she wailed dismally. 'How could he? How could your father leave us like paupers?'

Amy blew upward at a darkish blonde tress that had fallen from beneath the peak of her riding hat. Was Mother about to have another of her vapours? And where was that dratted bottle of smelling-salts? 'He pays us to stable his horses,' she said reasonably. 'There isn't enough room in the Grange stables. It's jolly decent of him to allow us to ride Cleo and George.'

'Stupid names for horses,' spat Louisa.

Amy studied her mother. Thin to the point of emaciation, Louisa Burton-Massey was, Amy suspected, as tough as old rope. She had been accustomed from birth to having her own way, and she had taken to poverty as a gourmet would relish tripe and onions. 'Mother, Mr Mulligan spoke to me and—'

'You are not to deal with him,' Louisa snapped. 'How many times must I tell you not to associate with that . . . creature?'

Amy reeled in her temper and held it tightly. 'He seldom speaks to anyone, as we all know to our cost. Had he been more forthcoming, his intentions might have been clearer. He wishes to return the house to us.'

'Really?' screeched Louisa. 'Really? After all we have gone through? Remember the pity, the pretended sadness and sympathy of our friends. Where are our friends now? Disappeared, gone off to richer pickings. I absolutely refuse to be a victim of that man's charity. How should we maintain the place? We have very little capital, no investments to speak of—'

'He has a business plan,' said Amy quietly. 'The income

25

from the properties in town would help, then there's the possibility of opening up the Grange.'

'Opening it up? Like a stately home? It may be a splendid house by local standards, but it's hardly the seat of an earl.'

'I know, but—'

'Amy,' said Louisa, the name squeezed through tightened jaws. 'We have our pride.'

Amy dropped into a chair, dragged off her hat and placed it on a side table. 'We could live in one part of the house and let the other rooms out as a sort of rest home. Well, more of a health hydro, I mean.'

Louisa Burton-Massey was suddenly bolt upright in her chair. 'I see. So our grand Irish neighbour wishes to give back the house, the inn, the business premises in town – oh, how terribly kind he is. And I am to share my home with the sick?'

Amy glanced at the ceiling in the manner of one seeking assistance from the Almighty. 'No, with people who need respite from their everyday lives. Wealthy people, Mother, who would enjoy the countryside, the lake, the woods. We could have a swimming-pool, a Turkish bath, perhaps. There'd be horse-riding, a bit of putting for golfers, a beautician for the ladies, mud baths, tennis in season, walking on the moors, a gymnasium and so forth.'

'Over my dead body,' muttered Louisa, with an air of finality.

Amy slumped downward and placed her right foot on her left knee, sitting exactly as her father had used to sit. Knowing that this annoyed her mother, she sniffed and folded her arms determinedly. She knew that her own behaviour was childish, knew also that her mother was acting like a two-year-old, all tantrums and cross looks.

Louisa closed her eyes, saw him walking up the steps, watched her broken husband struggling to stay on his feet. In the year of Our Lord 1915, Alex Burton-Massey, an officer and a gentleman, had returned prematurely from the war. From that September day, he had been a stranger to his family. What had he seen? What had turned him into that reckless fool? The leg had improved, as had a shrapnel-shattered arm. But his mind, his brain . . .

'Mother?' Amy saw the tears as they began to drip down

Louisa's cheeks. There was no point in upsetting her any further, so Amy placed both feet on the floor, drawing them slightly to one side in the manner of a lady. Not that anyone could look graceful in riding breeches, she supposed.

The eyes flew open, crocodile tears drying miraculously. 'Here you are, Amy, talking as if you agree with Mulligan about the future of your father's family home . . . and to think that you were the one who found his tortured body.'

'Yes.'

Louisa still failed to understand her eldest daughter's composure. Amy had discovered her father's body more than five years ago, when she had been just sixteen. He had hanged himself from a beam in the Grange stables, his face distorted by asphyxia, a note still clutched in a cooling hand. 'I am sorry, my dear girls. This time, I went the whole hog and have disgraced myself completely. Our house, the lands and our properties in Bolton now belong to Thomas Mulligan. I managed to hang on to one of the farms and I must advise you that you will be living at Caldwell after my funeral . . .'

Amy watched her mother's face. Given Louisa's upbringing, her reaction to Father's death was understandable. Louisa had been cosseted, adored, indulged *ad nauseam* by her husband. An only child, she had been the centre of her parents' universe. Now, all that remained was a small part of their legacy. On interest from the remains of her dowry, Louisa was keeping three daughters and two servants, not to mention this house. Yet Amy had always known that her female parent had a special strength, born of stubborn determination and sheer bloody-mindedness. And, after all, Father had been dead for years. For how long was Mother going to mourn? Was Louisa indulging herself? 'Mother?'

'Yes, dear?'

'Mr Mulligan was talking about a partnership.'

Louisa's eyes clouded again at the sound of that dreaded name. 'I have no son to run a business.'

'You have three daughters. And I am as capable as any man, I'm sure.'

'I will not have you working.'

Amy looked at the ceiling. It wanted plaster and two coats

27

of paint. The whole house was in need of repairs – plumbing, window frames, dry-rotted wainscoting. In truth, Amy loved this old place. Pendleton Grange was terribly grand, a fairytale mansion built by her father's forebears. It was not the sort of place where one might slide down banisters or play ping-pong. She bit her lip. 'If you want to return to the Grange, this might be your last chance. As Mr Mulligan said not half an hour ago, we are the bigger family.'

'No,' screamed Louisa, all thoughts of manners completely abandoned. 'I will not creep back like a mange-riddled animal seeking a bolt-hole. Have you no finer feelings? What would people think? What would they say about us then?'

Amy did not know, did not care, offered no response.

'And your father would turn in his grave if I put you and your sisters out to work.'

A puff of sooty smoke billowed out of the fireplace. Automatically, Louisa pressed a perfumed handkerchief to her nose to save it from taking offence.

'So, what are we to do with our lives?' asked Amy. 'Everyone works these days. What about Margot and Eliza? When we were landed, there was, perhaps, a chance of us marrying well. Even so, the daughters of many good families are working now, so why should we be different? In fact, we have a case stronger than most, because we three need more than simple occupations to while away the years before marriage. We must earn money, Mother.' Amy bit her tongue. She had determined not to upset Louisa, yet these words had to be said, so she might just as well hang for the full sheep. 'I am twenty-one,' she stated now.

'I am well aware of your age.' The words were edged with frost.

'And I am legally entitled to make my own decisions.'

The grandmother clock chimed. Elspeth Moorhead staggered in with morning coffee. She waited until Amy had removed her hat from the table, then set the tray down on its surface. 'Will I pour, ma'am?' she asked.

'I'll do it,' said Amy. Poor old Elspeth had so much on her plate. She and her husband were the only resident staff, though a woman from the village came in twice a week to do the heavier chores.

28

Louisa shook her head and waited for the coffee. What on earth was she going to do with this wayward daughter? And what sort of example was Amy setting the other two girls? It was hopeless. Amy had put rather less than her whole heart and soul into exploring the social circuit. Not that Bolton's environs held a lot of possibilities, but these three beautiful girls were surely capable of ensnaring decent, affluent husbands?

Amy could read her mother like an open book. Louisa imagined that marriage was the cure-all for every ill, that her daughters' supposed beauty would overcome every other obstacle in the wedding stakes. Well, it didn't work that way. Money married money, trade married trade, the working classes sought partners within their own spheres. Amy and her sisters did not fit into any category – they belonged nowhere. She handed a cup of coffee to her mother.

Louisa sipped, pulled a face. 'As weak as dishwater. Ask Elspeth to make some more.'

Amy began to bubble inside. She tried to ignore the feeling, told herself to remain calm, but she realized quickly that Mother had gone too far. 'No,' she answered, her voice low. 'I shan't. You take far too much for granted. This house needs caring for, and Elspeth cannot be in two places at once. We are very lucky to have kept her, because she and her husband could earn far more elsewhere. She will be preparing vegetables now, for lunch or for this evening. The coffee will just have to do.'

Louisa's jaw dropped, but she righted her expression quickly.

'And, Mother, when you judge the coffee to be dishwater, I wonder how you manage to know? I daresay you have never contended with dirty crockery.'

'How dare you talk to me like this?'

Amy placed her cup and saucer on the tray, then rose to her feet. 'Because I must. The facts have to be faced squarely. Look at me, please.' She paused until she had the older woman's attention. 'My father gambled away everything he had—'

'I need no reminder of that.'

'Listen, please. For once, stop grieving and hankering after the past. He killed himself. I loved him and I love you so very much. But, oh, you are annoying, blinkered and negative.' She walked to the window in case tears began to flow. 'When I found him, my first feeling was one of intense relief.'

'I beg your pardon?'

'Relief,' Amy repeated. 'His suffering was too great, too huge to be contained.'

'And how would you know?' Sarcasm trimmed Louisa's words.

Amy swivelled, looked her mother in the face. Yes, five years was long enough for Mother to have lived in ignorance. 'Because he talked to me. You were his wife, while I was a chit of sixteen, but he came to me because he knew that you would be upset by his agony. His love for you was boundless.'

Louisa blanched.

'When Father was . . . injured in battle, the chap next to him was blown to kingdom come. Not to put too fine a point on it, there were bits of flesh and bone everywhere – in Father's hair, on his face, even in his mouth. He drank and drank to take away the taste, but he never succeeded. Then he gambled to stop himself thinking and remembering. That one moment of war finished him.' Perhaps Mother might worry rather less about weak coffee now. It was time for her to grow up, time for her to stop reading silly magazines. There was a lot more to life than Worth, Chanel and the level of this year's hemlines.

Louisa remained motionless for several seconds. 'And he told you this,' she said eventually.

'Yes.' She recalled how he had ranted and wept, how he had clung to the hand of his oldest child. In death, even with his face contorted, he had looked comparatively serene. 'You know only too well that the drinking and the gambling were not a part of his true nature, Mother. He was enduring unimaginable mental torture. So he put an end to it.'

Louisa absorbed this unpalatable information. 'He should have told me,' she said at last. 'Me. I was his wife. I might have stopped him.'

'He could not have been stopped by anyone.' Like her father, Amy had tried to take away the taste, had hidden her own terrible anguish from this childish parent and from her sisters. Eliza, twelve months Amy's junior, was a sensitive soul, while Margot, not quite fourteen at the time of her father's

30

suicide, had been far too young to witness Amy's shock. 'It really is time for you to mature, Mother. Finding him like that devastated me but, like him, I was unwilling to cause you further distress. We have nursed you for long enough.'

Louisa focused on her daughter. Of the three girls, this one had the most interesting appearance. Slender yet strong, with dark blonde hair and huge brown eyes, Amy might have been described in theatrical terms as a show-stopper. Eliza, paler and more ethereal, was possessed of her own fine beauty, while Margot was all sunny smiles and bouncing curls.

'I have to move on, Mother.'

'Move on?'

'Make plans.'

'Ah.' Louisa stood up and smoothed a skirt that was at least three years old. 'I am sorry that I have been such a dreadful mother. I am also sorry that I allowed myself to believe that you were unmoved by Alex's death.'

'You had your own grief to contend with. We all knew that you and Father had a good marriage.' This was, without doubt, one of the most awkward moments in Amy's life. Attempting to teach a parent good sense was not usually the task of a daughter.

'I depended on him.'

'I know.'

'Too much, perhaps.' Louisa picked up her magazine and tossed it into a wooden rack. 'I shall go upstairs for a while,' she said evenly. She gazed at her daughter for a few seconds, then left the room and ascended the flight. She needed to think. But one resolution remained untouchable, non-negotiable. She would never throw herself on the mercy of a man whose father had taken away property and money at the turn of a card.

She sat on a wicker chair at her bedroom window, her eyes turned towards Pendleton Grange. She could not see her old home, but she did not need to. Every creak of a floorboard, every sound of a closing door, every sight and smell was etched deep into memory. Louisa had not set eyes on the Grange for five years. She avoided it like a plague, causing Moorhead to drive the pony and trap the long way round whenever his mistress left Caldwell Farm.

31

Two defining moments, then. The first had arrived courtesy of the German army, the second had been delivered from a pack of cards. The king of hearts had not been good enough; the ace of spades had won the day. That blackest of cards had been a suitable choice for Thomas Mulligan, now deceased. The king of hearts? Alex had certainly been the ruler of her heart. Now, a dark, secretive creature resided in luxury at Pendleton Grange, a proud and unapproachable sort with a soft accent that did not match his hard interior, his forbidding face.

Amy was probably in the right, as usual. The girl had been born sensible, knowledgeable. The more Louisa concentrated on the recent past, the more she realized her own deficiencies. 'Poor Amy has been mother to me, to Eliza and to Margot,' she whispered into the silence. 'She is not wayward, she is merely direct.'

Louisa considered her own failings, knew that she should be pulling herself together. 'But how does one change quickly, radically? What must I do to improve myself? Oh, Alex, where are you?' Silly question. Had Alex been here, she would not have needed to change. Or . . . or what if he had remained disturbed, out of order? She would have been forced to alter her ways, had that been the case.

She leaned back against the chair's hard shoulder, thought about her relationship with Amy, with her other two girls. The children had raised themselves, she supposed. Oh, there had been a succession of nannies and governesses, followed by education at a good private school, but Louisa could not remember spending time with the girls. When had she taken them for walks, for dentistry, for a theatre outing? When had she last kissed them, hugged them?

'So selfish,' she muttered. 'So close to him, so far from them.' At the end of the day, what was there? Just children, then grandchildren. There was Amy, backbone of steel, heart of gold. Then Eliza, excellent musician and painter, designer of clothes, seamstress, poet. Margot, vigorous and silly, winner of sporting trophies, remarkable horsewoman, fluent in French, funny, a performer who, as a child, could sing, dance, keep an audience happy for hours.

Louisa walked to the bed and laid herself flat on the

32

eiderdown. They had lost a father, and a father was supposed to be so important to a girl. The male parent had a hand in helping choose a husband. The qualities in a father were often echoed by the son-in-law. May God grant that the three Burton-Masseys would seek husbands who reflected Alex's real characteristics, the ones he had displayed before the war.

For five years, Louisa had simply allowed life to happen. The girls would marry reasonably well, she had believed, so everything would turn out satisfactorily. Money was tight. Much of her dowry had been invested in improvements at the Grange, and she was left now with just a few thousand, the capital sum of which she dared not touch. The quarterly income, handled by Amy, was paltry.

Even so, Louisa Burton-Massey knew that she could not change herself overnight, was possibly incapable of changing at all. At forty-five, she was not old, but her wool was dyed sufficiently fast to preclude the application of new, brighter colours. So, it could well be Amy's task to better the family's financial status. Amy, again.

Sleep beckoned. It was scarcely noon, yet Louisa was tired to the bone. Alex had spoken to Amy, only to Amy. That beautiful voice, deep, yet soft and tender, had poured itself into his daughter's ears. Yet Amy had retained her sanity, had held herself in check, so solid, so sure. Louisa must try now to turn herself into another Amy. It should have been the other way round, she thought sleepily. What sort of a role model had she been . . .? Thoughts slowed, became disjointed.

Chanel. *Vogue*. A nice little number edged with squirrel fur. Eliza. Louisa was suddenly bolt upright on the edge of her bed. What had Amy said earlier this morning? It was quite respectable to earn money these days. Hadn't Helen Smythe's daughter gone into catering? It wasn't common-or-garden food – no sausage rolls and sandwiches for Camilla Smythe. No, Camilla's exclusive range was for moneyed folk whose domestic staff had gone off into factories and so forth. If Camilla Smythe, daughter of one of the wealthiest chaps in Blackburn, could cook for the gentry, then why not . . .?

Louisa was off the bed and down the stairs before taking breath. She entered the drawing room, scarcely noticing that

33

Amy still wore riding clothes, that Eliza was at the piano, that Margot was missing, as usual. Louisa snatched up her magazine and left the room.

When their mother had returned to the upper floor, Eliza swivelled on the stool and spoke to her older sister. 'What happened then?' she asked.

'Mother happened.'

'Ah.'

This morning's diatribe seemed to have fallen on deaf ears, mused Amy. Mother was plainly intending to live in the past, her attention cornered by trends in fashion, her mind centred on what might have been had Father lived, had the Kaiser died, had Germany slept. Oh, well, let her read her silly magazines. Amy had tried her best.

Upstairs, Louisa sketched furiously, outlining the shapes of skirts and coats, changing details, drawing a handbag, a hat, a scarf whose width varied to fit with a collar. She had always been a designer at heart, and Eliza had inherited the ability. An excitement simmered gently inside a woman who was too much of a lady to allow joy to show. She stopped for a moment, pencil poised. 'I'm not a lady any more,' she informed the dressing-table. 'After all, I did say "damn" and "hell" today.' Perhaps there was hope for her yet.

Downstairs, Amy stared at her riding boots while Eliza practised a bit of Chopin. Much as Amy disliked James Mulligan, she had to allow that he had shown some decency in trying to present an olive branch to Mother. His plans for Pendleton Grange were not settled, had not yet been engraved in stone, but at least he had an eye to the future.

Mother, deeply embedded in her yesterdays, was not prepared to listen to reason. She saw Mulligan's proposition as charity, while Amy viewed it as an act of conciliation. Thomas Mulligan, dead for several months now, had been the owner of the ace of spades. James, his son, had simply inherited his father's ill-gotten gains. Underneath the mop of black, tangled curls and behind that sullen face, a corner of conscience seemed to linger.

What now? wondered Amy. A secretarial course for herself, a job in a stables for Margot, a position in music teaching for

Eliza? A little voice inside Amy's head suggested that all three girls should go in with Mulligan. She could tackle administration, Eliza might like a place in a string quartet, would, perhaps, play soothing music to the guests at Pendleton Grange during afternoon tea or just before supper. As for Margot, well, she could make herself useful at organizing outdoor pursuits.

But there was Mother. Who would want to come home to her sulks after a hard day's work? The fire breathed again, puffing smoke in the manner of a dragon preparing to belch flames. Eliza's sweet music trickled into the soot-laden atmosphere, the clock declared that lunch was a mere fifteen minutes from now.

Margot fell in at the door. Amy grinned. There was no real need for timepieces at Caldwell Farm, since Margot's stomach was always on red alert at lunch, tea and supper.

'It was amazing, truly wonderful,' cried Margot. 'He had to put his arm right inside the cow, tie a sort of rope thing to the calf's hoofs, then pull like blazes. And there it was, a whole cow in miniature. I was there, I saw everything.'

Amy shook her head gleefully. Margot often happened to be around when something unusual was happening.

'Of course, Mr Mulligan never said a word, strange man. Just took off his coat and got stuck in.' She giggled. 'The farmer said that the calf took one look at Mr Mulligan's face and decided that this was a grim world. That was why it took so long to be born.' She paused for breath. 'Actually, I like Mr Mulligan. He's very good-looking, almost handsome, I'd say. There's something about a man who frowns a lot. What do you think, Amy?'

'I think you and I should get cleaned up,' said Amy.

Margot, to whom dirt clung like glue, glanced down at herself. 'Gosh,' she hooted. 'I must pong like a midden.' She smiled her wonderful smile before wandering off in the direction of soap and water. Amy got up and followed the youngest towards the bathroom. Like Mother, she was beginning to wonder what would happen to them all.

35

THREE

'I don't know who the blooming heck he thinks he is.' Tilly Walsh's several chins shivered with indignation. A small amount of colour was paying a brief visit to suet-pudding skin, twin circles of red anger situated just below brightened button-eyes. 'Carrying on as if he's somebody, throwing his flaming weight about.' She sniffed, causing her chest to expand even further until it threatened to burst right out of her blouse. Had the sisters been in the presence of an audience, someone might have made a comment about weight being thrown about, because the Walsh ladies were massive.

'I miss Mr Burton-Massey,' agreed Mona Walsh, anxious, as always, to keep both peace and pace with her older sister. 'All you got was your quarterly visit and a couple of quid for a night out. Did us proud, he did. See, Tilly, he were a gentleman through and through. He knew how to treat folk, how to get the best out of them. Very kind, he were, when you think back. Just used to let us get on with it, no messing.' Gentler in nature than her sister, Mona strove to keep up with Tilly, to be as tough as Tilly, who did not believe in being pleasant, humorous or even overly civil. 'Women in business has to be tough,' was Tilly's motto. 'We give no quarter, Mona. Remember that – no quarter.'

Tilly grunted with the effort of taking two steps sideways to allow a customer to reach the door. 'We got a lovely chicken at Christmas, plum puddings made by his staff. And what have we got now?'

'An Irish lummox,' replied Mona, parrot fashion.

They stood together in the wash-house doorway, twin remnants of Victoriana, white blouses, black floor-length skirts, hair cordoned off severely with the aid of pins and grips.

'Well, we'll not be safe now.' Mona pulled the grey shawl across cooling shoulders. 'And he's bringing the blinking thing right into the yard, and all. Some poor devil'll get run over. I don't hold with these fancy ideas. What's wrong with a horse and cart, eh? Or a bloody tram, come to that. At least a tram stays on its rails. You know where it's going and you know where it's been.' Mona was genuinely disturbed by the arrival of their landlord's car. She had seen cars about, of course, but she had not expected to have a motor vehicle parked so close to the laundry. 'What if it blows up?' she asked darkly. 'We'd all be killed.'

They stared at the black Austin. All shiny and new, it was sitting outside the inn's stables. Chrome headlights, little windscreen wipers, spare tyre housed at the back, sweeping mudguards, lined running-boards beneath the doors.

'Frightens the horses, too,' complained Tilly. There weren't as many horses as there had been in the Walsh sisters' youth, but those in the Red Lion's stables were in for nervous breakdowns what with all the honking and belching of exhaust.

'Eeh, but times is changing,' Tilly continued. 'I can't keep up at all. Wind-up gramophones, electric irons, refrigerators. There's washing-machines as well, you know. I mean, they're not the sort of stuff everybody can afford, but I reckon our days is numbered. And there he is with his motor car.' She tutted. 'Makes you think, eh? All this lot – and more – won after a poker game on a single cut of the pack. I mean, he should have give it all back, that Thomas Mulligan, because it weren't fair.'

Mona shook her head. 'Too much of a gentleman, he were, our Mr Burton-Massey. Man of his word, you see. They say a gentleman's word is his bond, Tilly. King of hearts, Burton-Massey had in his hand. And that drunken bugger come through with an ace.'

'From up his sleeve, I shouldn't wonder.'

37

'Aye, we could put money on that.' Mona looked across at Mulligan's office. He presided over the yard most days, his watchful eye making mental notes of comings, goings, who kept the place tidy, who left a mess. He ran his own business, too, something to do with Irish racehorses and breeds of cattle he wanted to introduce. 'Miserable sod,' declared Mona, before placing a pinch of snuff on the back of a hand. She inhaled, sneezed, passed the snuffbox to her sister who went through the same ritual.

'Well, if he says one more word to me, I'll punch his face for him,' declared Tilly, once her sinuses settled. 'Clean me windows? What's the point of cleaning windows every day when they just mist over with all the steam? I mean, he never speaks, then when he does open his ignorant Irish gob, it's just to gripe and complain.' She pointed to Mulligan's window. 'Look, he's stood there now watching us. Flaming cheek.'

Mona glanced across the yard. 'As long as he gets his rent, why the hell should he care what we do? Thirty year we've been running this laundry – ever since Mam died. He should learn a few manners. Why, the gob on him'd curdle milk from forty paces, I'll bet. Dairy farming? His cows'll be giving nowt but cheese if he has owt to do with it.' In spite of the harsh words she spoke, Mona's heart skipped a beat. Eeh, James Mulligan was a bonny-looking man, that was for sure.

Both sisters swept a glance around the yard. The undertaker next door was always quiet, but that was the nature of his trade. Next to the funeral parlour and at right angles, the stonemason carved out his trade. He laboured under strict instructions not to hammer after nine in the evening, so any rush jobs had to be done during the day, just a bit of polishing and quiet chiselling after hours. Between the mason and the clockmaker, stables stood parallel with the rear of the Red Lion, then, after the turn, there was a nightwatchman's shed and Mulligan's office. A sweets and tobacco, a fabric shop and a grocer's backed on to the yard, their main entrances on Deansgate, one to the left of the inn, two to the right. Those shopkeepers didn't know how lucky they were, because Mulligan could not oversee their ongoings.

'Shall I get the leather and wipe the windows?' asked Mona.

'Not yet. Let the swine wait,' replied Tilly. 'Him and his car and his fancy clothes. He dresses like summat out of an old book. God knows where he got that hat, but I swear it's one of them they wear at the opera. I bet it goes flat so it'll fit in a cupboard.'

'It's him wants flattening,' declared Mona, though she didn't know whether she meant it. But even his father had been easy in comparison with this bloke. Thomas Mulligan had been too drunk most days to notice whether the yard buildings still had roofs and walls. Mr Mulligan Junior might be something of an oil painting, but he was a hard man.

'He'll get his comeuppance,' Tilly remarked. 'If there's a God, yon feller'll not thrive. Catholics? All that dressing up, bowing and scraping – the service they call Mass is like a three-ring circus or a pantomime. And they know how to hang on to their money. Show me a rich Catholic and I'll show you a miser. Oh, aye, he'll not prosper.'

As if their movements had been choreographed, the sisters turned simultaneously and re-entered the wash-house, Tilly leading the way, as ever. A few poor souls lingered, folk who couldn't afford a morning session. Mornings were dearer and busier, and the Walshes managed to get an extra penny per sink from early birds. Some of the early washers used the dryers, too, whereas these remnants of the local populace would carry or push wet bundles home, contents to be hung in kitchens overnight or saved for tomorrow, God and the continence of rain clouds willing.

Mr Dobson from next door came in with a box of shrouds. These had been used to house bodies until families turned up with a suit or a dress. He pushed the plain white items across the counter. 'He's been on the rampage again,' he said mournfully. 'Could I be a bit more discreet with my coffins. That's because I had three arrivals at once, and I left two outside for five minutes.'

Tilly and Mona shook their heads in sympathy.

'Then, he started on about my horses. They've got to do it somewhere, haven't they? I mean, I pick it up regular and put it in the manure bucket. There's folk queuing up to get their hands on my manure. Nowt but the best, my horses get.

39

There's a fair few prize-winning roses come out of the back ends of my beasts. There I am, seeing to the needs of the newly departed, and all he can think about is keeping the yard clean and uncluttered.'

Tilly picked up the shrouds and pushed them under the counter until morning. 'Usual, Mr Dobson? Boil and a light starch?'

'Aye.' The undertaker fiddled with his watch fob.

'I were just saying afore,' volunteered Tilly, 'I don't know what the world's coming to. Have you seen his motor?'

'I have,' replied Seth Dobson. 'Just a big piece of swank on four wheels.' He leaned forward in a conspiratorial fashion. 'I've heard some say as he had nowt as a lad. No back in his trousers, no boots on his feet.'

'Eeh,' said Mona, joining the other two in their huddle. 'You don't say.'

'I do say,' Mr Dobson said emphatically. 'You can tell he's new to money, like. There's two ways they can go, you see. Now, one type'll take hold and spend the lot before you can say knife. But the other kind – and he's one of them – looks after every brass farthing as if it were a king's ransom.'

'Tight,' pronounced Mona.

'A right Scrooge,' agreed Tilly.

The undertaker looked over his shoulder. 'Then there's the cellar.' He straightened, smoothed his waistcoat, nodded three times, then bent his head again. 'Funny goings-on,' he whispered.

'You what?' Tilly's quadruple chin went into overdrive as she glanced furtively about the room. 'There isn't no cellar round here,' she said eventually. 'Unless it's where they keep the ale in the Red Lion.'

'Not here,' said Mr Dobson. 'Up yonder. Pendleton Grange.'

'Go on,' urged Mona.

'Nay, I'm saying nowt,' answered the dark-clad man.

Tilly grabbed his hand, then released it suddenly. The trouble with an undertaker was that you could never work out where his hands had been, but imagination filled in the gaps. 'Hey, you're not leaving us here with the tale half told.

That'd keep me awake all night, wondering about doings in a cellar.'

'Me and all.' Mona was not to be outdone in the gossip stakes.

Dobson continued reluctant. 'It's only summat and nowt.'

'Let me be the judge of that,' challenged Tilly.

'Me and all.' Mona pointed a fat finger at the customer.

'I don't know as I should rightly say. A man in my profession has to be discreet, same as a doctor or a lawyer.' He paused for effect. 'Only a friend of mine has a lass who works for Mulligan – a sleeping-in job. Mary, she's called. She comes home on her days off and she ... well ... lets a few things slip.'

'Does she?' Tilly's eyebrows were almost in her hairline. 'What sort of things?'

'Cellar.' Seth Dobson's voice was almost inaudible.

'What about the cellar?' Tilly was getting cross. It was nearly closing time, and this fellow was getting on her nerves. He was a miserable-looking bloke, with a squint. Thin as a rake, he was every inch the professional mourner, face like a smacked bum, stringy neck, not a muscle to brag about. And his skin was yellow like old paper, as if he was nearly dead himself.

He inclined his head even further. 'Well, the family – the proper family – used to keep wine in a part of it. Big house, big cellar, so most of it's been empty except for rubbish – worn-out furniture and that. Then there's coal at the back, near the kitchen. But now, nobody knows what's going on down there. First thing every morning, his nibs goes down for about an hour, then he comes back up, locks the door, wears the key on a chain round his neck.'

Mona shivered. 'Just once a day?'

'No,' answered Dobson. 'Sometimes it's twice, sometimes three or four times.'

'What does he do in there?' asked Tilly.

Mona clicked her tongue impatiently. 'If folk could see through doors, happen there'd be an answer.' She turned her attention to Mr Dobson. 'Can they hear anything while he's down there?'

'I don't know,' he replied.

41

'Ooh, heck,' exclaimed Tilly. 'He could have a mad wife locked up – like that feller in *Jane Eyre*, him that ended up burnt.'

'Bigamist, he were.' Mona's tone was disapproving.

'Mulligan might be a mad scientist doing experiments on animals,' offered Tilly. 'Or on people.'

'They'd scream,' scoffed Mona.

'Not if they were tied up and gagged.'

Tired of the women's prattling, Seth Dobson began to wish he'd kept the news to himself. The trouble with women was that they made too many boils out of pimples. Give them an inch and they ran a flaming marathon. He turned to leave.

'Hang on,' Tilly ordered. 'What do you think?'

'What about?' he asked.

'The cellar.'

He shrugged non-existent shoulders. 'It's a mystery, that's what I think. He must have something to hide. Nobody goes underground unless they've got to.'

The two women pondered. 'Photographs or paintings of naked people,' said Tilly, with the air of someone who has just conquered Everest. 'I bet he's one of them perverts. They do all sorts, perverts. They muck about with kiddies, look through bathroom windows, follow women all over the show. There were one in the paper a few weeks back, kept pinching unmentionables off washing-lines. Thirty pairs of wotsernames were found in his allotment shed up Tonge Moor.'

The undertaker returned to the fold. 'Careful what you say,' he warned. 'He's just the sort to have you done for defamation.'

When a cough was heard, all three froze. Tilly and Mona raised their heads and stiffened. The undertaker turned slowly. 'Mr Mulligan,' he uttered, his tone more shrill than usual.

The Misses Walsh appeared to shrink in height, though not in girth. Tilly, the elder and the leader, bent to tidy the under-counter shelf. Mona simply stood still and exhaled, fat fingers spread out before her as if the stretch of counter would support her if and when she fell completely. How long had he been there? What had he heard?

Seth Dobson swallowed audibly, his thyroid cartilage

seeming to scrape like sandpaper against the unhealthy, sepia-tinged skin of his scrawny neck.

Mulligan doffed his tall, dated hat and entered the wash-house.

The undertaker, galvanized, collected his own headgear and fled the scene.

Mona waited. Tilly was still fiddling with bleach and Oxydol washing powder on a low shelf. Tilly, always one for pushing herself to the front of life, was suddenly reduced to hiding. Mona was not going to take evasive action; she would show them both that she wasn't afeared of him.

The room was quieter. Only two clients remained, and they had reached the folding and packing-up stage.

Mulligan gazed around the building. It was vast, with twenty sinks, a large, coal-fuelled drying rack, dolly tubs, several boilers, benches for sorting and folding, a pile of washboards, a barrel filled with possers.

'Can . . . can I help you?' asked Mona.

He turned and looked at her. 'Perhaps,' he replied.

Mona and Tilly were not experienced with men. Both claimed to be unaffected by them, each declaring frequently that marriage was drudgery. But this man was . . . different, Mona decided, with extreme reluctance. She could well imagine young women falling all over him – if only he would take an interest.

'How much would you charge to do my domestic linen?' he asked. 'You do provide such a service, I take it?'

Mona cleared her throat. 'Yes, Tilly and I do laundry for people who haven't time. As for the cost, that depends on the number of items.'

He nodded gravely, acting in the manner of a diplomat at the signing of a treaty, all deep thoughts and internationally important clauses.

'Not on Mondays, though,' continued Mona. 'We get a bit busy on Mondays.'

'Yes.'

It was as if he had to consult some invisible dictionary before uttering a single syllable. He wasn't shy, Mona thought. He didn't blush, didn't go to pieces when approached. And

43

what a sight for sore eyes, especially in here, where attractive men were as rare as Welsh gold. He had shoulders broad enough for Atlas, dark brown eyes surrounded by thick, curled lashes. His limbs were long, probably muscular under the black cloth, while teeth, skin and hair were all better than merely satisfactory. If he had a visible fault, it was his tendency to frown.

'Miss Walsh?'

'Oh, I'm sorry. Did you say something?' And what a voice.

'I suggested Tuesdays.'

'Right.' She could feel the heat in her face. Fancy a woman of fifty-odd having her head turned by a man half her age, a miserable blighter into the bargain. She was already in enough trouble with Mr Wilkinson for swearing. No way would she and Tilly enter the Light Eternal if they kept using bad words. But eyeing up a man? Ooh, that was probably the biggest sin of all.

Tilly surfaced at last. 'Oh, you're still here,' she informed the new customer.

Mona vowed to tackle her sister later. Five minutes with her head down, then all she could do was state the obvious.

'Who does your washing now?' asked Mona. She flinched when Tilly's clog made sharp contact with her leg. It was a fair question, wasn't it? What was wrong about asking a fair question?

But he offered no reply.

Mona tried again. 'Course, you'll be able to fetch your dirty linen in your car.'

'Yes,' he managed.

Blood out of a stone, remarked Mona inwardly. She met his gaze, found no enmity in the features, noticed no friendliness, either. It was as if he felt nothing at all, as if he couldn't make contact with his fellow humans. He was a funny package altogether, a man whose childhood was reputed to have been poor, yet whose vocabulary – when he chose to use it – betrayed a better than average level of education. 'It's a very nice car,' she said, in yet another attempt to draw him out.

'It's convenient,' he replied. 'And faster than a horse.'

'Right,' offered Tilly. 'You just fetch your stuff and we'll see to it for you.'

44

'Oh – we have an ironing service for special customers,' was Mona's next little comment.

'I am not special,' he answered.

'But you're the boss, the owner, like,' said Mona.

Tilly wondered whether her sister might be on the verge of lying down on the floor and giving this jumped-up Irish fellow the chance to walk all over her. A right two-faced crate-egg their Mona was turning into. All against him till he turned up, then nice as pie with cream on top. Wanted her bloody head examined, did Mona.

'If you iron, I shall pay for that, too,' he stated.

'Naturally,' said Tilly, standing as tall as she could manage.

'There's nothing free in this life, is there?' he asked.

Well, blood and stomach pills, thought Tilly. He had made a remark, expressed a level of opinion, of judgement. 'We'll do you proud, Mr Mulligan,' she conceded. If he was prepared to make an effort, then so would she. 'There's no finer laundry in all England. We've been up to our eyes in soap and water since we could walk, me and our Mona.'

'A hard life,' he remarked. 'And a damp one.'

'It's not been easy,' agreed Mona, completely oblivious to the man's small quip. 'Especially when we first started and our Tilly mixed starch that thick – why, you could have plastered a full ceiling with it.'

Tilly bridled. 'Now, listen here, you,' she barked at her sister, 'that were nowt. What about you and that red scarf? Pink sheets, pink tablecloths. Mam went mad.'

A strange sound assaulted the women's ears. He was laughing. And, Mona decided after looking at him, he was the most beautiful thing she'd seen except at the pictures on a Saturday night. So, he had a sense of humour, then.

'By the way,' he said, his face settling back into its normal expression of hard, implacable lines, 'I am not in the habit of instigating litigation.'

Tilly's mouth fell open. 'Eh?' she said, before she could help herself.

'I don't sue gossips.'

The sisters avoided his eyes, Tilly going back to her Oxydol and chlorine, Mona shuffling off to help a woman pack her washing.

He turned, made his farewell, then left the building.

Tilly righted herself, a box of Dolly Blue still clamped in a rigid fist. So, he had heard the three of them discussing the mystery of his cellar up at Pendleton Grange. What had they said? She rooted about in the canals of recent memory. Photos of naked women. Experiments on living creatures, both human and animal. Oh, heck.

Mona was in a flat spin. Supposedly helping a woman to pack wet washing, she got towels mixed up with underwear, colours tangled with whites. 'Sorry,' she told the bemused client. What was he going to think of her at all? Mind, he didn't seem one to carry a grudge, because he had laughed and said something about not suing folk for gossip.

Tilly put down her Dolly Blue and began the business of cashing up. She kept an eye on Mona, who, once the stragglers had left, was making a bad fist of cleaning up. She was a bit on the hysterical side, was Mona. If she got herself over-excited, there might well be tears before bedtime.

When the money was safely tucked away in canvas bags, Tilly breathed her way across the floor, lungs struggling to take in enough oxygen to fuel her huge body. She swept, mopped, pulled some odd socks from behind a sink. There must be loads of men walking about Bolton with one brown foot, one black.

Mona polished the windows. She could see him across the way, seated at his desk, bending over, probably writing. He had such a lot of hair, unruly, it was. She experienced a sudden urge to run across with scissors and a comb, but she knew she daren't. There was something about him, as if he'd been hurt and had decided to clad himself in armour, all tough shell covering a broken heart. The hand clutching the wash-leather slowed. Why, if she'd been married, and if she'd had a son, he could have been about the same age as James Mulligan.

'Mona?'

'What?'

'Watch yourself. You'll be coming off that ladder in a minute. We don't want you getting a leg broke, do we?'

That night, as they sat by their range in the kitchen, each

46

with her skirt raised to welcome the heat, Tilly carried on where she'd left off before Mulligan's visit. 'I still wonder who he thinks he is,' she said, the words echoing into an almost empty cocoa cup.

Mona was looking at pictures in the flames, was dreaming dreams of what might have been had she been thinner, younger, prettier.

'Mona? Are you listening to me?'

'Of course I am.'

'Well, what did I say?'

Mona drained her cup. 'Something about who does he think he is.' She continued to stare into the fire. 'I don't think he knows who he is, or what he is.'

'Eh?'

Mona blinked slowly. 'He's got a lot on his mind.'

'Oh? And which crystal ball did you see that in, Mona Walsh?'

'His eyes,' replied the younger woman. 'I saw it in his eyes.'

'Rubbish.' Tilly clattered off to the scullery.

Mona dozed in her chair. She saw a little lost boy running round in circles. He had black hair and brown eyes and his clothes were torn. His father was drunk and his mother was dead. She saw a fine man with a frown and a load of responsibilities. These two were the same person.

'Mona?'

She woke with a start. 'What?'

'Another drink?'

'No thanks.' It was time for bed. Mona stood up and stretched. Who was he? And what was in that cellar?

FOUR

For the first time in her short life, Sally Hayes had a bedroom all to herself. It was high up in the roof, its dormer window overlooking the rear gardens and yards of Pendleton Grange, property of Mr James Mulligan, a silent, broody man of whom most people were terrified. He never shouted, never threatened anybody's job, but he seemed to have so much power, so much quiet strength, that everybody kept out of his way whenever possible.

But Sally Hayes wasn't frightened of him, not any more. He was one of the kindest, gentlest people she had ever encountered in her fourteen years. Brought up in an orphanage after the early deaths of her parents, she felt at home here. The room wasn't huge, but it was hers. There was a rule in the house about privacy, so every servant had a PRIVATE sign on his or her door, with PLEASE KNOCK printed underneath. Mr Mulligan set a lot of store by a person's privacy. On the cellar door, there was no sign inviting a knock: on the cellar door the notice read, DO NOT ENTER.

She snuggled down under the patchwork quilt, enjoying the luxury of being in bed during daylight hours. Her room had yellow check curtains, a wardrobe, a little table with drawers underneath and a mirror over it, a pine chest with a padded lid, a straight chair, an upholstered armchair, pictures on the walls, even on the wall above her bed. It was the pictures that made it homely, she decided.

Sally dozed, remembering the day when he had chosen her. Just another ordinary morning it had been, make your bed, dress the little children, do your chores. There had been no cruelty, no abuse, no whip to keep the orphans working. On that Monday morning, they had gone off to school, where Sally had been employed to help with lessons, teaching infants their letters, mixing ink for the juniors, giving out milk, making cups of tea for the six kind teachers.

And he simply materialized, like a ghost that drifted through walls. One minute she was on her own in the cloakroom, picking up shoes, hanging coats and wiping sinks, then there he was, tall, so big that he almost had to stoop to enter the inner room where the ten washbasins stood. He asked her about her future. She told him she liked to keep busy, that she enjoyed reading and drawing, that she could sew, knit and do plain meals.

He nodded a few times, asked her would she like a job in a big house, left her alone to think about it.

Sally hadn't needed to think. Miss Purcell, the headmistress, had shed a few tears, then everyone had clubbed together to buy Sally a beautiful handbag and some gloves, both gifts made out of the softest kid They lay now in white tissue, wrapped safely and kept in Sally's top drawer with her underwear.

Someone knocked at her door. 'Come in,' she called, expecting to see a member of staff.

James Mulligan entered the room. He carried a little vase containing a few freesias. 'They smell nice,' he explained.

Sally wished she had brushed her hair properly. 'Thank you, sir.'

He placed the vase on the windowsill. 'Two more calves,' he told her, before sitting in the armchair. 'Both well, both feeding.'

'Lovely,' she replied.

'And I'll take the washing to the laundry at the yard until your ankle is well again. The others have enough to do without tackling laundry as well.'

'Thank you, sir,' she repeated.

49

He sat for several minutes, seemed to be deep in thought.

It was his silences that frightened people, Sally decided. He was just one of those types whose brains were busy, the same as a painter or a writer, a bit absent-minded. He had picked her because she looked weedy, as if she needed feeding up and keeping warm. He had never said that, but Sally knew that there were better and hardier specimens in the Chiverton Children's Home.

'Are you happy here?' he asked suddenly.

'Oh, yes. I'm very happy, Mr Mulligan.'

'Is the work too much?'

'No, sir. If you mean my ankle, like, it could have happened to anybody. I just kecked over on a cobble.'

'Kecked over?'

She smiled. A lot of the Lancashire expressions were still mysteries to him. 'I think the right word might be "keeled", sir. Keeled over.'

'Ah.' Once again, he stared into space for at least two minutes. 'You're well-read,' he pronounced eventually. 'Don't hesitate to use the library.'

'Thank you, sir.'

He sighed. 'No need to thank me, Sally. The written word is for everyone, not just for those who can afford the paper on which it's printed. Like music and paintings – for all of us, you understand. When you read Shakespeare, or look at a Constable, when you listen to Mozart on the crystal or the gramophone, you are hearing a piece of a departed soul, a slice of his being. Those sights, sounds and ideas were bequeathed to the whole of mankind, because they were gifts from God, gifts to be shared.'

Sally was stunned, not because of what he had said but by his having strung together so many words all at once. She felt honoured, singled out by this very clever man.

'Sally?'

'Yes, sir?'

'Do they . . . talk about the cellar?'

She bit her lip. This was a difficult one to answer. Her loyalty to her employer was almost boundless, but she owed much to her colleagues, too. At the orphanage, nobody ever told tales. It wasn't for fear of dreadful punishment, but it was a law, like a commandment. She decided to compromise. 'I think most of us wonder about it a bit.'

'Mary Whitworth, I believe, has been putting stories about, in the town and so forth.'

'Oh.' She gulped audibly. 'She's young, sir.'

A smile threatened. 'Older than you, my dear. But, then, you've always been old, haven't you? Orphans are often wise.'

She attempted no answer, no comment.

'Am I a bad man?'

The girl shook her head quickly, emphatically.

'Do I look like your average mad scientist? Is my hair wild?' She couldn't resist. 'Yes, it's wild.'

Now, he really did laugh. 'You should see a painting of Beethoven, then. Looked like something from Greek or Roman myth, a head covered in snakes.'

'And if you looked at the snakes, you went blind, or died,' she said. 'You had to cover your eyes, then cut their heads off, but you couldn't see where they were, 'cos you were blind-folded.' She hung her own tousled head. 'I read about it somewhere.'

'Ah, did you, now? Well, I must be off and about my business. Keep the weight off that foot, whatever.'

'Yes, sir.' It was because of her that he had bought the car. He'd told her at the time that he had no intention of taking any poor soul to the hospital in a cart ever again, because the journey had been unnecessarily painful for the patient. This was definitely not a bad man. 'Sir?'

'Yes?'

'I don't care what you've got in the cellars.'

'Thank you, Sally.' He stood up and approached the bed. 'We all have a cellar, you know. Mine's made of bricks and mortar, but the cellars of the human mind are deep and in-visible. Each man has his secrets and his fears.'

She didn't know anything about all that, so she stayed quiet.

'Life's a battle,' he told her now. 'Gird yourself, be strong, read all you can and know all you can.'

'Yes, sir.'

He turned and left the room. As he passed Mary

Whitworth's door, he noticed that it was closing very slowly. 'Mary?' he called.

With her face beetroot red, the copper-haired girl crept out on to the landing. 'Sir?'

She had been listening at Sally's door, of that he felt certain.

'The yard in town is full of talk. Now, I don't want to gag anyone, but do you really need to discuss my arrangements with your family and friends? Don't be speculating about the cellar and its contents. Whatever goes on down there is my business, mine alone. Let me reassure you that I am breaking no law, Mary. Do you understand?'

She nodded quickly.

'And there'll be no more gossip? Did you know that gossip can hurt people? Is this an end to it, so?'

'Yes, sir.' She waited until he had gone downstairs, then pushed open Sally's door. 'God, I thought he was going to kill me. If I got the sack, it'd be my mother killing me and all.'

'You shouldn't talk,' said Sally. 'It's not fair, going behind his back. If you've anything to say, say it to him.'

Mary laughed mirthlessly. 'Oh, but I'm not his favourite, am I? I didn't get picked by him, so I'm not special. He doesn't come into my bedroom for cosy little chats. You want to watch yourself, girl. Some of them like scrawny bits of gristle on their plate.'

Taking into account a bad sprain and an overstretched ligament, Sally moved very quickly, jumping out of bed, feeling very little pain except for the fury in her chest. 'There's a sign on my door that says "Private". Get out, shut the door, and next time, knock.'

'Ooh,' exclaimed Mary, the syllable stretching through a couple of seconds and varying in pitch. 'Touchy, aren't we? Did I come a bit too near the truth?'

'You wouldn't know the truth, Mary Whitworth, if it hit you across the chops like a pound of cod. Well, just you listen to me for once. I might be quiet, but I take it all in. I used to wash four tablecloths a week, but there's only three now. Who's in charge of the table? You are. Well, I'm in charge of washing and it's time I counted his sheets.'

'What are you saying?' The blushing cheeks clashed very badly with Mary's deep red hair.

'Nowt I wouldn't say to him, that's for sure.'

'Are you threatening me?'

Years of living in a crowd had taught Sally how to fight her own corner. Too slender for physical battle, she used words and used them very well. 'Just so as we'll know how we're fixed,' she whispered, her face almost touching her companion's, 'I'll answer yes to that question. We none of us understand him, 'cos he's cleverer than most. He pays well and he doesn't moan. Now, you take one more thing from this house and I'll tell him. Better still, I'll tell Mrs Kenny, and she'll have you out of Pendleton before you can say knife or steal a knife. So it's up to you, Mary.'

At the mention of the housekeeper's name, Mary took a step backwards. Mrs Kenny was the fierce guardian of the master's interests. She had followed him over from Ireland, had taken the place of a woman who refused to work for any more Irishmen after the somewhat inglorious and untidy death of Mulligan Senior. 'Watch your step,' she muttered, burnished curls bouncing free of her maid's cap.

'I'll not need to,' Sally replied.

'Oh, yes? I'd not be too cocky if I were you, Little Orphan Sally. I'm not afeared of you.'

'Then,' said Sally, her tone low and controlled, 'you're even dafter than I thought.'

Mary opened her mouth, but no words emerged. Sally was a bit like him, Mary decided. Silent but deadly, and with an inner strength that poked its head out just occasionally, as if to check on the weather outside. Two of a kind, then. It might be best just to get away before real storm clouds gathered in the small bedroom. Nevertheless, Mary had to have the last words. 'I've two big brothers,' she warned. 'Watch your step.'

Alone at last and feeling more than one kind of pain, Sally got back into her bed. It seemed that Mary had not heeded her own advice, was not watching her own step, because Sally heard her tumbling down several stairs. Still, never mind. If Mary needed hospital, the master would take her in his car.

Mary rubbed a grazed shin, then made her way to the ground floor. In a kitchen bigger than most houses, Kate Kenny was throwing together a batch of soda bread. She looked up, stopped punishing the dough and glared at the maid. 'And where've you been these last weeks?' Sarcasm was Kate Kenny's forte. 'I was wondering did you go to Blackpool?'

Mary had the answer ready. 'I had to go upstairs, Mrs Kenny. It's one of my rag-and-pin days.'

Kate Kenny put her head on one side. The street-wise madam was not exactly the housekeeper's idea of a decent parlour-maid. Why, the young orphan with the bad foot had more decency than this supposedly more settled article of humanity. 'If you have your monthly ailment on you, just say that this is your time of the month. No need to go into details about the implements involved. Vulgarity has no place in this house, certainly not in my kitchen.'

'Right, Mrs Kenny. Sorry, Mrs Kenny.'

Kate heard the boldness, the audacity. 'Get that parlour polished. God help you should Mr Mulligan ever open up the rest of this house, because I've seen more shape in a potato cake than in yourself. Would it hurt to get a bit of a move on? I've known snails go faster. Go on, get on with the work you're paid for.'

Mary took her time gathering up the tools of her trade. She found beeswax and cloths, wandered about looking for a bowl, filling it with soapy water, letting the tap run slowly.

Kate shaped her bread. One of these days, she would shape that young woman's backside, really she would.

Mary ambled off, her footsteps echoing in the large, under-used house. She reached a vast, museum-like hallway, heard the doorbell. Sighing, she placed her small burdens on a table, then answered the door.

It was Amy Burton-Massey, the eldest of three girls whose father had allowed Pendleton Grange to slip into Mulligan hands. It must have felt funny, Mary thought, to ring the bell for admission to a house that was rightfully the Burton-Masseys' property. 'Come in, miss,' she said sweetly. 'Did you want to see Mr Mulligan?'

'Yes, please.' Amy stepped into her childhood home. Unlike her mother, Amy carried very little baggage from the past. She accepted all that had happened, felt only the merest twinge of sadness whenever she strayed on to the old homestead. Life went on. It went up, down, sideways, backwards, and humanity had been designed to cope with all its twists and turns. Except for Louisa Burton-Massey, that was.

Summoned by the maid, James Mulligan came out of his study to greet Amy. He held her arm and led her beyond the reach of the chatterbox maid's ears, taking her into the study and closing the door firmly. 'Miss Burton-Massey,' he said, once she was settled in a chair. 'So nice to see you.'

'Amy,' she replied, before getting on with business. 'I'm afraid Mother doesn't want to play. I tried to explain about the hydro, but she wouldn't listen. I think it's pride. Also, she would consider her territory thoroughly invaded if you opened up the house as a business. I'm so sorry.'

He placed elbows on the desk, steepled long, brown fingers and rested his chin on the apex. 'I do not intend to remain here, Miss Burton-Massey – I beg your pardon – Amy. My home is elsewhere.'

She awaited further explanation, received none.

He stared at a point above her head, went into one of his quiet stretches of time. 'I have given myself two years to get this place up and running,' he said, after a sizeable pause. 'There is potential here, but there is also much to be done. I should need a manager, of course, someone who could be trusted.'

It was almost impossible to discuss anything thoroughly with this man, Amy decided. His mind worked in its own mysterious way, taking a path that did not necessarily run parallel with anyone else's road through life. She wondered what he did with his time. Apart from his horses, cows and a few hours each day in town, he seemed to have no hobby, no interests. There was a handful of books on the shelves, some papers stacked neatly on his desk, a letter tray, a letter opener, pens, inks, blotters. The room was all but intellectually sterile.

'If I were to offer you the position, or if you were to become a working partner, your mother would not be pleased. You see, I wanted her to take the partnership so that we might all benefit from Pendleton Grange. Clearly, your mother is not thinking positively about the future.'

Immediately, Amy was on the defensive. Whatever her own opinion of Louisa, she would not allow anyone else to criticize her. 'My mother is a hurt woman, Mr Mulligan.' She could not quite manage to call him James, not just yet. One would certainly not address him as Jim, or Jimmy. 'Our father committed suicide.'

He nodded. 'A heavy burden for a widow.'

'It was not her fault. They adored each other.'

'I didn't mean—'

'Don't worry, Mr Mulligan. I know that you did not intend any harm. It's just that Eliza, Margot and I are all Mother has. We must look after her and protect her.'

He allowed a slight smile of encouragement to occupy his features for a split second. 'I shall put my cards on the table, as we—'

'Perhaps that metaphor is misplaced,' she said wryly. 'Since playing-cards were the cause of our changing fortunes.'

'I'm sorry.'

'Not at all.' She watched him. He seemed so ill-at-ease, so unused to the vagaries of everyday life. Yet he was intelligent – that much was plain. Perhaps the rumour that he had been raised in a remote part of Ireland was based in truth, then. He was clearly not fond of company, would rather have been alone. The books would be in the library, she decided obliquely. She remembered Father reading stories aloud in there—

'Miss Burton-Massey?'

'Sorry, I was miles away.'

'Miles away is often the best place to be,' he answered.

Emboldened by his slightly friendlier tone, she asked, 'What is your real job?'

'I teach,' he replied, after a tiny pause.

'In Ireland?'

'Yes.' He fiddled with a paperclip. 'Of course, I had to come over to sort out my father's affairs. It was only after his death that I heard about this house and all that property in Bolton. As far as I was concerned, he was still living hand to mouth and ... well ... drinking when he could get the price of whiskey or beer. I had no idea.'

56

It was her turn to smile encouragingly.

'I wish your mother would just take the place away from me. I don't want it, you see. But I'm not prepared to let it stand empty and wither away to nothing. I tried the partnership idea, but she scotched that straight away. So, unless you, or you and your sisters, will help me, I am at something of a loss.'

Amy knew that whatever she chose to do, the decision would not be easy. But she also realized that she wanted work, responsibility, a niche in the world. 'There's a lot of thinking to be done,' she told him. 'I shall be plain. We have very little money. We are living on interest only, as Mother dare not touch her capital. Therefore, Margot, Eliza and I must each make a living.'

'And your mother dislikes me, wants nothing to do with me.'

'She dislikes what happened between my father and yours.'

He shook his head very slowly. 'No, Miss . . . Amy. I am not easy with strangers. I don't seem to have the knack of communicating easily. Few people take to me.'

'Yet you teach? Surely communication is important in that sphere?'

'I am good with children.'

'Ah.' Perhaps he needed to be older than his companions, needed to be bigger, stronger and in charge. Yet in this man, there was a deep seam of something or other. Was it certainty? Was it arrogance? He was definitely beautiful. Not merely handsome, but carved to perfection, every line correct, every feature balanced and well proportioned. Amy wriggled in her chair. Assessing a man's physical attributes was not a comfortable occupation.

'Would you like something to drink?' he asked. 'Tea, coffee?'

She declined. 'I think you underestimate yourself, James.' She tried the name for size, saw that he did not mind, did not flinch. 'I have the feeling that you could make an excellent businessman.'

He raised a shoulder. 'I have to go home. Two years is all I have allowed to sort out the Grange.'

Amy decided to wade right into deep water. 'Sell it, then,' she challenged. 'If you don't want it, get rid of it.'

James Mulligan rose and walked to the window. 'Have you any idea of the damage an alcoholic gambler can do in a matter of months?'

'Well,' she answered thoughtfully, 'my own father drank a great amount after returning from the war.'

'Then there was the gambling,' he added. 'My father . . .' His voice petered away, then revived itself. 'My father died a horrible death in this very house, Amy. Both our fathers endured great torment.' He turned and faced her. 'His liver bled, poured away out of him. He was, or so I'm told, the colour of old, dirty vellum and his pain was intense, to say the least of it. However, before he got to that stage, he mortgaged this place just for gambling stakes.'

'I see.' She didn't really comprehend how anyone could spend so much on gambling, but she wanted him to continue the tale. James Mulligan had a habit of drying up and shutting down.

His face wore a strange expression now, as if it had snapped closed. His eyes were cold, his lips stiff as he spoke. 'You sell it,' he said.

'It isn't mine to sell.'

'But it will be. I have left it to you and yours, and you must not tell your mother. This is your future, not mine. I am merely trying to give back all that was yours, including the paying off of the mortgage.'

Amy almost bridled, was suddenly aware of how her mother felt. Yes, this was charity. 'I would rather honour my father's gambling debt.'

His lip curled. 'Legend has it that Mr Burton-Massey held a king, while my father had an ace. Out of fifty-two cards, Thomas Mulligan picked the one with the highest value. It's unbeatable, Amy. It wipes out all the other aces, certainly makes mincemeat of the king of hearts.'

'What are you saying?'

'That my dad was an alcoholic, a cheat, a fraud, a card-sharp. There wasn't a gambling den in Dublin would let him in. He got beaten up for cheating so many times that his nose was spread all over his face. So I'd say there is probably nothing to honour. He cheated you, stole from you.'

58

Amy stood up. 'She won't listen to any of it, James. It's down to me and you.'

'I know.'

'And you think that we could repay the mortgage by opening a hydro?'

'It's just an idea.'

She pondered for a moment. 'When you die, the place reverts to me and my sisters?'

'That's the crack. Sorry, an Irish turn of phrase there.'

Amy picked up her gloves. 'May you outlive my mother, then. Because she won't set foot in here again, I'm sure.'

'I am a mere boy of twenty-nine,' he said, before walking across the room and opening the door for her. When they reached the hall, both stopped as the bell sounded.

Mary Whitworth opened the door.

As if to make mockery of Amy's final statement, Louisa Burton-Massey marched into Pendleton Grange. Followed by her second daughter, she crossed the mosaic floor, tossed her gloves on to a side table, nodded at her host. 'Mr Mulligan,' she said firmly, 'I should like to have a word with you.'

FIVE

Margot, watching from behind a hedge while her mother and one of her sisters entered Pendleton Grange, was rather less astonished when, within seconds, Amy walked out through the same door. Mother and Eliza visiting James Mulligan? Amy was a different matter: Amy would have been engaged in some practicality or other, perhaps business connected with the horses or the leasing of Caldwell's acreage. But Mother? Mother actually entering the lion's den after saying that she would never see Pendleton Grange again as long as she lived?

Margot chewed at a blade of grass, her eyes fixed on the house. Amy dashed off homeward. The youngest of the Burton-Masseys remained where she was, hidden from sight, her sole companions a riding hat and a pair of binoculars.

Margot, strangely restless these days, was managing to dislike just about everyone she encountered. Mother got on her nerves, Amy was too bossy, Eliza was a dreamer with her head full of music and poems. They were all boring. So Margot had taken to staying out for much of the time, riding, helping in fields, wishing that she could . . . Could what? Stop having to act like jolly little Margot, the clown, the tomboy? Everybody and everything was suddenly so tedious.

But no, not everyone was the subject of Margot's contempt. He wasn't. He was her hero. She had seen him this morning on horseback, his spine straight, reins held with gentle but thorough control, the chestnut mount polished until its sides shone like mahogany. James Mulligan. He was everything a man ought to be – strong, confident, effective, handsome, clever, authoritative, tall, energetic. *Et cetera*, she said inwardly.

His face. She closed her eyes and saw him not as others saw him. When a calf was born, when an animal was sick, he wore an expression she had seen only on faces in paintings. He tried so hard to hide his feelings, but Margot saw through him and into him. No one knew James Mulligan. Margot was the only living person who understood him. He loved the outdoor life, he loved all living creatures, and she loved him.

James Mulligan was like a person out of a classic novel. Not Heathcliffe, because Heathcliffe was given to ranting, was all but insane. And not Rochester. No, James Mulligan would never try to marry a plain young girl while his mad wife was living in the roof. Or in the cellar. But Mr Mulligan was the sort of hero Margot might write about. Except that she wasn't a writer. If anyone turned out to be a writer, it would probably be Eliza.

She knelt and placed the binoculars against her eyes. Nothing. It was a big house with many rooms, and it wasn't easy to catch a glimpse of him. And Eliza, who was with him now, at this very minute, was so beautiful, so angelic – why, he might fall head over heels for her. Margot felt a dart of hatred for her mother and Eliza. They were talking to him, were clouding his mind, distracting him. Margot wanted him all to herself . . .

She flopped down on to her back, held up her hands and studied the nails. They were torn and broken, the quicks jagged, tips lined with all kinds of debris. She took a penknife from a pocket and poked about, scraping out soil and what looked suspiciously like horse manure. She hadn't looked at her face for ages. Every morning, she splashed about in the bath, always in a hurry to be off and out. But she didn't have what Mother called a beauty routine. Beauty routines involved Pond's cold cream and hand lotions, egg shampoos and beer rinses, potions, lotions and perfumes.

She held the knife away, looked in its surface, polished it on her riding breeches, peered at it again. A prettyish face stared

61

back at her, but she had to look at it in bits, since she couldn't see it all at once, not along this narrow blade. She supposed that she might have a look later in the bathroom, if she remembered and if she didn't get distracted. 'Farmer Margot,' she told the bright, long-lashed eyes. He, too, had long, thick eyelashes.

All Margot wanted, apart from him, was to have land and animals to care for. Well, if she could get him to like her, to love her and marry her, she'd get everything in one fell swoop. As lady of the manor, she would, of course, be gracious in victory. She would buy new furniture for Mother, a grand piano for Eliza, a horse for Amy. She would be a good wife, an excellent farmer and, if pressed, a mother to his children, as long as there could be a nanny to do all the worst jobs.

Her nineteen-year-old stomach growled. It must be getting towards feeding time. As she walked homeward, Margot caught the sound of music floating from Pendleton Grange. That would probably be Eliza at the grand in the music room. He would be standing next to her, no doubt, would be breathing in Essence of Wild Rose, a scent of which Eliza was inordinately fond. Yes, it was time to look in the mirror, time to start wearing a dress.

James Mulligan was not standing over Eliza. Eliza had been dragged along as moral support, but, within minutes, Louisa had dispensed with the services of her middle daughter. Eliza was not built to be supportive; Eliza was just a decorative accessory, like a good silk scarf or a decent brooch. 'Let her play on the grand, Mr Mulligan,' Louisa had asked. 'She's happiest when making music.'

Against a background of clinically correct Chopin, the adversaries eyed one another. James, who had never received so many visitors in one day, met Louisa's gaze without flinching. Louisa, having informed no one of her plans, stared into an uncertain future in trade. Even in its unspoken state, the word terrified her.

'And how may I help you?' he asked.

'I ... er ... I find myself at a disadvantage here,' she stammered, 'as I don't quite know how to express my thoughts.' Her thoughts? Emotions simmered near the surface. Here she sat in her husband's study, the room which had housed his guns, his collection of ugly toby jugs, his pipes. This room had lost its tobacco-and-brandy smell, was no longer an extension of Alex.

'Being here is distressing for you,' said James. 'Would you rather I came to you?'

She shook herself visibly, as if waking from sleep. 'I beg your pardon?'

English pride, he thought. Was it any worse than, any different from, Ireland's pride? He wanted to tell Louisa of his plans, but he dared not. She would honour her husband's word until she, too, lay beneath six feet of soil. So he could not say, 'This will go to your daughters . . .' Nonetheless, he had to say something. 'If you would rather discuss your business at Caldwell Farm . . .'

She eyed him frostily. 'My daughter – Amy – has pointed out to me that we need to acquire income. I wish to offer a service to people of means.'

'I see.' He awaited further explanation, watched this poor soul as she avoided looking around the walls in search of memories. 'I shall help you in any way I can, of course.'

'Amy tells me also that the fabric shop on Deansgate will soon be available.'

'Yes. Mrs Hooper will be retiring shortly.'

Louisa inhaled deeply and lifted her head high. Everyone was working these days, she repeated in her head for the hundredth time. She was not an old woman; she was capable of dragging herself into a century that had served almost a quarter of its time. 'Eliza is an excellent designer and seamstress, as, indeed, am I. My other two daughters are also competent in the field of dressmaking. It has been something of a hobby, but now . . .'

'Now it becomes a necessity.'

Her eyes narrowed even further. 'I could manage as things are, Mr Mulligan, were I alone. My children, however, are going to find their circumstances rather more straitened than we might have hoped.'

All from the turn of a card, thought James. All from

a card up a sleeve. 'So, you will be wanting the shop?'

'Yes.' She seemed to spit the word, as if it tasted bad.

'Then you shall have it.'

'And I shall pay rent at the going rate.'

He shuffled some papers, picked up a pen, laid it down again. 'Instead of rent, would you let me use your top field, the one furthest away from the house? I'm bringing over some more horses, you see—'

'That will be satisfactory. Thank you.' Again, the last two words were forced. 'I shall require the first as well as the ground floor of the property.'

'Naturally. The upper storey is already non-residential, as Mrs Hooper has always used it for storage.'

There was little more to be said, yet Louisa needed to justify herself. What was it about this man that rendered her so awkward? Although she was poorer than he was, she was definitely his social superior. Perhaps his discomfort was infectious – no, that was not the crux of the matter. At the age of forty-five, Louisa Burton-Massey had to confront the fact that she was disturbed by his extraordinary attractiveness. Why, he was almost magnetic. She brought herself out of the reverie. 'I shall not be in the shop all the time, of course. I shall need a manageress, someone who will wear my clothes with elegance, someone who will sell them.' She allowed a small sigh to escape. 'One of my daughters, perhaps.'

He nodded.

'The designs will be couturier-based, exclusive and very expensive. There will be no direct plagiarism, naturally, but once new Worths and Chanels hit the fashion press, I shall improvise and produce items for those who would like to pay rather less than they might in London and Paris. Clients will be interviewed and entertained. Ladies, you see.'

Again, he inclined his head for a moment.

'This will not be for the general public, you understand.'

'Of course.'

'Each item will be unique. For this sort of thing, the right woman will pay handsomely.'

'I'm sure,' he said softly.

He was criticizing her inwardly, she felt certain. It was as if he might even be laughing at her, after all. Women's fashions were probably not worth considering. 'There is money to be made, Mr Mulligan.' Why could she not stop chattering? He was staring at the wall, was sitting as immobile as a garden ornament. Louisa bit her tongue to prevent any more mindless prattle escaping from her mouth.

At last he moved, turning his head slightly and awarding her a half-smile. 'Yes,' he said thoughtfully. 'That seems an excellent idea. You have skills, as do your daughters. Women like good clothes and, I suppose, for some functions – weddings and so forth – a lady likes to feel that she can wear a dress in the sure knowledge that no one else will have the same. Good, good.'

Louisa exhaled. She felt as if a teacher had just awarded her the full ten points after a spelling test.

'Mrs Burton-Massey?'

'Yes?'

'Remember I am here whenever you or your daughters might need any kind of help.'

He had the knack, Louisa decided now, of turning a person's insides to water. First, there was his very disturbing tendency to say almost nothing. A mind such as his – and, whatever his beginnings, he had educated himself – was likely to be occupied all the time. Like an assessor of some kind, he would stare at someone, or in the general vicinity of a person, as if he were calculating value and potential. Then, when he did speak, those honeyed tones seemed to caress and hypnotize his target. 'Thank you,' she replied. 'You are very kind.' Was he? Why was she thanking him? Why was she justifying herself? 'I think it's time for us to leave,' she said, in a near-whisper.

He excused himself and went to the music room. Eliza was completely absorbed in her occupation, and James stood in the doorway for a while, allowing the sound to trickle over him. She made no mistakes, or so it seemed to him. Like a perfect doll, an automaton, she sat correctly, played precisely, seemed totally occupied by the activity. Eliza was a creature of tremendous beauty, but she seemed docile, almost without character. This was possibly most men's idea of a desirable companion, biddable, exquisite, accepting. He cleared his throat.

Eliza turned, giving her companion the full benefit of a serene

65

face and a neck of palest cream. The complexion was flawless, the eyes were huge, mouth and nose delectable. By no means impervious to a woman's charms, James stood still for several seconds. 'Your mother is ready to leave, Miss Burton-Massey.'

She blinked several times, as if processing and filing this small amount of information. Then a smile erupted, making the face into the countenance of an angel, beyond beauty, beyond words. 'Mr Mulligan,' she said softly, 'would it be a terrible cheek if I asked to come occasionally to play this instrument?'

He saw her then, saw what she really was. How many had misjudged this girl so far? he wondered. There was damped-down intelligence behind those eyes. Eliza had moulded herself, he guessed, to fit with her mother's pattern, to be the sort of lady Louisa would want to have as a daughter. 'Of course you may play here,' he replied. 'As long as your mother has no objection.' God, she was lovely. Not all the dictionaries in Christendom could possibly contain language to describe the young woman.

They had been born, these young Burton-Masseys, within a space of just over two years. Amy was twenty-one, Eliza twenty, Margot nineteen. Probably despairing of ever producing sons, the parents had stopped breeding after Margot's birth. But Alex and Louisa had created three stunning daughters, three different pearls from the one shell.

'Thank you.' She drifted past him, the perfume of a rose garden filling his nostrils as she left the room. She met her mother in the hall, then followed the servant to the front door. James said goodbye, standing to watch the two women as they were helped by their one remaining male servant into a small trap.

No sooner had they left than he was approached on the steps by yet another Burton-Massey. 'Hello, Margot,' he said casually.

Margot's stomach felt like the Grand Canyon. After walking half-way home towards sustenance, she had doubled back. Mr Mulligan could not be allowed to fall in love with Eliza and Chopin. He was hers. Although she was a mere nineteen, Margot was absolutely sure that she knew her mind. 'Thought I might help when the new horses arrive,' she mumbled.

With senses alerted by his recent encounter with Eliza, James was suddenly aware that this Burton-Massey, too, might easily be misjudged. Margot was pretty in a healthy but untidy fashion. Margot was in possession of an agenda that was difficult to hide, especially for one so unversed in the ways of the world. Naked adoration for him shone in her eyes. Immediately, he was on his guard, almost frightened of the child.

'I'm very good with horses.'

'Yes, I know you are. But these are unbroken and quite wild.'

'I'm not afraid,' she replied straight away.

'Then you should be. Irish and Arab blood can be a startling combination in an animal.'

She felt the change in him. So, he must have been taken in by Eliza. 'My sister and my mother – what did they want?'

'You might be better speaking to them,' he answered.

A knife twisted itself in Margot's chest. All her hopes and dreams seemed to be crumbling. She even glanced at the ground, as if expecting to see a sprinkling of dust around her feet. She didn't understand. She had helped him with lambing, with calving, in fields, in barns. Theirs had been an easy relationship, almost like brother and sister, or uncle and niece. No, perhaps uncle and nephew. Her boyishness had gone against her. 'I thought we were friends.' The tone landed just short of petulance.

'We are.'

'Then why are you so . . . so forbidding all of a sudden? I've been helping you for ages, haven't I?'

'Yes, but your mother may have plans.'

Margot hooted with false laughter. 'Mother? Mother never makes plans. Amy's the one for sitting down and working things out.'

'People change,' he said. 'Given certain circumstances, most of us make an effort.'

'Not Mother,' she insisted.

He didn't know what to do or say, so he simply stood, feeling foolish, his eyes moving over Pendleton Grange's gardens as if for the first time. People found him rude and brusque –

he realized that well enough – and he really was inept when it came to the small delicacies attached to social dealings among humans. With a cow, he knew where he was. Women, on the other hand, were—

'I'd better go, then,' said Margot plaintively.

Women, on the other hand, were forever altering. 'Right,' he muttered. 'I'll see you soon.'

'Will you?' Margot dashed off in a very bad mood.

When she reached home she stood in the hallway, breathless from running, listening to her mother and sisters.

'So,' Louisa was saying, 'if you really insist on running the business to begin with, Amy, then that will save us a manager's salary. And, of course, we need someone who can measure correctly. We know that you can.'

'And what will I do?' asked Eliza.

Margot could hear the smile in Mother's voice. 'Why, you will make these *pièces de résistance*. You shall be my right-hand man, dear. Margot can do her share, also.'

Margot dropped on to a monk's bench. What on earth was going on? Amy had started speaking about a hydro, was saying that she would also help Mother, Eliza and Margot to start the fashion shop. Fashion shop? Nobody had bothered to mention any fashion shop to Margot. Amy was announcing now that she wanted to be involved, eventually, with the hydro at Pendleton Grange. 'With rich clients there, Mother, you might get some commissions for clothes.'

The youngest Burton-Massey was beginning to feel more than just a little angry. Hydros and frock shops?

Mother spoke again. 'And Margot, you know, is a good little finisher. She does an excellent button-hole.'

The button-holer in the hallway was heartbroken and starving. Was it possible to be both? she wondered. It was certainly possible to refuse to do button-holes. What about her riding? What about Mr Mulligan's animals? And why should she have to work for a living? No, no, she didn't mind working. But she wasn't going to sit inside, with Mother and Eliza, making clothes for fat women in corsets and directoire knickers.

'Is that you, Margot?' Louisa called.

68

Margot felt too shocked to reply. There they all were, three women discussing the future of a fourth, a fourth who had not even been consulted. Sometimes, families were hateful. Shouldn't she have a say in what went on in the house? This was the trouble with being the youngest. She was expected simply to follow where others led. What about her own ambitions? She wanted to run a riding school, or a farm, or . . . or even a zoo. Yes, she could go to Manchester and work at Belle Vue . . .

'Come in, dear,' said Louisa.

Margot removed her riding jacket and hung it on the stand. She took a deep breath before joining her family in the drawing room. Amy was by the window, her face turned away from the rest. She was always thinking about something or other, always concentrating, calculating, concocting. Well, they could make all the plans they liked – Margot would sort out her own future.

'Margot,' Louisa began, 'we have been discussing an idea—'

'I know,' replied Margot. 'I've been listening. I'm sorry to interrupt you, Mother, and I'm sorry about eavesdropping. But really, I think you should have waited until everyone was here.' She threw herself into a chair. 'Mother, I do not wish to be a dressmaker.'

Amy swung round. 'Nor do I, Margot. None of us wanted the life we have. Mother lost a husband, we lost a father—'

'And he lost our house and our fortune,' snapped Margot.

In the silence that followed, Margot felt the anger of her companions. She knew that her comment was not appreciated, realized, too, that she should not have made the remark. She had loved her father so much, had been his nearly-son, his out-of-doors companion.

Amy nodded quickly. 'Spoilt,' she said quietly. 'The little tomboy, the amusing child. You are a woman now.'

'Only when it suits you.' Margot leaped up, marched across the room and stood in front of her sister, pushing her face forward until each could feel the other's breath. 'The rest of the time I'm too young. Well, make up your minds.'

Louisa lifted a hand. 'Stop, please.'

Margot confronted her mother now, striding past the

69

fireplace very quickly. 'I want to work with animals,' she said. 'I have arranged to help Mr Mulligan with the new horses when they arrive.'

Eliza looked at her mother. No one ever challenged Louisa. Since the death of her husband, she had been vulnerable, often tired or distressed. Eliza had done her best to be obedient, to agree with Mother, to humour her. It was tedious, and it was her daughterly duty, she supposed. Amy, though older and more confident, had also worked hard not to upset their frail mother. But Margot was making trouble, was causing pain to a woman whose agonies had already been immeasurable.

Louisa rose from her seat and walked to the door. Turning, she spoke to her daughters. 'I think we should postpone further discussion until Margot has composed herself.'

Margot had no intention of composing herself. She had been rejected today by the man of her dreams, had been placed in an impossible position by her mother and her sisters, and was not prepared to negotiate. Button-holes? Never.

When Louisa had disappeared upstairs, Amy rounded on her terrible sister. 'I have never known anyone quite as selfish as you are. And when did this happen? When did you change? You used to be a pleasant, generous girl. What on earth has come over you? You are petulant, rude, silly—'

'I am not silly. Just because I don't want to sit cross-legged on the floor stitching button-holes and finishing hems—' Her voice was cut off when Amy grabbed the front of her blouse and shook her hard. 'You will do exactly what is required of you. You are not on Mr Mulligan's payroll, are you? Are you?'

'No. But I should rather work free for him than earn a pittance making clothes.' She pushed her older sister away. 'I'm stronger than you,' she hissed, 'and I am quite capable of throwing you off and giving you a black eye into the bargain.'

Eliza, who had never seen a display such as this, turned on her heel and fled from the room.

Amy released her hold on Margot's clothing. 'Now see what you have done. Eliza will be upset for the whole day, no doubt.'

Margot tutted. 'What a shame. Poor, poor Eliza. She has it

70

easiest, you know. Mother's little beck-and-call, Mother's sweet, innocent right hand. Eliza is very, very clever – mark my words, Amy.'

The older girl spoke softly. 'You have no idea, have you? Eliza is just a bundle of nerves, because she loves our mother so much that she is denying herself all the time. Have you never seen her outside? Have you never followed her into the woods? No, no, since you care only for yourself, you won't have bothered.'

Margot allowed a single hoot of hollow laughter to escape from her throat. Then, noticing the ferocity of Amy's expression, she silenced herself determinedly.

'She sings and dances when she thinks no one can see or hear. You're not the only performer in the household. Eliza, when she's alone, becomes a music-hall artist, strutting about and singing songs she's learned from the theatre in town or from the phonograph. These are not the songs Mother might choose. Eliza is deliberately good, Margot. She would rather be on the stage of some dingy, smoke-filled theatre than sitting still, all sweet and demure, cutting out clothes. You are not alone.'

Margot quietened. 'So none of us wants to do it, then?'

'No, but beggars cannot be choosers.'

'Needs must when the devil drives,' said Margot. 'That was one of Father's sayings, wasn't it?'

Amy lowered her chin. 'It was. And look where the devil drove him.'

'To the end of his rope – in more than one way,' said Margot. 'All those sayings are so connected and so strange.' She put her arms around her sister's shoulders. 'I'm sorry,' she wept.

'We all are.' Amy comforted her naughty sister, wondered at the same time when Eliza would crack wide open. 'Just try to be good,' she admonished gently. 'And know this, Margot. Defining adulthood is easy. Being grown-up implies understanding of the feelings and needs of others. Being human is caring about those feelings and needs. Please remember all that.'

'I will try. Oh, I will.'

18 March 1921

Staying with my brother tonight. Stephen is not of the faith, but, like me, he is unmarried, so there are no women underfoot. He runs his little bakery and sells pastries to servants from the Grange, also to people from Caldwell Farm. My brother is a decent man, though unimaginative and not given to prayer.

I saw her again, the middle daughter of Burton-Massey. She is Eliza. She is unbroken and as fresh as spring blossom, as lonely as night. Naïveté untouched, voice mature and strong, music and arms lifted up to the sky as she praises nature.

Oh, child of dreams dancing on carpets of mist, I commend the God who made thee. This moment thou art mine, I hail and hallow thee. Woman-child, child-woman, loveliest creature sent for me to praise, I envelop thee in Light Eternal. Thou shalt come to me, as I shall come to thee. Glorify the Lord.

SIX

Mad Dog Duffy, property of one Daniel Duffy, was a cross-bred terrier with a disposition that was not always pleasant. He answered to Mad Dog, Duffy, Maddie, Full Moon, Hey You and various other titles with which he had been blessed during his eight earthbound years. Many said that he had 'been here before', because he was possessed of a remarkable insight into human nature.

Mad Dog always knew when people didn't like him. He urinated on the steps of folk who never fed him, left more solid deposits on the property of those with the temerity actually to shoo him away. Small, basically white but with black and tan patches, Mad Dog had elected himself monarch of all he chose to survey. Alsatians and retrievers kept their distance, because what the little terrier lacked in stature, he made up for in temper.

Danny Duffy and Diane Hewitt had been training Mad Dog for some months. They played to his strengths, made plans with an eye to the fact that Maddie was an ankle-nipper. In a crowd, he simply bit his way through, not bothering to discriminate between those who liked canines and those who did not. A throng confused him, made him fret. So, by the September of 1921, Diane and Danny had pushed him through the open market, the market hall, Woolworth's, Ashburner Street fish market and several smaller shops. The pickings resulting from the dog's ability to distract people had been fair-to-middling, a mixed bag of food, money and curses.

Now, it was time for the big one. Danny and Diane were giving Maddie his final briefing in a ginnel behind Deansgate. They squatted in the narrow alley, one each side of the dog, who moved his head in the manner of someone watching tennis, doing his best to award equal attention to his two instructors.

'Go for the two fat ones and all,' said Diane. 'It's their wash-house, you see.'

'Big but slow, they are,' added Danny.

'Get folk away from the counter, 'cos that's where all the money is.' Diane's tone was deep and serious. It was plain that her belief in the dog's comprehension of language was strong. 'Bite everybody you come across,' she continued. 'Then go out the back road and run like hell.'

'And bark a lot,' said Danny.

Diane looked with contempt upon her human companion. 'No need to tell him that,' she said scornfully. 'He always barks. Barking's his proper job.'

Danny made a half-hearted attempt to square up to her. 'Whose bloody dog is he?'

'Yours, I suppose,' she answered. 'Only we all feed him.'

'Aye, but he lives in our house. If I tell him to bark more, he'll do it. He takes notice of me.'

The dog yawned, scratched an ear and stretched out on the flags.

'He's gathering his strength,' said Diane now.

'That's right,' agreed Danny. It was safer, on the whole, to concur with Diane Hewitt's statements. Although she was thin and only a girl, she could deliver a fair wallop when riled.

Diane went through it all again, using a crumb of chalk to delineate the plan on paving-stones. She drew the counter, the sinks, the dryer, showed Danny where to direct the dog. This was the first Monday of September wakes week and, since most folk went away during the June fortnight rather than during the autumn week, the wash-house would be packed. Monday was 'uncle' day, too, so purses were likely to contain pawnshop pickings. 'Keep your head low, so as they'll not recognize you,' she ordered Danny. 'Chase Maddie up and down, up and down. While everybody's screaming and mithering, I'll get behind the counter, grab the takings and the purses, then I'll nip out the front way. You just look after yourself and him.' She pointed to the snoring terrier.

'Now for the disguise.' Danny was not looking forward to this bit. Maddie was not beyond biting nearest and dearest when pushed to his limit. 'You do it,' he said, handing the tin to Diane.

Shaking her head in despair, Diane grabbed the shoe blacking. Danny Duffy, like most blokes, was a flaming Mary Ellen when it came to courage. She took some tissue paper from a pocket and stroked it across the polish, then applied it to the dog. Maddie sniffed, whimpered, closed his eyes. This female usually meant business, so he put up and shut up.

'That'll do,' she announced, after thirty seconds.

'He looks daft,' commented Danny.

Diane's eyes travelled the length and breadth of her human accomplice, a journey that took a mere split second. Danny was all angles and scabs, a small scarecrow crowned by a lifeless pudding-bowl haircut. 'If looking daft were a crime, Dan Duffy, you'd have been in prison for years. Come on.'

The dog allowed himself to be dragged along on the length of washing-line that served as a leash. He was fed up, because he knew he smelt wrong, yet he sensed something at the end of all this rope, perhaps a bone or a meat pie, so he went along with it.

Diane was already disguised in so far as she was wearing other people's clothes, items culled from washing-lines earlier in the day, some of them not quite dry. She cut a strange figure in her over-long skirt, baggy jumper and headscarf. Danny Duffy wore his usual, rather scruffy garments together with his dad's flat cap, which was pulled low over his eyes. Far from promising to blend in with their environment, the pair looked like something from *Oliver Twist*, underfed, weirdly dressed and a mile or two short of clean.

The next few minutes were a blur of frantic activity. The dog did his duty, pausing only to cock a leg against a washing-board. He bit several ankles, barked shrilly, got mixed up in a sheet. He was still wearing this item when he left the building by the rear door, his lord and master in hot pursuit.

Diane did not get as far as the counter. As ill-luck would have it, Maddie failed to bite either of the Misses Walsh, who guarded their interests throughout the riot, finally emerging from behind their counter to make a citizen's arrest.

Diane hung from Miss Tilly Walsh's clenched fists, each of which had found purchase on the shoulder of the 'borrowed' jumper.

'I've seen her afore,' announced Mona, ripping the scarf from Diane's head.

'Me and all,' responded Tilly. 'She's from the temple, should know better, but her's never been up to much good.' She glanced at her sister. 'Give that lot the first-aid box.' She nodded towards the customers. 'Then you'd best fetch Wotsisname.'

'Mulligan?'

'Aye,' said Tilly grimly. 'For summat as serious as this, we go right to the top.'

Diane felt the blood draining from her head towards the floor.

'This were meant to be a robbery, weren't it?' Tilly asked.

Diane swallowed hard.

'All dressed up and nowhere to go,' continued Tilly. 'Disguised, I'd say. Even the bloody dog didn't look right. And it's made off with somebody's sheet into the flaming bargain. Well? Nowt to say for yoursen?'

Diane watched Miss Mona as she left the wash-house to fetch the boss.

'You were after my takings and all these ladies' purses, weren't you?'

The customers had sorted themselves into an audience, two ranks, tallest at the rear.

'Thou shalt not steal,' said Tilly. 'And you a laudator and all. Just you wait till Mr Wilkinson gets a grip of you, girl. It's a commandment is that one about stealing.'

The audience, having transformed itself into a congregation, muttered about the young, about sin and about Ada Carter's double flannelette sheet.

'Well?' Tilly shook the child. 'Any more dumb insolence out of you, and I'll give you a good smack.'

The gathering shouted words of encouragement. Its members would have liked nothing better than to watch Miss Tilly Walsh tanning the backside of somebody who had disturbed washday. Washdays were sacred. They were for gossip, flasks of tea, the cleaning of clothes and household linens; most of all, washdays were a chance to get away from home and all its problems.

The whole place fell silent when James Mulligan arrived. Big burly housewives strode back to their business, while the scrawny ones, strangely braver, hung on to watch the show for a few more seconds. When no great drama occurred, they, too, scuttled off to sinks and washboards.

'Well?' James Mulligan raised an eyebrow.

Mona, behind the great man, touched his sleeve tentatively. 'Her and a lad come in with a dog,' she said. 'Like I said before, they were after money.'

'Were you?' he asked the child.

Diane gulped again. For a reason she could not have expressed in a month of Sundays, she was unable to lie to this man. It was as if he could see through the stolen green jumper and right into her sinful heart.

'Well?' He tapped a foot on the flagged floor. 'Give her to me,' he told Miss Tilly.

'What about Mrs Carter's sheet? What about clothes what has to be washed again 'cos of all the black stuff on the dog? I mean, they shouldn't get away with it, should they?'

He pushed a hand into his pocket, withdrew some coins and tossed them on to the counter. 'If that is not sufficient, be good enough to let me know.' He wrenched Diane from Tilly's grip, then marched her across the yard and into his office.

Dumped without ceremony into a leather chair, she studied the floor. It was brown. Most floors were brown, usually oil-cloth, but this one was tiled in small squares, like very posh flags. She couldn't look up. There were two rugs on the floor, both red with light brown bits in the pattern. There was a desk with thick wooden legs. Slowly, she raised her eyes to look at the top of the desk. It was very neat, just a few papers, some pens, a pair of ink pots and a square blotter.

'Look at me.'

He was seated at the desk. He wore a black coat, a grey waistcoat and a very dark blue tie. She could not look at his eyes. Behind him, the window was dressed with maroon curtains and a green blind at half-mast. She glued her eyes to his chin. It was strong and square, with a little dent in the centre.

'Diane?'

'What?'

'Why?'

She shrugged listlessly. It was over and she had failed. If the police found out, she might get put away. Then Joe might well starve. Diane could not quite bring herself to worry about her grandmother.

'There has to be a reason,' he said quietly.

The door opened. Diane felt cold air fanning her ankles.

'Later, please, Miss Burton-Massey.' He waited until the intruder had gone. 'Tell me,' he persisted. 'Who looks after you? Didn't I hear that you live with your grandmother?'

'That's right.'

'Who cooks, Diane?'

'Me.'

'Because your grandmother has no heart.'

'Aye.' Questions, questions. They wanted to know everything or nowt, only started taking an interest if you were in trouble for trying to take something off them. 'I've already told you about six month ago – folk have got to eat.' Let them come for her – she had had enough.

He watched her face. She was older than the hills, cleverer than the Blarney Stone, a woman-child with no hope, no pattern to build on, a past worth forgetting, a future already darkening. 'What am I to do with you? This is my yard, Diane. All the buildings in it, including the inn, are mine. It is my duty to protect those who work here from thieves and vagabonds like yourself.'

She felt almost hypnotized. Were she to live in Ireland among folk with voices such as this, she'd be in a permanent stupor. Even though he was telling her off, even though the tone had an edge to it, she wanted to stay and hear more. No, she wasn't hearing it, not really. She was feeling it, letting it flow through her like warm cocoa, silky, smooth, comforting.

'Diane?'

'What?'

'Are you hearing me?'

She went for the truth. 'Not really. You're putting me to sleep.'

A smile tugged at his mouth, but he bit it back. 'You're a thief, child. A common thief. Listen to me, please. The women whose money you meant to steal are not rich. You steal from them and you steal from their children. How do they buy food? Will they have to become thieves so that their families might thrive? The disease called theft is very contagious – that means it spreads. So, while you use their money, they are forced to take someone else's. Am I clear?'

She was listening now. 'Yes.'

'So, what are your immediate needs?'

She had never thought about any of this before, had never worried about those she deprived. The main driver behind Diane's behaviour was a picture in her mind, an image of Joe with his little crooked legs and his thin white face. Feeding her brother, getting clothes and shoes for him and for herself – these necessities had been the mothers of Diane's inventiveness. 'Food for our Joe,' she replied thoughtfully.

'And fuel? Who pays for coal?'

She raised her chin. 'If we can't buy it, I pinch it.'

He saw the defiance colouring her cheeks. 'You cannot continue like this. Eventually you will be caught, then you will spend years in a variety of institutions. Who will care for your brother when that happens?'

She folded her arms. This was all very well – she even agreed with the man – but what was the alternative to stealing? 'All right.' Her voice was low. 'So can you tell me how we manage on parish pennies and a few bits from the temple? What would you do if you got up in a morning, no coal for the fire, no bread, no milk? And if you had a little brother, could you look him in the face and tell him that he'd just have to get on with it and starve to death?'

79

He tapped on the blotter with his fingers. 'How old are you?' 'I'm eleven – just.'

Eleven and going on fifty, he mused. 'I shall not inform the police as long as you comply with certain conditions.'

She sat rigidly still. 'Go on, then.'

'I must speak to your grandmother.'

Diane almost cried out, but she managed to overcome the urge.

'How old is she?' he asked.

'Very old,' she answered. 'She must be going on sixty.'

Yes, sixty would be aged to a child of eleven. 'And she never gets out of the bed?'

She shrugged. 'She goes down the yard, gives herself a bath in front of the fire one night a week. But she's not been out of the house for years.'

It was time to introduce himself to Diane's grandmother. It was time for Diane's grandmother to be introduced to her granddaughter's way of life. Something had to be done. He stood up. 'Come with me,' he said firmly.

Diane left her chair. 'Where to?'

'Number thirteen John Street,' he answered. 'In my car. We shall arrive in style, my dear.'

They entered the house together. There was a tiny vestibule, then a small parlour through which they had to walk to reach the kitchen. Furniture in this 'best' room was sparse – just an old table, two straight chairs and a black horsehair chaise. The kitchen was warmer, certainly fuller. It contained a large dresser, a central table, some chairs, a rocker, a black range fire and a bed under the stairs. In this tumbled item sat a woman with hard eyes, greying scraped-back hair, a mouth set in a rigid line, a faded blue shawl clutched at the throat with a large safety-pin.

'This is Mr Mulligan,' said Diane, after a few tense, silent seconds.

Ida Hewitt's hands clasped each other on the greasy quilt. She did not encourage visitors, was certainly not in the habit of allowing drunken Irish gamblers into her house. 'What do you want?' she snapped. 'I don't remember asking you to step inside.'

80

'You could hardly invite me in when you don't leave your bed,' he replied easily. He sat at the table. 'Mrs Hewitt,' he began.

'I don't know why you've let him in, Diane,' said Ida.

'She brought me in, since I fetched her home, you see.'

Ida looked from Diane to him, from him to Diane. 'What's going on?' she asked eventually.

'If you will listen, madam,' he said slowly, 'then I shall tell you.'

Ida Hewitt almost growled, but she felt something in the air, a threat, almost. Diane had a face on her like a week of wet Mondays, all damp, downcast eyes and quivering lips.

'You have no work, I take it?' he asked.

The woman in the bed looked up to heaven for guidance, her eyes snagging on a pulley-line of washing that was not at all clean. 'How can I work when I'm like this?' she asked. 'The road I am, I'm lucky to carry on breathing.'

'Mrs Hewitt, Diane is resorting to methods of acquiring the wherewithal . . . methods that are not honest.'

Ida fixed her gimlet stare on Diane. 'You what?'

'Not to put too fine a point on the matter, Mrs Hewitt, Diane is stealing.'

'Never.' The woman sat up with a show of alacrity that was remarkable in view of her supposed condition. 'We are members of the Temple of Light, Mr Mulligan. Our faith does not allow stealing.' She glared at the child. 'Tell him. You tell him, love.'

Diane said nothing.

'She does not earn all the money and food she brings home,' said James Mulligan. 'There is very little work for a child of her age. At eleven, she should be concentrating on her education. Outside school she ought to be playing games, not trying to work out how to feed her little brother. This cannot continue, Mrs Hewitt. If it does, I shall take steps to have her and her brother removed from your care, since you are clearly unfit to look after them.'

Ida's skin darkened to a deep shade of magenta. 'How dare you?' she snapped. 'How dare you come over here to my country,' she beat her breast with a closed fist, 'my country, and tell me how to carry on? Where were you lot when my lad died in the mud, eh? What did your country ever do to save the world?'

He gazed into the flames for at least thirty seconds. The only sound in the overheated room was provided by Ida's rasping breaths. 'I was there,' he said softly. 'As for my countrymen, many fell in the fighting alongside your son, Mrs Hewitt. Not all of us sat at home drinking beer and chewing the cud.' He turned his head with excruciating slowness and met her fierce gaze. 'Oh, I was there, all right. And now I am here, looking to the welfare of your son's children while you lie there waiting for death.'

Diane was transfixed. Nobody ever took Gran on; nobody ever took Mulligan on, either, so here was an interesting situation. As the tension grew, the child almost forgot her crimes. The reason for the Irishman's presence was no longer significant. Daggers were drawn and both contenders seemed keen to see blood.

'You'll not take mine away from me,' Ida whispered.

'Is that a challenge, Mrs Hewitt? I do have some clout in this town, some influence. My father may have been a drinker and a fool, but I was not cast in the same mould. However, I did not come here to explain myself. The purpose of my visit is to inform you about Diane's behaviour. She is worried sick about her brother. She steals to feed him and you. Now, I have no idea regarding the nature of your illness, so I shall send a doctor to look at you.'

'You'll do no such thing.' Ida was shaking with temper.

'As you wish.' He stood up. 'But if you will not see a doctor, I shall go straight to the Town Hall and advise the appropriate department about the situation in your house.'

The front door opened, clattered into the closed position. 'Diane?' called a thin voice.

'In here, Joe,' she answered. Her younger sibling's arrival appeared to have fractured the tension.

Yet when the boy entered, James Mulligan sat down again, the movement almost involuntary. He had seen many such children in his time, but none had stood so close to him. Joe was very small. He had white skin, dark hair and frail, bowed legs. The smile, though, was huge. The lad ran to the bed and handed some coppers to Ida. 'I did three steps, Gran. And I went for Mrs Hardcastle's powders and for Mr Hardcastle's baccy.' He turned and looked at the visitor.

'Joe?' James threw him a penny. 'Would you do me the great kindness of watching my motor car?'

'Yes, sir. Thanks, sir.' He dashed out as quickly as deformed limbs would allow.

Ida stared malevolently at James.

Unmoved by her expression, James returned the cold gaze with interest compounded by a deepening frown. 'His legs will not get strong if he's cleaning steps and running messages all the while. So.' He leaned an elbow on the table, cupped his chin in the hand. 'What do you intend to do about Diane and Joe?'

'Why should you care?' Her tone continued defiant.

'It must be in my nature.'

The sarcasm did not go astray. 'You just get out,' she yelled.

'That's a strong voice coming from such a weak woman.'

'Get out,' she repeated.

Diane gulped. Things had ceased to be merely interesting: she was starting to feel a little shaky, knees wobbling, stomach fluttering. It was like a big boxing match, two adults staring one another in the eyes, each trying to be powerful enough to knock sparks off the other. But these two didn't need to try. There was more to be said, more to be done. She imagined that the air in the kitchen was filled with unspoken words waiting to be plucked and thrown from one to the other and back again.

'The doctor will visit you on a Friday evening,' he said, his voice ominously low. 'I cannot be sure which Friday, as he is a busy man. If you refuse to see him – and I'm sure you need medical help if you cannot get out of bed – then I shall take this matter to the highest authority.'

Ida's chest was heaving with barely contained rage. 'Please yourself,' she barked, 'but the Lord will provide through the Eternal Light.'

He shook his head. 'No. Diane will provide through shoplifting.'

'Irish pig,' she answered smartly. 'What would you know?'

'Enough,' he said. 'I know enough.' He knew that Diane was suffering, as was young Joe. He saw that this woman had vigour, far too much fight for a person who had stayed in bed for almost five years. She was probably very unhappy, possibly depressed and out of sorts in a general sense, but the children had to come first.

'You're a Catholic.' She delivered this as statement rather than as question.

'I am.'

'Then you'll not know about the Light.' Her delivery of the last word ensured that the receiver would be aware of its initial capital.

'Ah, but I have, indeed, heard about the sect.'

'Sect?'

He raised a shoulder. 'Religious group, then.'

Ida sniffed. 'You think we're cranks, don't you? Well, we're not. That religion of yours is a joke.'

'I'm glad it amuses you.' He had won. He knew it, she knew it and the child, too, probably realized that her grandmother was out of her depth. Ida Hewitt could attack every cardinal, bishop and parish priest, could lash with her tongue at the Pope, the saints and all Catholics living and dead – he didn't mind. The Church had stood in spite of criticism heavier than this, and was likely to continue for all time. As long as the confounded woman would give some thought to the minors in her care, she could do her worst in all other areas. 'I am glad we understand one another at last,' he said, rising from his seat.

'Oh, I understand you, all right.'

He reached the door. 'I wish you better health, madam.' In the parlour, he slipped a half-crown into Diane's hand. 'When this business is resolved, you will visit me again in my office. If you want work, we shall find you some.'

She stood with her brother and watched the car leaving John Street. 'Come on, Joe,' she said. 'Meat puddings today.' They ran off towards the chip shop, mouths wet with anticipation. This day, and for a couple of tomorrows, they would eat well.

SEVEN

Helen Smythe, long-term friend of Louisa Burton-Massey, was in her element. As chair of the Blackburn-based Women of Industry, she was fully armed when it came to the setting up of businesses. Her philosophy was simple: men fought wars, women kept the fires burning. If males intended to carry on dying in their millions, then the female of the species needed to be in charge on the domestic front. Having preached all over Lancashire, she was only too happy to step back into the life of a friend who had, it seemed, resigned from the human race several years earlier.

It had been a difficult few months for Louisa. Originally she had intended to take a back seat, but she had gradually picked up the reins, and was now at the point where she realized that she had to remain involved. Amy, the most sensible of the three Burton-Massey daughters, had agreed to manage the business, which, after many discussions led by Helen Smythe, was to be named A Cut Above. The innovative label sat rather less than comfortably on Louisa's shoulders, though she had been drawn in by Helen's infectious excitement. And, after all, this was Louisa's money, so she had to keep watch. Sitting at home thinking, sewing and worrying would not have been enough.

After four months of planning, the scene was finally set. Helen was thrilled to pieces with Louisa's progress. 'You look wonderful,' she declared, after a sip of coffee. 'This is the

answer for so many of us, my dear. Why, think of Camilla –
she has never looked back since I set her up. Women have to
cash in on their own abilities. If we have no abilities, then we
simply invent them. And don't forget, I am always at hand if
you need me.'

Louisa gazed around her domain. She was finally out of the
house, was sitting in an upper room of the shop, the area where
cutting, fitting and detailing would take place. She supposed
that A Cut Above summed it up, since the real work would
take place on the top storey. Because customers would need to
come upstairs to choose fabric and for fittings, the floor was
carpeted in a rich blue, the walls papered in ivory, sprigs of
bluebells repeated in the pattern. There were chairs, tables,
fashion magazines and, beautifully racked and colour-graded,
yards and yards of the finest materials.

'Exciting, isn't it?' asked Helen.

It was more than exciting, thought Louisa. It was absolutely
terrifying, because a good fifty per cent of her capital was
wrapped up in linen, cotton, silk and wool.

Just off this main upper room, another of similar size housed
sewing-machines, patterns and cutting-tables. Three excellent
women had passed rigorous tests, one making an outfit for
Louisa, the next sewing for Helen, the third dressing Camilla
Smythe. In three days, the shop would be open for business.
Already, through the hard work of Helen and Camilla Smythe,
no less than five women had booked appointments with A Cut
Above. Interviews would take place downstairs, in a drawing-
room setting, where women could discuss with Louisa and
Amy their clothing needs. The atmosphere was geared towards
relaxation. A comfortable woman, Helen declared, spent more
freely.

'I'd rather not have the party,' moaned Louisa.

'Don't be silly, dear,' replied Helen Smythe. 'Camilla needs
her chance to show off her catering skills.' She laughed rather
loudly for the wife of a decorated major. 'God, she couldn't
even boil an egg until I pointed out the gap in the market. Now
people would kill for her recipe for salmon mousse. By the
way, did you see Worth's new pleating on that spring
collection? So flattering, especially for the larger lady. And

there was a hemline with a slight dip, elongates the spine wonderfully – where is that confounded page?' She rattled about in a folder. 'Jennifer Turner wants a wedding outfit for April – blue, I think. Did the shoes come?'

Louisa put a hand to her aching head. An overdose of Helen was just what she needed. Oh, for a moment alone . . .

'Fabulous bags Chanel has just now. Scarves are in, of course, so flattering and mobile – excellent for hiding a bit of looseness on the neck and throat. And I found some wonderful costume jewellery in a dinky little factory in Manchester, all hand-set, some semi-precious stones, a bit of jade and so forth. Lapis is so nice, cheap and cheerful, a bit of coral, perhaps—'

'Helen, do be quiet.'

Helen glanced at her friend. 'Sorry. I do go on, don't I?'

'Yes. Yes, I'm afraid you do.'

The two women stared at one another. 'Good grief,' exclaimed Louisa after a few seconds. 'What have I done?'

Helen pondered. 'I suppose it must be a bit daunting, old girl, but let me answer your question. You've caused employment. There's the little jewellery place I just mentioned, then the shoe factory in Liverpool – yours won't be the only outlet for designer shoes.'

'Copies,' Louisa reminded her companion.

'Who gives a hoot or a boot? If a woman can kit herself out for thirty pounds, why should she spend hundreds? Who's going to ask to see the labels? This is the future, Louisa. You are an event, a happening.'

'I am a migraine.'

Helen reached out and slapped Louisa's hand. 'Go home, have a rest, then come back tonight and enjoy yourself.'

'I shan't know anyone.'

Helen tutted in mock despair. 'There always has to be a first time for something to happen. Otherwise there would be no second, third or hundredth. Break out, old girl.' Lack of oxygen caused a brief pause in the diatribe. 'There are one or two widowers on the scene at present. In fact, I think I know of four at least, two of whom are eminently suitable, financially and physically.'

'Helen—'

'I know, shut up. But you should put yourself back on the market.'

'As a real label or as a copy? As second-hand, remodelled, slightly used?'

Helen clicked her tongue. 'We are sharp enough for the cutlery drawer, aren't we?'

Louisa smiled faintly. Mixing with Helen Smythe over the past few months had honed her own tongue somewhat. 'I thought the idea was for women to stand alone, Helen. Isn't that what your organization is all about?'

Helen tapped the side of her nose. 'It's still nice to have wallet and cheque book somewhere in the background. Husbands are occasionally useful. If you manage to catch a handsome one, he can be a rather nice accessory.'

Louisa actually laughed. 'Get that magazine out, Helen. Look at what Lanvin has to say. If husbands are in, I'll order one in emerald green and another in navy. They're next spring's colours, aren't they?'

Shaking her head and a fist, Helen left A Cut Above and went home to gird her loins for the evening fracas.

Louisa closed her eyes, wished that the headache would follow Helen and leave her in peace. A strange mixture of excitement and fear had lodged in her stomach like a huge, indigestible ball. She was going to stand alone. Well, alone except for Amy, Eliza and Margot. And Helen. Which was hardly alone, she supposed. But, at the end of the day, the quarter, the financial year, Louisa's was the name on the books. 'I am a business,' she whispered, into the elegant room. The unmistakable smell of new carpet drifted up her nostrils. 'I'm very new and very inexperienced.'

Margot entered. Margot was a worry. She wore a pretty little wool-crêpe suit in rust, a cream blouse, pearls at her throat and two spots of natural colour on her cheekbones. Still rather untidy, Louisa's youngest was making an effort on the fashion front, was looking less like an ostler and slightly more like a woman of almost twenty. 'Margot,' breathed Louisa, 'what on earth are you doing up here? Weren't you supposed to be helping Camilla?'

The girl snorted. 'Camilla's all done. She's going home to

Blackburn with Mama in the new car. After Mama has done a bit of last-minute shopping, that is. I'm sure Mrs Smythe has a first-class honours in spending.' She sidled closer to her mother. 'Must I come to this . . . event?'

'Yes.' Of late, Louisa had decided that explanations were not always strictly necessary.

'But I want to . . . well . . . I thought I might—'

'No.'

'Mother, you don't even know what I was going to say.'

Louisa knew. She had watched this silly madam coming home all hot and bothered after fruitless pursuit of James Mulligan, who was too old, of the wrong faith, miserable, foreign . . . and extraordinarily handsome. Now, Margot had set her sights on one of the more worthless young men of her own generation. Rupert Smythe, son of Helen and brother to Camilla, was a rake and a wastrel. A tall, lean and hungry-looking specimen, he was possessed of a charm that was given to very few youths. Outwardly compliant, forever in agreement with his elders and betters, Rupert had the ability to court the approval of all females between the ages of nine and ninety. With the exception of one, mused Louisa, one whose youngest had recently fallen under the Rupert Smythe spell.

'Mother—'

'No. You are not haring around in Rupert Smythe's motor car this evening. You will be here to support the rest of your family.' Unconsciously, Louisa straightened her spine, pushing herself against the back of the chair. 'Going into trade is not easy for any of us. Like musketeers, we must stand together. I had not intended to be so involved on a personal level, but the Burton-Masseys are in need of money, so the Burton-Masseys must, as a clan, go out and earn it.'

Margot stamped a foot. She had been so good, was intending to be good in the future, but all she wanted—

'I will not have this, Margot. Rupert will ruin your reputation. Helen has indulged him absolutely, and he passes on the ruination. His parents have, I understand, dug him out of many a hole. Do not become his next victim, I beg you.'

'But I—'

'Must I speak to Helen about this? Because if I do, I shall lose a valued friend.'

The trouble with Mother was that she seldom allowed a person to explain herself. Rupert had not yet popped the question, but Margot felt quite sure that it was just a matter of time. He loved her. She, the youngest of three, was on the verge of becoming engaged. Rupert would take her away from all this. She would not be cutting out and stitching, as would Eliza and Louisa. She would not be fronting a shop on Deansgate, would not be an Amy, all dressed up and nowhere to go. No, Margot would make a very good marriage.

'It's a dream,' whispered Louisa. 'Only a dream.'

Margot, who felt close to explosive, marched out before saying anything untoward. Rupert could drive her home, at least. Mother, waiting for Moorhead to return with the trap, would travel to Caldwell Farm by a slightly less comfortable means.

Louisa, wearied by the persistent headache, leaned back and rested her head against the wall. Downstairs, over two hundred pounds' worth of shoes were racked and waiting to be sold. She had made a similar investment in gloves, bags and scarves. It had to work. Earlier in the day, she had looked out on Deansgate, had seen women bustling past in old coats and headscarves. Whence would purchasers of her goods arrive?

From Chorley New Road, from Heaton and Smithills, she reassured herself now. From houses on the moors, even from the town, surely? Yes, the wife of a doctor or a lawyer could afford a good, decent and inexpensive copy of a fashion item. So far, she was resisting ready-to-wear, though it was an option, she supposed. Wages to pay, too. The headache was worsening.

Amy had been an absolute darling, taking as much weight as she could from her mother's shoulders, urging Louisa along towards confidence, towards faith in herself. Eliza, God bless the child, was like an over-excited two-year-old, exclaiming over colour and cut, choosing the best scissors, sewing-machines, threads. Eliza seemed to be coming to life at last.

Margot? Gloves might hide the bitten nails, but the youngest of the three was still wild at heart. God alone knew where she got to these days. She had paid lip-service for a couple of months, had even escorted her mother on shopping expeditions

90

for furniture for the salon, but that state of affairs had been temporary. Rupert Smythe did not fool Louisa, Amy, or even Eliza.

Trying to be wise, Louisa had not laboured the point. She had forced herself to sit back and hope that Margot would not get in too deep with Helen's son. But waiting for Margot to come to her senses was a thankless task. Louisa would have to talk to Helen. Dreading such a confrontation, Louisa picked up her bag and gloves, taking one last look around the peaceful area. By this evening, the business would have been christened.

Downstairs, Camilla was putting the finishing touches to her buffet. 'Hello,' she called cheerily. 'Going home to put on the warpaint?'

Louisa smiled. She had a soft spot for poor Camilla, whose vibrant red hair and equine features did not attract many suitors. 'Yes, time to go,' she answered.

Camilla blew a rusty tress from her homely face. 'See you later, then, Mrs Burton-Massey. *Nil desperandum.*'

Louisa walked out and allowed Moorhead to help her into the trap. It had been a tiring day. And it wasn't over yet.

If noise measured success, then the opening of A Cut Above was an event to remember. Helen Smythe's bush telegraph must have done its job, because the place was packed. Elegant ladies sipped sherry from crystal glasses, while their husbands, most of them looking as dazed as freshly landed trout, lined the walls, brandy globes twisting, watches making regular appearances, half-told jokes cut off before vulgar punchlines could offend a female ear.

Margot, smiling graciously in defeat, hung from the arm of Rupert Smythe as if she were a fixture. Mother had refused permission for Margot to be elsewhere with Rupert, so she would be here with him, on show, in public and for all to see.

Louisa, whose headache showed no sign of abating, tried not to look at her disobedient daughter. Instead, she circulated and spoke to almost everyone, was polite, slightly distant, and she avoided Helen's widowers as if running from plague. One in particular seemed quite taken with Louisa, who steered him in the direction of an avid spinster from Westhoughton, leaving the poor man to the tender mercies of a woman whose desperation was clearly visible.

In a corner near the door, James Mulligan oversaw the situation. As usual, he wore dark and rather unremarkable clothing, which seemed slightly dated, as if he had stepped out of a recently deceased age. Unfortunately, Helen Smythe, drawn by a magnetism she didn't even recognize, decided to interrogate him. He listened for a quarter of an hour to a lecture on fashion, was quizzed about his marital status – was he engaged, had he ever been engaged, didn't he think it was time he settled down, there were plenty of Catholic women in Bolton, what did he think of the shop – until he excused himself and stepped outside for a few moments.

Amy followed him. 'Well done,' she said.

'What?'

'You threw her off. Helen Smythe is something of a limpet, I fear. She'd have you married and buried within the hour.'

'Yes.'

Amy drew breath. This taciturn man should really have stayed at home, since he was obviously ill-prepared for social occasions. She gazed upward, counted twenty stars between clouds, noticed an unlit gas lamp outside Woolworth's, looked sideways at him. What was this man? A teacher, a Catholic, a hard worker, a person of scrupulous morals? Those were qualifications, qualities and choices, easy to express and illustrate, yet his essence remained elusive. What did he think about? 'James?'

'Yes?'

'What are you thinking about?'

He looked at her as if noticing her existence for the first time. 'Your sister,' he replied.

It was like tapping a stone and expecting blood. 'Which one?'

'Margot.'

'Ah.' Amy waited. A coal cart ambled by, then a tram clattered along its rails. A pair of policemen strolled past, trying doors and peering into darkened windows. Life continued, though there was little sign of it in the man at her side. What had made him so quiet? she wondered. Had he grown up in a cave, a one-man tent, on a deserted island just off the coast of Ireland?

After at least two minutes, he spoke. 'That's not a very pleasant young man.'

Amy decided to take an obtuse angle. 'Who?'

'The Smythe boy.'

'Rupert.'

'And the sister's so jolly,' he volunteered unexpectedly. 'Many plain young women are sweet, as though they are apologizing for their appearance. When she smiles, she's almost pretty.'

The boys in blue stopped, lit cigarettes in a doorway, watched the couple across the street. They also surveyed the carry-on in A Cut Above, probably wishing that they could pop in for a quick drink.

Amy continued to wait, wondering when she would take root. It was plain that James Mulligan had gone into one of his reveries. 'If you marry and change your mind, we shan't be upset,' she said. 'You don't have to return the house or the yard to us. Mother would have a fit if she was aware of your intention.'

He turned to study her. 'What was that?'

'Do you have a problem with your hearing?'

'No. No, I do not.'

She repeated her statement.

'Don't worry about that,' he mumbled. 'I shan't marry.' The next pause was mercifully short. 'He fell in with a bad lot at university, or so I'm told. But I still think he's been spoilt by his mother in the first place. You must urge Margot to stay away from him.'

Back to Rupert, then, mused Amy. He never wanted to talk about himself, did he? 'Why won't you marry?'

He cleared his throat. 'If you'd had a daddy like mine, if you'd seen a marriage like my parents', I'm sure you would opt for single status. I am better alone.'

'Oh.' She didn't know what to say. Even when he was forced to talk about his personal life, he remained unmoved, detached, strangely non-involved with himself.

93

'He caused trouble with a dancer at the Theatre Royal,' said James. 'There was a scandal.'

Back again and again to Rupert Smythe. 'Yes, I know.' Amy smoothed her cashmere shawl. 'It was very visible. Not everyone keeps secrets in the cellar, Mr Mulligan.'

'There is no dancer in my cellar, Amy.'

She decided to go for the full sheep. 'What is in your cellar, then? Buried treasure, dead people, a mushroom farm?'

He laughed. 'Perhaps all three.' He crooked his arm. 'Shall we go back inside, Miss Burton-Massey? The air is becoming chill.'

'Thank you.' She took the proffered support and moved towards the door of A Cut Above.

Inside, loud confusion reigned, but just for a few seconds. A sudden silence ensued, then the air was shattered by a dreadful, drawn-out scream. 'That's Eliza,' whispered Amy, a hand straying to her throat.

James Mulligan, taller by several inches than most men, looked over the heads of those in front of him, turning quickly to Amy when he had pinpointed the trouble. 'I think your mother has fainted,' he said softly. 'Stay here till I find out.'

The policemen, having heard the scream, barged in and cleared a path which closed behind them, blocking Amy's way. But Amy was staying nowhere. She pursued James and the police, pushing aside any obstacle in her path, human or inanimate. Dr Jones, a friend of the Burton-Masseys for many years, was on his knees beside the prone form of Louisa. Two women were trying to comfort Eliza, who was almost as white about the face as the woman on the carpet.

Margot clung to Rupert Smythe's arm, her mouth open in an almost perfect O.

'Quiet,' said the doctor. 'And give me some space, please.'

The crowd stepped back, the two officers shooing them away with waving arms. Gordon Jones felt for a pulse, even placed his ear against Louisa's chest. He placed his hand near her whitening lips, feeling for the slightest emission of breath. Instinctively, Amy grabbed James Mulligan's hand.

'Hold tight,' said the Irishman. The woman was dead. James

had seen enough of death to recognize its signature. 'Be brave, Amy.'

She clung to him as if he were a life-raft. Mother was so still and so pale. But surely she was alive? People did not die so quickly and so young.

Dr Jones rose to his feet and looked at the three girls in turn. 'I'm sorry,' he said, the words fractured by emotion. 'She wouldn't have known a thing. Your mother was dead before she hit the floor.'

Eliza screamed again, and people clustered round her, gathered her up and took her away. Margot sobbed in Rupert's arms. Amy wrenched her hand free, dropped to the floor and hugged the lifeless body of her mother. So brave and so strong Louisa had become of late. And she would not see the fruits of her labour.

James knelt beside Amy. 'I am so, so sorry,' he said.

For a reason she could not have explained or justified in a million years, Amy turned on him. 'Look at your father's handiwork,' she cried, as she held her mother's body. 'He killed both my parents. Get away. Go on, go home.'

'Amy—'

'Don't touch me,' she screamed, hysteria bubbling up into her throat. When Rupert Smythe stepped forward, she screamed at him too, opening fire with both barrels. 'As for you, just stay away from my sister. Go and find another chorus girl, because that's just about the correct level for you.'

Silence weighted down by shock and grief hung in the air. Rupert Smythe and James Mulligan backed away towards the door. Rupert left before anything else could be said, but James remained by the door. Helen Smythe joined him. 'It will be the shock,' she told him, in an effort to explain Amy's accusations against her son.

James shook his head. 'Shock releases truth,' he whispered. 'Amy spoke from the heart. What she said about my father was perfectly correct.' He nodded, as if counting the seconds as they passed. 'Your son is a wastrel, Mrs Smythe, but this is not the time to discuss the skeletons in our cupboards. Three young ladies have lost their mother just now.'

Helen bit back remarks that might have served to improve

the reputation of her beloved Rupert. The Irishman was right – this was scarcely the time or place to defend the living.

Amy, Eliza and Margot were shepherded out by police and many willing chaperones. As they passed James, Amy looked straight through him, as if she could see nothing at all. Eliza had to be carried, while Margot, so recently happy in the presence of Rupert, was now in a state bordering on the hysterical.

James, after making sure that the doctor had gone with the Burton-Massey girls, took it upon himself to clear away stragglers and to wait with Helen Smythe for the ambulance. Just one constable remained, the second having run across the road to Bolton's main police station.

Helen picked up a scarf and spread it across Louisa's stilled features. 'She had a headache,' she announced, to no one in particular.

The policeman sighed loudly. 'It'll be one of them brain bleeds, a bit of a stoppage what's burst, like,' he said. 'Aye, we see a lot of this kind of thing in our line of work. She won't have known what hit her.'

James sat with his head bowed, hands clasped between his knees. All he could hear was Amy's voice, the accusation, the anger. Thomas Mulligan, gone but not forgotten, continued to do his worst.

EIGHT

The funeral service for Louisa Burton-Massey was held at the Church of St Augustine on Thicketford Road at the bottom of Tonge Moor. The main cortège consisted of a horse-drawn hearse and two carriages for family and household staff. Behind these vehicles, others tagged along, a mixture of motor cars and carts in many shapes and sizes.

It occurred to Amy, as she followed her mother on this final journey, that death prompted people to remember those they had ignored for years: several faces from the past had decided to put in an appearance on this sad day. In death, Louisa deserved a visit; in life, she had been relegated to the rear seats of memory, just another penniless widow trying to offload three daughters before following her husband into the great beyond.

The service was beautiful, Amy supposed. St Augustine's was high Anglican, its speciality the quality of its choir. The singing was excellent, almost inspirational. Amy fixed her gaze on the coffin and allowed 'Abide With Me' to flow over her. She could smell incense and flowers, while the scent of beeswax rose from highly polished pews.

It was a proud church, cared for as well as any fine drawing room. This was the house of the Lord, a comfortable extension of everyone's home, a place where one could visit and think about life's problems and joys. The clergy's attitude was that

97

there was no harm in coming in to check a shopping list or to rest weary feet. Jesus's house was like any other, except that the Host here was invisible, precious and deserving of total respect.

Amy remembered how Mother had answered when questioned about St Augustine's. Why did she travel so far on Sundays? Could she not have used a church nearer to the village of Pendleton? Wasn't St Augustine's rather Roman in its celebrations?

Louisa's reply had always been the same. 'God is special, so we should dress up for Him. Had I wanted a drab Christianity, I should have become a Methodist.' Oh, Mother, Mother. How you tried, how you changed, how you battled to set up the business. And how you loved this beautiful, glorious little church.

The first real tears followed gravity's path down Amy's cheeks. Busy with arrangements, tired from comforting her sisters, she had squashed her own grief. But now, in this place which had always made Louisa and her family welcome, the oldest of the dead women's children was finally overcome. Sweet voices of young choristers, excused from school for the funeral, enveloped her, penetrated her inner self. Mother had gone, and no one would see her like again. In recent months, Mrs Louisa Burton-Massey's true colours had shone through, had been as bright as the sunlight now piercing stained glass in St Augustine's windows.

Margot's arm crept around her older sister's shoulders. Amy was in charge now. At twenty-two, Amy would have to become the pilot, the navigator, the sailor in the crow's nest. Margot, heartbroken on her own account, was further stricken by the knowledge that Amy would now be forced to look after everyone and everything. While the older girl was used to running the home, a new business was a huge responsibility. Mr Mulligan had promised to do all he could, but Amy was scarcely speaking to him. The business would be closed for a while, closed before it had opened properly.

Mr Mulligan had offered Pendleton Grange as venue for a post-funeral buffet, but he had been thanked and refused. The Burton-Massey girls did not want to drink tea or sherry after their mother's burial, so the congregation could simply disperse and fend for itself.

Margot withdrew her arm and fiddled with a glove. She was an orphan. Scarcely out of her teens and with both parents dead, she felt terrified. Rupert was in the church, had been dragged along by Helen and Camilla, Margot suspected, but he had made no move to comfort Margot in the days since Louisa's death. Just a dream, Mother had said. Both Eliza and Amy had agreed that Rupert was a waste of time and space, though Eliza had been slightly kinder than Amy. A thousand button-holes stared Margot in the face. How many miles of stitching was that? Hems might make a less than welcome change. How many miles in a thousand hems? Poor Mother was in that box, crated up like fruit from foreign parts. It was fancy, polished, decorated with brass, but it was still a wooden container.

Eliza simply breathed. Since Louisa's death, she had felt strangely liberated, as if expecting that her own life might now begin in earnest. She missed her mother, had been shocked by so sudden a departure, yet she retained a calm that did not match the seriousness of this occasion. Unable to weep, she found within herself little need to mourn. Sometimes, she did not know who or what she was; this was one such time.

At the rear of the church, James Mulligan leaned on his cane. He wore his everyday clothes, but tie and gloves were in plain black, not the greys and blues he usually favoured. Like a dagger twisting in his son's stomach, Thomas Mulligan's sins refused to be digested. James Mulligan's father had caused all this.

He closed his eyes, smelt burning peat, whiskey on his father's breath, on his clothes, even in his sweat. Mammy running across the yard, screaming when the shovel winded her, curling like a foetus as she tried to protect her face and belly. The day had come, of course, the day when James, albeit still in his thirteenth year, had throttled the man to within an inch of total asphyxia. 'Touch my mammy again and I'll see you in hell.' Even when young, James had dwarfed most adults.

So Mammy had sent her beloved son away to be educated

99

in Dublin by Christian Brothers. The money to support him had come from the Church, a fact that had been intoned regularly whenever James had failed at his books. The brothers had not been cruel; they had simply sought to remind him that the Catholic Church was his sponsor and that he should repay his betters by working hard.

Mammy had been found dead in a field, supposedly trampled to death by a bull whose temperament had been remarkably good. Even as a ten-year-old, James had spent many happy hours talking to Samson, leading him about, answering the loud snorts, which always managed to sound tame when compared to the bellowings of other male cattle. Samson had loved Kitty Mulligan above all other beings; Samson had not killed her.

Thomas Mulligan had murdered his wife. The product of the union between Kitty Gallagher and Thomas Mulligan stood now mourning another of that wild man's victims. Had Alex Burton-Massey lived, he might have recovered from the wounds of war. Had Mulligan Senior not cheated his gambling partner, the man would probably not have killed himself. And now, his widow was on her way to everlasting joy.

James opened his eyes and stared at the backs of three young women. Amy, tough on the outside, tender beneath the veneer, was crying. He could tell from the movement of her shoulders that the sobs had erupted at last. Eliza, unnervingly beautiful, had drawn herself to one side, as if separating herself from this grievous occasion. Eliza's grief was internal, he judged, and she retained a strength that showed sometimes in her face, often in her movements. Eliza, James decided, was possessed of a degree of self-management that would help her to survive. Margot, the youngest, seemed to be staring at the floor. James knew that he could not return to Ireland until these girls were settled. The sins of the father had, indeed, been visited upon this particular son.

How to atone? Would they accept the return of their property more easily now that Louisa was dead? And what would they do with it? There was a mortgage to be repaid, and would the sale of the inn cover that? Why should they sell the whole yard? Those businesses could keep them in comfort.

No – he had to free the Grange of debt before returning it to its rightful owners. As for the inn, that would probably have to be sold whatever – it was not making money. He closed his eyes and counted the hundreds, possibly thousands, needed now to put Pendleton Grange to rights. Giving it back was not enough: the house should support itself, should make its own income. Otherwise, it would surely become a millstone far too heavy for the necks of three young women. Sighing deeply, James opened his eyes and bade his mind break free of its circular thinking. The house, the farms, the yard and the inn must rest awhile.

The vicar was speaking. 'Louisa Burton-Massey was a true lady. Had it not been for her and others of her ilk, St Augustine's Church would not be here. She and her husband gave unstintingly so that both church and vicarage could be maintained.

'After the premature death of her husband, I visited Mrs Burton-Massey frequently, as her grief was immense. I can only hope that I gave that good woman a degree of comfort. Just prior to her own death, Mrs Burton-Massey set up a business in an attempt to provide some security for Amy, Eliza and Margot, her three daughters. The last time I saw her, she was laughing and happy. I am sure that she meets her Maker now in a state of grace.

'She had a very strong faith, a total belief in God and His Holy Trinity. There is a soul newly arrived in Heaven this day.

'I leave you now to pray silently and inwardly as we all thank God for sending us such a wonderful human being.'

Amy could not pray. She tried to tell God of her gratitude, but she resented Him for taking Mother so early. Louisa had spent five solid years in torment, a mere four months as a tangible person. Still, Heaven had no time. Heaven went beyond all known dimensions; it was a state of simple happiness. Was Father there? Did God allow suicides to grace Paradise?

James left the church, the vicar's words echoing in his mind. The untimely deaths of two people made him guilty by proxy, since he was the son of a wicked man. Louisa might not have worked so hard, might not have died, had he, James Richard

101

Mulligan, found a way to force the woman to take back her property. The ace of spades, the devil's card, the— Who was that? Staring down Thicketford Road towards Tonge Moor, he saw a short fat man. He had seen him before, quite recently, too.

Ambling along slowly in an attempt to look casual, James went towards Peter Wilkinson. An insurance agent, Wilkinson might have been on his rounds, but he was standing so still, his piggy eyes seeing nothing, it seemed, except for the church in which Louisa's service was currently taking place. 'Looking for someone?' James asked, when he reached the side of this oily, repulsive Guardian of the Light Eternal.

'What?' Like one waking from a dream, the man almost shook himself.

'Your brother keeps the Pendleton bakery and post office, does he not?'

'That's right.' Small eyes raked over the Irishman's face. 'And you are James Mulligan.'

'I am.' James shuddered involuntarily.

'You were at the funeral?'

'Yes.'

'And your culpability made you leave early. Had it not been for your father . . .' He shrugged, lifting fat hands in a gesture of despair. 'But we can't be responsible for the misdeeds of our fathers, I suppose.'

James leaned against the wall. The father of Peter Wilkinson had produced a strange creature. James suddenly felt very cold, as if the temperature had plummeted within these few seconds. He had noticed this man lurking on the edge of Sniggery Woods, had investigated, had discovered Eliza singing a sad song. Peter Wilkinson had been watching Eliza Burton-Massey, of that fact James was certain. And then there were the rumours, quiet whispers, words spoken in hushed tones by people who had chosen not to linger within the long shadows cast by Wilkinson's Light.

'Aren't you a Catholic?' the man asked now.

'I am indeed.'

'And you've attended a C of E service?'

James nodded.

'A sin for you, isn't it?'

James forced himself to meet the malevolent stare. 'There are sins and sins, Mr Wilkinson. I can be cleansed quite easily.' He paused for effect. 'The cleansings in my Church do not involve the laying on of hands.'

Wilkinson staggered back a pace. 'What do you mean by that?'

James remained quiet for several seconds. 'I mean whatever you choose to make of it, sir. But you would be wise to watch your step.' He turned as if to leave, then swivelled on his heel. 'By the way, an American friend sent me some cuttings from a Dallas daily. Every time one of your burning bushes ignites, there seems to be a strong smell of paraffin in the vicinity.'

'The – the bush burnings are a mystery,' stammered Peter Wilkinson.

'So is your hypocrisy. Watch yourself. One of these days, you'll go too far. Oh, by the way, I own the woods known as Sniggery. Stay off my land, please.'

Crooked teeth were bared in a travesty of a smile. 'You own nothing, you Irish thief.'

James agreed, noticing at the same time how quickly Wilkinson's anger rose to the surface. A fragile personality, then. 'We arrive with nothing, and we leave the world in the same condition,' he said, with exaggerated patience. 'Our value is contained in what we choose to do with the years between those two events. So look after your Light, Mr Wilkinson. Lights have a habit of extinguishing themselves. Mrs Burton-Massey is today's illustration of that certainty.' He mustered his strength and walked away.

Peter Wilkinson felt the blood draining from his head. He had done nothing wrong. He had never done anything wrong. He simply performed the tasks required within his ministry. Boys, less vulnerable than young females, cleansed themselves by doing good works within the community. But girls could not be left to wander in the wilderness. They were tomorrow's mothers, producers of laudators and bearers, even of guardians. The guardian had to be the first to touch the flesh of innocents, the first to guide them into the Light and away from danger.

103

His collar tightened. White dresses, pale limbs, warm bodies, trusting faces. Nothing ever happened, nothing unseemly. He simply poured his spirit into them by praying and soothing, words and sympathy, no more than that. It was not sexual, he reminded himself yet again. His particular guardianship went above and beyond all that; he was as virginal as the girls he blessed. But, oh, if only he could . . . if only.

He made sure that Mulligan had disappeared completely before returning his attention to the church. They would come out in a minute, those three beautiful girls, grief in their eyes, loveliness on their faces. Perhaps one day, he might help to save them. If only . . . Dear Lord, if only somebody would . . . would love him for himself, for who and what he was. He could not help his appearance. Being ugly did not remove need or desire; being almost impotent did not render him numb. If only, if only.

The Light was his hope, his faith and his life. The Light had given him dignity, a place in society, the chance to make contact with his fellow man. And woman.

They were coming out now. All three girls were blonde, though each head of hair was individual in its shade. The youngest was pretty enough, alive, wayward, he suspected. Eliza was perfection; like a goddess, she seemed untouchable. Amy was his favourite, yet he recognized that she lived beyond his sphere, that she was less biddable than the others.

But it was almost noon and there was money to collect. After allowing his eyes to soak up beauty for a few more precious seconds, he set off again on his rounds. The rain continued to hold off – there was even a bit of sunshine peeping through the clouds. All was well, so Peter Wilkinson praised the Lord.

'I can find very little wrong with you in the constitutional sense.' Gordon James shook his head. 'It's a mystery to me, Mrs Hewitt. Your muscles are, perhaps, a little weak, but that is only to be expected, since you spend ninety per cent of your life in bed.' He pushed the stethoscope into his bag. 'You will need a tonic, fresh air, good food and exercise. To begin with, walk just the length of your street and back.'

Ida was not best suited. Doctors knew next to nothing these days. How could anyone guess how she felt and what went on inside her head and body? And what did he mean by fresh air? The industrial core of Bolton had not suffered an invasion of oxygen for more than sixty years.

Dr Jones snapped shut the clasps on his case, then turned to look at her. Having lost her son, the woman had resigned her position as a member of the race. In a sense, she reminded him of poor Louisa, who had reacted in a similar way after the death of Alex. The difference was that Louisa had still possessed a mite with which to feed herself and the girls, whereas Ida Hewitt was just a breath away from starvation. Still, this one was alive, at least, while Louisa had passed away younger and, to the naked eye, apparently healthier. Doctoring was a strange job.

She glared at him balefully. 'I can't go back in that mill,' she said. 'I couldn't stand the din nor the heat before, so I'm sure it'd be even worse after so long away from it.'

He sat on the edge of the bed. 'It's your soul that's sick, Mrs Hewitt.'

She bridled visibly. 'There's nowt wrong with my soul. I'm of the Light, so the miracle comes to this house at least once a week.'

'Ah.'

What did 'ah' mean? she wondered.

'Do you feel tired all the time?' he asked.

'Aye, that's right. And I get shooting pains in my legs.'

'Exercise,' he reminded her.

She met his enquiring gaze, insisting inwardly that she should not feel ashamed. She was constantly exhausted, permanently sad. It was as if there was nothing sufficiently important to make her want to stay alive. 'If it weren't for the Temple, we'd be in a right mess,' she informed him. 'Then our Diane earns a few bob and—'

'And the boy?'

Ida shrugged. 'He does what he can, bless him.'

'His legs are terrible.' Gordon Jones had sent the two children into the parlour, had noticed that Joe's legs were badly misshapen due to rickets. 'Those two young ones will be

105

taken from you if you make no effort. I've seen it happen before. Then, there would be no one to help you if the children left.' He paused fractionally. 'As for the Temple of Eternal Light, in my opinion that is a sect that does nobody any good.' He held up his hand when her mouth opened to air her objections. 'My opinion, Mrs Hewitt. I do know of others who share my view, but that does not mean that we are right. However, I have to say that Mr Wilkinson and others of his ilk do seem to draw in the more vulnerable members of society.'

'You're wrong.'

He pondered for a moment. 'I hope that you will not regret having thrown your lot in with the Light. These minority religions are often well to one side of the beaten track – rather strange, in fact.'

'There's nowt funny about the Temple,' she insisted.

He patted her hand. 'Just concentrate on getting well and looking after your grandchildren. I shall see you again just before Christmas.'

'What for?'

'To report on your progress, of course. Just in a general sense, that is. I shall divulge nothing that is personal, though I shall have to say whether you are up and about, whether the children are still fending for themselves.'

Ida stepped out of the Light for long enough to swear under her breath. Bloody Mulligan. 'I suppose his lordship will want that report?'

'He's paying the bill.'

'Aye, that's about the size of it. Money talks, money rules the world. If I'd sent you to look at him that'd be a different story, because I can't pay. Whichever road round you look, they've got us. They run the factories, the town, even the country. What about our rights, eh? Nobody takes a rich man's kids away if he's ill.'

'True,' replied the doctor. 'But I'm sure Mr Mulligan has the welfare of your family at heart. In fact, he is outside in my car at this very minute.'

Ida blanched. 'Under the wheels of your car might be a better place for him, Dr Jones.'

106

He suffocated a laugh with the back of a closed fist. 'That's hardly a charitable attitude, Mrs Hewitt. He's actually a very fine man, does a lot for orphans up at the Chiverton Children's Home. From what I've heard, he did not have a very good childhood himself.'

Ida groaned. 'I can't be doing with do-gooders. They do a lot of harm – they'd happen be better called bad-doers. And he's picked me – me and my grandchildren.' She lay back and closed her eyes, listened as the doctor left the room. Five minutes later, doors opened again. Ida took a deep breath. 'I suppose that'll be you.'

'That's the truth of it, so,' James replied.

'Sounding bog-Irish, as ever.'

'Another truth.'

She opened her eyes and, oh, he was a sight for them, all right. Straight as a ramrod, broad-shouldered, eyes full of . . . laughter? He was just about the best-looking bloke she'd seen for years. But then, as she reminded herself quickly, she hadn't been out of the house for years, so how was she to be the judge?

As before, he sat down uninvited. 'I hear you're planning on getting better.'

She emitted a sound that was suspiciously like a growl. 'I wish you'd get yourself back to Ireland where you belong.'

'That would suit me fine, so it would.'

She eyed him up and down. 'Any road, a nice-looking fellow like yoursen should be thinking on settling down, couple of kiddies, nice wife with a sense of humour.' She sniffed. 'Let's face it, she'd need one.'

The corners of his mouth twitched. 'Will I tell you something just now, Mrs Hewitt? Something I've never told another living soul?'

She sat on her curiosity. 'Please yourself,' she replied, with laboured nonchalance. 'I can take it or leave it, but it'd go no further and that's a promise.'

He studied her for several seconds. She didn't like him, while he was not very fond of her, but there was a strange kind of trust between them, as if they had known each other for a long time. 'One of my earliest memories is of my father trying to kick the life out of my mother,' he told her.

Ida caught her breath, held it for a few beats of time.

'I would stay with her when I should have been at the village school. I'd brush her hair for ages – she had thick black hair – unless he'd beaten her about the head, of course, in which case I'd hold her hand instead. She never said much, you know. I suppose I've been a bit like her, though I seem to be coming out of it just lately. In fact, I'd talk the back leg off your horse compared to . . . compared to how I was.'

Ida saw the trouble in his face, the pain these memories were giving him. A grudging respect for him was threatening to put in an appearance. She squashed it determinedly. Let him tell his tale and be off – she was dying for a mug of tea.

He paused, looked into the flickering fire, recalled a white cottage with a huge fireplace where peat was burnt, where pots hung from iron rods, where Mammy sat, day in and day out. 'She just sat. Days on end, she looked into the fire while I brushed her hair and peeled the spuds and waited for her to move.' He swallowed a lump of agony. 'At about the same time every afternoon, she would jump up and do his dinner. Then he'd come home, eat it, beat her, eat and beat almost every day, eat and beat.'

Ida blinked. She could not hate such a man, could she?

'No one else knows this. I am telling you because I feel that these truths will help you. You are like my mother.'

Ida blinked again. 'Nay, lad. Nobody's ever laid a finger across me. If they had, they'd have finished up in a coffin, no time for questions or police. I might be short, but I wield a fair poker and a man has to sleep. It's easy to clout a man while he's sleeping.'

He spoke softly now. 'Your boy died and your daughter-in-law was a disappointment. You got all your beatings at the one time. It's easy to think of you as lazy, but I know different. You've dead eyes, Mrs Hewitt. Like my mammy's.'

Ida gulped audibly. This Irishman, this papist, understood her. He was the only one so far who really empathized, who knew how long-term sadness felt. 'Is your mam dead?'

He nodded.

'Was she took young?'

'Aye, she was. She sent me off to boarding-school, because

108

she knew I couldn't watch the goings-on much longer. I was growing big enough to choke him. So, off I went. By the time I was sixteen, she was dead. He never informed my school until after the funeral, so she was buried over a fortnight when I found out.' He gazed silently at the wall for a minute or so. 'I didn't go to his funeral, either.' He lowered his chin, was obviously deep in thought. 'When I got my degree, Daddy heard about it and came to Dublin, drunk as a lord, bragging about my honours. I did not attend the ceremony.'

Ida tutted. 'What did she die of, your mam?'

He lifted his head slowly. 'A farming accident, they called it. He murdered her. She was thirty-eight years old.'

'God.'

'Exactly. I was raised a member of the strongest Christianity on the earth, yet I doubted God for years after her death. Where was He? Why was Mammy's life so terrible? Why did Thomas Mulligan thrive?'

'Then he died, too.'

'Yes.'

A sob rose in the woman's throat. She changed it to a cough, but the result was a very poor imitation. Soon, she was crying openly. When she looked at him through saline-misted eyes, she saw that he, too, was not an inch away from tears. Why had he chosen her?

'I loved her so much,' he managed finally.

'I know you did, lad.'

'Really Irish, she was, with that clean milky skin and clouds of soft dark hair.' His voice threatened to crack, then steadied. 'I could never marry, just in case he might be in me. I do have a temper.'

Ida was too choked for speech.

'So.' He rubbed at his eyes with a sparkling white handkerchief. 'I do what I can when I can. You and yours are my latest project, Mrs Hewitt.'

'Ida.' The single word was fractured on its way out.

'You'll come and stay up yonder for a while, I hope. Diane and Joe can go to the village school while you learn to milk cows.'

Ida's tears disappeared as if by magic. 'You what?'

109

'I'll get you a cottage, then you'll be able to walk about in your little garden. We'll soon have you on your feet.'

'Cows?' Ida had never seen a cow, except in a photograph or a film at the Lido or the Regent. Cows' produce simply appeared via the milkman or the Co-op. 'I don't know as I'll take to cows.' But a country cottage? Yes, she would have something to live for, wouldn't she? The children would be healthier, too.

'I'll leave you to think on it,' he said.

She didn't need to think. 'I'll take it,' she said impulsively. 'Ta very much. A cottage'd be lovely.'

He picked up his hat and made for the door. 'What about the Temple?'

Ida looked at James for a long time before answering. 'Diane and Joe first, eh? They've been neglected long enough by me.'

'Depression's a terrible thing, Ida. Still, the cows will kick it out of you.' He left the house.

Ida dried her damp cheeks on the flannelette sheet, then called out to her grandchildren. For ages all she'd needed was a leg up. Well, she had one now. God bless him, he wasn't bad. For an Irish Catholic.

110

NINE

Sally Hayes was fed up to the back teeth with Mary Whitworth. The job would have been wonderful except for the red-haired madam with her loud opinions and her sticky fingers. The house was almost closed, because Mr Mulligan used just a small part of it, but Mary and Sally were expected to clean the closed rooms on a rota basis. Up to now, this had meant that Sally and the dailies did the cleaning, while Mary messed about, talked a load of rubbish and flicked the odd duster when she felt like it.

The two girls sat in the kitchen with their morning tea, Mary slurping loudly from a saucer, Sally trying to be rather more ladylike. Kate Kenny, the fierce Irish housekeeper, had gone shopping, so Mary was taking her ease, feet up on the fireguard, skirt lifted to allow coals to toast her rather plump thighs.

'She'll kill you,' said Sally. 'She doesn't let anybody put their feet up on her bit of brass.'

'She won't see me. She'll not be back for a good half-hour.'

Sally bit into a piece of shortbread. 'If they open this hydro, you'll have to shape.'

Mary snorted. 'If they open the bloody hydro, you'll not see me for dust. Can you imagine it? Fat old women lolling about all over the place, their dirty old husbands trying to grab hold of us. Some life that would be. Any road, I'm fed up working for the queer fellow. He's off his rocker.'

111

Sally kept her counsel.

'There's summat not right in that cellar,' continued Mary. 'He takes food down. Why would he want food in a cellar, eh? And sometimes he comes straight back up again, so who's eating it? He's not, I can tell you that for no money. But you don't take food down and just leave it there. Somebody has to be eating it. Who's he got locked in his dungeon?'

Sally took another bite.

'You don't care, do you?' Mary's voice had risen in pitch.

'I care about the tablecloths and sheets,' answered Sally. 'And you'd best start caring and all, because Mrs Kenny's going to have what she calls a stock-take.'

Mary pursed her lips. 'Well,' she said, after a pause, 'nowt to do with me. I don't wash and iron, do I? You'll be the one getting asked questions.'

Sally knew that Mary was up to no good. A few ornaments had gone missing, too, and a couple of Mr Mulligan's shirts. Not that he would notice, she mused. He wouldn't care if he was got up like a tramp on fire, because he didn't seem to bother much about appearances. As for the cellar, well, that was his business and nobody else's. Mind, it was a rum do . . .

'What are you grinning about?' Mary asked.

'I'm not grinning.'

'Oh, yes, you are. You fancy him, don't you?'

Sally decided not to reply to the stupid question, as an answer would have awarded dignity to its silliness. She did have a secret, but it was nothing to do with Mr Mulligan.

Mary pulled off her cap to scratch her scalp through its dense covering of red hair. 'I hope I've got no walkers,' she said. 'My mam'll kill me if I take nits home.'

'But not if you take a nice china figurine home,' stated Sally baldly. She stood up. 'I've had enough, Mary. Now, you can either fetch all that stuff back on your day off – tomorrow – or I tell.'

Mary jumped up. 'Who do you think you're talking to? I've been here longer than you.'

'Bring it all back. Every bit of it.'

Mary swallowed. 'And what if it's been sold?'

'Buy it back.'

'What with? Buttons? Mind, I'm not saying I stole owt. But if somebody has been pinching, there could be a good reason, like hungry people.' She nodded vigorously. 'It'll be a daily woman. It's usually a daily woman that steals.'

Sally gave not one inch. 'Just you listen to me, Mary Whitworth. I'm not having anybody accuse me of thieving. Now, think about it, try to be sensible if you're going to blame me. If I've been pinching, where's the stuff? I never go anywhere to sell it. I've no family to give it to.'

'Big house, could be anywhere.'

'We'll see.' Sally crossed the room to place her flat irons on the grille in front of the fire. If necessary, she would tell Mr Mulligan what had been going on. After all, she was an orphan, and orphans had to fight for a place in the world.

'So, I have changed my mind and decided that the children should carry on at their school in Bolton,' said James Mulligan. 'For the time being, at least. You will recognize the girl, I suppose, though her school might well have forgotten what she looks like. I daresay her teachers have seen less of her than we have.'

Amy could scarcely bring herself to look at him. All she could recall was a vague notion of kneeling over her mother's body and accusing this man of causing her death. She sat in his yard office, her eyes fixed to the half-mast blind at the window. Her mind was elsewhere, as if she didn't really exist in the here-and-now any more. Dr Jones said it was the shock and that she should take things at an easy pace for a while. Being other-worldly was odd and confusing. But Dr Jones said it would clear up after a while. He might have been talking about a rash or a head cold.

'You came in here once while I was telling her off. It was that business with the dog and the sheet and a lad we never caught. Diane had laid a plan to rob the wash-house. I have to admit that the Misses Walsh are not my favourite cup of arsenic, so I found the whole thing rather amusing.'

Amy missed her mother. There was a gaping hole in her life, a bottomless pit into which she had felt like jumping for several weeks after the funeral. Eliza had been quite composed given the circumstances, though Margot, like a two-year-old with an uncontrollable temper, had taken to absenting herself again. The oldest Burton-Massey was at a loss. She was a sensible girl who knew her own limitations, and she had to admit to herself that she was not capable of managing Margot. Then there was money – or too little of it – wages to pay, food bills—

'The grandmother reminds me of my mother – and of yours.'

At last, Amy forced herself to look at him. 'I'm sorry. Tell me again, please.' Wasn't this a man who never said much? He seemed to be making up for lost time . . .

So he retold the tale of Ida, Diane and Joe Hewitt, emphasizing Ida's depression and the children's plight. Outwardly calm and constructive, he was heartbroken in the presence of Amy. All three girls had been shattered by Louisa's death, but here sat the one with the world's weight on her shoulders. Not only did she have the home and the business to think about, she was struggling to keep Margot on the straight and narrow. Also, she was the cleverest of the three girls. The brainy inevitably suffered most.

'They'll live for a while at Bramble Cottage,' he said. 'And, in case it doesn't work out for them or for me, I'll bring the children to and from school. Some townsfolk can't settle in the country.'

'I see.' She didn't really. Amy could not understand how the world had the temerity to continue without her mother. The business of clothing women would have drawn Louisa out, would have given her so much joy. Amy could imagine her mother losing herself in a length of silk, becoming excited when a dress worked properly for its owner. Mother had been about to flower, had been on the verge of something wonderful. It was all so unfair, yet everything carried on apace, as if no one cared.

'You're not hearing me,' James said.

'What?'

He jumped up. 'I know your mother is dead and that you blame me. Well, I give you permission to blame me, full and absolute permission. But I cannot stand by while you allow yourself to be dragged under like a sinking boat.'

She had never heard him shouting before. What on earth was wrong with him?

'I watched my own mother being destroyed by life, by her own silent acceptance. I would talk to her for hours, but she never heard me. I understand that your mother was like that for five years. Ida Hewitt is a similar case. And now you, a young woman of twenty-one—'

'Twenty-two,' she interspersed.

'Whatever. Open that business, Amy. Get Eliza and Margot to help you. You cannot separate yourself from life in this way. Even from a practical point of view, there is a great deal of money tied up in that shop. How will you live?'

Why should he care? she wondered. As far as she was concerned, A Cut Above could remain idle for all eternity. They would manage financially, though details remained vague. But Eliza might teach music, while Margot could work with horses. Margot. Where was she now? Where had she been last night until almost eleven o'clock?

'Well, Diane could sweep the floors after school, pick up bits and pieces for you, while Joe might be useful here. Not that he can do much.'

'What are you talking about?' She had missed several more minutes, she guessed. 'You expect me to open up the shop just to give your vagabond child a sweeping-up job? For goodness' sake, we've just lost our mother.'

'It's November,' he said.

'What's that supposed to mean? It could be the ninety-eighth of January for all I care. Mother died in there. And I'm no longer interested in clothing the idle rich.'

'I see.' This had to stop. Louisa Burton-Massey had been dead for almost two months. 'Then what were you doing in the shop when I saw you just now?'

'Picking up the post.'

He sat down again. It seemed that he had spent his whole life among sad women, that he was condemned to talking them round, bringing them back into the realm of the living . . . only for them to die? No. Mammy and Louisa were dead, but Ida, Amy and Eliza were still of this world – physically, at least. Margot was another matter. Margot, parentless and silly, was

115

spending time with Rupert Smythe again. For all James knew, Margot could be on her way to becoming a very lost sheep. James needed to talk to someone about Margot, but there was only Amy, and Amy seemed to be unreachable. If James had measured the Smythe boy correctly, Margot might well be misplaced for ever. The cad knew that Margot had no real guardian, so—

'Mr Mulligan? James?'

'Sorry.' It had been his turn to go absent without leave this time. 'Sorry,' he repeated. It occurred to him in that moment that he and Amy were similar in some ways. She, like him, was inclined to quietness when troubled.

She thrust an envelope under his nose. 'I found this. It's addressed to you.'

He stared at the writing. It was a beautiful copperplate hand in black ink and was addressed to him 'in the event of my death'. Strangely unwilling to open the letter immediately, he picked it up and pushed it into his breast pocket.

'It's from my mother. I found it in her davenport a few days ago. Aren't you going to read it?'

'Later.' Her tone was flat, he noticed, as if she didn't care one way or the other. 'Amy?'

'Yes?'

'You need to be doing something. Try to open A Cut Above in the New Year.'

She blinked rapidly. Christmas. How was she going to face Christmas without Mother? 'When . . . when is New Year?' she asked. When was anything? When was morning, night, noon? When was peace? 'How many weeks?' she asked.

He consulted the calendar. 'About seven.'

Amy folded her arms neatly on the edge of his desk, placed her head on them and wept. She didn't know what to do about the shop, about Margot, about Christmas, about money . . .

James froze. His hands clasped themselves together like a pair of small animals seeking warmth and companionship. Knuckles whitened. A signet ring dug deep into flesh. James remembered Ganga, his mother's father, who had given him this ring while lying on the deathbed. 'Look after your mammy,' Ganga had implored. Amy was still sobbing. An

116

unseasonal fly bumbled about on the windowsill. The pain in his finger joints increased. He must not weep.

'I . . . can't go on,' she mumbled into her forearms. She had not expected to miss Mother so badly. In fact, until a few months earlier, Amy's affection for Louisa had been eroded by the awful lassitude that had surrounded Louisa for years. But the new Mother had been so lively, so strong and likeable.

The room darkened. James realized that the darkness was not real, that it came from within himself, an imagined dusk, an internal veil. He was reacting to the tears of a woman, was hearing the sobs of his own mother, too. A small spark of fury ignited in his head, turned quickly into an inferno. No, no, he must stay quiet. But the roar was too big. It erupted in his throat, forced his jaws apart, spilled itself into the room.

She sat up abruptly. 'James?'

He heard nothing. When his arm swept items from the surface of his desk, the remaining corner of clarity in his head was grateful for the desk's relative emptiness. Red and blue inks stained a rug. James saw the red and called it blood.

'James?'

'Hating a dead man is never easy.' The words hissed their way past clenched teeth. 'Especially when that man is my father. This is his temper, his temper in me. Thomas Mulligan was a murderer, a thief and a cheat. I am his son.'

This latest and completely unexpected happening dried Amy's tears like a piece of magic. James Mulligan, too quiet, too sober, too rigid, had exploded. She could see and hear that he was terrified of himself. 'Stop it,' she ordered softly. 'You are nothing like him.' They must have been like chalk and cheese, she mused. This man was buying and selling horses just to make a hydro, to make a living for three girls to whom he owed nothing. James Mulligan was kind, generous and very angry. Anger and temper were not the same.

He glanced sideways at the debris on the floor.

'Things,' she told him, 'they're only things. You would never harm a living soul, James.'

He turned his gaze on her. 'I killed your mother. Had I found a way to put her life back together, had I—'

'The Burton-Masseys are a stubborn, proud lot,' she said.

117

'You are to blame for nothing. The responsibility for my mother's health and happiness was never yours.' Amy was feeling something at last. She was angry with the man's opinion of himself, guilty because she had contributed to his sadness and fury. 'You didn't kill my father or my mother. I know I've said things in the past, unkind things, but you are not a cheat or a liar.' She watched his face for several seconds. 'Why are you so afraid of yourself?'

'Because I almost killed him when I was a boy. Because I know that I can be stirred up beyond reason, just as he could.'

'And as a result of this you stay alone?'

'That's a part of the reason.'

'Then you are sillier than I am. None of us is responsible for our parents' behaviour. Do you really believe that you must be a drunkard and a gambler because your father was? You are far more likely to steer away from those particular weaknesses. As for me, my mother has been dead just a few weeks. Her death does not imply that I am going to mourn, like she did, for years on end.'

He found himself relaxing. It occurred to him that he and Amy seemed to have swapped places in recent moments: he had been urging her on, now the boot was on her smaller, younger foot.

She tried a faint smile, wiped the remaining tears from her cheeks. 'We're both hopeless, aren't we?'

'Perhaps.'

Amy realized that she had, at last, achieved comfortable eye contact with James Mulligan, that troubled, secretive owner of Pendleton Grange. Without knowing him, she understood him. There was a deep, almost unbearable sadness in the man, a gap in his armour. 'You're selling the inn?'

'Yes.' James got out of his chair, knelt to pick up pens and ink bottles. 'I hope you don't mind.'

'Why should I?'

'Because it is yours. Anyway, with whatever the inn yields, I should be able to think about the hydro, also pay off a bit of the mortgage on Pendleton Grange. If the hydro is successful, we shall all benefit.'

Tired of arguing about who owned what, Amy dried her

118

eyes and steadied her breathing. James Mulligan seemed to be an amazing person. He had dragged her back into the land of the living without her consent, had forced her to react, to feel. During the later months of Mother's life, he had drawn her out, too, had even encouraged Eliza to practise on the piano at the Grange. Yet nobody truly knew him.

Having recovered the items from the floor, James picked up the letter. 'Shall I read it now?' he asked.

'No.' Amy gathered up bag and gloves. 'Had Mother wanted me to know the contents, she would have read it to me, I'm sure.'

'Amy?'

'Yes?' She prepared to leave, fixing her hat at a straighter angle, adjusting a scarf.

'Spend Christmas with me at the Grange – all of you.' He waited for a reply, received none. 'And if you need help with . . . with anything at all, you know where I am.'

Amy nodded to convey that his message had been received. She didn't know what to do about offers of help. Helen Smythe and Camilla were always calling at the farm, usually laden with savoury tarts, casseroles and words of advice. James was here, eyes full of sorrow, mind brimming with thoughts he couldn't bring himself to frame. 'You can manage women only one at a time,' she commented, no judgement in her tone. 'You win us round singly.'

James achieved a tight smile. 'I had just the one mother,' he replied softly. 'And after her, I lived in an exclusively male environment.'

She gazed at him for a second or two. 'Yes, that would fit the symptoms, I suppose.'

'Symptoms?'

Amy walked to the door, turned. 'Your awkwardness with company probably stems from being incarcerated with men and boys. As for the cellar – that is where you vent your anger. I envisage a row of desks covered in pens and inks, all ready for you to attack.'

'And to reach those conclusions about me, you had to think for a moment about something other than your loss.'

'True.'

119

He joined her at the door. 'You and yours are welcome at Christmas – or at any time. And open that business. Give yourself three months to see does it go well.' He decided to aim below the belt. 'If you don't, all your mother's efforts will go to waste. Think of the designs she left, her cleverness in creating one basic style, then turning that into ten different dresses just by careful choice of trimmings.' He smiled, nodded at her. 'Oh, yes, your mother explained to me about tucks and braiding and lace. In fact, she left me quite educated in the fashion department.'

Amy thanked him, stepped outside, then walked out of the yard and up the alley towards A Cut Above. The windows needed cleaning. Ah, well. After Christmas, perhaps.

Caldwell Farm
19 August 1921

Dear Mr Mulligan,

I used to refer to you as the Irish upstart and I apologize most sincerely for voicing my uninformed opinion. Please forgive me and read the following with open mind and heart.

I am dead. Were I living, you would not be reading these words. I cannot understand fully why I am writing to you, but a partial reason may lie in the fact that I have come to trust you more than anyone else – with the exception of Amy, my oldest daughter. My death will have brought her a great deal of grief and responsibility, so I beg you to bear with me.

There is a sickness in me. When I grow tired, my whole body shakes and shivers. Sometimes, my head hurts so badly that it threatens to explode. In spite of this, I feel I should continue to work towards opening a business for the girls. None of us envisaged a future in trade, but I must leave my daughters a degree of security.

I ask you to keep watch on all three. Help them to make a success of A Cut Above. Although you owe us nothing, I appreciate your need to make amends for the behaviour of your father. Do bear in mind that my late husband played no small part in reducing us to our current state of embarrassment. The truth is that Pendleton Grange would probably have been sold by now, as poor Alex was out of control after his return from France.

Amy is a pleasant, clever girl, with a good head for business. She has been a dutiful daughter and has worked extremely hard. However, she is rather too selfless and pays little heed to her own wants and needs. She rarely smiles these days. It seems hard to believe that I had to chide her only six months ago for spending too much time with your horses. If only I could see her now draped across my furniture, her clothes covered in mud. My Amy needs encouragement and someone in whom she might confide. Of the three, she is the most sensible and, I believe, the easiest to deal with. I pray that you will talk to her and make her aware of her own true value.

Eliza is not as ladylike and correct as she chooses to appear. She has a giddy side and might easily be led astray. While Eliza has tried to be the perfect daughter, she does not fool me. She wants bright lights and music, bangles and beads. In Eliza, I have been truly blessed, since she has given up so much just to please me. Mr Mulligan, this girl wants settling before she is much older. She requires a good man, a decent house and some children. I know that you cannot supply those needs, but if you would kindly try to keep her away from the theatres in Bolton and Manchester, she may calm down and find a nice husband. I have heard her singing in the woods; the songs she performs are popular in variety theatre. I cannot bear the thought of her dashing off to seek her fortune on the stage.

So now I come to Margot, apple of everyone's eye, a treasure and a torment, a worry. She is headstrong and spoilt, a great sportswoman. There is an energy in Margot, which, if not properly directed, will lead her to ruin. She does not belong in A Cut Above, so please, I beg you, use her in your stables. Margot is capable of mastering the most difficult of beasts, as she is gifted in calming animals. She has recovered from her shallow passion for you and, of late, has thrown herself at Rupert Smythe. There is every chance that he will abuse and abandon her, as he is not a man of good character.

Having just read through the above paragraphs, I realize the enormity of these tasks. There is no one else to whom I might turn. We have no relatives in the vicinity and most acquaintances turned away after we came to Caldwell Farm. If, however, you cannot help my girls, do not blame yourself.

Finally, I want to thank you for the assistance you have already given. I was pleasantly surprised by your character, your wisdom and generosity, your unexpected warmth. These intimations of mortality under which I currently labour may be nonsense; nevertheless, knowing that you will read this only if I have left the world, I shall be bold in telling you that you are quite the handsomest man I have met for some time. Even your religion does not prevent me from declaring that you would make an excellent son-in-law. Now, that *is bold!*

I wish you good health and happiness for the future.

Yours sincerely,

Louisa Anne Burton-Massey

He folded the letter and sealed it in a new envelope. What next? he wondered. Turning towards the window, he watched the stonemason with hammer and chisel, the undertaker grooming a horse, two women emerging from the wash-house. The clockmaker was struggling to carry a grandfather through a doorway too low for the task. A child dropped small stones into the horse trough.

It seemed that James Mulligan Esq. had inherited more than the yard, the inn and the large house. Now, he was expected to supervise the lives of three young women. 'I seem to have become a father,' he muttered under his breath.

He began to stride about the office, fingers combing through the tangled mass of dark hair, head shaking occasionally as he pondered the future and its difficulties. How on earth could he be expected to orchestrate the lives of others when his own was such a mess? He already accepted that he had to stay in England until the estate was up and running properly. The inn was lost – nothing he could do would save it. There was the mortgage on the big house, the hydro to think about, the yard, the clothing business . . .

'Yes, the hydro is a good idea,' he insisted aloud. Managed properly, a hydro could finance Pendleton Grange, thereby allowing the girls to move back into a part of the house, or to remain at Caldwell if they so wished. What about the yard? Should he sell it as a job lot? Should he offer each business separately to its tenant? Should he leave things as they were? No matter what had to be done, he remained resolved to return Pendleton Grange to its rightful owners.

It was time to go home, time to visit his own secret, the cellar about which everyone seemed to have an opinion. If they only knew. The space under Pendleton Grange contained something far smaller, yet far bigger than most could imagine. In those underground rooms, James Mulligan kept the evidence of his sinful soul. But his own confusions were nothing compared to the weight of Louisa Burton-Massey's requests.

Sighing resignedly, he picked up his hat and cane. It was a hard life, and it promised to become no easier.

TEN

Sometimes, Sally was glad that she had no family to lose. Miss Amy had taken Mrs Burton-Massey's death badly, as had Miss Margot. The former didn't seem to want to do anything about anything, while the latter, wild and headstrong, was running around trying to pin down a man called Rupert Smythe. If this was the result of a parent's death, there was something to be said for being an orphan.

Sally knew all this because of her secret. The secret's name was Miss Eliza Burton-Massey, though the young lady insisted on being addressed as Eliza. 'We all come into the world naked and afraid,' Eliza had said, continuing with, 'and we breathe our last as equals in the sight of God. During the in-between years, we spoil all that. Let's be different. Let's be the same.'

In Sally's opinion, Eliza was unique. She looked and sang like an angel, made wonderful clothes, was kind, generous and forgiving. Of the three Burton-Masseys, Eliza had been the least affected by her mother's demise. She expressed some concern about Amy and Margot, but her own recovery from shock was unusually swift. She was quiet for two or three weeks, then she set about the business of retrimming the contents of her wardrobe.

Several times each month, Eliza came to Pendleton Grange to practise on the grand piano. While there, she had started to converse with the sensitive little maid, thereby discovering quite by accident that someone wanted to talk and listen to her. Margot was conspicuous by her absence, while Amy had retreated into a state where monosyllables seemed to be the order of the day. But little Sally Hayes, an orphan tossed about on the cruel tide of life, was in want of a surrogate sister, an adopted relation who would listen, at least.

Mr Mulligan, by no means a snob, ignored the unusual liaison. Kate Kenny, the housekeeper, famous for her sharp, sarcastic tongue, did not question or rebuke Sally for stepping beyond the bounds of her class. But Mary Whitworth was livid. Coal scuttles rattled, feet stamped, doors closed emphatically. Sally was the recipient of a thousand black looks, though she bore such treatment stoically. She was special by association, because she was learning decent manners. In the privacy of her own room, Sally copied Eliza's movements, facial expressions, and made a real effort to improve her own speech.

'Trying to talk proper?' gibed Mary on the stairs, after listening at Sally's door.

Too much a lady-by-proxy, Sally no longer heeded this feeble and oft-repeated remark.

'My brothers'll get you,' came yet another warning.

'Tablecloths,' replied Sally sweetly. 'Tablecloths, good shirts and a few ornaments. You've brought some back, but not all.'

'At least I've got a mam and dad.'

'Really? I thought you lived with two drunks and a few scarecrows.'

'While you crawl up the bum of the so-called gentry.'

Such confrontations ended only when Sally stalked away to get on with her job.

Towards the end of November, Mary Whitworth's brothers put in their first appearance. Wearing clothes that seemed to have come straight off the rag cart, the burly thirteen-year-old twins came to offer their services as wood-choppers. Kate Kenny, who knew only too well that Mulligan's farm labourers had not the time to perform this task, employed 'our Jack and our Harry' for two days. As the pair of reprobates had travelled all the way from Bolton to beg for work, they were allowed to sleep on mattresses in the scullery for one night.

While carrying laundry to the wash-lines, Sally had to pass these two scruffy articles as they chopped logs. At first, they laughed when she walked by, but by the second day that special bravery known only to cowards bubbled to the surface.

Normally, there would have been little washing on a Tuesday, but Mary Whitworth had 'accidentally' upturned a full pot of tea on the kitchen table. Sally pegged the cloth, heard them approaching from the rear.

'Hey, you,' said one.

With her heart banging like a hammer, she turned. They were a matching pair, two great lumps with matted brown hair, watery brown eyes and broad shoulders. 'What?' she asked. Each carried a wicked-looking axe.

'Our Mary,' said one.

'What about your Mary?' She was surprised to hear that her voice maintained its steadiness.

'You know,' spat the second boy.

Sally cocked her head to one side. 'Do you mean the stealing? There's linen gone, then some figurines and a china dish.' She paused for effect. 'Hey, your Mary didn't pinch anything, did she?'

Stunned due to lack of brain power, they stood open-mouthed for several seconds.

She lowered her head and shook it slowly, appeared to be deep in sad thoughts. 'It's always the one you'd never suspect, isn't it? Well, thanks for letting me know.' She tutted softly. 'Good job Mr Mulligan walks about without noticing much. He still doesn't know the stuff's gone for a holiday.'

Harry looked at Jack; Jack looked at Harry.

'Has any of it been sold?' asked Sally, her tone continuing light.

'Eh?'

'Ah, so it's no longer at your house.'

'The lady in the pink frock's still at ours, her with the frilly umbrella.'

The speaker was awarded a hefty kick from his sibling. 'Shut up, you daft bugger.'

The daft bugger bent down and rubbed his injured shin.

Sally grinned, picked up her empty wicker basket and

126

sashayed towards the house. Some families weren't worth having. An orphan was best placed since she could choose her own company without being lumbered with a crowd of morons. Just before going out of earshot, she tossed a final remark at the Whitworth brothers. 'It's not an umbrella, it's a parasol.'

'Now, isn't this a sight?' crowed Kate Kenny, who was developing as soft a spot as she could manage for this young maid. 'Is this you, Sally?'

'Yes, Mrs Kenny.'

'Are you certain? Did you check?'

Sally was becoming immune to Kate Kenny's brand of humour. 'No, I'm not really sure,' she replied. 'I could be somebody else dressed up as me.'

The housekeeper laughed. 'Ah, listen to you, now. And you've no Irish blood?'

'I don't know whose blood I've got, Mrs Kenny, but nobody never – I mean ever – said anything to me about Irish relations.'

'Never mind, but. There's a sparkle in your eye this morning. Surely you haven't taken a shine to one of madam's brothers?' She didn't need to speak Mary Whitworth's name.

'No, I haven't. They're horrible.'

'And that'd be the truth of it, I don't doubt. Here.' She passed a tray to Sally. 'Away and take that to Miss Eliza. She's playing the piano for himself, so there's an extra cup and saucer on the tray.'

For a few moments, Sally stood and listened to the sweetness of Eliza's playing, breathing in each note as it slid beneath a closed door. She enjoyed music, wished with all her heart that she could make those wonderful sounds. But Eliza had been to music lessons; it had taken years to acquire this level of expertise.

When she entered the room, Sally caught sight of an expression on Mr Mulligan's face. It was there only for a second, but it made Sally's heart tumble about all over the place. She set the tray on a side table, then turned to leave. She didn't want to be rattling china while Eliza was making such lovely music.

127

The playing stopped. 'Sally,' cried Eliza. 'Thank you for the tea. It's just what I need.'

Mr Mulligan muttered something under his breath before leaving the room. Sally kept her eyes fixed on him, but his features had settled back into their usual frame.

'That was Beethoven,' said Eliza.

'It was beautiful. I stood outside listening.'

Eliza jumped up and poured tea, handing a cup to the maid.

Sally backed away. 'No, I can't. That cup was for Mr Mulligan. We . . . the servants have to eat and drink in the kitchen.'

'My rules are different,' insisted the visitor.

'No. Please, Miss Eliza. This is my job, this is where I work. It wouldn't be right, not here. See, I have to call you Miss Eliza when you visit. I can't drink tea with you and I can't chat like we do in the stables or when we go for a walk.'

Eliza sipped her tea. 'Isn't life silly?' she asked, before returning the cup to its saucer. 'Sometimes, I just want to get away from here.'

'Where to?'

Eliza lifted a shoulder. 'There's none of this in the theatre, I'm sure, no master and servant. It's just one big family, everyone the same, everyone judged by the audience for what they can do, not for who their parents are.' She blew out her cheeks in a fashion that did not suit the delicate features. 'Let's run away, Sally.'

Sally was going nowhere, but she said nothing. At Pendleton Grange she had all the freedom she needed. There was warmth, security and a tolerant employer. If and when he went back to Ireland, good servants would be retained to work in the house or the hydro or whatever. Anyway, surely Miss Eliza was not serious about running away?

'Wouldn't you like to see London?' Eliza asked.

Sally pondered. The Houses of Parliament, that bridge that went up and down, boats on the Thames, Buckingham Palace. 'I suppose I would. Yes, I'd love to see a few different places like London and York and Chester. Only I'd want to come back.'

'But that's the beauty of theatre. Variety acts move about all over the place – we'd return to Bolton, work at the Grand or the Theatre Royal.'

'And what would I do?' Sally asked.

'Well . . . you could be my dresser.'

A short pulse of time passed before Sally replied. 'That's a servant, isn't it?'

Eliza looked confused for a split second. 'But we could practise dance steps. You might become an act in your own right.'

Sally didn't want to be an act. She wanted to be a good housemaid, a good housekeeper in the fullness of time. If she met a nice man with a job, she might even get married, have children and give up being a servant. If no one came along, she'd be quite happy with her lot.

'No ambitions, Sally?' There was disappointment in the voice.

The young housemaid had seldom given thought to the long-term future; she was grateful for her good fortune so far, happy to have been treated well at the children's home, to have been chosen to work here, in a decent house and for a decent man. 'I don't think I'd like that sort of life,' she answered at last. 'I need to know where I am and where I'll be tomorrow.'

And that, thought Eliza, was where the difference lay. It was not so much cultural as elemental, essential. Had Sally been born the daughter of a duke, she would still have been a stay-at-home, a goodly soul programmed to find a man to lead her into a similar existence with no changes except for an address. Eliza Burton-Massey was a different breed altogether. A consummate actress, she had the ability to shape herself to fit any scenario. For Daddy she had been a tease, a plaything who had sung and danced to order. For the widowed Louisa, Eliza had been soft-spoken, dutiful and correct. Never, ever, had she been herself.

'Why do you want to go?' asked Sally. 'Aren't you happy?'

Eliza turned her head slowly and looked through the window. November light, always meagre, poked dull, short fingers past curtains and into the room. She was not unhappy, and she still retained a sense of duty towards her family. Should Amy decide to open the business, Eliza would stay to

129

help until . . . until the time was right. 'I just don't want all my life to be like November,' she said. 'Is it wrong to need a little fun?'

'No,' answered Sally.

'Don't tell anyone about this, please.'

'I won't.' Sally turned to leave, stopped suddenly.

'What is it?' asked Eliza.

The young maid returned to the tea tray. 'Shall I take this?'

'No, thank you. Sally? What is it? What's on your mind?'

Sally could not say it, could not find the words. The way Mr Mulligan had been staring at Eliza, the light in his eyes . . . Did he love her? And wouldn't it be wonderful if they married? A kind master, a good mistress, this house ringing with the laughter of children . . . No. Pendleton Grange was to be a hydro, Eliza wanted to go on the stage, and Mr Mulligan needed to find his own way of expressing feelings. He didn't need a housemaid to be running around and talking about his facial expressions.

'Sally?' enquired Eliza once more.

There were areas that must be avoided even by friends – perhaps especially by friends. Sally poured a second cup of tea for Eliza. 'It was just a thought,' she said finally. 'One of those silly thoughts that just stays for a minute and then gets forgotten.'

'A butterfly moment,' said Eliza.

'Aye, that's it. Just a butterfly, Eliza.'

The day had come at last. Ida Hewitt, packed and ready for off, sat on the rocking-chair next to the struggling remains of her last fire in 13 John Street. Having decided not to die after all, she had practised walking, had even ventured upstairs several times to organize the gathering of her family's sparse belongings. But Ida was uneasy with herself, unsettled in her own company. She had neglected the children for years, had never been ill at all. Misery was not a disease. A woman such as she would be unlikely to see the face of the Lord, would not receive the ultimate blessing of Light Eternal.

Joe was already sitting on the front doorstep waiting for Mr Mulligan's car and a dray cart hired to carry bits of furniture up to Bramble Cottage near the village of Pendleton. 'We're going to be villagers,' said Ida. 'It's posher, living in a village. I hope our Joe's sitting on a cushion, Diane. We don't want him catching piles on top of everything else he's got. Still, we'll soon be gone, eh?'

Diane was in several minds. Even Daft Danny Duffy and his dog had begun to look attractive of late. She had started noticing things, stuff that had never mattered before. The lamp-posts were interesting shapes, the Town Hall clock was beautiful, the market was exciting. And what was she going to find up yonder? Fields, trees, cows, more trees, a couple of sheep. It would be good for Joe, she reminded herself repeatedly. It was already good for Gran, because she'd perked up no end just lately.

Ida stared into failing tongues of fire in the grate. She wasn't a decent woman. This realization had come to her gradually, had been born when she had started to frame herself a bit better. The promise of a cottage in the country had goaded her to move; she could have moved earlier, could have helped their Diane. 'I'm sorry, love,' she mumbled. 'I really am.'

Diane studied her grandmother for a few seconds. 'It weren't your fault,' she said. 'Mr Mulligan's explained it to me. He said life knocked you down.'

'And he's picked me up. A flaming Catholic and all.'

'Gran?'

'What?'

Diane sidled to the chair. 'I'll still see my friends, won't I? You know, with coming to school here, I'll not be lonely.'

Ida closed her eyes, but could not close her ears. It was plain that her granddaughter depended more on her playtime fellows than . . . than on her own folk. 'Aye, you'll still go to the same school. And make sure you do go and all, eh? No playing truant, no stealing. Our Joe'll be at the school and all, so I'll get him to make sure you stay put. If you like it up on the moors, you can change to the village school.'

Diane swallowed a huge lump of pain that contained Queens Park, Manfredi's ice-cream parlour, Mad Dog, the boating pond at Barrow Bridge, the Tivoli cinema, the Bolton holiday fairs. No, no, she chided herself. She would still be here most

131

days. But she would be living in the country, sleeping at Bramble Cottage. 'I bet it's dark at night.'

'Aye, it will be. I hadn't thought, but you're right enough.'

Diane cast an eye over bug holes in the walls, remembered cockroaches and silverfish, mice, even the occasional rat. Perhaps vermin didn't thrive up on the moors. And Mr Mulligan was nice in his own way, so that was another bonus. The shock of finding a nice Holy Roman was beginning to fade, especially since Gran had admitted that Mulligan was all right as far as bead-counters went. Gran even prayed for Mr Mulligan, begged God to help him see the Light before it was too late.

The Light. Diane perched on the edge of a chair and thought about Mr Wilkinson. Her feelings towards him had changed immensely over the past few months. Having started off as reluctantly respectful, Diane had travelled through tolerance, impatience, distrust and dislike before reaching ... was it hatred? There was something about him, something nasty. She didn't like standing near him, and it wasn't just the smelly hair stuff that put her off: it was inside him. What was inside him, though?

To take her mind off the confusion, she placed the last few paper-wrapped cups in a cardboard box. Mr Wilkinson's brother had a shop up in Pendleton. She spotted Gran's other shoe under the dresser, dragged it out and put it with the cups. It was something to do with girls, to do with cleansing. Gran's shoes were going to need new laces. Joe wanted a new vest. The Guardian of the Light did things to girls. The girls didn't say much. He spent some weekends up at Pendleton. There was no getting rid of him, it seemed.

'Diane?'

'Yes, Gran?'

'We'll be all right, won't we?'

It wasn't just children who feared the unknown, then. Gran, too, was afraid of the new life. Having imagined that adults were usually sure about everything, Diane was startled. What chance was there for the young if grown-ups didn't have solid answers? 'Yes,' she sighed, 'we'll be all right.'

Ida was genuinely tired, though the daily shifting of herself

132

had made her bones and muscles stronger. She could never give back Diane's childhood, could never repay that huge debt. From now on, though, she needed to be positive. The Hewitts could not depend for ever on Mulligan's generosity, so Ida would need to find work. Where? There wouldn't be much going up yon, even if Mr Mulligan had made a joke about cows.

The kitchen door opened. Ida turned, expecting to see James Mulligan, Joe, or both, could not manage to wipe the disappointment from her face after identifying the visitor. 'I thought you'd be at work,' she said.

Peter Wilkinson placed the Light on the dresser. 'I'm collecting round here today,' he said, 'so I thought I'd call in to wish you well. Of course, I'll see you at weekends.'

Diane could not be bothered to look at him.

'Art thou well?' he asked.

Diane sniffed loudly. Why couldn't he stick to 'you' instead of 'thee'-ing and 'thou'-ing all over the shop? In fact, why didn't he just beggar off and leave folk in peace?

'Diane?' His voice was low. 'You have been chosen.'

She moved her head and looked at him. 'Chosen? Chosen for what? I'm not even a bearer yet.'

Peter Wilkinson bared teeth that imitated a row of ancient gravestones after an earthquake, all stained and out of alignment. 'Some of us will be emigrating to Texas,' he said, his chest puffing out like the upper half of a pouter pigeon. 'We shall live simple lives where everyone will be the same. Except for guardians,' he added hastily. 'The Great Guardian has his own house, of course.'

'Of course,' mimicked the child.

Ida rose to her feet. 'When did all this come about?' she asked. 'Nobody's never told me about America.'

'Makersfield, Texas, is our spiritual home,' he replied gravely. 'Just a chosen few will go there to serve the Great Guardian.'

Ida Hewitt folded her arms and stared at the man. 'I'm sorry,' she said firmly, 'but no, thanks. Our Diane is not going to live in Texas.'

'It's an honour to be picked,' he spluttered.

133

But Ida cut him off. 'Has America not got enough folk of its own? Why do they want people from England?'

'Because we are international, therefore every country should be represented. Come on, Mrs Hewitt, the Temple has cared for you and yours for years. This is the way to pay back.'

'She's my granddaughter.'

'She belongs to the Light,' he insisted.

Diane looked from one to the other, felt as if she might be watching some game of bat and ball, her turn, his turn, back and forth, to and fro. Had she been sold, then? Had Diane Hewitt been bartered for a few quarters of potted meat and boiled ham?

Ida's cheeks sported twin areas of darkening colour. Flustered, she was doing her level best not to let bewilderment show. Even this was her own fault, because she had run to the Temple, had taken gifts of food when she ought to have been out working to feed the kiddies. 'If you had told me that our Diane was going to be the price, I'd never have touched your Friday food parcels.'

Wilkinson took a small step back towards the dresser. If he wasn't careful, this little family would be entering Mulligan's lair. Mulligan's Catholicism must not be allowed to influence the Hewitts. 'I have to find my quota to send over there,' he muttered. 'Most people round here would be glad of a future abroad. They want ten. I've found eight girls who will never go hungry, who will dwell within sight of the miracle, who—'

'What about lads?' Ida asked.

He offered no reply.

'They don't need boys,' said a new voice.

Ida nodded at James Mulligan, whose broad shoulders seemed to fill the doorway. His handsome face, clear eyes and white teeth made Peter Wilkinson uglier than ever. Not for some considerable time had Ida been so pleased to see anyone.

James entered the room. 'Go and sit in my car,' he told Diane quietly.

Disappointed because she would hear no more, Diane left the house. Children were often forced to disappear just when life got interesting. But Mr Mulligan was not a man to be dis-obeyed, so she sat in the Austin with her brother while less

134

fortunate children peered through the glass at the lucky Hewitts.

Inside, James took charge. He placed himself directly in front of Guardian Wilkinson, his own brown eyes welded to the pupils of the shorter man. 'I await proof,' said James softly, 'but I already believe that girls are being collected and stored for breeding purposes. Rather like my racehorses, in fact.'

Ida fell back into her chair. 'You what?' Her voice was thin.

James's gaze remained on Wilkinson. 'Bearers are trained to respond only to guardians. The Great Guardian gets the pick of the crop, naturally.' He paused to rein in his anger. 'Impressionable girls from poor families are initiated by creatures like yourself. They are trained to accept as part of the creed that their minds and bodies belong to you and that through you they will find a better life and ultimate salvation.'

Wilkinson's face was puce. Sweat dripped down his face, while the carefully arranged strands of hair suddenly slipped in wetness born of fear. 'Would you dare to repeat all that in court?' he asked squeakily.

'Whatever,' answered James. 'But if any girls disappear from this part of Bolton, I'll remove your skin and leave you like a peeled tomato on the floor of your temple.' He glanced at Ida for a second, then addressed Wilkinson again. 'You are a member of an evil cult. One day, a cleansed child will speak out against you.'

Wilkinson picked up his lantern and ran from the house.

Ida swallowed audibly. 'Were all that true?' she asked.

'I'm not sure,' James replied honestly, 'though I do have my suspicions.'

Ida gulped again. 'Why did he run?' she whispered, a hand to her throat. 'If there's nowt in what you say, what made him scarper like the devil were on his tail?' She saw them then in her mind's eye, young girls with scrubbed hands and faces, white frocks, small flames in glass jars held reverently as each made her individual, solitary journey into the Sanctum. Diane had described the service, had related to her grandmother all that had happened at the temple. 'Does he touch them?' Ida asked. 'Does he touch our girls?'

James said nothing.

135

'The burning bush,' she babbled, 'it just set itself afire one day. Then, about a year later, another one flared up. Everybody said it were like something from Exodus, a Bible story come to life all over again, a wonderful mystery.' Her voice tailed away, died on a sigh of near-desperation. For a full minute, she sat in silence, unseeing eyes fixed on the middle distance. 'They take the Light from the bush, then bring it over on a ship to be spread through all the temples.'

'And if it gets blown out half-way across the Atlantic?'

'You what?'

'Does the guardian have to go back if his flame goes out?' asked James. 'Because if he were to relight it with a Swan Vesta, who would know the difference?'

Ida blinked slowly. 'I don't know,' she replied.

'Texas is a dry place,' said James. 'The first so-called miracle might have been caused by a fragment of glass under the noon sun. Subsequent events ... well, I don't think Moses would have been impressed. God does not carry paraffin and matches.'

'So it's all a lie?'

'I think it might be just that.'

Ida stared through a window that had not been cleaned properly in years. Like her own inner vision, the pane had clouded over, had not allowed the light of day to enter. The light of day, the Eternal Light – which? 'Am I a stupid old woman?' she asked.

'Not old.'

She spun round, saw a tiny glint of mischief in his eyes. 'I'm nearing sixty,' she announced. 'Am I stupid?'

He raised his shoulders. 'Misled. Looking for something, grieving for all you've lost.'

Tears stung her eyes. 'No excuse for neglecting the children,' she said hoarsely. 'Sat there in bed like a stuffed animal, no care for nobody except myself.' She dabbed angrily at her cheeks, then straightened her spine. 'But that were then, and this is now.' Her mouth set itself in a grim, determined line.

'There's the spirit.' He glanced around the small area that had been Ida Hewitt's home for so long. Women got ground down in their hundreds – perhaps thousands – but few were

136

noticed. Even married ones ceased to be significant once the gilt wore off the gingerbread. Widows, it seemed, were beneath contempt, non-existent, not worth considering. 'Never apologize, Ida, for becoming too sad to cope. Tomorrow's a new beginning.'

She didn't like Catholics, wasn't particular about Irish folk, either. But by heck, this man was a presence, a force, a calming influence. He put his money where his mouth was, didn't want thanks or fuss. She reached out and took his hand. 'All right then. Lead us through to tomorrow, son.'

Without a backward glance, Ida Hewitt, who had lost all heart and all hope, placed her trust in the hands of a papist. He was a good man, was James Mulligan. Her feet were killing her and her coat was too thin, but she stumbled and shivered her way to Mulligan's car. His arm was strong and sure, the children's faces were bright with expectations. A new page, a fresh start. And this time, there would be no blots in Ida Hewitt's copybook.

ELEVEN

The virgins are chosen bearers of the Light, bearers of our future, who will receive the seed and bring forth laudators, workers, more bearers. The Great Guardian hath given forth the word, praise the Lord. We are to be as an apiary in which only the faithful shall survive, though there will be no queen bee, since all our females will be crowned, blessed while pure, then led to guardians, agents of the Light, carriers of life.

The men, our worker bees, shall toil in shed and field. The strong, the good and the brave shall be allowed to mate; all guardians will be expected to do their duty. I am a guardian and I cannot mate. Women in the Sisterhood Chapter will bear children and no child can be mine.

I have glorified the Lord and His Light, have begged to be blessed, yet the power has not been granted. Please, please, let me not be a drone condemned to live among venerables in the Chapter of Ancients. My mark must be made, my loins must bring forth fruit so that the Light will continue to shine through me and my issue.

Now, I shake and shiver in fear and horror, for eyes of a darker fire have seared my flesh until it tries to rise from the bone. On this day, I have met with the devil in Sister Hewitt's house; the demon is taking away the woman and the children to dwell within sight of his unholy kingdom. He spake to me and cursed our faith, our miracle. Just as he once tempted the

Saviour in the desert, he has seduced the simple mind of Sister Hewitt and she, a poor, weak soul, has followed in the path of evil. This time, he comes as a handsome man, but Beelzebub has many guises.

I pray that I shall look on thee no more, Satan, lest thou enter me and make me thine. The Lord could rise above thee, but I am mere mortal tissue, vulnerable and finite. Lord grant me strength through Thy Light. Let me not be tempted by the pomp and incense of Satan's creed.

Praise the Lord.

The air was crisp, sharpened by frost, while views on all sides were like pictures borrowed from Christmas cards. Every tree and field bore the marks of thin white ice, as if a cook had dressed her baking with a layer of sugar to make it pretty.

Diane Hewitt remained unimpressed. It was freezing, colder than the bitterest day in Bolton, a town that nestled beneath moors, its atmosphere clogged by cosy dirt and the warm emissions of several thousand chimneys. What the heck was she going to do up here? She thought of a carol whose words contained the term 'bleak midwinter'. Well, it was bleak, all bare and silent, motionless, boring. No street lamps to swing from, no children playing, no trams.

'Are you all right?' asked Ida.

Diane shrugged. Did it matter whether she was all right or not? Up here was for Joe and Gran, for folk who needed their lungs filling with sharp air. She was a town girl, and town girls did not go in for wide-open spaces, frosty hedges and walls built of crooked bits and pieces of stone.

'Diane?' There was a plaintive edge to Ida's voice.

'Yes, I'm all right,' lied Diane.

Joe was using a finger to draw patterns on breath-misted glass.

'Give over,' chided Ida. 'You'll make everything sticky.'

What would happen? Diane wondered. She and Joe were going to be employed in Mulligan's Yard after school, but what about Gran? She was still a bit wobbly, still not ready for work. Would they continue to get parish money? Would the Temple help when Gran had refused to send Diane to America?

'There's the Grange.' James Mulligan waved a hand towards a massive pile fronted by sweeping lawns. 'And that's where you'll be working, Mrs Hewitt. Just peeling vegetables and so forth, guide yourself in gently.' She would have company, at least. He had primed Kate Kenny, had begged her to be kind. He grinned ruefully. Was good old Katie capable of kindness? Of course she was; she was the only one who understood him. The cellar? Oh, yes, Katie had all the facts, all the details of her employer's unhappy secret . . .

'Mr Mulligan?'

'Yes, Diane?'

'What do folk do up here? It's so empty and bare. It's like . . . it's as if everybody's died. There's no picture house, no pubs, no—' Her voice cut itself off as the car slewed round a bend.

'Does this answer your question?' asked the man at the wheel, once the car was stationary.

Ida actually laughed. 'Well, if they're all dead, then this is heaven. I've never seen such a lovely place. Is this where we'll live? Oh, say it is, please.'

Joe stopped his finger-painting. 'They're playing out,' he cried, pointing to a group of children. 'They've made a slide in the ice.'

'You're not sliding, not with your legs,' said Ida.

James promised himself that he would speak to Ida. Little Joe should be allowed to let rip, to test himself, to grow physically and mentally. 'That's your house.' He indicated a white cottage with small-paned windows and a green gate. An end-of-terrace, Bramble Cottage was fastened to three more. Several other groups of houses edged the lane, one made into a bakery-cum-post-office, another selling groceries. At the top of the gentle slope sat a church with a school attached. 'Pendleton village,' James announced, 'complete with people, Diane. Past the school, there's Pendleton Clough, which is really the same village, though residents keep the two places separate for the battles.'

Several seconds elapsed. 'Battles?' asked Ida eventually.

'Every summer,' replied James. 'It's a very serious business, not to be taken lightly.'

140

Ida looked at Diane, who looked at Joe.

'Greasy pole over the water,' continued James. 'Tug-of-war, fastest knitter, best bramble jam, quickest plough, bull-taming, wrestling, tastiest hotpot, clog-dancing, best-groomed horse, longest daisy chain and so on and so forth. The losing village buys kegs of beer for the winners.'

Diane perked up. At least they wouldn't be on their own, stuck in the middle of a field with nothing to do, nobody to see. And Gran used to be a very fast knitter.

Ida's gaze was fixed on her new home. It was the bonniest place she'd ever set eyes on in real life. There were houses like this in books, but she'd never expected to live in a real cottage in a real village. She allowed a long sigh to escape her lips. 'Thank you,' she said softly. 'Let's hope we deserve it.'

James Mulligan cleared his throat.

'He's embarrassed,' Ida informed her grandchildren. 'Still, never mind, he's learning. He can talk to more people now – instead of just one at a time, I mean. Happen we can train him to be a Lancashire man.' She swept a glance over the driver, pretended to think hard. 'No,' she said, 'there's no cure for an Irishman, is there? And definitely no mending a Catholic.' Having pronounced, Ida opened the door and stepped gingerly into her new, rather slippery life. She had better get a fire going: then there'd be cinders for the ice.

Tilly and Mona were having a row. There was nothing unusual about this since the Walsh sisters worked together, lived together, seldom enjoying time apart. When explosions occurred, nobody in the vicinity took much notice. The reality was that these two saw far too much of one another, with the result that they fought like a married couple. The neighbourhood closed its doors and got on with life; the warring pair was no longer of interest to the community.

'You've done nowt only sulk,' yelled Tilly, massive chins wobbling, face scarlet with temper. 'Anybody'd think Mulligan were an old flame, the road you're carrying on. What would Guardian Wilkinson say if he knew, eh? It's disgusting, him a Catholic and all. You know what the Light thinks about Catholics.'

Mona opened her mouth to speak, thought better of it, snapped her dentures into the closed position. There was no reasoning with their Tilly, not when she'd come out of the wrong side of the bed with a chip on her shoulder and ants in her knickers.

'Cleaning bloody windows every five minutes just so's you'll be able to have a dekko whenever he shifts himself. You've wore yon glass thin enough to shatter in a breeze, you have. Well, just listen to me, Mona Walsh. I'm not carrying you. The laundry's our bread, butter and jam, so shape. That service wash you did today was more of a wash-out. Underwear inside out, socks mixed up, no starch in the collars. We'll be losing trade.'

Mona poured herself a cup of tea and sat down at the kitchen table. A cat could look at a king, she told herself resolutely. She wasn't doing any harm, wasn't making a nuisance of herself. And she'd seen other women looking at him the same road, a bit like hungry dogs with their eyes pinned to sirloin steak. Well, bitches rather than dogs, she supposed.

'You're thinking about him now,' accused Tilly.

This time, Mona caught the bait and chewed on it. 'What I think about is my business,' she answered. 'Even you can't get into my head, Tilly, though God knows you've been up to your armpits in everything else that was mine.'

Tilly's bosom swelled until it developed a strong resemblance to a double-bed bolster. 'Making a fool of yourself, you are. Showing me up and all.'

Mona was fed up right to her porcelain molars. She couldn't breathe, spit, swallow or break wind without Tilly making a comment or offering a suggestion. Well, Mona had come to the end of this particular road. Up to now, it had been more like one of those cul-de-sac avenues, only one way out, one way in, and everything the same day after day. She and Tilly were wearing one another down, picking and moaning, no joy, no rest.

'Even if you were twenty-five, he'd never look on your side of the street,' continued Tilly. 'You were never much to look at.'

142

'Then I'll find another bloody street,' snapped Mona.

Tilly's upper body deflated visibly, like a balloon with a slow leak. 'You what?'

'And I want half the furniture.'

The older Miss Walsh stumbled into the wooden rocker. 'Half the . . . ? What are you on about at all?'

Mona drained her cup, inhaled deeply, set the cup back on its saucer. 'I've got my own place,' she announced, with the air of one who had decided to divulge a state secret. 'It's being decorated and done up for me, just me, on my own, new lino and a gas cooker.'

Tilly gulped.

'It's time we had separate lives,' continued Mona. 'It'll do us both good, I reckon. We'll still work together, like, but twenty-four hours a day, seven days a week – it's too much. I'm getting on your nerves and you're getting me down.'

'My mother will be spinning in her grave,' said Tilly.

Mona shrugged. 'If she is, then she's having more fun than me, I can tell you that for no money. You won't let me do nothing. I can't go on the fair when it comes, mustn't be seen eating black peas or trying to win a coconut. If there's owt on at the Tivoli – owt as I want to see – you have to find out if the film's suitable.'

'But the guardian says—'

'Bugger the guardian,' shouted Mona. 'He's ugly, stupid, and his religion stinks. Collecting children to send to America? Running round with his lantern what was lit off the burning bush of Moses? Daft. I'm thinking about going back to chapel, so shove that in your pipe. I've had enough of you, the Temple, the Light and Peter Wilkinson. But mostly I've had enough of you. So I'm off.' There, it was said. Mona had nursed her resentment for years, so it had grown until the pressure had got too much for the lid to stay screwed down.

For the first time in many a year, Tilly Walsh was very nearly lost for words. Their Mona couldn't live on her own: their Mona had what might best be called a nervous disposition. If somebody looked at her wrong, she got upset. When she'd been a kiddie, she'd had to walk round big puddles in case she fell downwards into the reflected sky.

143

'You've never in all your life slept in a house by yourself.'

'First time for everything, as they say,' replied Mona smartly. Inside her chest, her heart was flailing about like a trapped rabbit, but she wasn't going to let her sister know about the fear. Mona had enough put by to allow her to live a simple life, no worries about rent, plenty of pennies for the gas, for little outings to the pictures, for her snuff, for the little romance magazines that she had always hidden from Tilly.

Tilly's mouth hung open as she considered the prospect of Mona living on her own. Who would tell her what to do? Mona was a follower, not a leader. 'So where is this new house?' she asked.

'It's the Hewitts'. Number thirteen John Street.'

'It'll be a hovel,' Tilly pronounced.

Mona smiled. 'It is, but it won't be. I'm getting a back boiler put in, a hot tap in the scullery, new flooring, decorating. And because I'm paying for the improvements, my rent's been halved.'

'What about fleas and bugs?'

'That's all getting sorted out as well.' Mona took a bite from a scone. 'You'll have to get a lodger, someone you can boss about,' she spluttered through a mouthful of crumbs.

Tilly closed her mouth. She cursed herself inwardly for all the times she had wished Mona far away. The boot was suddenly on a different foot, Mona making the rules, Tilly sitting helplessly while the balance shifted. 'You'll not thrive,' she promised, her voice quieter. 'Half the time, you don't know whether it's Sunday or half past three. If I weren't here, you'd be walking about in odd shoes and with your curlers still in. Right.' She shook her head emphatically. 'I suppose I'll have to move with you if you're set on going.'

Mona finished her scone, wiped her hands on a pot towel. 'No,' she said, when the perfunctory ablutions were done. 'I have to be by myself. You see, I've something special to do. You wouldn't like what I'm going to do.' She grinned impishly, making her round face younger.

'You don't half talk some tripe at times,' said Tilly. 'What have you got to do? Is it something to do with Mr Holy Roman flaming Mulligan?'

144

'No,' lied Mona. 'It's nowt to do with nobody excepting me.' She decided to soften the blow. 'Look, we can visit one another for our tea – you cook on a Monday, I'll do it on a Thursday. And I'll not leave the Temple, not yet, so we'll see each other there.'

'What about Sunday dinner?' asked Tilly. 'It's always been a big tradition in our family.'

When Mona thought about it, the Walsh family's life had revolved around food. At the end of a meal, plates had been so clean that they'd hardly needed a dip in the bowl. Bits of gravy had always been scraped up with bread, because the leaving of God's gifts on a plate had been a huge sin in the eyes of Mr and Mrs Walsh. As a result, both girls had burgeoned, had been overweight all their lives, often berated by their peers, sometimes ignored, never chosen to join in games. 'There's only us two left, so that's hardly what you might call a family,' said Mona. 'Sunday dinner was all right while Mam and Dad were alive, but we don't need a load of meat and veg now. I'd be happy with a chop. No, I think Sunday dinner's a thing of the past, Tilly. Any road, I'd forget to cook without you at the back of me, so you'd arrive at an empty table if I were in charge. Didn't you just say I never know whether it's Sunday or half past three?'

Tilly held her tongue, put her temper on a leash.

'We've ate too much all our lives,' continued Mona. 'Porridge, then eggs and bacon for breakfast, pies, pasties and chips at dinner time, great big teas, then suppers. If you get any bigger, you'll not fit in a chair with arms, and I'm not much thinner than you.' She nodded pensively. 'If we're separated, that mould'll get broke. Mam fed us wrong, now we feed ourselves wrong.'

Tilly was shocked to the core. She hadn't bargained for this sort of thing, not from their Mona. And what was it about, anyway? There was Mona, two feet under the table as usual, face stuffed with scone, yet going on about too much food? 'I'm not talking to you no more, not until a bit of sense manages to float out of your gob. Looking for trouble, you are. We've got this nice little house, a bedroom each, and you decide to pike off down John Street. You are on your own,

145

Mona Walsh.' On this note of high drama, Tilly left the room and stamped upstairs.

Mona experienced a few minutes of discomfort, her symptoms including palpitations, sweating, a bit of a headache and a sick feeling deep in the pit of her stomach. She and Tilly had never been separated, not for a day. They'd been in different classes at school, but, from the age of fourteen and fifteen, they had been a team, a pair of workhorses. Well, it was no use carrying on tied together if they were arguing and pulling in different directions. Mona needed her own cart. He'd told her that. He'd told her to get herself sorted out.

She smiled. They'd met twice in his office, had discussed A Cut Above, the new business that hadn't even started up yet after the death of poor Mrs Burton-Massey. She'd promised to be the presser, the ironer in a very high-class establishment – if it ever opened, that was. It had been nice, talking to him on her own like that, as if she were important. Once his little maid's foot had mended, Mr Mulligan had stopped fetching laundry in, but Mona still saw him, oh, yes.

Then, one day when she'd pretended to be at the dentist's, she and Mr Mulligan had enjoyed a good long natter. He was looking for somebody mature and sensible, a kindly soul from the Deane and Daubhill area, because he was worried about the Temple of Light. He'd decided to speak to Mona, because she had confided in him, had told him that she was a member of the Temple, but that she had been dragged along by her sister.

On that day, Mona's mind had made itself up. She had decided there and then to live on her own. She'd even managed not to blush when he'd expressed his fears for young girls who were being prepared for export. Mona was now a spy. She could work from inside, as well as from outside the Temple. Best of all, she would report to him, to James Mulligan. 'Eeh,' she breathed now. 'I should never have said owt to our Tilly about going back to chapel. Never mind, I'll pretend I said it all in temper.'

She stood up and looked in the mirror. Wanting to be prettier was nothing to do with him, yet everything to do with him. He was too young for her, yet she needed to look better

146

because . . . because he existed. It was daft, and she could not have explained it in a century of years, but she had to lose weight and perk up a bit.

She smiled at her reflection. 'Tilly's right,' she said happily. 'You want your head testing.'

Margot Burton-Massey longed to tell the world about her lover, but she dared not speak a single syllable. Bright-eyed and living on the edge of her nerves, she did not realize that some of those about her recognized the symptoms. When she wasn't singing, she was daydreaming; when she wasn't in a trance, she was curling her hair, trying out new makeup, trimming blouses.

Rupert was waiting for the right time. Christmas would arrive soon, and he did not want to make any announcements during the festivities. When New Year was over, he and Margot would begin to make plans for their future. Sometimes, a tiny cloud of doubt appeared on Margot's horizon, but she blew it away repeatedly. Rupert was right – the engagement needed to be made public when everyone stopped being so busy.

Margot sat in her bedroom at Caldwell Farm. She was in a giggly mood, was laughing inwardly because she, the baby of the family, was now a woman, fully fledged, initiated by Rupert, who would be the one and only love of her life. The feelings she had entertained for James Mulligan had been shallow and childish. Now, she knew all about real love. Real love was needing to give oneself away whenever possible, in barns, in a car, in the woods. Real love was cursing inclement weather, waiting breathlessly for opportunities, for families to go out so that precious moments might be snatched.

When separated from her beloved for more than a day, Margot would walk through fields and over moors, just to use up her energy, just to stay away from Eliza and Amy – the latter especially, since Amy had started to ask questions. Margot was above questioning, because she had her own man, someone who would take care of her and love her for the rest of time.

It was almost the end of November. Rupert was engaged in

147

family activities, trips to Manchester and Liverpool in the company of his mother, Christmas shopping excursions, visits to theatres and cinemas. He wasn't avoiding Margot, could not, would not do that. But life without him was so dull, especially here. Amy was improving, was talking more, yet this house was so quiet.

When Amy entered the room after knocking, Margot was surprised. She looked up, saw her sister hesitating in the doorway. 'Come in,' she said.

Amy closed the door and sat next to Margot on the bed. She didn't know where to begin, but it had to be done, had to be said. The anger she felt on Margot's behalf still simmered, so she slowed her breathing before embarking on the speech she had tried to prepare. She cleared her drying throat. 'Margot, I . . . I do hope you haven't gone overboard for Rupert Smythe. People do strange things after the death of a family member.'

Margot made no reply. She and Rupert had been 'doing things' long before Mother's death . . .

'Mrs Smythe came to visit me this morning. You were out walking, I think.'

'Yes.'

This was so difficult. Amy did not want to hurt her little sister, but Amy had to hurt her little sister before anyone else damaged her. 'Mrs Smythe was very clear, Margot. She wants Rupert to stop seeing you.'

Margot leaped up. 'What? Why?'

Amy, bone weary after worrying about Christmas, about A Cut Above and about Margot, closed her eyes for a second or two. Mature enough to realize that she was too young for all this, she wished with all her heart that a long-lost family elder would appear and take the reins for a while.

'Amy?' Margot's tone was just a fraction quieter than a scream. 'Why?' She had lost her mother – was she about to lose Rupert, too?

'Because we are poor, I suppose.' Helen Smythe had not mentioned money; she had simply stated that, in her opinion, Rupert and Margot were not suited. 'Compared to the Smythes, we are church mice,' said Amy.

'That's silly and cruel,' exclaimed Margot. 'And we are of

148

what Mrs Smythe would call good stock.' What would she do without him? And surely Rupert was not going to obey his mother? Rupert was of age, was old enough to decide for himself.

As if reading Margot's mind, Amy spoke again. 'Mrs Smythe is an interfering, domineering sort of woman, dear. Remember how she was always there when Mother was preparing to open the business? Mother had a knack of pretending to be guided by her, though she never allowed Mrs Smythe to make a final decision.'

Margot sat down again and grabbed Amy's hand. 'But Mrs Smythe is all modern. She allowed Camilla to start a business, she's always lecturing women about taking charge of their own lives. So what makes her dislike me so much? Am I a bad person? And would she have dared to do this to me if Mother had lived?'

'No, you're not bad, Margot, not at all.' She was silly, stubborn and a bit selfish, but Margot could never be described as bad. In fact, she would probably turn out well in time.

'What exactly did she say, Amy?'

'That she wanted Rupert to spread his wings and fly south.'

'London?'

Amy nodded.

'That's part of our plan. He and I have talked about moving to London. Amy, why is she doing this?'

The older girl suppressed a shudder as she remembered her earlier conversation with Helen Smythe. A lady to the core, Amy had distressed herself by yelling, like a fishwife, 'No, I should not choose Rupert as husband for my sister, or for anyone of my acquaintance. It is he who is not good enough, Mrs Smythe.'

'Amy, what am I to do?'

Amy drew her sister close, pulling the tousled head on to her shoulder, heard the words she had delivered so recently to Rupert's mother. 'You are a fake, Mrs Smythe,' Amy had announced. 'Modern women are supposedly encouraging their children to find their own feet, yet here you sit, dictating like a mid-Victorian father, forbidding this, insisting on that. If Rupert were a man, he would not listen to you. And his record

149

is not exactly clean, so perhaps you would do better by sending him to London. After all, he has ruined no chorus girls in that part of the world. Yes, pack him off to where he is unknown.'

'Amy?'

'Yes, dearest, I know how difficult this is for you. I realize, too, that you will not want advice, yet I must tell you that I believe Rupert to be a thoroughly wretched young man. Mother didn't like him at all. And Camilla is so nice. I think Mrs Smythe has doted on her son—'

'Because Camilla is ugly,' sobbed Margot, 'while Rupert is so good-looking.' She rubbed at her eyes. 'I shall see him tomorrow and find out what is going on.'

'No, please don't chase after him, Margot.' Was it too late for such advice? Had Margot wasted her precious body on that bone-idle, stupid, self-indulgent creature? 'You are too young to settle down just yet. Look, Mr Mulligan is determined to open the hydro in a few months. Think of all the people you would meet there. You could be in charge of the stables, riding lessons and so forth.'

'Please, Amy.' Margot did not want to think or talk of anything except her dilemma. Panic flooded her veins, causing her heart to beat fast, her palms to sweat, her pores to open. 'I'm scared,' she whispered. 'And please, I beg you, Amy, don't discuss this with Eliza.'

'May I ask why?'

'I'm not sure.'

Amy had not been sure about Eliza for some time. Since gaining partial rein on her own behaviour and reactions, Amy had become more acutely aware of the behaviour of close companions. Eliza was deep. The happy-go-lucky girl who had sung in the woods, the sweet, well-behaved darling daughter of Louisa Burton-Massey, the demure pianist, the seamstress – was any one of these the real Eliza?

'Amy?'

'What?'

Margot wiped her eyes. 'I think I don't trust Eliza. It's as if I don't . . . as if she's a person I've only just met. She has changed since Mother died, she is a stranger.'

150

'The consummate actress,' mumbled Amy to herself. 'Like the two of us, Eliza has probably been in shock,' she added, in a clearer voice.

'If everything goes wrong between myself and Rupert, I don't want Eliza running around me and being kind. It would be too much to bear.'

'I understand.'

Elspeth Moorhead knocked on the door. 'It's Mr Mulligan,' she said. 'I've put him in the drawing room.'

After a final glance at her distraught sister, Amy followed the ageing housekeeper downstairs and found James Mulligan pacing in front of a roaring fire. When Amy entered, he made a cursory bow, then placed his tall, unfashionable hat on a tea-table. 'The inn is sold,' he said, without preamble.

Amy placed herself in a Victorian nursing chair just inside the door. 'Good,' she replied. 'But why are you telling me?'

He opened his mouth, closed it, glanced at the ceiling, then at Amy. He wished with all his heart that he could be some-where else, but he was here and he must get on with his business. With his eyes fixed on a point somewhere between the picture rail and Amy's head, he began again. 'The inn is sold,' he repeated lamely.

Amy decided not to encourage him. Occasionally, the annoying man drifted back into his old, silent ways, but when talking business involving the Burton-Massey family, he was sometimes at his dramatic worst. She knew that he was capable of normal – well, of near-normal – behaviour, so she simply waited.

'The estate will, eventually, revert to you.' He cursed him-self, knew that he sounded like a phonograph needle stuck in a scratch on a record.

She nodded. 'Yes, you have said that before.' It was plain that he continued guilty and embarrassed about the misdeeds of his father. 'It is very generous of you,' she added, trying to put him at his ease. Where James Mulligan was concerned Amy often disliked herself since she knew his kindness was real, yet she persisted in tormenting him. This had to stop, she ordered herself. Why was he here on this occasion? Just to repeat himself yet again?

151

He shifted about, moved the focus of his attention lower until he was looking at his companion's hair. 'The yard businesses bring in a living, but I fear that Pendleton Grange would bleed you dry. The roof needs fixing, then there's some dry rot and the—'

'I am aware of the state of the house, James.'

At last, he looked directly into her eyes. 'I am sorry to keep labouring these points, but I must beg you to listen, since I know that you will soon run out of money. If you continue here, turn the Grange into a hydro which can be run by others, open the dressmaking business, then—'

'Then we shall all die of over-exertion and nothing will matter.'

'You will be comfortable,' he said, rather sharply. 'And occupied. Now, the price I have received for the inn will pay off some of the mortgage on the Grange, though it will not stretch to cover improvements. The choice is between paying off a proportion of the loan or using the money to make a hydro. Which is it to be? Or shall I sell the Grange and give you the money?'

Amy raised a shoulder. 'This is very kind of you, but it is not my concern. Do as you will.' She pulled herself up again. 'Look, I don't mean to be unkind or to sound ungrateful, but it is so long since we lived in the big house that I can hardly imagine owning and running it. As for selling it, would you get a good price while it is in need of modernization? And . . . well, I do have other concerns.'

'I know.' He lowered his tone. 'How is Margot?'

'Head over heels in love with Rupert, I fear.'

'And Rupert?'

'Head over heels with himself. His mother, in spite of her emancipation, is keen to marry him to someone with better expectations.'

James stood up and walked to the window. 'Would you have me tell Mrs Smythe exactly what Margot's prospects are? After all, were you to sell everything after I go home, or were we to sell up now, you might even be rich.'

'Tell her nothing,' said Amy. 'He doesn't deserve my sister.'

'And you feel I may renege on my promise and keep everything myself?'

Strangely, that possibility had never occurred to Amy. This man said what he meant, meant what he said. 'There are few trustworthy people in this world, James Mulligan. You happen to be one of the few. But, as I have said before, the property is yours. Should your circumstances change, then your priorities would shift.' Amy lowered her tone. 'You are not like your father. Wipe that idea from your mind, marry if you wish.'

He walked back to the fireplace. 'Eliza played very well today,' he said.

Amy felt tension settling in her spine, making her stiffen against the back of her chair. She had mentioned the possibility of him marrying; immediately, he had spoken of Eliza. Why did the concept of a marriage between James and Eliza bother her?

'She sings well, too,' he added.

'Eliza is gifted,' she replied.

He picked up his hat. 'You will come for Christmas, I hope. We are to celebrate in the kitchen, because that is more homely. It will be a mixed bunch, no ceremony, no master, no servants.'

'I see.' She rose and followed him into the hallway. 'Then who will cook the meal?' she asked.

'Mrs Kenny. She will have help.'

'So the servants will cook?'

At the front door, he paused. 'Will you go through the rest of your life splitting hairs, Amy? Does everything have to be so carefully thought out, analysed and criticized? No matter who cooks or cleans or washes dishes, we shall be a family on Christmas Day. In fact, I may decide to do the cooking myself.'

'I'm sorry,' she whispered.

He smiled, then placed his hat on his head. 'Never mind, so,' he smiled. 'There's only one of you, then the mould got broken.'

When he had marched off, Amy closed the door, closed her eyes, leaned against the wall. He disturbed her. She didn't know why. She didn't want to know why.

153

TWELVE

Margot was feeling out of sorts. She was experiencing nausea, headaches and a general lassitude whose sole benefit was a marked diminution of anger. There was no space, no energy for temper. When aimless thoughts landed on the subject of Rupert Smythe, the resulting resignation was completely alien to the character of the youngest Burton-Massey. He did not want her. She could do nothing to force him to love her. Amy was right, as usual – few affluent young men would choose to be connected with a family as impoverished as theirs.

She sat as still as stone at the window, her gaze floating loosely across the snow-covered stretch of lawn and flower-beds. Beyond the boundary walls, heavy cloud seemed to be sinking on to moortops as if threatening to drop a cargo of lead. The house was cold. Winter had moved in without invitation, had settled his refrigerated essence in every corner, spreading ice-tipped fingers along thin glass, breathing frosty air throughout the rooms. Fires had little effect, warming just a small apron in front of each hearth, leaving Winter to do his dramatic worst.

She sighed gloomily. She didn't want to be here in this sooty parlour with its walls stained by smoky exhalations from a faulty chimney. Parlour? Elspeth Moorhead had christened the room, and the housekeeper was right. At Pendleton Grange there had been drawing rooms, warmth, light, space. Here, there was no fire in Margot's bedroom until evening, while even the dining room was unheated. These days, meals were taken in the parlour, served on a wheeled table with semi-circular wings. 'Poverty,' she mouthed. 'I bet it's warmer outside.' Yes, perhaps the house might feel more cheerful after a stroll.

In the hallway, she dragged on coat, hat, scarf and boots. Dusk was beginning to descend as she closed the door in her wake, but the silvery-white earth seemed to produce a light all its own as she crunched her way alongside footprints left by her sisters. Amy and Eliza had gone to town in search of Christmas presents. They had travelled with Mr Mulligan who, Margot felt sure, was falling in love with Eliza.

The woods were beautiful, bare trees dripping crystal icicles, leafless limbs stretching upward to embrace a clear sky. Margot kicked the ground, creating tramlines in four inches of white carpet. She sat on a stump and worried about not being worried. The concept of pregnancy should be terrifying, yet she remained so stupidly calm. It was almost as if she watched someone else, as if the problems were not connected to her at all. Even when she concentrated on the idea of her family's further ruination, she continued unmoved. But was she truly concentrating? Was she capable of that?

Rupert. He was the only one; he was the father. Counting the months, Margot decided that her baby would be due in the middle of June. She was almost three months pregnant, yet her belly remained as flat as it had always been. Amy would have to be told, of course. What then? A home for mothers and babies, adoption? Margot harboured no sentiment for the child or for its father; she simply breathed, ate, slept, tried not to vomit. The trouble her predicament would cause meant nothing at this point. Just occasionally, a mild unease would creep over her, unattached, unconnected with anything real. Although she was in trouble, she was not particularly troubled.

She thought about the spring and summer, her silly obsession with James Mulligan, her passion for Rupert Smythe. Six months ago, Margot Burton-Massey had been alive, vibrant, mobile. She had wanted to work with horses, not with fabric and thread. There had been dirt under her

155

fingernails, a sparkle in her eyes. Mulligan's stables were now filled to bursting with fine, pure-bred horseflesh. Eliza still visited the Grange to play that rather fine piano while he listened and lusted, no doubt. Margot had not been near the big house for weeks – even the wild, unbroken horses could not drag her in that direction.

It didn't matter, any of it. Sometimes, Margot wondered whether she would experience any pain at all, even if run through by a sword. 'I'm dead, I suppose,' she told a nearby tree, 'and still talking. Talking to a tree.' She was a fool. Like a witless schoolgirl, she had twice imagined herself in love, each time with an unsuitable person. Mulligan, taciturn and, on occasion, as cold as tonight's frost, then Smythe, that self-centred mother's boy with no thought for anything save his own comfort. 'A fool,' she declared aloud, the two syllables emerging on a small cloud of breath.

Something moved. She turned her head, half expecting to see a cow bent on escape, but it was a man, a stranger. He was quite the ugliest creature she had ever seen. Shivering, Margot rose from her uncomfortable seat and backed away. The chill in her bones came from the inside. She was feeling something; she was experiencing fear. 'What . . . what do you want?' she asked, the words stumbling on their way out.

He smiled. She was a snow queen, alabaster-skinned, finely etched, a living expression of all that seemed magical in the world. Weight seemed to have melted away from her face, rendering her more fragile than she had seemed earlier in the year. Oh, what a prize. The Guardians in Texas were content for the time being, happy to receive young women capable of toil. But the Light needed to attract the educated, too, people like the Burton-Masseys, those who had attended excellent schools, folk with good manners. In spite of the cold, Peter Wilkinson's palms were slick with sweat. 'Are you all right?' he asked. 'I saw you sitting there so still. That can be dangerous in low temperatures. Frost can kill. You should be inside or, if you insist on being out of doors, keep moving.'

Margot's teeth chattered.

'I love the woods in winter-time,' he continued, 'so pretty, like a Christmas card.'

Terror gripped her heart. It wasn't just his appearance – there was something in his eyes. He looked like . . . like a dead salmon before a slice of cucumber covered its dead eye. When had the Burton-Masseys last enjoyed a full salmon? She shook herself. There was no expression in the man's countenance. Yet evil lived in his face, almost unnoticeable but definitely there.

'So I'm trespassing,' he continued. He delivered what he imagined to be a reassuring grin.

Margot cleared her throat. 'Sniggery Wood belongs to Mr Mulligan,' she said. The teeth were horrible, she noticed, stumpy, uneven and stained.

'The woods were yours until the gambler took them,' he snapped. 'Double standards, double dealings, double Dutch.' He bared the incisors once more. 'Latin. I ask you, who wants to hear Latin in church? They use it to fool the congregations, you see. Plain English is good enough, wouldn't you say?'

It was clear that he expected an answer. 'I don't know,' she managed finally. 'We're C of E.'

'Quite.'

Spurred on by a panic for which she could find no real reason, Margot rushed off in the direction of home. Why was she running? It was his ugliness, she decided, and ugliness, like beauty, was merely skin deep. The eyes, though. Oh, those hideous orbs belonged in the face of some cloven-hoofed creature . . .

He was not following her. Relieved beyond measure, she leaned against Caldwell Farm's boundary wall. It was the relief that finally touched her core. For a few seconds, Margot looked at her home from the outside, was happy to see lamps and firelight. She wanted to live, wanted to see tomorrow with all its glaring faults and disappointments. After Christmas, she must confide in Amy.

Eliza smiled tentatively at her companion. They were in a little coffee house next to Bolton's Moor Lane bus station, a hut erected by some entrepreneur with an eye to profit and poor taste in coffees. 'Amy's shopping,' she said, in an attempt to break the ice.

'And Mulligan?' Eliza's companion raised an eyebrow perfect enough to belong to a woman.

'In his office,' she answered. 'Dealing with racehorse pedigree papers. I am to meet them both there in twenty minutes.'

Rupert Smythe placed his cup in its saucer. 'So,' he drawled, 'are you game, Eliza?'

She pondered, dusted a cheap napkin across her lips. It was true that Margot seemed to care no longer for this young man, yet the situation remained awkward. 'I can't,' she replied, after a short pause. Yes, she could. Surely, she must? Why couldn't life be simpler? she asked herself.

'Why not?' He raised creamed and manicured hands. 'It's London, Eliza. London. I shall be doing something or other in the City, living in a flat provided by darling Mama . . .' He drew breath slowly, elegantly. 'Two bedrooms. There will be no hanky-panky, darling – please be reassured on that front. What is there here for you? And why should I be lonely in a city of strangers? We can help one another out.'

She stared into the middle distance, allowing his narrow, handsome face to blur at the edges. If Amy decided to open A Cut Above, who would help to run it? Margot's sewing was acceptable, no more. And what about design, cutting, fitting? But London, with its theatres, bright lights, concerts, markets and cinemas, was a powerful magnet. This might well turn out to be Eliza's sole chance in life. She focused on him again. Rupert Smythe's reputation was far from unsullied. 'How can I be sure?' she asked.

'Sure of what?'

She hesitated momentarily. 'Of your intentions.'

Eliza was lovely, so much more beautiful than her younger sister. Eliza would take some persuading, he felt sure of that. Margot had been easy, too easy, no challenge at all. But this one would not step readily into his arms. Ah, well, anything worth having was worth fighting for. 'You have my word as a gentleman,' he told her.

Eliza sipped at her muddy coffee. It seemed that she had two choices, neither of which promised to be perfect. She could remain at Caldwell Farm, safe, secure and bored, the only chance on the horizon a possible job in a possible fashion store. Had Mother lived, Eliza would have felt obliged to settle for

158

that. But here sat the physical embodiment of a second opportunity, a totally unsafe option. By its very nature, London
could never be safe. Rupert Smythe would always be
dangerous.

'Well?' he asked.

'I'll probably come,' she said. 'On condition that you understand that I shall return home if I am unhappy.'

'Certainly.' He managed, just about, to keep the excitement
from his tone.

'And I can't disappear from Lancashire when you do. You
must go first so that no one will guess that you have aided and
abetted. Should anybody suspect that you are involved in my
running away, your mother will know where to find me. There
must be no scenes, Rupert. I will not tolerate scenes.'

He inclined his head in agreement.

'Rupert?'

'Yes?' His heart leaped at the thought of bedding this one.
She looked frail, too delicately formed for a physical relationship. Yet there was a hint of cold blue steel behind the eyes, a
promise of hidden depths, stored passions. Oh, yes, here sat a
soul that waited to be stirred from sleep.

'If you touch me, I shall kill you. That is a definite promise.'
These words, spoken in a whisper, managed to be harsh.

Rupert shivered, blinked twice. God, she meant it, too! The
determination to deflower Eliza Burton-Massey grew stronger.

'I have saved my pennies for years,' she told him now. 'I
haven't a great deal of money, but as soon as I get work I shall
find a place of my own.'

'London is expensive,' he advised.

She fingered a teaspoon, allowed it to shiver in the saucer.
'So am I,' she murmured. 'I'm certainly worth more than your
wallet, more than your mother's cheque books.' She paused for
a second. 'Do you still want to house me, Rupert?'

'Yes.'

Eliza leaned across the table, watched as his pupils dilated.
'I daren't tell Amy – not yet, at least. She would try to force
me to stay. When I arrive in London, I shall write and put her
mind at rest.'

'Good.' He wondered briefly about Mama's visits, decided

159

not to worry until the problem pressed. 'You'd better go now,' he suggested reluctantly. 'We don't want to become a talking point, do we?'

Eliza rose, donned hat, scarf and gloves. This disreputable young man had fallen in love with her. She noticed how his mouth, slackened by desire, gaped slightly as she turned to leave. The eyes, full of plans, were widened by expectations. But Eliza was no chorus girl. Miss Elizabeth Burton-Massey, excellent pianist, accomplished singer, had plans of her own. With a certainty whose source she would never choose to fathom, she realized that she could cope with men, especially those as obvious as Rupert Smythe. Should he attempt something distasteful, she was more than a match for such a transparent, puerile creature.

She walked towards Mulligan's Yard, her step light and unhurried, her mind scarcely touched by guilt. For Mother, Eliza might have hesitated. But now it was every woman for herself, because the world was cruel, especially for a parentless woman with no dowry. She was going on the stage; she was going to be a star. As for the feckless youth in the coffee shed, he was a vehicle, no more, no less.

Gradually, Amy Burton-Massey regained her equilibrium. Really, it was a case of having to, because everyone else seemed to be what Elspeth Moorhead called 'out of flunter'. Margot had taken to walking about in all weathers, while Eliza became more thoughtful and secretive by the day. Amy adjusted her own 'flunter' and tried to get through each day without dwelling too closely on her mother's tragic death.

Sometimes, though, when dealing with a certain person, Amy felt like a donkey in pursuit of a carrot, a dumb beast forced to go round in an everlasting circle. All she wanted was the truth; all she needed was to know a little more about the man whose father had ruined her family, the fellow who strove endlessly to turn around the fortunes of the Burton-Massey girls. He was, she supposed, just another donkey, another part of the mechanism called life. But surely they could converse, find common ground, a sense of comradeship, even? After all, they both seemed to be treading the same

160

piece of ground. Were donkeys capable of communication?

Bending over paperwork, James felt her eyes boring into him. The question-and-answer session had reached half-time. He compared himself to a member of a football team, a captain waiting for the referee to blow the kick-off whistle. 'I'm the goalkeeper,' he muttered.

'Did you say something?'

He raised his head. 'Do we add on injury time at the end?' he asked, deliberately obtuse. This woman was an accurate shot. Bolton Wanderers might find her useful in attack.

She gazed at him. Making sense of James Mulligan was rather like attempting logarithms without a set of tables. He would open up, allowing her a glimpse of a decent, thoughtful human being, only to slam back into the closed and bolted position. The man was his own jailer, or so it seemed. Did the cellar at Pendleton Grange house his dungeon, his personal torture chamber? 'I was just thinking that we were a pair of mules condemned to create power by perpetual motion. Perhaps we are tethered in the goalmouth at Burnden Park.'

He processed this piece of misinformation, filed it away in the miscellaneous section of his brain. 'Look,' he began, patience edged deeply into the syllable, 'you know perfectly well what I'm doing, Amy. With the inn sold, some of the mortgage on Pendleton Grange has been paid off. The rest of that debt can be cleared in a relatively short time as long as the estate works for itself. Now, if we open a hydro, the income will allow you and your sisters to live in reasonable comfort, while rents from the yard should provide extras, small luxuries like—'

'You're still not telling me why,' she said. 'You've explained things over and over, yet the real why, the reason for insisting on returning everything to us, is still unbelievable. You owe us absolutely nothing. You seem to be suffering from an overdose of altruism, too generous for your own good.'

'I don't need the yard, the house, the business rents, the farms or the cottages,' he replied. 'And I certainly don't want to stay for ever in England.'

'Then sell everything.'

'I can't.'

161

'Why?'

He raised hands and eyebrows. 'Another why?'

'It's the same why,' she answered, through gritted teeth. 'You could return to Ireland a rich man.'

He smiled tightly. 'With my father's misdemeanours suspended from my neck like the Ancient Mariner's albatross? Catholics are born with a heightened sense of guilt. By the time we're confirmed, we know we're the sinners, the perpetrators of each and every ill that visits the world.'

'Like volcanic eruptions, earthquakes, outbreaks of typhus?'

He nodded gravely.

Annoyed without and beyond reason, Amy stood up and walked to the window. Steam poured through the wash-house doorway and from the nostrils of two jet-black geldings who waited between the shafts of a hearse. The stonemason chipped away at a slab of marble; Miss Tilly Walsh emerged from her chores to inhale drier air and a pinch of snuff.

On James Mulligan's table sat the facts, the figures, costs, an account of the inn's sale, income from rents, expenditure for repairs. Those papers contained the future according to the gospel of Mr Mulligan. Amy had said little, had absorbed some.

'Just resign yourself,' suggested James Mulligan.

'I don't understand you at all,' she answered, without looking at him. 'You're a teacher from Ireland. I don't know anything at all about Irish teachers, though I never met a wealthy English one. Why don't you take your money and run? Scruples? Think of all the poor you could help.'

He tutted, let out a long sigh. 'It would be wrong.'

'In whose book?'

'In my own – in a book I've neither read nor written yet.' These words were edged with a hint of impatience.

'And if we won't accept your charity?'

'Margot will. Eliza, too, I think. Do what you will with your own portion.'

She swung round. Their eyes clashed, locked, narrowed. 'I think we are very alike, you and I,' he said. 'The mule was a good creature to think of, as we are both stubborn and proud beyond stupidity.'

162

'Immovable,' she agreed, noticing that he would not lower his gaze.

'You will allow this,' he said quietly. 'I am returning your history to you.'

'Only if you accept a small salary, enough for your own provision. I shall send it to you in Ireland.'

Silence reigned for several very long seconds. 'Open that shop, then,' he said at last. 'Do something to occupy yourself and the other two. Remember how much your mother invested in that business. At this rate, the materials will have gone to dust before ever seeing a sewing-machine.'

Amy was acutely uncomfortable. She knew him, didn't know him at all; she liked him, didn't like him one bit. 'Eliza seems to have lost interest,' she told him.

Determinedly, he kept his opinion of Eliza to himself. 'Then find another designer, somebody who can't get a job in a city, perhaps a mother of schoolchildren. Eliza's not the only creature in Bolton who can draw a frock or copy one from a magazine.'

'She's up to something.' Immediately, Amy wished that she could bite back the words. She did not want any more of his advice.

'Yes,' he answered. 'She's deep.'

'And talented.'

'That, too.'

Amy stood her ground until he averted his eyes. Like a stupid child, she had resolved to win the staring-out contest.

Eliza entered the office. There was an atmosphere, but she chose to ignore it. 'I found very little in the shops,' she declared, arranging herself gracefully in a leather chair. 'I just had to buy what was available. So, if Christmas presents aren't quite up to the mark this year, blame the tradesmen of Bolton.' She offered the man a sweet smile, was unmoved by the lack of response. 'Of course, financial restrictions make the job harder.'

James looked at the pair of them. Amy, bright-eyed and angry, tapped her foot in the manner of an impatient horse. Eliza, folded correctly and neatly in her seat, wore the air of a woman who knew that the world was hers to have and to own.

163

Her devastating beauty gave her a confidence that was almost supreme. Amy was right – Miss Eliza was up to no good.

Eliza studied the man covertly, played with the idea of setting her cap at him. No, no. She wanted to get away – and wasn't he planning to return to Ireland? If he did manage to repay his father's debts, everything would be invested in the estate, she supposed. She could not imagine Amy selling up and splitting the money three ways. And even if A Cut Above did ever open, Eliza did not want to be involved, not yet. Oh, let them all stay here, she mused; they would be hovering and worrying in the background should she ever need or want them. 'We need to get something for the Moorheads,' she told Amy, whose feathers seemed to be settling into a smoother mode. These two did nothing but quarrel, it seemed.

Amy picked up her basket. 'Come along, Eliza,' she said, almost snappily.

'I'll drive you home later,' offered James, 'if you would kindly return by five o'clock.' He walked them to the door.

The cold one, the devastating beauty, swivelled and looked straight into his face. 'I understand that we are to spend Christmas with you,' she said. 'That is a very thoughtful and generous gesture.'

'You will all be most welcome,' he answered.

Amy pulled at her sister's arm. 'Hurry,' she said. 'Presents to buy.'

When the two women had walked away, James Mulligan re-entered his office, closed the door and leaned on it. 'Stop it,' he bade himself. 'You can never marry.' He had not reckoned on falling in love so desperately, so stupidly. All men window-shopped, he supposed. But he, above all men, was in no position to purchase. 'Catch yourself on, Mulligan,' he muttered, 'just do the job, then get off home where you belong.'

Mona Walsh's new house was coming on a treat. It boasted a back boiler, new plaster and paint, a mended roof and a solid front door with 13 in brass at the top. Their Tilly could do as she liked, but she wasn't moving into John Street, oh, no. Their Tilly was stopping in the family home where both women had been born and raised; Mona was going up in the world. Slowly, surely, she intended to improve her lot whether or not Tilly liked the idea. For too many years, Tilly had been the leader, had made all the decisions. Mona was getting divorced from her own sister. This concept made the younger of the two Walshes smile as she set off to visit her home on John Street.

Mona waddled down Derby Street, her winter coat flapping slightly in a chill breeze. The coat was a bit bigger on her these days, as Mona had begun to shed some of her weight. Her intention was to be thinner and fitter, because life was short and she had determined to make the best of her remaining time. In a couple of years, a nice little endowment would mature; in a couple of years, Mona would add that money to her savings. She had it all worked out. She was going to buy a nice house up Swan Lane, Accrington brick, electric lights and a flushing lav.

She stopped outside the second-hand furniture shop, placed a hand over her eyes so that she could examine the darkened interior of Samuel's Quality Used Furnishings. Squinting slightly, Mona identified her 'new' dresser, table and chairs, making sure that the word SOLD was affixed to each item. 'After Christmas,' she promised her dining set, 'after Christmas, you'll be moving to a good home.'

'Hello, Miss Walsh.'

She almost jumped out of her skin. 'Good God!' she exclaimed. 'You'll be giving somebody a heart attack.'

James Mulligan grinned. 'Are you off to see your house?'

'I am, that.' She straightened her hat.

'Get in the car and I'll take you.'

Mona hesitated for a split second. She had never ridden in one of these mechanical monsters. 'Tilly'd have a blue fit,' she said.

'And wouldn't that be a sight for the world to behold?'

She found herself laughing. If only people knew what he was really like. And if only he would stay in Bolton and allow Mona to be his second mam. Once she was thinner and prettier, she might look good enough to be related to this handsome man.

'Is this you losing weight?' he asked.

165

Oh, she could have died happy, right here and now. 'Tilly says I look ill.' He had noticed; he cared.

'Will we go for a little spin?' he asked. 'Give your sister something to get her teeth into? Just imagine what she'd say if somebody told her about it.'

'Aye,' said Mona. Then a thought struck. 'This here road's a bit slippy, isn't it?'

He pointed to the tyres. 'You can't see much in this light, but these have a tread like wellington boots. Come on, take heart.'

She sat in the passenger seat, watched him as he walked around the car.

James climbed in, blew into his hands, then set the car in motion.

'Oh, heck,' breathed Mona. She was sitting in a tin box that was fuelled by a highly explosive substance. All sorts of whirrings and wheezings were going on under the bonnet.

'Open your eyes,' he suggested. 'There's nothing to fear. Don't you trust me?'

She nodded vehemently. 'Course I do, but I don't trust this blinking motor. It's not natural, is it?'

'It's progress. And we're doing ten miles an hour, so.' He waited until she seemed more relaxed. 'How is the Temple?'

Mona shrugged. 'Same as ever, loads of preaching about building a new world in America.' She paused. 'He did a couple of them cleansings last week. I've found out a bit about the cleansings, like you asked me. He washes their faces and hands with a white flannel, dries them with a white towel. Then he does their feet.'

James gave her a few seconds, but she said no more. 'Faces, hands and feet. What about areas in between? I hope I'm not embarrassing you.'

'Course you're not.' She was glad that darkness hid the colour in her cheeks. 'He's a right funny man, that Wilkinson. Mind, like everybody else, I got took in at first. He likes the young girls, always does the cleansings one at a time. It's what he calls a secret ceremony.'

'Yes, it would be.'

Mona turned and looked at the handsome profile. In the

poor light provided by street lamps, he looked like one of those sideways-on cameo portraits. 'Do you think he interferes with kiddies?'

He changed gear, turned on to Deane Road. 'It's a possibility. He seems . . . unstable, thwarted in some way.'

Mona inclined her head thoughtfully. 'There's a rumour . . .' Her voice died.

'A rumour?'

'Oh, this is hard for me,' she complained. 'I'm not used to talking to men about . . . personal things, things to do with folk's carryings-on and all that sort of stuff.'

'Tell me.' He stopped the car near a gate leading to Haslam Park. 'Just say it, Mona.'

She marked the fact that he had used her Christian name. James Mulligan made her feel valuable, important. He had chosen her to find evidence against Peter Wilkinson. At first, she had felt a bit guilty about her mission, but it had become a labour of love, almost. Had he asked her to investigate the King himself, she would have done this Irishman's bidding.

'Well, Mona?'

She took a deep breath of cold air. 'They say he's not quite up to scratch, if you get my drift. See . . .' She rooted about her head to find the words. 'If he'd got married, there wouldn't have been any babies, because he can't . . .'

'Save your blushes,' he said. 'I take your meaning, right enough.'

'It is just a rumour, though. People say all sorts, don't they? What I'd like to know is how do they find out he's not the full twelve pennies to the shilling? Especially in that . . . department. And if he's not a proper man, what's he doing messing about with young lasses?' Now that she had started talking, she couldn't seem to stop. 'It doesn't make sense,' she concluded.

'Impotence does not always remove desire,' James said.

'He'd a terrible childhood,' Mona continued. 'His mam kept him in pinafores till he started school – his brother, too. Five years old and still dressed like girls, the pair of them. It were normal to keep lads in frocks up to three. That was to cheat the devil, because the devil only took boys. But most of them were breeched long before their schooldays.'

167

'So he was a figure of fun.'

'Ooh, you can say that again. And she were cruel, specially to him. She used to lock him in the coal-hole under their stairs – Emblem Street, they lived. She flayed him with his dad's belt till there were no skin left on him. It was because he was so ugly, I think.'

James drove down Deane Road. Peter Wilkinson had probably hated his mother. She had humiliated and belittled him, had locked him up, had beaten him. The man had travelled through life despising and fearing women. That was the reason, but it was no excuse. 'His brother seems a decent enough man. Runs the post office up in Pendleton, sells groceries and cakes. Stephen Wilkinson's a talented baker.'

'Aye,' replied Mona thoughtfully, 'but, looking back, Stephen got better treated, because he were quite a handsome little lad. He always did what he were told. Mrs Wilkinson used to say as how Peter looked at her wrong. As far as I can work out, she'd no love at all for her eldest.' She turned to look at her companion. 'Does that mean he can't help what he does – if he does owt, like?'

'No, it means nothing of the sort. The man has free will, just like the rest of mankind. He knows the difference between right and wrong.'

She shivered. 'I'd never have thought but for you mentioning it. If you hadn't asked me to keep my ears and eyes open, I'd have carried on with them shut. I mean, with it being a religion, it's supposed to be about making you a better person.'

He pulled the car into John Street, stopped outside number 13. He remembered earlier visits when he had met Ida and little Joe Hewitt in this very house. 'It isn't a religion, Mona. The Temple of Eternal Light is a cult. Inventors of cults find people who are needy, some rich, some poor. The unloved rich provide funds, while the poor provide manpower. Texas is a big empty state with too few women. For the promise of enough food and a roof, girls are enticed across the Atlantic Ocean. They are used as brood mares, cooks and cleaners.'

Mona gulped audibly. 'How do you know all this?'

'Friends in Dallas who write to me.'

'So . . . so the Light is bad through and through?'

'Possibly. But that doesn't make all the members bad. Most of them don't know what the Light is really about. If my suspicions are correct, any unsuitable females travelling to Texas could be thrown straight into the arms of uncouth cattlemen or oil workers, men who live hard and drink hard.' James lowered his chin. 'I know what it is to live in the wilds with a dangerous drunk. The Light has to be extinguished.'

Mona felt a sudden dryness in her throat. 'Do you fancy a cuppa?' She could show off; she could let him see all she had done to the house. More than that, she could get the subject changed. She didn't fancy thinking about poor girls lost in a country full of foreigners and Red Indians. 'I've got gas rings to boil a kettle, and two stools in the scullery. If we leave the gas on, we'll be nice and warm.'

'Promise you'll keep an eye on him, Mona.'

'I will.'

'Good.' He got out of the car, then helped Mona across the slick pavement. She opened her front door, turned to welcome him.

'What's the matter?' he asked, when the woman stopped dead in her tracks.

She put a finger to her lips. There was no sound in the house, yet something felt different, as if the air had been displaced by recent movement.

'Mona?'

'Shush.' She took his hand and walked through darkness into the living room. 'There's been somebody in here,' she whispered, moving away to light a mantle.

James struck a match and entered the scullery. 'Sweet Jesus!' His legs almost buckled at the knees. He sensed that Mona was standing behind him. 'Go away,' he ordered shakily. 'Get a blanket—'

'I've got no blankets yet.'

'Find something – anything.' He struck another light and applied it to a candle on a small table. Slowly, he knelt and reached out a hand. 'Don't be afraid,' he mouthed quietly. 'You're safe now, safe with us.'

Mona ran round almost aimlessly until she happened on some curtain material. It was not as warm as blanket, but it was all she had. When she returned to the scullery, James made no attempt to prevent her entering the room. 'My God,' she murmured.

He took the cloth and placed it over the girl. She was lying on a pegged rug, her eyes and mouth covered by two scarves. 'You take off the gag and blindfold,' he told Mona, 'so that the first face she sees is a woman's.'

When the scarves were removed, the girl made no sound. She simply continued to lie without moving, without attempting to escape, eyes closed, limbs motionless. The only sign of life was the movement of her chest as she breathed.

Mona bent down and touched a cold hand. 'Hello, love. What are you doing here? Who brought you in, eh?' The poor kiddie was stark naked. 'What's that sickly smell?' she asked James.

'Chloroform,' he replied, his voice thickened by anger. 'She's been doped. Put the kettle on, then I'll go and fetch the police and a doctor.' As he spoke, he massaged the girl's hands.

Mona straightened, filled the kettle, lit both gas rings so that the room would warm up. As she turned to leave the scullery, she noticed something in the corner. 'Look here,' she said. 'Come and see.'

The clothes were folded in a perfect pile, had been arranged in the order in which they had been removed – coat at the bottom, underclothes and stockings on top. 'Who the heck would do a thing like this?' asked Mona. 'Leaving her here, too, in the freezing cold.' She shot a glance over her shoulder, looked at the sleeping child. 'She can't be more nor thirteen. Has she been . . . ?' Mona clapped a hand to her mouth, plainly seeking to hang on to words and suggestions that were far from palatable.

'A doctor will have the answers.' James stood up. 'Will you be all right? I'll have a look round before I go, make sure whoever did this has gone.' He checked the doors, found an unlocked window in the living room. The perpetrator had come in through here, then. 'Is the scullery door unlocked?' called James.

'Yes,' came the answer. 'I left the key in the inside lock.'

So, a criminal had paid a visit tonight, had entered via a sash window, had opened the back door, had ... So much reckoning had gone into the preparation. Premeditated crime, thought James, as he searched two bedrooms. This place had been made ready by the hunter, then he had gone to seek his prey.

After looking upstairs and in the front parlour, he left the house. When the Austin shuddered to life, he drove towards the police station, his hands almost too unsteady for steering. 'She wasn't touched,' he muttered. 'Wasn't raped, at least.' With a certainty that was almost uncanny, James Mulligan knew who had committed this crime. It was a man who both feared and worshipped women, a man who could not cope with female adults. Guardian Peter Wilkinson, respected pastor of the Temple of Eternal Light. 'And who will believe that?' he asked. 'Who on earth will listen to me?'

He ran as fast as his shape would allow, bouncing off a wall, colliding with a lamp-post in his haste. He needed the Light, the shining purity of Moses' legacy, that eternal flame carried so far across the seas from a land of cactus and dry earth, from Texas, from the original miracle, breathing was so hard.

I had to look, to see the female body, another temple, sacred part of our faith. She was not beautiful, was not like the Burton-Massey girls. My body failed me yet again; I am arid, dry as bone bleached in the desert sun where the flame flourishes.

The bottle bounced from a pocket, hit the flags and smashed into a hundred pieces. Could he get more? Would he need more? The idea of dealing yet again with a criminal was unpleasant. Five shillings for a small amount of the drug, five shillings to remind himself that he was still less than a man.

Less than a man? Or do I need a certain kind of woman, a special creature with spun silk hair and features carved in porcelain? Running, running, a stitch in my side, pain in my legs. She folded me into a cage once, a crate made to contain fruit. She poked food through the gaps and called me Fido. Why did you hate me so, Mother?

He was home. Home was not with a sister or a brother; home was a sanctified shed, part of a mill. Once inside, he would be safe. Nothing, no one could hurt him while he stood near those dancing flames.

171

He slammed the door and made for the centre of the room. Here stood a large dish in which the sacred fire danced, fuelled now by kindling and coal, the resulting smoke drawn up a flue created specially for this purpose. Several times each day, the Light was taken, stored in lanterns, guarded while the dish was cleaned and reset. On every occasion, the new fire was created by the original flame.

She did not see me. With the scarves over my face, she would not have known me, anyway. I crept up behind her and placed the pad over her mouth. Oh, how quickly she fell. Dragging, dragging up the yard and into that empty house. Unconscious, how heavy she was. No white towels, but I blessed the sleeping girl and cleansed her head and feet. Nothing. Again, nothing.

He spoke to the Light. 'What is my mission? Am I to live in Makersfield, Texas, a male who is not a man, and must everyone know of my plight? Will I serve with the old and stagnant, those who weave cloth and tend gardens? Or should I remain here, continuing my role as a seeker of virgins?' He prayed for guidance, then sat and looked at his temple. It was so calm, so peaceful.

When a draught of cold air wrapped itself around his ankles, Peter Wilkinson scarcely noticed. It would be one of the night-watch, people who took turns to come and tend the Light. Footsteps approached, then he was suddenly dragged upward by two very strong hands. 'Don't hurt me,' he wailed.

James swung the man round and threw him into a seat. 'What are you?' he asked. 'In God's name, what kind of creature have you become?'

The Guardian of Bolton's Eternal Light was terrified. 'I . . . er . . . what do you mean by coming in here like—?'

'I mean business. That poor girl – why?'

Wilkinson swallowed. This was one of Satan's cohorts, a Catholic, a man damned to an eternity of suffering.

'Number thirteen John Street,' continued James. 'Mona Walsh will be living there shortly. Tonight, she and I visited the house and found your handiwork in the scullery.'

I washed her, blessed her, cleansed her mind and body.

'Why?' James persisted. 'Tell me why.'

'I don't know what you mean.'

172

James bent over the cowering figure. 'Oh, you do, but. You climbed in through an unlatched window, opened the scullery door, then lay in wait for a victim.'

'No.'

Before he could check himself, James Mulligan was shaking the man, rattling him back and forth until the jowls shook like setting aspic. 'I am going for the police,' he promised now. 'And I shall mention your name.' Furious with himself for touching Wilkinson, James left the building.

Guardian Wilkinson let out a long sigh. Who would listen to an immigrant Catholic, one whose father had destroyed an old family from these parts? Who was going to heed the son of Thomas Mulligan, a gambler, a drunkard who had died in his own faeces, whose destroyed liver had spilled on to the floors of Pendleton Grange?

James drove away, wheels spinning on ice, brain burning with fury. The Guardian of the Light was a do-gooder, one whose hideous face appeared quite often in the pages of local newspapers. He gave to the poor, collected food parcels, begged scraps from shopkeepers who were only too glad of free photographic publicity. On paper, Peter Wilkinson saved bodies and souls; in truth, he sought a place for himself, forgiveness for his appearance, a cloak behind which he might hide his true nature.

'God forgive me, I should pity him,' breathed the driver, as he pulled up outside the main police station. 'But I pity his victim more.' This was just the beginning. The man was on a mission, was attempting to prove his manhood. While shaking Peter Wilkinson, James had glimpsed madness in the man's eyes. Not sheer lunacy, but obsession, a terrible, terrible need. 'To be normal is all he asks.' He left the car and walked towards double doors. 'And he will never, ever be that.'

THIRTEEN

'And where have you been?' Kate Kenny stood in front of the kitchen range, arms akimbo, the usually obedient hair sticking up in places like the wig of an ill-kept doll. 'Isn't there enough for me to do without worrying about you in that motor car, in icy weather, in the dark, and in case you've had a crash? The trouble with men is they've no thought for anyone.'

James lowered himself into a chair next to Ida. 'Is this you still here?'

'No,' replied Ida Hewitt. 'I'm just a shadow of me former self. You said you were going up Daubhill to find some woman for that there Amy Burton-Massey's shop. Well, it's took you long enough. Kate's been fretting herself daft. Wore holes in her slippers and the mat, she has.'

He closed his eyes. 'I'll explain in a minute, so I will. Where are the children?'

'Playing marbles in the second drawing room,' answered Kate. 'With Sally. And, in reply to the next question before it jumps out of your mouth, your supper's in the pigs.'

'I'm not hungry.'

'Good.' Kate, still muttering under her breath about wasting good food while people starved in Africa, clattered about with cups and saucers.

Ida, more content than she had been in years, carried on with her knitting. If she had anything to do with it, Pendleton

Clough would not do well in next summer's two-horse race. When it came to working with wool and needles, Ida was confident of an outright victory for the village of Pendleton. Then there was the cake competition. Ida had a few recipes of her grandmother's up her sleeve, banana bread, carrot cake, sponges that floated off at the prod of a fork. All she needed was her legs back; once she got her legs, she might even take part in the tug-of-war. She was so grateful to her host that she was determined to get better even if the effort killed her.

James watched her. Ida was coming on in leaps and bounds. He had been bringing her up to the Grange each morning, and she had made a good friend of Kate. Kate, who did not make friends easily, had grown fond of the 'poor soul' with the weakened legs and the sad past. Ida was now capable of peeling vegetables, washing dishes, a bit of polishing. And knitting, of course.

Kate slammed sugar bowl and milk jug on to the table's surface. 'Did you find the woman?'

He looked at her vaguely.

'The woman,' she repeated, her mouth exaggerating each syllable. 'The woman from that fashion house in Manchester, fancies herself as a designer.'

'Oh, her? I did, yes.'

'Good.' Kate glanced meaningfully at Ida, who looked sideways at James. 'Well, you took your time.' There was sarcasm in Kate's voice, but James was used to that. 'Did she look as if she might be some use, then?'

'What? Oh, yes, yes. I'll get her to visit Amy after Christmas,' he said, with the air of a man whose thoughts are definitely elsewhere. 'Louisa Burton-Massey left a lot of sketches to be worked on, so that'll give them a head start.' He paused, drew a hand through his thick, dark hair. 'Then I met Mona Walsh. You'll know her, Ida.'

'Her from the wash-place? Her what's taking over our old house? Big fat woman with a face like a stewed prune?' Ida had even managed to stop knitting. 'Been in laundry for years, her and her sister. Didn't you say she was supposed to be helping out with the ironing if the frock shop ever opens?'

175

'Yes, to all the above,' replied James. 'She wanted to show me the house, so I drove her there.'

Ida winked at Kate. 'He's been out courting,' she said mischievously.

'Him?' The Irishwoman laughed, though the sound was hollow. 'Nobody'd have him, and that's the rock bottom truth of it.'

'Kate?' James shook his head slowly.

'What?'

'Shut up, there's a good woman.' He told them the story, omitting just the scene in the temple. 'The girl's in shock, but she's not been seriously damaged,' he concluded.

'Good God.' Ida's knitting now rested on the table between teapot and biscuit tin. 'In my house?' It was plain that she took this as a personal insult. 'Who the hell would do a thing like that to an innocent kiddie?'

James shifted his chair until he faced Ida. 'The behaviour was strange to say the least of the matter. The man – she never saw his face – drugged her, removed all her clothes, then . . . just looked at her, I suppose. This is a sick fellow altogether, one who is driven by some terrible poison in his brain.' He paused, looked straight at Ida. 'I think . . . I'm ninety-nine per cent certain that it was Peter Wilkinson.'

Ida shut her mouth with an audible snap, opened it immediately. 'Get away with your bother. I know you don't think much to him, but he does a lot for folk – he did a lot for us.'

'And he wanted a great deal in return.' He paused for a second. 'He wanted your granddaughter.'

Ida closed her eyes for a moment. A sudden headache was drawing jagged lights across her vision. 'What did the police have to say about it?'

'They managed not to laugh at me. The girl was unhurt, confused, but in one piece. Ida?'

'What?'

'Mona says he'd a mournful childhood.'

'So did you,' snapped Kate. 'I mind the time when—' She stopped herself, reminded her tongue of the rules James had set down when she had arrived in England. She was to say nothing, nothing at all about his past. Feverishly, she

176

back-pedalled. 'I mind the time you told me a little about yourself.'

'Ida knows about my early life,' he said, the emphasis on the 'early'.

'All I'm saying is that your childhood didn't make you bad. You can't go about making excuses for people just because their young years were a bit uncomfortable.' Kate poured the tea.

Ida Hewitt remained silent for several minutes while James accepted a sandwich from his housekeeper, while he ate it, while the table was cleared. Then she spoke. 'When you give up on life like I did, when you ignore your family and neglect them, it's a selfish way to carry on. I grieved something shocking when my lad died, but I weren't the only one to suffer a loss. Trust me to make a song and dance of it. So when Guardian Wilkinson came to my house, he made things a lot easier, bringing food and soap, bits of clothes, all kinds of stuff. In a way, he helped me to . . . what's the word? . . . to indulge meself.'

James placed a hand on Ida's. 'You must also forgive yourself,' he begged.

She blinked rapidly. 'I hope you're wrong, but he is a bit peculiar, like.'

'Mona told me about his childhood.'

'He never had no childhood.' Ida's tone was sad.

'So now he tries to steal the childhood of others. I think he may also be trying to become a man.' James squeezed Ida's fingers. 'There's a rumour that he's impotent.'

'Aye.' Embarrassed, she paused for a few seconds. 'But . . . but we all thought that were a good thing, as if he'd dedicated all his energy to the Light, nowt to distract him.' She sighed, shook her head slowly. 'Same as Catholic priests if you think on it. But there were a price, eh? See, folk same as Mona and Tilly, they give money and food. When it comes to people like me and mine . . . well, they want our girls. But as for what happened down John Street tonight, I'm not sure you can lay that at his door.'

James decided to hang for the full sheep. 'Ida, I went to the temple and I accused him face to face. Looking at him,

177

listening to his terror, I knew I had the right man. Later, when I told a police sergeant my opinion, I got a lecture about blackening the name of a man whose charitable works make him a legend in his own lifetime. But the police were not there earlier, in the temple. They didn't see the fear, the trembling.'

Kate blessed herself hurriedly before speaking to Ida. 'If Mr Mulligan's convinced of the man's guilt, then he's probably right. He's a knack of knowing folk better than they know themselves.'

Ida gripped the edge of the table. There'd been talk, but she'd not heard everything, as she had depended totally on visitors. 'The cleansings,' she whispered now.

'Yes?' James leaned closer to her.

'The cleansings only work if they're not talked about. Far as I can make out, most lasses just get their faces and feet washed. But our Diane said the odd one came out a bit shaky, like. Usually quiet girls in borrowed frocks, girls from poor homes. Happen they got tret different. I mean, our Diane used to say she didn't like him and wasn't going in for cleansing. Ooh, it makes you wonder.' She stopped speaking, was plainly deep in thought.

'Could we talk to some of those girls?' asked James.

Ida pondered for another moment. 'No. Even if something did go on, they'll likely say nowt, because they'll want to go off abroad for a better life. And they'd be too embarrassed, most of them.' She paused again. 'No, no, it can't be right. He wouldn't do something as bad as that. Would he?'

Kate took a rosary from her pocket and twisted it about like a set of worry beads. There was something in James Mulligan's eyes, in his voice, in the set of his jaw. She cast her mind back through the years, remembering the hardships he had overcome, the sheer, dogged determination that had driven him onward until he had become the finest and best-educated of men. He had several gifts, one of which was the ability to teach, another the talent to absorb and analyse information at the drop of a hat. He had most folk summed up within minutes. She shivered. Her nephew, the person she loved most in the whole world, had come upon evil tonight.

'I'm all right, Kate,' he whispered.

There he was again, reading her mind, understanding her soul. 'What will happen?' she asked him.

'Oh, he'll strike again. The police will talk to him, but unless the girl remembers something, he'll get away with it. As for my opinion, I obviously carry little weight with the guardians of the law. I'm just another immigrant. No, worse than that – I'm the foreigner whose father was a vagabond.'

'Won't he get caught?' asked Ida.

He lowered his chin, pondered for a moment. 'In the end, he will. But how many young women will he target in the meantime?'

'You might have scared him off,' ventured Kate uncertainly.

'His sickness is too deep for that.' James drained the last dregs from his cup. 'He will follow where his uncontrollable fantasies lead him. We'd need to be watching him twenty-four hours a day and seven days a week.'

Ida gulped. 'What if he kills somebody?' she asked.

'I did all I could,' replied James. 'The police probably think I'm the cracked pot, not him. Ah, well.' He stood up. 'Away now, Ida. I'll drive you and the young ones home.'

When James and the Hewitts had left, Kate Kenny lit a candle and placed it in a blue dish at the feet of the Immaculate Conception. The statue, serene and beautiful, always calmed Kate. Mary had been Kate's strength when her husband had died, when her little boy had been stillborn just weeks later.

'I've a terrible foreboding,' she said aloud. 'Mother of God, I beg you to watch over James. After all my brother did to him, he surely deserves some peace.' Then Kate Kenny knelt on the kitchen floor and said her rosary. Soon, it would be Christmas, the time of the greatest of all miracles. She placed herself where she had always sought to dwell, in the hands of the Blessed Virgin.

Camilla Smythe had a homely face, and hair that looked as if it had been left to go rusty in the rain. She was her own woman, with her own style and a set of morals that would have been a credit to any practising clergyman. As an unpretty female, she had long owned the knowledge that a queue of suitors was not likely to form, so she made the best of her life

179

by running a successful business and by staying loyal to her friends.

In Camilla's book, family was another matter altogether. Had she been offered a choice, she would certainly not have picked a father who wandered towards retirement via the golf course, a mother who preached one thing and did the opposite, and a brother who . . . who was beneath contempt.

She stared at her reflection, saw large, white teeth, a too-big nose, freckles and a new, angry spot on her chin. Rupert was so beautiful on the outside, an alley-cat within. She didn't know what to do about him; she did know that she would like to take the biggest whip from the stables and lash him to within an inch of his aimless, stupid life.

What to do? she asked herself for the umpteenth time. Tell Mother and watch while that not-so-good woman stopped Rupert from going off to London? Tell poor Amy? Father? Father was more interested in his handicap and making 'good contacts' via the nineteenth over at Birkdale.

Rupert, daft boy, was planning to run away with Eliza Burton-Massey. Camilla, astute when it came to measuring people, was not fond of Eliza. The girl was odd. She seemed to alter whenever she felt so inclined, one minute the dutiful daughter, the loving sister, the next moment a calculating monster ready to take off into her own future with never a backward glance at her sisters. Like a chameleon, Eliza Burton-Massey changed her colours to accord with her background; now she was intending to change her environment, too. Well, let her.

Camilla dabbed eau-de-Cologne on her aching temples. She wished with all her heart that she had not overheard a certain conversation between two people who were not worth the worry. But she had heard. At approximately four o'clock this afternoon, while Mother and Father were safely out of the way, Rupert had brought his latest lady-friend home. They had not entered the house; they had sat in the stables discussing plans for Eliza's escape from Caldwell Farm. Camilla, trapped in the stall belonging to her favourite mount, was now in possession of facts that would upset several applecarts in the New Year.

180

'Perhaps I am not such a good person after all,' she told her reflection. A plan was forming almost of its own accord, and she was concerned about her attitude towards the subject of Rupert and Eliza. The plan was simple: all she needed to do was . . . nothing. They deserved one another. Rupert, only too recently allied to Margot, was now about to run away with Margot's sister. Eliza, so precious, so treasured by Amy, was, in truth, a selfish and untrustworthy piece of work.

'Eliza will go off anyway,' she muttered. 'She might just as well be with Rupert. Then she will know somebody in the city.' As for Rupert, let him sink or swim – it was time for him to make a go of things beyond the reach of his mother's restraining embrace.

'What about Amy, though?' Amy had taken her mother's death badly, then Camilla's mother had waded in to separate her beloved boy from Margot. Even so, Eliza and Margot were old enough to do as they pleased. In the long-term, Amy was going to suffer anyway. Why should Amy have the responsibility of Eliza and Margot? Of the three sisters, Amy was the most practical, the nicest. There was no chance of her getting on with her own future while Eliza and Margot held her back. 'Let them all go,' Camilla said firmly. It was with Amy that Camilla's loyalty lay; she would be on hand to offer comfort to Amy when the time came. There, the decision was made.

Nevertheless, there was one thing she had to do. She brushed the hated hair, failing to be impressed by its sheen, washed an uncomely face without seeing the intelligence in her own eyes, the generosity of the mouth. Burning with an anger that lit up her features, Camilla crossed the landing, knocked, waited for her brother to allow her to enter his sacred space.

He was lying face downward on the bed, bare feet dangling over the edge, hair ruffled, hands flicking the pages of a magazine on his pillow. 'Ah, dear sister,' he drawled.

Camilla sat in a bedside chair, wriggling until she achieved some comfort among the discarded shirts and trousers. 'Do you never clean up after yourself?' she asked.

'What? And disappoint the servants? They'd have nothing to do if we all looked after ourselves.'

She studied him, took in the long, lean bones, the handsome

181

face, the silk pyjamas. He was the very embodiment of the term 'fop', all polish on the outside, and inside, just a shallow, muddy pool instead of a soul. 'Will you have servants in London?' she asked.

'Not sure. I expect Mater will have fixed something.'

'Just as she always does.' Camilla's tone was harsh.

He rolled over and sat on the edge of his bed. 'Ooh, I say,' he hooted. 'Who rattled your cage, old thing?'

'She even got the job for you.'

'Jealous?' he asked.

'No.' She wanted to hit him and hit him until the silly smile disappeared. 'I could never be jealous of a person as mean-minded and facile as you are. But I want you to know this. Eliza Burton-Massey is another just like you. She'll get what she wants even if she has to leave a trail of corpses.'

'W-what?' he blustered.

'You expect to share her bed, I take it? Is Amy on your list, too? After all, it should be fair shares. I don't doubt that you took the youngest one's virginity, so why not all three?'

His jaw hung slackly.

'Eliza will have her own way, Rupert. I very much doubt that your wishes will come under her consideration.'

At last, brain and mouth clicked into gear. 'What on earth are you talking about?'

'The stables. Today. About fourish.'

'You – you eavesdropped?'

She noticed his heightened colour and a vein throbbing in his temple. 'Yes. By the way, your temper is showing.' Used to getting his own way for most of the time, Rupert was not enjoying this confrontation. Camilla smiled. 'Bank clerks need to be servile, you know. Pull your horns in.'

'I shan't be a clerk for long.'

'But Mother will not be there to push you onward and upward. You will be forced to fend for yourself for the first time in your life. How on earth will you manage?'

His lip curled. 'She's done a lot for you, too. I never heard you complaining when she set you up in your little cookery business.'

'I know, and I'm grateful. But if Mother were to interfere in any relationship of mine, I would tell her that she is a two-faced mess. I mean, she preaches equality of the sexes, pleads the cause of women, yet she could not allow you to associate with Margot Burton-Massey. Worse than that, you allowed Mother to separate you from a girl you supposedly loved.'

Rupert sniffed. 'Margot was a mistake.'

Camilla laughed. 'You're the mistake.'

'So what are you going to do about it?' he asked.

'Nothing.'

'What?' The clearly defined eyebrows shot upward.

'Nothing,' she repeated. 'Except this. I tell you now that Eliza has a rather special kind of power. She will eat you for breakfast and spit out the bare bones. Really, I look forward to news of your life in London, because it promises to be quite interesting. In fact, I shall visit you – perhaps at Easter?'

'Don't bother,' he barked.

'That's a terrible thing to say to a sister who is concerned for your welfare.' She paused for a few seconds. 'You know, the greatest favour I could do for you would be to tell Mother. She would certainly refuse to pay the rent on your *pied-à-terre* if she knew about Eliza. But I intend to do nothing for you, Rupert. Eliza is an extraordinarily beautiful woman who will fare very well in London. She can sing, dance and play the piano extremely well. When her name is up in lights, she will surely be beyond the reach of a simple little bank teller.' She smiled, nodded thoughtfully. 'You are in for a wonderful time.'

Rupert, all bravado on the outside, was secretly afraid of venturing into the big city. Eliza was a necessity – he could not possibly make the move on his own. Knowing his own weakness and worrying that it might show in his face, he retrieved his magazine and flicked the pages.

'There's always been a woman, hasn't there?' said Camilla. 'Mother has been your cushion, and you cannot go to London by yourself, so Eliza is going to be your soft landing when things go wrong. Well.' She stood up. 'Eliza hides her prickles beneath a layer of softness. Take care. Take very great care. After all, we don't want you getting hurt, do we?'

Rupert watched his sister as she left the room. She was a great ugly carthorse who would never get a man in a million years. She was also clever, bright enough to see right through him. Camilla knew his faults, his Achilles' heels; she knew that he was afraid to go south alone. 'Bitch,' he spat.

Camilla prepared for bed, her thoughts fixed on Amy and the New Year. She could not remember a time when she had wished anyone ill, and a part of her failed to understand her current attitude to Rupert and to the Burton-Massey girls. Was she turning bad? Oh, what a mess. She went over and over the problem, yet always returned to the same point. She felt guilt-ridden, amazed at herself. But although she tossed and turned all night, Camilla's resolve stayed firm. Amy would survive. Rupert? Never.

Sally Hayes was alone in the kitchen and drinking her cocoa when James Mulligan returned from Ida Hewitt's cottage. Her eyes smiled at him over the rim of her mug. 'Mrs Kenny said to tell you she's had enough and she's gone to bed.'

'I see.' He sat opposite the girl. She was about the same age as the naked child in the scullery at 13 John Street. His blood boiled at the thought of Peter Wilkinson walking freely in the world. 'Sally?'

'Yes, sir?'

'Never go out alone at night, especially at the weekends.' Wilkinson often spent weekends with his brother in the village of Pendleton. 'Take someone with you.' Diane Hewitt now lived in Pendleton. Wilkinson had intended to prepare Diane for emigration. Surely he would not touch a child so young?

'Right, sir.'

'Do you still go for walks with Eliza Burton-Massey?'

'No. She doesn't bother with me any more.'

James heard the sadness. 'Where did you walk, Sally?'

'To the stables or through the fields. Sometimes, we went into the woods.'

'And did you ever meet anyone?'

She shook her head.

He arranged his next question carefully, as he did not wish to alarm Sally unduly. 'Did you notice anybody? Not someone you'd meet or talk to, just . . . a man hanging around. I think

184

he's related to Mr Wilkinson at the post office, the man who sells those wonderful cakes.'

Sally frowned. 'I know who you mean – he's the ugly one. Miss Eliza used to laugh and pretend not to see him. Oh, he stared so hard at her, but that's because she's very beautiful. Miss Eliza said he was the frog and she was the princess, but she'd no intention of kissing him to turn him into a prince.' Smiling, she paused. 'But that was when she was my real friend, before I said I wouldn't go to London with her and ...' The words melted away.

'Sally?'

'I wasn't supposed to say about London. Please don't tell anyone. She wouldn't be my friend at all if she knew ... Oh, please. Miss Eliza hardly ever comes to play the piano now. She'd stop altogether if she knew I'd said about running away.'

'You have my word.' Perhaps Eliza would be safer in London. Perhaps all the young women of Pendleton and Pendleton Clough should escape while the going was good. Was it possible that Wilkinson might be planning to spread his wings outside the town? Could he be working his way north towards the villages?

'Thank you, sir.' She rose and took her cup to the sink, rinsed and dried it, walked to the door. 'Good night,' she called.

'Good night, Sally.'

He sat alone with his thoughts, bone weary after an evening that had seemed to go on for ever. Now he carried the knowledge that Eliza was probably planning to go away. He could not warn her family because he had made a promise, and he had no intention of betraying Sally. What a disaster.

Had it not been for his own father and Mr Burton-Massey, James would still have been in Ireland. His life there had been so easy, simple, predictable. What would he not give now to be planning lessons, chasing boys away from the orchard, listening to young voices raised in song or in laughter?

Businesses, mortgages, hydro, farm management – he was not designed for this sort of life. Even so, he knew that he had to stay here until wrongs had been righted, until life had been made viable for the descendants of the Burton-Massey line.

185

Yet, oh, he was in so much danger. His heartstrings had been tugged by all three girls who lived at Caldwell Farm, but one in particular caused him much discomfort.

Discomfort was his forte for now, he concluded. With a heavy heart, he entered the pantry to pick up the necessary provisions. From a pocket of his jacket, he took a large key, then made his way to the cellar. The key groaned in its ageing mechanism, the door hinges screamed for oil, his mind screamed silently for peace.

He descended into darkness, feet made sure by habit, a hand reaching out for the oil lamp. When the wick was lit, he placed the lamp on a table and stared for several seconds into the near distance.

In here, in this private place, James Mulligan faced his own secrets. In the cellars of Pendleton Grange, the man's conscience, raw and sore, waited to be nourished and appeased.

FOURTEEN

On Christmas morning, Mona rose early. This was to be her last Christmas at home: next year she might be a visitor, or she might play hostess to Tilly. So, this was to be a special celebration, though Tilly refused to regard it as such. Deeply resentful of Mona's impending 'desertion', the older sister had been less than co-operative with preparations for the feast.

Mona made little patties of sage and onion, remembering that Tilly did not like the chicken to be stuffed. She pricked pork sausages, which were to be toasted in jackets of crisp streaky bacon, then peeled sprouts and carrots for steaming, potatoes and parsnips for roasting, set the pudding to boil.

At about ten in the morning, with everything ready for oven and hob, Mona had a nice sit-down with one of her penny dreadfuls. Since her declaration of independence, she had displayed her reading matter fearlessly – in spite of their Tilly's sniffs and grunts. Mona liked a good story. These were comforting tales, where the hero and heroine inevitably came together in the end. Upon reaching the last page, Mona always heaved a sigh of relief, gladdened to the core because true love had won through yet again.

She reached a bit about two lovers on a sinking boat, then found herself elsewhere. In the dream, she stood in the scullery at 13 John Street, found the tiny room crammed with naked girls and piles of clothing. Mr Mulligan was running about in the next room trying to find which frock fitted which girl, then Tilly decided to wash everything. Mr Wilkinson arrived with the Light in a glass jar, two more unconscious females and a copy of *Illumination*, which was the Temple's magazine.

Mr Mulligan clouted Mr Wilkinson, who fell out through the door and banged his head on the opposite wall. Seth Dobson, the undertaker from Mulligan's Yard, brought enough coffins to fill the house. Mona screamed and tried to explain that the girls were not really dead, but no one listened, though Tilly said, 'They might as well be dead, after what's happened to them,' while Ida Hewitt walked unaided into the house and reclaimed it as her own.

Mona woke shivering from head to foot. What a nasty dream that had been. Was it an omen? Should she not move to John Street? Was Mr Wilkinson bent on some terrible errand that involved stripping young women of clothes and dignity? She blinked herself back to full consciousness, looked at the clock on the mantel. It was nearly twelve. The chicken sat raw and white on the table, while a nasty smell from the scullery advised Mona that the pudding pan had run out of water. She ran to rescue the pudding, returned to the kitchen, stoked the fire, placed the chicken in the range oven.

'Tilly?' Mona stood at the foot of the stairs. 'Do you want a cup of tea and a biscuit, put you on till Christmas dinner?'

No answer floated down the stairwell.

Mona called again. 'Tilly? Are you stopping up there while the cows come home?'

Still no reply.

A cold finger of fear traced itself the length of Mona's spine. Tilly liked her bed, but she had never stayed upstairs till noon. Worse than that, Mona was possessed of a feeling that she was completely alone in the house. 'Tilly?'

Mona sat on the second stair. Mathilda Joan Walsh had been born in this very house, as had Monica Jean Walsh. They had travelled through life with the same initials, had been welded together in the family business, had buried their parents, had stood firm during trials and tribulations. 'Dear God,' prayed Mona, 'I know she's a pest, but don't take her from me. We're all we've got. There's nobody nowhere who cares about us.'

188

It was about ten past twelve now. Mona needed to go upstairs to check on Tilly, was determined to climb the flight. But her head and her feet seemed to have differing opinions. She stood up, tried to move up the stairs, could not manage it. Things would be all right, she insisted. But whatever she did, Mona's feet would move in one direction only – back to the kitchen.

Strangely, Mona found herself calculating that the small chicken would take about an hour, so she had better put the par-boiled spuds in soon. And the parsnips. Carrots and turnips twenty minutes on the hob, sprouts fifteen. The sausages could go in the top of the oven for half an hour, and she could fry the patties if pressed for time and space.

She smoothed back her hair, straightened her cooking apron. It had been a really bad nightmare, that one. And it had pushed its way into reality to make her imagine now that her sister was dead. The best thing was to get on with the job in hand instead of standing here like a lemon. Lemon – there was a thought. She would make a jelly to have for pudding after chicken sandwiches for supper. If she put the mould in the back yard, it would soon set out there in the cold. A lemon one. Tilly loved lemon jelly.

Margot didn't feel at all Christmassy. She had a lump in her belly that had suddenly burgeoned into slight visibility, causing her to let out skirts and dresses, making her hold herself stiff and straight in order to look as normal as possible. Soon, people would begin to point fingers at her. Really, she should visit Rupert, since this lump was his as much as hers, but she couldn't be bothered.

On Christmas morning, she sat in her bedroom, relieved that the feast day had merited a small fire in the grate. The Moorheads, faithful old retainers, had lit fires in every room. Having turned down Mr Mulligan's all-embracing invitation, they would have Caldwell Farm to themselves today. Margot wished with all her heart that she, too, might stay at home, but she did not want to draw attention to herself.

Somewhere, she had read about a pregnant woman who had gone horse-riding. Bouncing up and down in the saddle had caused the foetus to come away, prompting the same woman to write an article about the dangers of riding. 'My kingdom for a horse, then,' Margot whispered. She harboured no grudge against the unborn – in fact, her feelings in general seemed to have gone on strike. But if a simple gallop could rid her of the burden, then a simple gallop would be employed as soon as this terrible tiredness lifted.

Eliza, in the room that had once been Mother's, lay stretched out on the eiderdown, her mind far away from this dull, grey place. Lancashire was not a very exciting county, she concluded. The north was not inviting at all – even the cities were centres of smoke and boredom. London, however, was scarcely industrial. She perceived the capital as a huge bank, a bustling metropolis where all the money was stored, some of it spilling out of vaults and into the silk-lined pockets of gentlemen, the sort of males who treated women with respect.

She stretched out her hands, studied elegant long fingers with nails coloured a soft, ladylike pink, the kind of shade that would look well on the arm of one of those City gentlemen. She would be snapped up, of course. After she had served a few months as the star of some show in the West End, her admirers at the stage door might very well include a baron, even an earl or a duke. He would whisk her away to his stately pile in Hampshire or Herefordshire, and she would be married in a private family chapel with Amy and Margot as bridesmaids. Though it could be in a cathedral, she supposed. Many of the gentry got married in cathedrals. She would be beautiful in a gown of white gossamer, with real flowers threaded through a diamond tiara, silk slippers on her feet, a long veil suspended from neatly coiffed hair. Yes, the ethereal look would definitely suit her.

Rupert was going to be a bit of a bind, but she would find a way to be rid of him. He was hilariously funny, his eyes practically on stalks every time he saw her. His puerile devotion was pathetic, as were his clearly visible expectations of success in the seduction scenes he was planning. Let him try, she mused. Just let him try.

Amy, in her bedroom, was staring at herself in the mirror. She had decided to make an effort, and was applying makeup cleverly, in accordance with instructions contained in a fashion magazine of Mother's. The trick, of course, was to have a finished product that looked as natural and unmade-up as possible. After a fourth attempt, she threw in the towel and scrubbed her skin with Pond's. She looked better without warpaint, so she opted for a mere touch of lipstick, a dab of powder and a thin film of rouge to disguise the pallor of winter.

She wondered how she would look with shorter, in vogue hair, wondered why she was considering such measures. It was the fault of James Mulligan, she supposed, as he was bullying her to open up the shop in a few weeks. Perhaps, as the 'front' woman, she should be up to date in the couture stakes, but the cutting of hair was probably a step too far.

Christmas – the first without Mother. Of course, Mother had not been much fun in recent years, but, had she survived, she might have enjoyed the holidays this year. 'Stop it,' Amy told her reflection sternly. 'Onward, not backward.'

She found her shoes, placed all her gifts in a shopping basket. Then she sat by the fire and gazed into the flames, looking for pictures in the red and yellow tongues. Father had played this game with her when she was a child. Father's final game had placed his whole family in dire trouble . . . 'Onward,' she repeated.

The future. A Cut Above? Margot had flatly refused to consider working there, while Eliza just looked vague and secretive whenever the subject arose. Eliza made Amy rather uncomfortable these days, as did Margot. The former seemed to be living in a dream world and was reticent about her movements, while the latter, suddenly sickly and troubled by indigestion, kept running off outside in all weathers, almost as if trying to escape from herself.

Amy knew that she could not be a mother to her siblings. Had there been an aunt nearby, she might have sought advice, at least, but there was no one. 'I have to do something,' she said. 'The money will run out altogether soon.' Mother had invested a chunk of capital in the business, and the interest on the residue would not keep the residents and staff of Caldwell Farm beyond a matter of weeks.

191

She rose and walked to the window, looked out on a Christmas scene, a light sprinkling of snow decorating fences, walls and trees, crisping the grass. James had found someone, apparently. A young designer who had worked for a good house in Manchester was in need of employment. She had children and no husband to support her. Local folklore had it that he had gone off with a barmaid, leaving his wife and two small sons with no real means of support. 'Which is all well and good,' muttered Amy, 'as long as she can design, cut and fit cloth.' Of course, Eliza, too, would settle down. She would see sense and come to work in what was to become the family business. Margot? The bit of savings Margot had managed to acquire over the years from her paltry allowance would run out soon. Amy hardened her heart against both her sisters – no work, no pocket money.

The world was so pretty today. Christmas promised to be interesting, too, as James Mulligan had made the unilateral decision to do all the cooking. Kate Kenny, his housekeeper, had been muttering darkly for days about food poisoning, gravy solid enough to slice and a goose so underdone that it would find its own way to the table without much encouragement. She had promised that all who partook would go down with the ague, which word she pronounced as 'aygew', making it all the funnier.

'I'm noticing life again,' Amy said. 'That has to be a good thing.' It was not a sin to laugh, enjoyment was no crime. Perhaps Eliza and Margot were still grieving deeply. If that was so, it was time for them to look ahead occasionally. The trite adage about life having to go on was suddenly a piece of wisdom. Amy made up her mind there and then to enjoy the day, to treat the Christmas period as a time for pleasure, a chance to laugh and rest before opening A Cut Above. The shop would be Mother's living monument, a tribute to her genius.

Amy closed her eyes and daydreamed not about the past, but about a future that had to succeed.

Ida Hewitt, stronger by the day, looked out across her little patch of front garden, a squarish area edged by boundary walls of stone. It boasted a pathway made of hammered-down brick, with a full stop at the end in the form of a green wooden gate. The grass, still thick with hoar, stood to attention like a thousand tiny soldiers dressed in white. It was beautiful, almost overwhelming.

The Hewitts had been here for just a few weeks, but Ida was already worrying about returning to Bolton. Mr Mulligan would go back to Ireland, as would his housekeeper. What would happen to Ida and the children then? she wondered. James Mulligan had given her some pride, too, had got her working at the big house. Oh, why couldn't she just grab this time and make the best of it? After all those years in bed, she was now experiencing real worry, as if she had merely saved it up until now. God was punishing her for carelessness and idleness, it seemed.

The children were outside, both wrapped up against the weather, each engrossed in games. Diane was sliding with the older children, while little Joe, his legs already surer, was helping others to build a snowman from a few remaining banks of drifted snow. The Hewitt children had received books, toys and clothes, all bought by Mr Mulligan. He was so kind, such a good man. Only months ago, Ida had dismissed him as another flaming Catholic, all booze, Latin and gambling, but she knew better now. And, as she had taken to admitting begrudgingly, perhaps other Micks weren't as bad as she had once believed.

She fingered a scarf at her throat, knew that it was silk, for hadn't she tested it by crunching it in a closed fist? When her fingers had opened, the cloth had jumped out immediately. So, Ida Hewitt, late of 13 John Street, owned a silk scarf, all pastel shades and fringed at the ends. Mr James Mulligan had bought the scarf for her. He valued her, and she was more than grateful.

She turned away from the small-paned window and looked at her new life. It was so cosy, just two rooms down and three up, the latter having been made from one long space in the roof. In that area, weavers had toiled at looms, had made cloth from yarn spun in other cottages. They had slept on the ground floor, Ida supposed, spread about on straw mattresses in front of the fire, under the stairs, beneath tables.

Now, the house was truly comfortable. In the front room, there was a cast-iron fireplace with tiled sides, a proper dining-table, some chairs, a small sofa, a dresser, an occasional table with a plant standing on a lace mat. There were pictures on the walls, little ornaments dotted about, a brass-framed mirror, shelves with plates balanced along their surfaces. The kitchen was a dream, with a proper porcelain sink, cupboards, a big range oven with a large copper, pans hanging from beams . . . oh, when the time came, she would not be able to give this up.

She walked to the front door and called the children. Soon Mr Mulligan would arrive to ferry them to Pendleton Grange. Today Ida would be a guest, not a worker. Kate had been in a bit of a mither just lately, because Mr Mulligan was going to cook the dinner. Well, let him, thought Ida mischievously – it was time men realized that food didn't arrive by magic.

Diane turned. 'Aw, Gran. Just another five minutes – please?'

Joe waited. He always left complicated negotiations to his sister.

'All right,' called Ida. She watched while a big lad picked up Joe and allowed him to put coal 'eyes' in the snowman's face, while Diane skated on glassy ice at a very fast pace. They were safe here, so settled, unthreatened.

'Hello.'

Instinctively, Ida Hewitt drew back. 'Oh,' she mumbled, 'hello.'

Peter Wilkinson leaned on the green gate. 'Just taking my morning constitutional,' he said. 'My sister Doris and I are spending the festive season with our brother. He has the post office and the bakery.'

'Right.' Ida's hand crept of its own accord to her throat. There was something very reassuring about the feel of Mr Mulligan's silk scarf. She thought about Guardian Wilkinson's brother, Stephen, who seemed a decent enough fellow. Doris, the sister, Ida had never met, though she had heard of her. Doris played the piano at the temple, and she had the reputation of being a miserable sort.

'Happy Christmas, praise the Lord,' added Mr Wilkinson.

'Same to you, I'm sure.' Ida waited for the man to go away,

willed him to be off, to stop putting his weight on the hinges of her little green gate.

'I've brought the Light to my brother's house,' he told her now. 'Would you like me to fetch it here later on? We could pray together and thank the Light for your recovery.'

She coughed nervously. 'Well, that'd be nice, only we won't be here, me and our Diane and our Joe. We're going out.'

'I see.' He paused, waited for further information, received none. 'Are you going somewhere nice?' he asked.

Ida's grip on her scarf tightened. 'To Pendleton Grange,' she replied, after a short but measurable pause.

'Ah.' The ugly man stroked his chin thoughtfully. 'And will you be joining in the rosary, the Catholic blessing of the food, will you be praying to plaster statues?'

'I doubt it.'

He lowered his head and his tone. 'You owe everything to the Light, Mrs Hewitt.'

Ida could feel her dander rising. She released the hold on her scarf and folded her arms. 'But I don't owe anybody my grand-daughter. Nobody with any sense would send young girls off to a foreign country as payment for a few loaves and the odd scrape of butter. How do you know what'll happen to them? They could get raped, beaten up or whatever.'

He blanched, stepped away from Ida Hewitt's anger. Temper in a woman had always terrified him. It wasn't meant to be like this, because men were supposed to be the dominant ones. He wasn't even a man; at times such as this, he realized all over again that he was inadequate, incapable of fulfilling his function as a creator of life. Even so, Ida Hewitt should be grateful, compliant. They should all be servile . . .

'Did you hear about that poor young girl in my house down John Street?'

He felt his Adam's apple bobbing about like a cork in a bath, tried to swallow, was appalled when a groaning sound escaped his lips. She was staring so hard, so coldly.

'Some damned fool drugged her, took all her clothes off and left her freezing in the scullery. Mr Mulligan says it's likely one of them impotent men, them who can never be real husbands.' She left a pause. 'Whoever it is is having a look and trying to

195

work himself into a lather so's he can perform, like. Disgusting behaviour that. Don't you think so, Mr Wilkinson?'

He stepped further away from her. 'He blamed me. Did you know that? Did you know that he brought the police and gave them my name?' God, why didn't the woman say something? She was staring and staring, not blinking, just fixing him with her eyes, poleaxing him to the spot. 'Mrs Hewitt, I—'

'Go away,' she said plainly. Mr Mulligan was right: this was the one. 'I'm done with you.' Her grandchildren were not as safe as she had imagined, then. While creatures such as this roamed the earth, no one was truly out of danger. 'Stay away from me and mine,' she advised.

He pulled himself together. 'Are you implying that you believe that man's accusations? He has poisoned you against me – I can see that. How could you listen to him?'

'With my ears,' she answered. 'The same way as I'm hearing you now. And my eyes are seeing things in your face – guilt and fear, Mr Wilkinson.'

He took yet another step backwards, lost his footing, hit the ground hard. Children ran to help him up, but Ida spoke to them. 'Leave him,' she said. 'His precious Light'll look after him.'

'I damn you and yours for all eternity,' he growled.

She leaned over the little green gate. 'Only God Almighty can do that. He's the judge in the end.' She shooed the children away. 'You'd best lift yourself up off the floor,' she said, 'but never try to lift yourself above God. And remember, He sees everything you do. Oh, and your hair's come undone.' The side-pieces, grown to cover his bald pate, were dangling towards his shoulders.

He got up, made a feeble attempt to cover the barren area of scalp.

'Am I forgiven?' Ida asked sweetly. 'One of the main things Jesus preached was forgiveness. All Christians are told to love their neighbour. Do you love me, Guardian Wilkinson? Or am I not young enough? Am I too old for you to practise on?'

He felt the blood in his face, heard it buzzing in his ears. Words collected, but they refused to slide from a tongue as dry as dust. The ground, thick with frost, threatened to drag him down again. While attempting to regulate his breath, he allowed his eyes to slide across the lane to where Diane Hewitt played with half a dozen others.

'Don't even think about it,' said Ida.

He hadn't been thinking about anything.

'You're crackers.' Her tone was even, conversational almost. 'The craziness pushes you on, I know that. But if I had a mad dog, I'd have him put to sleep for the sake of safety. So next time there's a full moon, you'd best keep your eyes peeled, because I might just be at the back of you with a loaded shotgun.'

He bent to retrieve his hat, turned to walk back towards his brother's shop. Then he felt the foot as it pushed its way into his lower back. For a brief moment, he looked over his shoulder, saw Ida Hewitt standing outside her green gate, triumph burning in her face, then he slid several yards down Blackberry Lane's mercifully gentle slope.

The children, imagining that this queer-looking man was making a slide, dashed across and helped him on his way, every last one of them whooping and yelling, pleased that an adult had joined in their Christmas games.

Ida did not stay to watch. Diane and Joe, too, walked into the house, mouths and eyes round with disbelief. 'Gran,' ventured Diane.

'What, love? Hey, Joe – fill that kettle, I'm clemmed.'

'You kicked him, Gran.' Diane's voice was small and high.

'Ooh, I did, didn't I?'

'You did, Gran. And his hat was off and his hair was long enough for plaits.' The child's mouth twitched.

Ida felt a pain in her chest, was forced to open her mouth wide in search of breath. A howl of laughter escaped her lips, and she doubled up in agony. 'I'd ... I'd never noticed how ugly ... no oil painting, like, but ... ooh, it hurts.'

Diane threw herself on to the sofa, lay on her back, limbs paddling in the air like the legs of an over-excited puppy. At first, she was laughing because Guardian Wilkinson had met his match in Gran, then she was laughing at Gran laughing.

Joe came in and looked at the pair of them. 'I've put the kettle on,' he said. For a reason he could not fathom, this

197

simple statement resulted in near-hysteria. Diane sounded as if she might be ready to vomit, while Gran, tears coursing down her face, folded herself up in a rocker near the fire.

Joe smiled tentatively, transfixed by the scene. His family was happy at last. Gran was doing a little job, he and Diane were helping at the yard after school, bits of sweeping and polishing. They had a lovely house, nice neighbours and a real Christmas dinner to look forward to. He felt a smile breaking out. If Gran and their Diane wanted to carry on like a couple of daft things, let them. It was Christmas.

He went upstairs to one of the three cubby-hole bedrooms, put on new shirt, jacket and trousers, spat on a hand, smoothed down his hair. In a pitted mirror, he gazed at his reflection. The upper half seemed normal. If it hadn't been for his legs, he'd have looked quite a toff. Never mind. In a few years, he'd be in long trousers; in a few years, he would be a real toff.

Laughter floated up the stairwell, children played outside. He saw a snowflake floating earthward. In Joe Hewitt's book, all was well with the world.

Mona could not bring herself to venture up the stairs.

The chicken sat in the centre of the table, all golden and moist. She knew it was cooked properly, because she'd shoved a number twelve knitting needle in just above a leg, and the released juices had been clear. Sausages wrapped in bacon overcoats lay around the bird, punctuated by clusters of sprouts and carrots. Mona believed in presentation. A colour-ful dinner always looked more appetizing.

Tilly's sage and onion patties had been placed next to the gravy boat at Tilly's side of the table – she was a beggar for gravy and stuffing, was their Tilly. The pudding was all right, just about. There was brandy sauce to go with it, then some nice mints bought from the market hall last Friday.

Mona took a sip of sweet sherry, gazed into the cheerful fire. The Walsh family had always had a good do at Christmas, especially during Mother's lifetime. She'd been a bit grim and grizzled, and very chapel, but she'd always laid on a decent spread. Turkish Delight. Eeh, what had made Mona think of that? Dad had made quite a ritual of bringing out the circular box of thin, splintery wood, taking care not to rupture the frail timber while removing the lid.

Everybody except Dad had hated Turkish Delight. It was rubbery pink stuff, perfumed, covered with icing sugar. But no one would have dreamed of telling him that they didn't relish the horrible, glutinous stuff. Even Tilly hadn't liked it, and she enjoyed nearly everything that was edible.

She still couldn't go up the stairs.

They'd had a melodeon in those days, a squeezebox that had been left to Mother in the will of some long-dead aunt of hers. Carols after supper had been the nearest the Walsh family had got to entertainment. With parents who were dyed-in-the-wool Methodists, Tilly and Mona had enjoyed a regulated childhood.

She had to be dead. No way would their Tilly have stayed upstairs till half past two on Christmas Day. 'Whatever shall I do?' For a suddenly independent woman, Mona was seriously devoid of ideas. She went through a list of acquaintances, crossing off each one as unsuitable. What a blinkered life she had led.

Really, she should fetch the doctor. But what if Tilly was just in a deep sleep? What if she was seriously ill? No. Tilly was a noisy sleeper, and the house was silent. The doctor, then. No. It was Christmas. Mona didn't want to cause a song and dance for nothing. She could feel the hysteria rising in her throat, knew she was getting into what Tilly called a state and a half.

Then a thought struck. She rummaged in the sewing-basket and came up with a small card, white with black print. 'Seth Dobson, Undertaker, 24 hours a day, 365 days a year.' Seth would know the difference between dead, ill, or just asleep. As well as the yard address, Mr Dobson's home was listed with a telephone number. Mona had never used a telephone, wouldn't know where to start. So she lit the mantles, just to make the house a bit more welcoming for the undertaker, pulled on her outer garments and made for the door.

As she stood in the street, she noticed the sounds of Christmas floating out of other houses. She and Tilly had never bothered much with neighbours, and Mona regretted that for the first time in her life. An understanding friend would have been a bonus today.

She dragged her way up Deane Road, was grateful that she had shed some weight. Half an hour later, she stood just inside the gates of Seth Dobson's detached but modest home. All the lights were on. She could see the family sitting in the parlour, noticed that Seth Dobson managed to look sad even when he laughed.

She pulled the bell and waited.

Seth opened the door. 'Mona?'

She gulped down a draught of oxygen. 'I made the dinner.'

Immediately, Seth Dobson realized that there was something very wrong with the younger Miss Walsh. Used to people in grief and shock, he played along with her. 'Did you, love? Well, that's nice. Just step inside and tell me all about it.' He guided her into the hallway, placed her in a chair, closed the door. 'Now, then,' he began. 'Start at the beginning.'

'Has it gone three, Mr Dobson?'

'It has,' he replied. 'It's going on quarter past, I shouldn't wonder.'

'See, she's still in bed. I even made her sage and onion patties, 'cos she doesn't like scraping stuffing out of a bird. And gravy, I made that. But she never came down, Mr Dobson.'

'Seth. You can call me Seth, Mona. We've worked next door to one another for a fair few years, eh?'

Mona removed her gloves and placed them on a table. 'I think she must be dead.'

'Your Tilly?'

She nodded mutely.

'Have you ... felt for a pulse, tried a mirror near her mouth?'

This time, Mona shook her head. 'I've not been upstairs. I tried, but I got stuck after about three steps, couldn't go no further. Like I was frozen. Like me feet weren't listening to me head any more.'

'You should get the doctor,' he suggested. 'You're not the only one feared of going in a room with the deceased. I come across this all the while. The doctor's your man, love. I don't come into it until the certificate's signed.'

'I'm sorry,' she moaned. 'She might not be dead. I think she

200

is, though. I couldn't work out what to do for the best. I know it's Christmas and I shouldn't be disturbing a doctor or you—'

'You can forget that before the kick-off, Mona Walsh. I've been called out twice today already. Death doesn't stop for Christmas, and Christmas mustn't stop for death. We do what we can, all of us.'

She closed her eyes. 'Will you look at her for me? See, you'll know whether . . .'

'Course I will, you know I will.' He called over his shoulder. 'Janet? Fetch a sherry for this lady, will you? I'm getting me coat and hat on.'

'I'm sorry, I didn't mean to be a trouble to you.'

He placed a hand on her arm. 'Mona, you're no bother at all. My job is to look after folk when they're at their lowest ebb – some of them dead, many grieving. Let me go now and get my boots – it's cold out yon.'

Janet Dobson brought Mona a sherry. 'Here you are. Put yourself outside of that, it'll take the chill off.'

'I'm sorry,' repeated Mona.

Mrs Dobson tutted. 'Look, in a business like ours, we have to be prepared at all times. This isn't a job, it's more what you might call a vocation. We none of us mind, I promise you. My Seth'll look after everything. Would you like me to come and all? I don't mind, you know, I've done it in the past.'

Mona felt a huge sob bubbling in her throat. She wasn't used to kindness. There was a bit of banter at work sometimes, the odd joke, some gossip. But in the normal run of her domestic life, all Mona got was caustic comments and criticism from their Tilly. To hide her hysteria, she gulped at the sherry, accidentally allowing some into her air passage. The resulting coughing and choking filled the time until Seth came back with his cart.

'You're sure you don't want me?' asked Janet Dobson.

'We'll manage.' Seth kissed his wife on the forehead. 'You play with the grandkids,' he advised. 'I'll be back in two shakes.'

The sherry made Mona dizzy as they walked down Deane Road, so she concentrated on listening to her companion's attempts at conversation.

201

'. . . and we're going motorized,' Seth Dobson was saying. 'I'll keep the horses, because some folk prefer them, and I can't afford more than one motor hearse. I never thought I'd see the day, but I've thrown my cap in with the rest. Price of progress, eh?' He was talking to himself, but this was all a part of the balm he applied to wounds of the recently bereaved. Even so, he could not help worrying about Mona Walsh. Tilly was the driving force. Although Mona had made a great noise about leaving home, Seth had entertained reservations on the subject. In fact, he had been running a book, taking bets on whether or not Mona would move out when the big day finally arrived.

At last, they reached the house. 'Do you want to stop out here?' he asked. 'Fetch one of the neighbours to be with you?'

'No. I'll wait in the kitchen,' she answered. She allowed him to help her into the house. When the front door was closed, Mona heard, felt and almost tasted the silence. Even a full brass band could not have swallowed up this deafening noiselessness.

She heard Seth ascending the stairs, tried not to listen. The dinner was cold; a thick skin had formed on the gravy, and all the vegetables looked sad and neglected. A little Christmas tree drooped on the dresser, its arms weighted down by small, silver-wrapped chocolates. All movement above had ceased. He was looking at Tilly now.

Mona's eyes settled on two parcels, one from Mona to Tilly, the other from Tilly to Mona. Tilly should have been opening hers now; she always got her present before supper, then Mona would open her gift from Tilly after supper had been cleared. It was tradition. 'I got you a beautiful blouse,' said Mona. 'Lovely blue, it is, with pearl buttons and a high neck.' He was coming down the stairs.

Somewhere, there was a nice little cameo of Mother's. Dad had bought it as a birthday present years and years ago. It would look lovely at the throat of Tilly's Christmas blouse.

'Mona?' He placed a hand on her shoulder.

'Open my present for me, Seth.'

'Eh?'

'My present from Tilly – it's there, wrapped in green tissue.' The bemused undertaker did her bidding. It was a heavy linen tablecloth. He read from the enclosed card. ' "To my sister, Mona, for the new home." '

'She didn't want me to go,' said Mona quietly. 'Right against it, she was. But she bought me that cloth to show there was no ill-feeling. Oh, Seth, I killed her. I killed my sister as if I'd stuck a knife in her heart.' Mona grabbed the man's hands and sobbed. 'God forgive me, oh, God forgive me.'

Seth Dobson, who, since the arrival of adulthood, had handled more funerals than he'd eaten hot dinners, felt a pricking behind his eyelids. There was something really pathetic about this woman, as if she'd missed out on life altogether. Tilly, the brains, the pilot, lay as dead as a dodo upstairs.

'I shouldn't have got that house,' cried Mona. 'She thought I needed her, but it was the other road round. She needed me, Seth. She was frightened of being on her own.' The sobbing settled, turned into shuddering breaths. 'See, I'm the nervy one, she's the rock. But Tilly keeps it all inside.' Mona blinked away a few more tears. 'She is . . . dead, isn't she?'

He inclined his head. 'Aye, she's gone, love.'

'Did she suffer?'

'I'm no doctor, but I'd say she went in her sleep, never felt a thing. She looks really peaceful.'

'Right.' Another deep breath shook its way out of her lungs.

Seth tightened his grip on her fingers. 'Now, it's up to you, but I've had a lot of experience, as you know. I always advise folk to say goodbye properly – face to face. You don't have to do it now. You could visit her in my little chapel if you'd prefer, but it's important to do it if you can.' He pulled away and picked up his hat. 'I'll fetch the doctor now. Shall I get a neighbour?' he asked again.

'No. And thank you. I don't know what I'd have done without you, Seth.' She listened as his footfalls died in the lobby.

After making herself a cup of tea, Mona sat by the fire and drank deeply, enjoying the taste of sugar after many weeks of self-denial. She realized with a sudden jolt that she was hungry, almost starving. There was plenty of chicken and bread – she could make herself a sandwich later on.

Placing cup and saucer on the mantel, she smoothed her

hair, checked in the mirror. For such a momentous occasion, she wanted to look her best.

Slowly, Mona Walsh climbed the stairs and entered the front bedroom. She sat in the wicker chair next to her sister's bed, laid the new blouse on a bedside table. 'I'll find your best grey skirt, the one with the pleats. I hope you don't mind if I don't put Mother's cameo on your new blouse, Tilly, only I think it should stay up top, not six feet under.' A thought struck. 'Oh, you won't be getting buried, will you? It'll be that brand new crematorium for you with a bit of your Light fed into the furnace. It's not my religion any more, Till. I've been watching Mr Wilkinson for Mr Mulligan.' She sighed deeply. 'Looks like Wilkinson's a bad lot. Looks like the Light's a load of cow pats and all.'

She stroked Tilly's hair, pushed a few strands off the cold face. 'If I've killed you, I didn't mean to. I only wanted a bit of a change, love.' She still wanted a change. The prospect of working in the laundry until she retired was not an attractive one. 'I think I might still move,' she told the body. 'Don't believe that I didn't love you, because I did.' They'd got on each other's nerves, that was all. It was what happened when folk lived and worked together all the while – only to be expected.

Mona stayed next to Tilly's bed until Seth returned with the doctor. The undertaker followed her downstairs, sat her in a rocker, made her a fresh pot of tea. 'Now, look,' he began, 'you don't want to be stuck here on your own, do you? I'll be moving your Tilly as soon as the doctor gives me a certificate.'

Mona had nowhere to go.

'I've taken a liberty,' he continued. 'While I was at the doctor's, I telephoned the post office up at Pendleton. The sub-postmaster took a message, promised to pass it on.'

'Oh.' She remained mystified.

'He'll look after you.'

'I don't know anybody as works for the post office.'

Seth frowned, making his eyes look all the more out of alignment. Then the light dawned. 'Nay, I don't mean him. Though he will be telling his brother, because the funeral'll be at the temple. The sub-postmaster's Peter Wilkinson's brother. No, I mean Mr Mulligan. The message was for him.'

'Oh.' She was well past caring. Her sister was dead, she was starving hungry and she would go where she was put.

'I know he has a soft spot for you, Mona. Now, nobody's forcing you to go, but it might take your mind off things if you do.' Just keep away from the cellar, his mind's voice said.

'I want her to wear her new blouse. She's a nice grey skirt, too.'

'All right, love. We'll just sit here and wait for me to fetch the carriage. I shall take you up to Mr Mulligan.'

Mona sat and waited. She was numb, alone in the world and hungry. This had been the worst Christmas in her whole life.

FIFTEEN

'Look, will you listen to what I'm saying? I never knew a man who wasn't pig-headed, but you, James Mulligan, are the whole hog.' Kate Kenny cast an eye over the assembly. 'There is no dinner,' she advised them. 'I told him twenty-five minutes per pound for the goose, plus a further twenty minutes for good measure and crisping up of the skin.'

The disappointed diners tried not to laugh.

'It's raw, man,' cried Kate.

The dour, miserable, accidental master of Pendleton Grange adjusted his hat. The starch was wearing off, so the chef's headgear was beginning to droop sideways at the top. He opened his mouth to speak in his own defence, found no words to frame reasons or excuses, closed his mouth again.

'Saints preserve me this day and for many more to come,' muttered Kate. 'Go and sit down, will you?' She pushed James towards the kitchen table where he sat, head in hands, pretending to weep. 'Do they ever listen?' Kate asked Amy, though she clearly sought no response, as she took a breath and continued, 'I might just as well try talking politics to the fire-back.' She waved a dish-towel in the direction of the range. Unabated and unforgiving, she carried on. 'He would insist on entertaining in the kitchen, of course. We could have used the dining room and saved some of his blushes but, oh, no. The kitchen was nicer, more homely, he said.'

206

James raised his head and removed the silly hat, casting a mournful glance in the direction of Eliza. 'Do you know the funeral march?' he asked.

'Yes,' she replied.

'Well, wait until I fetch my shroud and a couple of candles, for I shall not survive the day.'

Kate Kenny bustled around the room, produced coffee, cheese and biscuits. 'You'll not mark the cloth,' she warned the gathering. 'It is the very best Irish linen embroidered by the hand of my own sainted mother.' She blessed herself quickly. 'Your Christmas dinner is now postponed until this evening. You've himself to thank for that, but. He'll make the dinner? Huh.'

James stood up. 'Come along now,' he said, to everyone except his housekeeper. 'We shall leave the martyr to her own devices while Eliza plays and we sing.'

Sally Hayes made a move towards Kate, who whooshed her away. 'Isn't this your holiday, too? Don't mind me, because I intend to take tomorrow off. I might take tomorrow off for three weeks, so. Carry the cheese with you, child. And some milk for the little ones.' She muttered on about English ways, about heathens who took their dinners late in the day, about stupid men who thought they could rule the world, about geese having far too much fat in them altogether. 'And no crumbs on the rugs,' was her parting shot just as the kitchen door closed.

In the music room, Eliza draped herself on the piano stool, legs correctly to one side, ankles together, skirt flowing grace-fully, hands folded in her lap. Margot, who hoped that the goose would never be ready, made herself small in the corner, while Amy searched through sheet music.

Ida had never seen such a grand room except in magazines. 'Ceiling's very high,' she announced. 'Must take some keeping warm, a place like this.'

Diane and little Joe, who had been warned by their grand-mother to be 'a mile better than good', pretended to read their books. In truth, they were so overawed by the grandeur of the place and the number of adults it contained, they would have behaved well without Ida's intervention.

James Mulligan stood with his back to the fire and surveyed the scene. Margot Burton-Massey looked about as cheerful as seven wet Sundays. Eliza, breathtakingly beautiful as ever, was clearly detached from the situation, while their older sister was making a valiant effort. Yes, Amy was a grand soul altogether. There she was now, kneeling next to little Joe and teaching him the words in his Brer Rabbit book.

Sally sat with Diane; despite the disparity in their ages, at a stage when eleven and fourteen were miles apart, they seemed to be forming a friendship. Eliza the Cool had no further use for Sally Hayes, it seemed.

'Bread and cheese all round, then.' James made and distributed sandwiches, noticed that Margot refused. 'Are you all right?' he asked.

'Yes, thank you.'

She wasn't; he knew full well that she wasn't. Surely she couldn't be . . . ?

'I shall eat later,' said Margot, wishing that he would not stare so. He was changing, she decided. He was opening up, noticing, deducing. And in spite of everything, the man still made her heart lurch a bit. 'I don't want to spoil my dinner,' she offered by way of explanation.

James turned away. Margot had dark smudges under her lovely eyes. She was sitting with her arms crossed over her abdomen; she had refused food. God, he was gossiping with himself, as if he had a couple of fishwives trapped in his head. But, oh, she was so pale and . . . and damaged. Rupert Smythe?

Eliza watched the man's movements, found herself assessing him. If only she could run away to London with someone like James Mulligan; but the Mulligans of this world did not run away with young women. Idly, she played with the concept of conquering him just as a mountaineer might tackle Everest, but there would not be time. In a matter of days, Eliza would be two hundred miles away.

Amy settled the children, then helped James to pour coffee and milk for distribution. 'So, you'd be no good as a ship's cook, then?'

'Ah, don't you start on me now. Sure, I wasn't to know the weight of the bird.' He spooned four sugars into his own cup.

'That'll be like treacle,' she told him.

'After two rounds with Kate, I need the glucose.' He took a sip, grimaced. 'We've another guest to come shortly. It seems that the Smythes have gone visiting, but Camilla wanted none of that. I think she's had a bit of a contretemps with her brother. I expect her shortly.'

'I'm glad,' said Amy. 'She's a good sort, worth a dozen of Rupert. I wonder what they quarrelled about?'

James allowed his eyes to travel to Margot's corner. She was fast asleep, her arms still protecting her abdomen.

'That's all over,' Amy told James. 'She hasn't seen Rupert for weeks.'

But was it over? he wondered. Here was Margot Burton-Massey on Christmas Day, in her old house, in relatively new company, sleeping like a . . . like a baby. Exhaustion and tension were etched deeply into features far too young to be so drawn. 'Amy?'

'Yes?'

'Has Margot been ill?'

Amy looked at her sister and frowned. 'She's been quiet, I suppose. And she spends a lot of time walking. The main problem is food – we can't seem to find anything that interests her.'

It was the festive season, he reminded himself. If he wanted to start airing any sobering thoughts, he would do best by saving them for another few days. 'Well, it's been a hard year for all three of you. Perhaps Margot still hasn't recovered from the shock. However, I'm glad to see that you are getting a little better.'

She remembered the scene in his office, felt embarrassment staining her cheeks. 'I sometimes wonder what normal is.' She noticed that he was staring now at Eliza. Most men fell for Eliza, she thought, with a slight trace of envy.

'Eliza, too, is withdrawn,' he commented.

'Yes.'

'Have you any idea why?'

'Ah, who knows anything where Eliza is concerned? I often feel that she isn't truly with us. She lives in a dream world, James.' Amy raised her voice. 'Coffee is poured. Come along, everyone.'

James carried his cup to the window while everyone bustled about behind him. Everyone except Margot, that was. In spite of noise and movement, she remained asleep, her head sliding down on to the wing of her chair. There was something very wrong with that young woman.

So, here he was, master of nothing he surveyed, playing once again the part of comforter to distressed and displaced females. First his own mother, then Kate after those two awful deaths. Louisa Burton-Massey had opened her heart, Ida Hewitt had needed help. He'd housed Sally, the young orphan, Diane and her little brother. And, as well as all the above, he was concerned about the Burton-Massey girls. Concerned? And, to top all that, Stephen Wilkinson had brought a message about Mona needing help, about Tilly dying. Perhaps Mona would arrive, another soul seeking comfort. James had told no one the bad news – let them have their Christmas.

He turned so quickly that a pain shot through his neck. The woman he loved was in this room. Remember your father, the voice of conscience said. Remember your own temper; above all, remember the cellar.

Diane knew that this was the happiest day of her whole life. She had a brand new friend called Sally Hayes. Sally was an orphan, and she had promised to visit Bramble Cottage on her days off. There was another young maid called Mary, but she had gone home for Christmas, and Sally had said that was a good riddance, too, so there would be some interesting stories there, no doubt.

Mr Mulligan had crawled about on all fours with Joe on his back. Diane remembered the first time she had met the big man, that day when she had planned the wash-house job. Oh, he'd been so grand with his cane and his good clothes. Fleas, they'd talked about. Funny way of getting to know somebody, talking about nits and bugs. So correct, he had seemed, advising her to go home and get clean. Yet he had really let his hair down today.

Diane didn't like Eliza. She was proud and spoilt and she played the piano as if she didn't really mean it, a bit half-hearted. Margot seemed all right as a person, only she wasn't

210

very well, didn't fancy food, but she was probably good fun on her better days. Amy was great. She'd organized Musical Chairs, Pin a Tail on the Donkey, Pass the Parcel, then a cut-throat game of cards called Newmarket. They had played for matches, because the Burton-Massey family didn't approve of gambling for money.

An interesting woman called Camilla had arrived. She had the reddest hair and the friendliest smile Diane had ever seen. Camilla was what Amy called a 'hoot'. Camilla was the one who had introduced Diane to Charades. Camilla was absolutely wonderful.

The best thing about today, though, had been hearing Gran laugh, watching her joining in and having a fine time. She'd even done a solo, a song about the boy she loved up in a gallery, or something. The voice had been a bit thin and weedy, but Gran could hold a tune. Oh, everything was lovely, and here Diane sat now, surrounded by good people, her stomach full of excellent food, Joe next to her all bright-eyed and joy-ful. 'I'm full,' she announced, during a lull in conversation. 'I'm full of food and I'm full of being happy.' Strangely, her eyes pricked, as if she was getting ready to burst out crying.

James gazed around the table and wondered how he would ever be able to go home again. He liked these people, loved them, even. One in particular . . . And the child had said it all. She was full of being happy. 'Is this a good Christmas, then, Diane?'

All eyes were on her as she searched for the word and tried to pronounce it well. 'Hexceptional, Mr Mulligan,' she pro-nounced.

No one laughed.

'That's right,' he said, after blinking away a bit of moisture. 'This is, indeed, hexceptional.'

I was put on this earth for a reason, and I thank my Maker for every breath I take. My God-given task is to lead people into the Light, to guide them in wholesomeness towards the thin mem-brane between life and death. Therefore, I must procreate, pass on these gifts to my children. My penance has arrived in this difficult form because I am to be made Supreme Guardian. I charge myself now, therefore, with the burden of fulfilling my function as a man, as a husband, as a father.

The girl was not suitable. Because of my future role, I must choose my partner from more elevated pastures. Nothing must stop me. Once impregnated with a Son or Daughter of the Light, the partner of my life, receiver of the holy fruit of my body, will have the knowledge inside her, will bow to the will of the Light.

Doris has cooked the dinner for this feast day. In my brother's house, I have broken bread and taken meat. Stephen is not blessed in the Light but, as a brother of mine, he will be forgiven. Doris praises in the temple, so she is already placed at the right hand of God. Today, I take my rest. Soon, soon I shall find the bride of my future, she who will sit at my right hand. Mulligan, the evil one, will be overcome.

Praise the Lord.

Seth Dobson's horses came to a halt outside Pendleton Grange. The undertaker squeezed Mona's hand before stepping down to ring the front-door bell. She had spoken scarcely a word for the last five miles, simply sitting next to him and staring straight ahead. Would Mulligan thank Seth for bringing this problem to him? But who else was there? Mona minus Tilly? The answer was zero.

The door opened. 'Can I help you?' asked Kate Kenny.

'I'm looking for Mr Mulligan.' He hesitated when he noticed the stern look on the woman's face. 'I know it's Christmas, and I'm so sorry – but would you do me a big favour, missus? By the way, I'm Seth Dobson. I work down in the yard.'

Kate nodded. 'And the favour?'

He jerked a thumb over his shoulder. 'Her name's Mona Walsh. Her sister died today, and she's got nobody in the world. If I could just go in and talk to Mr Mulligan, could you keep an eye on her? Only she's been a bit funny today. First she's with us, then not with us, if you get my meaning.'

Kate got his meaning. 'Wait there, now.' She darted off to fetch a shawl, then to get her nephew.

When Kate had left the house to go to Mona, Seth entered and saw Mr Mulligan approaching him. By, this was a grand

212

place, black-and-white tiled floor, big fireplace, furniture every-where – and he'd only got as far as the hallway. 'Mr Mulligan,' he began, 'I didn't know where else to take her.'

'I see. Do go on, Mr Dobson.'

Without waiting for an invitation, Seth sat down. He was hungry and cold to the bone. 'Tilly Walsh died,' he began, 'and Mona went into shock, I'd say. Even though she knew her sister had gone, like, she wouldn't go up to check, and she made a full Christmas dinner, all the trimmings. Anyroad, long story short, Mona came to my house. I took her home and made sure Tilly was deceased, then I fetched the doctor. I couldn't leave Mona there, Mr Mulligan. And my own house is full with the grandchildren, our daughter and her husband.'

'So you brought her here. Yes, Stephen Wilkinson told me some of the story.'

'Sorry, sir.'

'Ah, no, I'm not taking offence. I think you've done the right thing altogether. Kate – that's my housekeeper – will see she arrives at no harm. That's a desperate thing to happen at Christmas, is it not? Look, go through to the kitchen,' he pointed to a door, 'and get yourself a cup of tea and a bite. I'll fetch Mona in.'

Mona allowed herself to be led into the study. James placed her in a leather armchair, poured her a small brandy. 'Come on, now, Mona,' he coaxed. 'That's good stuff, emergencies only.'

Coming from a strict Methodist background, Mona remained unacquainted with hard liquor so the Cognac hit her hard. When she stopped coughing, she wiped her eyes and looked at him. 'I've left the dinner on the table.'

'Have you? Well, given the circumstances, I'm sure that's understandable. Will you take another drink?'

'No. No, I don't think I will, thank you all the same.'

He folded his arms, leaned back in his seat. So, here came the next needful woman, and he could find no resentment for this added encumbrance. He could sense her emptiness, her isolation. It was as if she scarcely existed at all, except that her body took up space on the earth. Even that was shrinking. Was she planning on disappearing altogether? Was she capable of planning anything?

'I think I killed her, Mr Mulligan.'

'What?'

'I didn't stab her or shoot her, but she went downhill after I got that house on John Street.'

'Ah, come on, now—'

'I apologized to her, but she was already dead, and she'd bought me a beautiful tablecloth and all. I got her a blouse to go with her grey skirt.'

'Mona, you've killed nobody. You're in shock and . . . when did you last eat?'

She raised a shoulder. 'It's still on the table, waiting for Tilly to come downstairs. She'll not come down ever again, will she, except for her funeral?'

'No, she won't.' It was plain that although Mona remained rational, she was not coping emotionally with the day's events. 'Will you sleep here tonight?' he asked.

'I don't mind.'

She didn't care. She had probably spent just a few nights away from home, as most working-class families tended to stay close to the soil in which they'd been planted. Even folk like Tilly and Mona, who earned decent wages, were not inclined to go off on seaside holidays. What to do with her, then? And for how long?

'Mr Mulligan?'

'Yes?'

'The funeral should be at the temple. And I don't want it to be. I don't want my sister being prayed over by a bad man.'

He knew exactly how she felt, yet he could not come up with an answer for this dilemma. The important thing was to get some food into Mona, then to encourage her to rest. 'We'll think about all that tomorrow. Now, I'll get Kate to make up a bed for you in one of the many spare rooms. Food, too.'

'I'm hungry,' she admitted.

Well, that was a good sign.

The door opened. 'Mr Mulligan?' Seth Dobson's miserable yet funny face insinuated itself into the room. 'I'll have to be off. There's . . . you know . . .' He nodded in Mona's direction. 'The body to be moved.' The last five words were mouthed noiselessly. He addressed Mona now. 'Don't distress yourself

214

about your house, love. My Janet'll shift all the food and stuff, clean round for you.'

'Thank you,' said Mona.

'All part of the service, Mona. I don't want you worrying about anything. It's a very distressing time, is this. People get distressed. So don't distress yourself any more than needs be.'

James waited for forms of the word 'distress' to continue, but the undertaker had clearly said his piece for now. 'Will you see yourself out, Mr Dobson?'

'Aye, no bother. I hope you'll be all right, Mona.' He disappeared.

Kate brought tea and sandwiches, said that she had prepared a bed with three hot-water bottles and a shelf out of the oven. Mona ate mechanically, as if aware that she needed fuel, though she seemed not to enjoy the procedure. She drained her cup and looked James full in the face. 'I want some help,' she stated very positively.

'I know you do, but first—'

'Not the funeral arrangements, nothing like that.' She heaved a great sigh. 'I know you'll think I'm awful, talking like this when my only sister, who I helped to kill, isn't even cold. But, ooh, I want rid of that place.'

'Your house?'

She put her head on one side, as if working her way through a puzzle. 'No, the wash-house. I don't care if I never see another posser or a boiler as long as I live. There's an endowment nearly ready, then our Tilly's insurance is a fair amount. I need somebody to sell the goodwill, or to rip out all the stuff and sell that for me. I shan't set foot in there again.' A slight quiver in the voice was the only sign that Mona Walsh was not in a business meeting.

He was amazed. Obviously, Mona Walsh was distraught, though her mind seemed to have cleared itself to the point where she was already planning for the future. Yet, only minutes earlier, he had doubted her ability to plan for the next hour.

She gave him a watery smile. 'I'm getting on, you know. I shan't see fifty again. From when we were still at school, our Tilly and me were soaked in soapy water, up to our necks in it. I doubt we were long out of our prams when we learned to fold sheets, mix Dolly Blue and starch.' She stopped for a while, her lips moving as she framed thoughts. 'Tilly dying means ... well ... it means what I were thinking before can happen now. I've never been me before. I've always been our Tilly's sister or one of the fat women from the wash-house.'

'I see.' He didn't, but everyone reacted differently to death.

'Will you help me, Mr Mulligan?'

'You know I will.'

Mona rose to her feet. 'All right, then. I'll go to bed now.'

He followed her from the room, found Kate in the hallway. 'Take her up,' he said, before returning to his study.

James Mulligan poured himself a small brandy. Soon, he would have to take Ida and the children home. Still, he had learned something today. Women were intricate people. Where they were concerned, he had better expect the unexpected.

SIXTEEN

Camilla Smythe had not seen Margot for some time; because of that, changes in the girl were immediately apparent to her. Deeply uneasy, Camilla refused the offer of a bed and set off for home at about ten o'clock. The party had begun to break up anyway, as the two children and their grandmother needed to go home, and a bereaved Mona had arrived to put something of a dampener on the proceedings.

As she drove her new little van towards Blackburn, Camilla could not rid herself of mental pictures of the tortured Margot Burton-Massey. Rupert was a cad. Planning to run away with Eliza, he was leaving her sister heartbroken, a shadow of her former self. Camilla's fury, which was very much in line with the colour of her hair, simmered all the way home. She could scarcely wait to sink her claws into him. 'Damn and blast the man,' she cursed, as she parked her motor in one of the disused stables. 'One day, some poor woman will swing for him, stupid, uncaring rascal that he is.'

On entering the house, she offered polite responses to her parents' trite questions – had she enjoyed herself, how was Mr Mulligan, had the country roads been icy and so forth. As soon as possible, she made her way upstairs. This time, she did not knock, simply burst into Rupert's room without preamble.

He was seated by the window, a cigarette in one hand,

brandy globe in the other. 'Ah, Camel,' he drawled. 'Good to see you. Have you enjoyed your day?'

Camilla crossed the room in three strides and hit his face with the flat of her hand. Made strong by dealing with horses and by carrying endless amounts of food from van to table, she almost knocked her brother through the window.

He righted himself and touched a sore cheek. 'Steady on,' he mumbled. 'No need for that sort of behaviour, old girl.'

Anger made her breath short, so she inhaled several times before speaking. 'You are a rat, a thing from the sewers.'

'Really?'

'Absolutely.' She ran the tingling hand through her hair. 'Have you any idea of the state Margot is in? Here you sit, idly flicking ash all over the rug, not a care in the world. That Eliza creature is hanging round like a cat with a secret supply of cream, when all the while Margot is suffering.'

Rupert allowed his tongue to search for loose teeth. This sister of his packed a stroke that might have found a place in the repertoire of a heavyweight boxer. 'And what, precisely, do you expect me to do about that?'

She glowered at him. 'A gentleman would not need to ask such a question. I think I shall have to tell Mother about your intentions regarding London and Eliza. As much as I should like you both to disappear, you cannot be allowed to get away with this.'

'With what? For God's sake, what have I done that is so terrible? Margot was a mistake—'

'Eliza is the mistake in that family. Oh, I know Margot has her faults, but Eliza is secretive, selfish, manipulative. She shapes herself to suit her circumstances.' Camilla paused. 'In fact, I am quite convinced that she will bring you down.'

'Then let her,' he answered. 'Let her. You stay here, a virgin saint, watch from a safe distance while I crumble. Given your opinion of me and Eliza, perhaps you should just allow us to go to the dogs together.'

She took a pace back in order to watch him. 'Is Margot a virgin?' she asked, taking note of a brief flash of panic as it crossed his face. The ensuing pause stretched to fill two or three seconds. 'That is all the reply I need, Rupert Smythe—'

'Come on, Camel—'

'And don't call me that!'

'But don't you admire those beasts? Haven't you always praised their staying power?'

'Do not attempt to change the subject. Have you had intimate relations with Margot Burton-Massey? Well? Have you?'

He took a sip from the glass, stubbed out his cigarette, turned his face towards the window. 'That is none of your business,' he replied eventually.

'Then you have. Right. I may sleep on this, brother, but do not be in the least surprised if Mother grills you tomorrow.' She shook her head sadly. 'The poor girl. Margot looks terrible. She slept half the time, had trouble keeping up with the rest of us when she was awake.' Camilla stood perfectly still for a while. Oh, God. 'Good grief!' She slapped a hand to her forehead. 'How stupid I am.'

'Don't expect me to agree with you,' Rupert grumbled. 'I don't want another slap.'

'I should not be at all surprised if Margot turns out to be pregnant,' said Camilla.

His shoulders sagged. 'Nonsense. Even if she is, it isn't anything to do with . . . no,' he finished lamely.

Camilla dropped into a chair. 'Margot may be silly, but she is by no means loose in her habits. You have taken her virginity and, unless I am greatly mistaken, you have left her pregnant.'

Rupert was beginning to feel rather hot under the collar. If Camilla went to Mother with these trumped-up charges, London might become an impossibility. As for Eliza, well, he would have no chance. 'What do you intend to do?' he asked.

'I don't know. I haven't had time to work it out. But you are not getting away with this, Rupert. Believe me, I'll have your scalp if that poor girl is expecting your child.'

'Could be anyone's,' he blustered.

'No,' she shouted. 'If there is a baby, it's yours. And you will stand by Margot or you will answer to me.' She banged a fist against her breast. 'From me, Rupert, there will be nowhere to hide. Ever.'

He was suddenly terrified. Camilla was not the type to issue empty threats. Furiously, he back-pedalled his way through the conversation, from the slap to her threats. 'I'll do a deal with you,' he offered, his voice made unsteady by fear. 'If Margot is pregnant – and there's no proof of that – I shall return from London and . . .'

'And what? Marry her? In which event, will you take her back to London with you? Where will you hide her sister?'

'Let's work that out if and when it happens.'

Camilla pondered. How could she go along to Caldwell Farm and accuse Margot of expecting a child? What was she intending to say to Amy? 'Amy, my brother has impregnated one of your sisters and intends to run away with the other . . .'? After all, there was a chance that Margot might not be . . . Oh, what a mess.

'Are you going to talk to Mater?' he asked.

She gazed at him, wondered how it could be possible to hate her own brother so strongly. Her mind clicked into gear. 'Go to hell your own way and take Eliza with you. But if Margot is having a baby, I shall drag you back from London myself. Do you understand?'

He inclined his head in reluctant agreement.

'I shall be judge and jury, Rupert.' Her tone was frighteningly quiet. 'You've known me for long enough. Tread softly, old fruit.'

She left his room and walked across to her own, her brain a tangle of bewilderment. As ever, her first loyalty was to her friends, those she had chosen over the years. Amy, a good egg, was probably going to suffer no matter what. Eliza, too interested in herself to care about her sisters, would go her own way sooner or later. And God forbid that little Margot should be carrying Rupert's child.

'I can do nothing,' she concluded aloud. 'I can't say anyone is pregnant, not without proof. As for Eliza and my cretinous brother, it will be farewell and thank God. For a while, at least.'

Mona struggled through the next few days, sometimes guilt-ridden and tearful, often deep in thought, occasionally walking

220

all the way to Ida's house, which was over a mile away from Pendleton Grange. Although she did not quite realize it, Mona was in the process of making her first two friends – Kate Kenny and Ida Hewitt.

Then, in response to an invitation, Mona paid her first visit to Caldwell Farm. Moorhead picked her up in the trap, left her at the front door, giving her a chance to study the place before knocking. Mona liked the look of this house. A lot plainer and smaller than the Grange, it looked used and a bit tired. Sturdy, weathered and surrounded by fields, Caldwell Farm was Mona's idea of heaven.

Amy opened the door. 'Good to see you out and about,' she said. 'Here's Elspeth. Elspeth, this is Miss Mona Walsh – I told you about her.'

'Sorry to hear about your loss, Miss Walsh.' Elspeth relieved Mona of her outer garments. 'The coffee's ready,' she said, before bustling off towards the kitchen.

As the two women entered the parlour, its chimney performed one of the belches for which it was fast becoming notorious. 'Just like ours at home,' declared Mona. 'Open the door and you get fumigated.' This broke the ice, and they sat drinking coffee and chatting about general matters for ten full minutes.

'So, how are you feeling now?' asked Amy, once the ground felt steady enough.

Mona considered her reply. 'Less like a murderer. The doctor told Mr Mulligan that our Tilly was a time-bomb just ticking away – she'd already lived a good bit longer than he expected. Mind, if I hadn't gone after Ida's old house . . .'

'A bit of advice,' offered Amy, 'as long as you don't mind taking it from a younger person. Start looking forward. Peering over one's shoulder all the time can never be a good thing.'

'Aye, well, I suppose I'll feel different once the funeral's over.'

Amy agreed. 'You will feel a change, but the mourning takes a bit longer.' She paused. 'The great news is that you are trying to think about your future.'

'I was doing that afore.' Mona placed her cup and saucer on

221

the winged table. 'See, I'm past fifty. Me and our Tilly, we never knew anything apart from the laundry. It was left to us by Mother and Dad, and we worked there all hours – after school, Saturdays, all through summer holidays. There's got to be more than that in life.'

Amy watched while a variety of emotions visited the plain, colourless face. 'I understand that Mr Mulligan has hired two women to run the laundry for the time being.'

'That's right. Now, see, there's a good man if ever there was one. Nice-looking too, but his packaging's wrong because he looks so stern.' Mona sighed, shook her head. 'What he really is doesn't show till you know him better. Now, take me. Inside all this blubber I'm still a young girl, Miss Burton-Massey.'

'Amy.'

'Amy. It's a nice name, is that. Short, but pretty. Where was I up to?'

'You were still young and Mr Mulligan was wrongly wrapped.'

Mona amazed herself by laughing. It wasn't a giggle or a chuckle: a huge belly laugh broke out with no warning. 'Eeh,' she breathed, when the laughter calmed, 'aren't I awful? I should be crying.'

'Not at all. Laughter is a form of medicine. Go back to what you were saying before.' Unless Amy was very much mistaken, this lady's laughter had been held back for too long, possibly for a lifetime.

Mona eyed Amy Burton-Massey, wondered whether this young woman would take her seriously when all had been said. It was probably a daft idea, anyway, but why not hang for the full sheep? 'Are you opening that there Cut Above shop? Made-to-measure fashions, isn't it? I'll still do all the pressing if you want me to.'

Amy nodded. 'Once again, Mr Mulligan has stepped into the breach. He has found a clever designer who will work on Mother's patterns, then on her own ideas. My sister, Eliza, will possibly help, too. Why do you ask?'

Mona ordered herself to take the plunge. 'Right, you just shut me up any time you like, Amy, only I've been thinking. Look at me. Go on, look at me good and proper. Not much

222

to send a letter home about, am I? Just an ordinary plain fat woman in an ordinary plain fat frock.'

Amy looked, said nothing.

'There's thousands of me. Not all fat women are poor, you know. So, I'm setting you a bit of a challenge. I love clothes, always have done. Me and our Tilly have usually made our own, because there's not much off-the-peg in our sizes. The challenge is this – try to make me look good. I don't mean just a suit and blouse. Get a hairdresser in – there's room downstairs at the shop. Make my face up, find me a decent corset and some shoes that don't make my little toes bend in under the rest. Take the ugly and make it . . . well . . . better.' After this long speech, Mona helped herself to a plain biscuit.

Amy sat back. 'You'd never have mentioned this had Tilly been alive. Am I right? Did she hold you back?'

Mona, with a mouthful of crumbs, simply nodded.

The younger woman rose to her feet and paced about the room, finally settling near the window. A hairdressing salon? Makeup? What about manicures, facial treatments, a complete package?

'You think I'm daft, don't you? Our Tilly would have laughed at me. She always did that, ground me down one way or another.' Mona paused for thought. 'Not that I want you feeling sorry for me, you understand. What I mean is, I'm not frightening. Most folk down town know me, I'm not unusual. There's nothing to lose, love. If you can make me look nice, if you can give me a job, I can get ordinary women with a few bob to feel at home in yon shop. You could advertise a specialist service for the lady with a more generous figure. And I suggest you have an economy department, too. There's girls out there who'd save up their pennies for a frock from A Cut Above. You could have them paying so much a week and all – like a savings club. And remember, they don't all want silk and jersey wool.'

Amy returned to her seat. She stared at Mona for several seconds, weighed up pros and cons, took in the grey, unremarkable hair, ran her eyes over skin that had been incarcerated for decades in the damp air of a laundry. Mona was, indeed, a challenge. 'Your hair will have to be done

223

elsewhere,' she said. 'Jumping into hairdressing before we've even sold a single outfit would be rather reckless. But . . .' But Mona had a gentleness of manner, an attitude that might draw out the damped-down egos of plump women.

'But what?'

'But we might just give your brainwave a go, Mona. Yes, you can press clothes, but you can also sell them. Hmm, larger ladies – yes, yes.' This woman had mental energy and imagination; she was also possessed of the experience of running a successful business. Could she be a saleswoman? Probably. 'We'll talk again after the funeral,' Amy promised, 'and—'

The door opened and Camilla strode in. 'Sorry,' she said. 'I sneaked in the back way, got past Elspeth – am I interrupting?'

'Not really,' replied Amy. 'This is Mona – Miss Mona Walsh.'

'Hello.' Camilla shook Mona's hand until it almost threatened to drop off. 'Caught a glimpse of you at Christmas – sorry to hear about your sister.'

'Camilla will be catering for A Cut Above – snacks and so forth for our clients,' Amy told Mona. 'Not every day, of course, but when we have our open days.' She explained to Mona. 'About once a month, we shall entertain our clientele in the parlour – the idea is to discuss trends and designs, allow the customer to have her say.'

'Good show,' cried Camilla. 'So you'll be opening up after all?'

'Of course.' She sent Camilla off to beg more coffee from Elspeth. 'Stay for lunch,' she asked Mona. 'We can talk a little more about your ideas. I'm sure Camilla won't stay all afternoon.'

The three women shared one of Elspeth Moorhead's famous Lancashire hotpots followed by the same county's crumbly cheese with crackers. They chatted about the shop, though Mona's idea remained for the present a secret between Amy and Mona, then Camilla had them all laughing about her family. 'Equality in the workplace?' she squawked, in a fair imitation of Helen Smythe's rather wearing voice. 'She pays our female staff less than half the wages of the men.'

They discussed this topic for half an hour, then Camilla rose

224

to leave. As she climbed into the high seat of her van, she remembered her reason for coming here. A firm believer in fate, she decided that Mona had been present for a reason. 'Let it take its own course,' she said to herself. 'I arrived in several minds, anyway.' And what might she have said? How could she accuse Margot of being pregnant when she might just be off-colour? 'Stay out of it, Smythe,' she ordered herself. 'Margot and Eliza are not your concern.'

While Amy was entertaining, Margot saddled Chloe, reined her tightly and set off through the fields, first building up to a canter, then driving the mare into a gallop. Life had changed so drastically in recent months, first with Mother's death, then with the arrival of this terrible, awesome problem. Normally, Margot would be more than ready for lunch, should now be eating in the kitchen while Amy ate with her friends, but food was no longer a factor in Margot's equation.

Willing her unwanted tenant to vacate the womb, she rode carelessly, brushing against branches at the edge of a field, urging the mare to take jumps that were high and difficult. As she turned into one of the upper pastures, Margot became aware that she was being watched, then pursued.

Within seconds, the man was upon her. He came alongside, took the head of her mount, dragged Chloe to a halt. 'What on earth are you trying to do?' he asked breathlessly.

Margot attempted no reply.

'Apart from anything else, you might have damaged my mare.'

'And that would never do, would it, Mr Mulligan?'

He dismounted, then dragged her out of the saddle. 'I realize that you are an adventurous horsewoman, but I never believed you to be reckless. You know your own limitations, and you know Chloe's.' He ran a hand over the mare's quivering neck. 'I have sold items from your old house, Margot. Valuable paintings have gone under a hammer so that I might use my expertise with horseflesh to enhance the fortunes of Pendleton Grange. The horses are the future of your family. Now, please look at me.'

She could not meet his eyes, could not have cared less about the survival of the Grange.

225

'What is going on, Margot?'

'Nothing.'

He placed a hand under her chin, turned her head until she faced him. 'This is not nothing. This is a piece of sheer lunacy. Chloe does not jump well – you know that better than anyone.'

'Perhaps I forgot.'

She never forgot, not where horses were concerned. Had she not been female, this one might have made a champion jockey. 'Amy is worried about you,' he said.

'Is she? I haven't been aware of that. She's too busy lunching with her friends to bother her head about me.'

'Rubbish,' he snapped, removing his hand from her chin.

As soon as he released his grip, she missed him. Rupert, that callow, selfish youth, was never going to be a man. Mulligan was a real man, the sort who would make a good husband. What chance had she of securing anyone decent while this pregnancy continued?

'Margot, your sisters are under the same roof as you, they are with you constantly, so they don't see what the rest of us see. You look unwell.' He left a pause, whch remained unfilled. 'What is the matter with you these days?' He felt like a father chiding his daughter.

Had she felt able to talk at all, she might have confided in James Mulligan. He was the type of man who kept secrets well; even so, Margot did not know where to begin. Panic bubbled in her throat. Soon, very soon, her problem would show of its own accord.

'If you wish to talk to me, please be reassured that the information will go no further.'

Margot perked up momentarily. 'You would protect me? Just as you protect your cellar? Now, there's a thing. You take yourself off several times a day, or so rumour has it. Into a cellar? When you have nothing to hide, Mr Mulligan, then you will be in a position to question and lecture others.'

'*Touché*,' he replied. 'But I believe that your difficulty may be more pressing than mine.'

He had guessed, then. How many others had reached the same conclusion? she wondered. Eliza and Amy probably judge her to be out of sorts, still grieving, perhaps. But those who saw her just occasionally might be achieving clearer and more accurate pictures. Something had to be done, and quickly. 'I shall ride Chloe back now,' she announced defiantly.

'If you must.' He helped her into the saddle, noticing that her agility was not as it had been. 'I daresay the damage is already done,' he said clearly, 'and I shall follow you.'

Margot gazed down on him. 'Damage?'

'To the horse,' he replied. 'Or . . . well, we shall see.'

She pulled tight on the rein, causing Chloe to veer away quickly. With her eyes misting over, Margot allowed the mare to choose the pace for both of them. It wasn't fair, any of it. The feelings she harboured for James Mulligan remained powerful – perhaps he was the man she loved after all. How was one supposed to separate infatuation from true love? Many women of Margot's age were married – how had they managed to choose, to know, to be absolutely certain? Was it a lottery?

Weary to the marrow, Margot Burton-Massey rubbed down her horse, found a dry blanket and some oats. She patted Chloe's flank. 'Thank you, girl,' she whispered. 'If that hard ride hasn't worked, it's none of your doing.'

Eliza waited at the tram terminus. He was almost twenty minutes late, and she was beginning to wonder whether she needed him at all. She hated being beholden to a man like Rupert Smythe, and she had been working hard to find a way of separating herself from him. Not completely, because even she was frightened by the thought of being lost and alone in the capital. Nevertheless, he needed to learn his place in her scheme of things.

A tram pulled in and disgorged its load. The driver changed ends, all the while glancing at the beautiful woman who stood so still and straight near the wall. 'Are you all right, miss?' he called.

She inclined her head.

Frozen out by the chill in her eyes, the man made no further enquiries, choosing instead to read his newspaper until the time came to clatter his way back into Bolton.

Eliza's measures had consisted of a two-pronged advance. First, she had got hold of Rupert's London address. This had

227

been easy, because the idea was that he would go first, accom-
panied, of course, by his mother, then Eliza would follow some
days later. Second, she had acquired what she considered to be
her share of Mother's jewellery, and had disposed of the same
in Manchester, thereby increasing her savings significantly.

She smiled to herself. She would be living in the same house
as Rupert, but not in the same flat. After corresponding with
the landlady, Eliza would shortly be the tenant of an attic
room with some kitchen facilities and the use of a bathroom
on a shared basis.

He arrived at last, a silly scarf streaming from his throat as
he braved the elements, his car hood pinned back, his face
reddened by an icy wind. 'Jump in,' he called.

The tram driver looked at the pair of young toffs. Off on a
jaunt, he shouldn't wonder, driving through the countryside at
breakneck speeds when gradely folk were doing a day's work.

Rupert was unusually quiet. Eliza wondered about that for
a second or two, then busied herself by tying a scarf over her
hair. She had no intention of being seen out and about while
resembling a badly constructed scarecrow.

'Eliza?'

'Yes?'

'I've decided to go down before the New Year.'

'Why?'

Why? Because his sister, who packed the punch of a prize
fighter, was on his tail. Because Eliza's sister, who was at least
doing him the courtesy of keeping her distance, might be
pregnant with his child. 'Oh, I've had enough of everyone,' he
said airily.

She knew exactly what he meant.

'Just want to see the bright lights as soon as poss,' he
concluded.

Eliza looked into a small mirror to check that her makeup
was surviving the ravages of Rupert's driving. 'I may go myself
later this week,' she said casually.

His gloved hands tightened on the wheel. 'But my mother
will be there. I've promised to take her to a show. Father will
spend the holidays playing golf, while Camilla – well, who
knows or cares what she gets up to? Catering, I expect.'

228

'And your mother must not catch a glimpse of me. Is that the case?'

'Sorry, but yes. She'll be paying our rent and—'

'No, she won't.'

'Of course she will. I could not afford a flat on the salary I've been offered.'

'I'll pay my own rent, Rupert.'

'Eventually, yes, you shall.'

'Oh, no,' she said clearly. 'I've found a room of my own in the same house. Naturally, I shall lie low whenever your mother is within forty paces. Shouldn't like to be responsible for upsetting the old girl.' She glanced at him. 'It's just as well that this is winter, Rupert. You'd be catching flies.'

He closed his mouth with a snap, slammed on the brakes.

'Take me back to the terminus,' she asked.

'But I thought we were going for lunch?'

'No. I think I'll just go home and pack. I know I shan't be travelling for a while, but it's best to be prepared.'

The tram driver watched as the little car slewed to a halt across the road. As he prepared to begin his journey townward, he saw the young woman crossing while the man drove off in a great hurry. Toffs. He had no time for them.

229

SEVENTEEN

The funeral of Miss Mathilda Walsh took place on New Year's Eve, 1921, at the crematorium. This compromise had been decided upon by Seth Dobson, who, on learning of Mona's sudden antipathy towards Peter Wilkinson, reached the conclusion that the Temple of Eternal Light was not a suitable venue. Because of Tilly's weight and the size of her coffin, extra bearers were brought in for the occasion, and the cortège assembled outside Tilly and Mona's house at nine thirty.

Mona had done nothing about the arrangements. Having stayed since Christmas at Pendleton Grange, she had been content to leave all dealings to the undertaker, who, to give fair credit, had made a fine job. The hearse shone, as did the two black horses whose job it was to pull Tilly from her home, across Bolton and to the crematorium. The coffin was made from the best materials, while Seth reassured Mona that Tilly was not in a shroud, but was dressed in her best grey skirt and the new Christmas blouse.

Seth spent some time with the bereaved sister, holding her hand in a comforting way, telling her that people got distressed at this distressing time, and not to distress herself about getting . . . upset. Mona heard little, saw next to nothing. She was sure of only two things: that she would get through today, and that she would not set foot in any buildings connected to her past.

Taking into account the fact that Tilly and Mona had

collected few friends on their conjoined journey through life,
the funeral attracted quite a crowd at all points along the
route. Neighbours, who had found the sisters aloof, now
declared that the Walsh family had been quiet, decent, and had
caused no trouble in the neighbourhood. They had quarrelled
occasionally, yes, but who didn't? And at least there had been
no fighting in the street.

In town, especially near Mulligan's Yard, people lined the
pavements, some with bags of washing in their hands or in
prams. Men removed their hats, women lowered their heads,
and Mona wished with all her heart that the whole thing could
be over and done with. She was cold, tired, and there was
nothing she could do for poor Tilly now.

The main party arrived at the crematorium, the living entering the building before the dead, as was the norm. Seth
Dobson hung about in the doorway, hoping against hope that
no distress would arise out of Mona's changed attitude towards
the celebrant, one Guardian Peter Wilkinson, who seemed not
to have bothered to turn up thus far.

Mona had many supporters on this sad day. Ida came,
though the children, judged too young to attend, had stayed
with neighbours. James Mulligan acted as chauffeur to Ida,
Amy and Eliza, while Margot was a passenger in Camilla
Smythe's van. James got the distinct impression that the two
younger Burton-Masseys had been press-ganged by Amy into
coming. Bringing up the rear of this party, the stalwart
Moorheads travelled in the trap.

Already inside the chapel, a representative from every business in the yard and several from Deansgate waited for Tilly.
It was when she saw these people that Mona had to bite down
hard on her lip. Some folk were nice, after all. There was also
a strong contingent from the Methodist chapel to which the
Walshes had belonged before the arrival from Texas of a flame
carried in the hold of a ship. Mona breathed a little sigh at the
sight of the Methodists. That august body, combined with the
presence of one dedicated Catholic man, would surely be
sufficient to drive the contaminating presence of Peter
Wilkinson back to the gates of hell.

The guardian arrived eventually, his presence announced by

the clatter of a bicycle in the porch. Some turned round in their seats to watch as he smoothed strands of hair to fill in the gaps. Half-way up the central aisle, he remembered the bicycle clips and was forced to stop in order to remove them from his person.

After such an undignified entrance, Peter Wilkinson was much disturbed to find himself facing a dozen Methodists, the beautiful Burton-Masseys and, worst of all, the man he considered to be the greatest enemy of all. James Mulligan. What was he doing here? Weren't Romans forbidden to attend services in churches other than their own? It was plain that Mr Mulligan was a law unto himself.

The coffin, borne by eight men, made its slow and stately way up the aisle. When it rested on a trestle, two girls in white appeared from a corner room. One bore a lighted candle, the other a book. Wilkinson placed the Light on Tilly's coffin, took the book and began to read from it.

He started with a collection of verses culled from various testaments, each piece lifted out of context to support the Eternal Light's message. While he spoke, the white-clad girls stood motionless, one at each side of Tilly's coffin. The original Light was praised for providing the dawn of creation, much was made of the Whitsuntide tongues of flame, then last, but never least, the burning bush of Moses was dragged into the arena.

Wilkinson managed to meet the unamused eye of James Mulligan. '"Hear and fear all ye who walk a path on which the Light shineth not, for ye shall not be admitted to paradise on the day of judgement. Come forth into warmth and joy, and ye shall be redeemed."'

Unfortunately, a latecomer arrived just as the guardian was getting into his stride. The resulting draught travelled through the room, blowing out the Light on Tilly's coffin. Wilkinson turned to one of the girls to ask that a second source of Light be carried in. Plainly, the girls had neglected to store a flame, and the guardian went into an immediate flap.

James turned to look at Mona, who sat by his side. Her face was contorted by an emotion he would not have cared to define.

232

'Er . . .' Peter Wilkinson searched for words. 'We shall have to adjourn while I go and fetch a flame.'

Seth Dobson stepped forward. 'I'm sorry,' he said, 'only there's another service in half an hour. We'll have to get a move on as it is, what with you turning up so late.'

'But the furnace must be fed by the Light,' babbled Peter Wilkinson. 'We must have a piece of the Eternal Fire so that Miss Walsh's soul can enter the kingdom.'

A strangled noise pushed its way out through Mona's tightly clenched teeth. At first, it sounded as if she might be choking, but, as her mouth opened, gales of laughter ripped through the saddened air. A neighbour crossed the chapel. 'It's the hystericals,' she declared authoritatively. 'She gets them. Summat to do with her being on the high-strung side.'

Mona rocked back and forth in her pew. 'Lead – lead kindly light,' she howled. 'It's stupid, it's all stupid.' She pointed to Wilkinson. 'As for him,' she paused to swallow a giggle, 'he's – the daftest thing, the most – most horrible man—' She jumped to her feet, the sobs of laughter diminishing. 'God sent that draught,' she declared. 'God snuffed you out, you miserable, nasty piece of work.'

'Mona.' James pulled at her coat. 'Come on, now, this is a funeral. Let the service finish.'

'Without the Light?' she screamed. 'Without the Light, there can be no service, no cremation, no nothing.' She pushed past James and into the centre aisle. 'There can be no virgins sent off to Texas into God alone knows what, not without the Light.' She turned. 'Mr Mulligan?'

'Yes?'

'You know how you were saying that anyone can do a baptism if there's no clergy around? Ordinary folk who aren't priests?'

James nodded. This was turning into a French farce.

'Well, can somebody do this for my sister?' She glared venomously at the guardian. 'Like, if someone dies and there's no pastor, can an ordinary person pray over them?'

James made no reply.

'I'll do it myself,' she declared, turning to the guardian. 'I'd advise you to pick up your bicycle clips, your holy

233

book, your virgins, and leave while the going's good.'

Wilkinson backed away. In spite of the loss of a couple of stones, Mona Walsh remained a figure to be feared. He wished he had never come; he wished that he had not been disgraced in front of Mulligan and within sight of three beautiful angels. They would be mocking him. Mona Walsh was mocking him now.

She stood next to her sister's coffin, sent the two virgins packing. 'I want to talk to you about my sister,' she advised the congregation. 'Now, I know she came over hard, but she wasn't, not really. See, we knew no life excepting the wash-house. When you do nowt but work, something happens, like a wall being built round you. In our case, you can see the wall, pounds and pounds of it, because nothing much is expected of a fat woman.'

James relaxed perceptively. She was not as out of order as he had feared.

'Tilly minded me. We minded one another, come to think. When she got sidetracked into that daft religion, I went with her and pretended to believe. Well, to be honest, I tried my hardest to believe. Now, if our Tilly died convinced that the Light shone on her path to Heaven, she will be saved. It's believing that counts, not what you believe in.'

Ida snuffled into her handkerchief. Her heart bled for Mona Walsh, who was merely stating her own faith, or the lack of it.

Mona addressed the coffin. 'Tilly, you are a good, God-fearing woman raised in the Methodist ways. We're all going to pray now, ask God to open His arms for your soul. There's a lot of Christians here, and they're all on our side, so their prayers will be very powerful. God bless.'

Tilly was pushed towards the furnace while all present prayed for her salvation. Many wept, because Mona's heartfelt tribute was far more touching than a sermon from a trained man. Her simple words reached the heart of everyone in the room, with the exception of Guardian Wilkinson, that was.

The insurance-man-cum-guardian picked up his book and stalked out of the crematorium, the two girls in white hot on his heels. Having reached the porch, he realized that he had forgotten his bicycle clips, so he sent one of the girls to retrieve them. Hatred burned hot in his heart, loud in his head. He had been made into a figure of fun, and his desire for revenge was strong.

Inside, Mona made her way towards the door, her hand in the crook of James Mulligan's arm. It was over; she had got through it in one piece. She shook the hands of everyone present, had a word with those who wanted to talk.

When various vehicles lined up to carry people back to their homes, Mona opted to travel in Camilla's van, while Margot, with whom Camilla had wanted a word after the funeral, got into the trap with the Moorheads. Seth expressed his gratitude to Miss Smythe, as she had released a driver who had been booked to carry the sole family mourner back to Pendleton.

Camilla sighed. She was not meant to say anything to anyone, she thought, as she began the journey towards town. Living in several minds was not easy, as she seemed to swing like a pendulum between the need to do something and the knowledge that she was powerless.

Mona sobbed quietly.

'A long hard cry'll do you good,' was Camilla's stated opinion.

Mona, who had done so well for days, realized that she had merely been in hiding. The space between a death and a funeral was an unreal dimension; now she would be forced to come to terms with life without Tilly. It was not going to be as easy as she had encouraged herself to expect. Thus far, she had concentrated on Tilly's bossiness; now she recalled the good times. 'We used to gossip by the fire,' she said quietly. 'We'd put the world right over cheese on toast and mugs of tea. She handled all the bills. I did baking.'

'But weren't you planning to break away?' asked Camilla.

'Aye, but not as finally as this.'

Camilla sought a clever change of subject when Mona's sobs abated. 'Margot is looking ill,' she said.

'She's not eating proper,' replied Mona. 'Going through one of them slimming phases, I'll bet. I've been dieting myself, only I'm being careful.'

No luck there, thought the driver. 'Whereas Eliza seems exceptionally well.'

235

'Aye, she does.'

There was, Camilla decided, no point in trying to drag blood from a stone, especially when that stone was so recently bereaved.

Back at Caldwell Farm, a small buffet had been arranged by Kate Kenny and the two young maids, Sally Hayes and Mary Whitworth, who were all on loan from the big house. People milled around having polite, meaningless conversations, while Mona, deep in thought, parked herself next to the fire and drank copious amounts of tea. Tilly would never again sit by a fireside, her skirt raised to allow heat to her legs, cup balanced on the fireguard, eyes glinting over a crumpet dripping with butter.

'I think it has finally hit her,' James told Amy. 'I shall tell Kate to keep an eye on her.'

Amy watched, almost dumbfounded when Margot made her way to Mona's side. This was the first voluntary movement Margot had made for ages.

'Hello.' Margot sat on the floor next to Mona. 'I expect you're feeling very sad and lonely.' Margot knew about sad and lonely, since each day of hers might be described by those very adjectives.

'I'll be all right.' Mona took yet another mouthful of tea.

'Is there anything I can do?'

Mona looked at the youngest Burton-Massey. 'You can start seeing to yourself,' she replied. 'The state you're in, you'd be best off getting to a doctor.'

Margot swallowed. She had begun to feel again, and the main emotion was sheer terror. Everyone was noticing; soon, the whole world would have its eyes on stalks, its fingers pointing in her direction. 'Have you seen that Burton-Massey girl? Pregnant and unmarried? What's the world coming to?' She felt Mona's gaze, realized that even these eyes were probing.

'Didn't you used to have a boyfriend?'

Margot nodded quickly. 'Rupert Smythe.'

'Ah.' It was Mona's turn to lower her head in thought. 'He went off to London with his mam yesterday afternoon.'

'Did he?'

'They're going to a theatre, Camilla said. He's got a flat with

236

two bedrooms so's his mother can visit him. Right mammy's lad from the sound of it. He's going to work in a bank.'

'I see.'

Mona's invisible antennae set to work. Thinking about someone else took her mind off her own situation, anyway. Also, after recent harrowing events, the niceties of life were suddenly unimportant. 'Margot?'

'Yes?'

Mona inhaled deeply. 'Right, lady. You and me are on that tram next week, we'll go and see my doctor. Nobody knows you down yon, if you get my drift.'

'Yes.' Margot's reply was spoken in a whisper. Perhaps this was what she had hoped for, that an almost-stranger would step in and help her.

'Promise?' Mona asked.

'I promise, Mona.'

The older woman gripped the younger's hand. 'Nowt's as bad as what it seems. In the end, it'll turn out for the best, you'll see. Look at me. My only relative's died, but I'll get over it.'

As she watched Margot wandering off to the other side of the room, Mona got to thinking again. It was a pity that Tilly had needed to die for Mona to notice how pleasant some people were. Take the Dobsons. They had cleaned the house, arranged the funeral right down to the tiniest detail, all for no extra cost, had fetched Mona's clothes up to Pendleton. Mr Mulligan had been a rock from start to finish, was arranging for both Mona's houses to be emptied and closed down, would return keys to the landlords. He had even offered to store Mona's bits and pieces in a loft above his offices at the yard. As for Amy, Ida and Kate – they had become real pals to Mona.

And now perhaps Mona could do something in return. If the youngest lass wasn't pregnant, Mona would eat the contents of a hat shop. It wasn't just the common folk who had problems like illegitimacy and abandonment. Life was hard; the alternative harder still. Poor Tilly.

Amy decided to try again with Eliza. The girl was growing more detached every day, was distancing herself from her

237

family, failing to turn up for meals, ignoring the little niceties like 'good morning' and 'good night'. Now, she was gazing through the window, a tiny smile on her face. 'A penny for your thoughts,' said Amy.

Eliza turned slowly. 'Amy.'

'I am so glad that you remember my name.'

'Sarcasm doesn't suit you,' said Eliza. 'You are far too sweet for it.'

'Well, while I hold you captive, so to speak, may I ask what you have been up to for the past few weeks?'

Eliza considered the question. Avoiding Rupert's mother was going to be a terrible bore; waiting for Amy to come in search of her would be even worse. 'I'm going to London for a while,' she said, after a pause of some seconds. 'Just to look around, see how the land lies. There is nothing here for me.'

Amy was cross, though she sat on several automatic responses. And was she surprised? Could she place a hand on her heart and say that she had never expected this kind of behaviour? But, oh, how many times she had shielded Eliza from Margot's bouts of adolescent temper, and here came the repayment. 'So, you have given no thought to your family. I have to open that shop, because so much of Mother's money – our money now – is invested there. With your eye for design, we could make a real success.'

Eliza raised her shoulders, said nothing.

'Give me a year,' Amy pleaded.

'I'll give you a year when I have one to spare.'

'Don't be clever,' Amy almost snapped. 'You have no money to start you off. You—' She staggered back a pace. Camilla's brother had just made his exit to the south. 'Does Rupert Smythe have a hand in this?'

'No.' The lie slipped so easily from Eliza's tongue.

'Then how are you managing to pay for accommodation? Come with me into the hall. This is no place for a discussion of this nature.'

'You started it.' Eliza followed her sister. Today, at last, she would tell the truth and shame Satan. She inhaled deeply. 'I took the fire opals and the sapphires,' she said. 'They were the pieces Mother wanted me to have. Worry not, I did not touch

238

yours or Margot's. The jewellery Mother had not mentioned individually I had valued and sold one third. The rest is upstairs.'

Amy was appalled. 'How could you?'

'Quite easily, I assure you. This grey, miserable place is not for me. I shall be working in theatre.'

Amy laughed, though the sound conveyed no merriment. 'You and a thousand other starry-eyed hopefuls. There are many talented people in London, most of them cleaning floors or serving coffee.'

'I shall not be one of them.'

Camilla stepped into the hall. Her beetroot-red face clashed wildly with her hair, and she was mauling a napkin in nervous fingers. 'Amy?'

'This is a private conversation.' Eliza was suddenly alert.

'And I've listened to one too many of those lately.' Camilla spoke now to Amy. 'I haven't known whether or how to tell you, and I'm sorry for eavesdropping just now, but Eliza has been plotting with my dear brother. They will be sharing a flat in Bloomsbury.'

'So,' Amy's eyes flashed dangerously, 'you are also a liar, Eliza.'

Eliza glared at Camilla. She was a great ugly lump of a girl with wild hair in an unforgivable shade of red. The face, too, had little to recommend it, while Camilla's large-boned body was almost as straight up and down as any man's. 'You know, Camilla, if you are going to spread gossip, you should try, at least, to keep up with events. I shall not – repeat, not – be living with Rupert. I have made my own arrangements.'

Camilla offered no response.

Amy, whose temper was rising towards the fury mark, stepped into the space between the other two women. 'In case it has slipped your mind, our mother is recently dead,' she said quietly. 'When she was alive, you behaved like a true angel, all sweetness and light. Well, there is no longer anything of the truth in you, Eliza. You refuse to help me and Margot, because you care for no one save yourself. Leave. Just go. And please don't bother to come back.'

Eliza raised perfect eyebrows. 'Oh, I'll be back. When

Mulligan hands back the house, the hydro, or whatever, I shall claim my share. We shall never live in Pendleton Grange again.'

Amy leaned against the wall, the movement unsteady enough to warrant a hand from Camilla. 'Careful, Amy,' she said, fingers cupping her friend's elbow. 'I decided weeks ago that neither of them is worth a candle.' She turned on the other girl. 'You, Eliza, are a selfish, foolish woman. My brother, who treated Margot so badly, is another damned idiot. You should do very well together.'

Eliza, slightly dismayed by Camilla's damning of Rupert, maintained her stance. Families like the Smythes never spoke badly of themselves. Why should Camilla break the mould by refusing to stand by her brother? 'Rupert and I simply happen to be departing at the same time, that is all. I have taken an attic room in the house where Rupert has a flat.'

Camilla laughed. 'My brother is probably interested in your body. He usually gets what he wants, then runs away.'

'He won't touch me,' declared Eliza firmly.

Amy broke away and ran upstairs. She was what Elspeth Moorhead would term 'sick to the back teeth' of everything. She sat on the edge of her bed, tears coursing down her face. And what would Mother have made of this? Margot decidedly off-colour, Eliza about to escape to London, Amy sitting in her bedroom while there were guests downstairs. It was hopeless, hopeless!

Someone tapped on the door. 'Go away, please,' she called.

The door opened. 'Amy?'

'I told you to go away. Is there no privacy to be had?'

James strode in. 'I saw you . . . I was concerned because . . . I saw you running up the stairs. Is this you weeping?'

'No.' She rubbed the heel of a hand across her eyes.

He sat next to her, placed a weighty arm across her shoulders. 'Come away, now, Amy, for you're tougher than this.'

'Am I? Is that how you see me? Oh, I'm the oldest, the most sensible. Amy Burton-Massey – she found her father hanging, you know, never batted an eyelid, looked after her mother, her sisters.' She turned on him. 'Well, it's not like that. Margot –

there's something wrong with her, and Eliza, the fragrant, beautiful Eliza, is going to live in the same house as Rupert Smythe. I've to open a shop, and I'm scared stiff. There'll be no help except for the woman you found—'

'She's good. I picked up her references and she's always up to date with the latest—'

Amy jumped up, pushed his arm away in the same movement. 'Oh, good for you. No one cares about how I feel, and I've had enough of everything and everyone.' She knew that she sounded childish.

'So, you've put your name down for a tantrum. Well, go ahead and scream, because I'm used to children.'

Her temper teetered, fizzed over into the room. 'Stop being so understanding. You might just as well stop all the hydro business, because Eliza is going to insist on an immediate sale if and when you return Pendleton Grange to us. So forget it, James. Sell up and go home.'

'I will not.' He could scarcely believe his ears. Eliza so cruel? She was capable of coldness and distance, he knew that. But would she go so far as to ruin her own family? Well, he would see about that. The Grange, the farms, the properties in town were all his, and he could cut Eliza off if he so chose. Couldn't he? Oh, why and how did these women wrap themselves around his heartstrings when he was so determinedly uninvolved?

Amy examined his face, saw pain there. 'Another of her many victims, James? I advise you to fall out of love with her at once, because she has no need of your affection.'

'What?'

'Ah, so you are in love with her.'

He didn't know what to say, how to answer without betraying himself. Sometimes, he longed for the peace and quiet of home, for the cold winds off the ocean, the bright sunsets, those famous mists that belonged solely to the west coast of Ireland. Even a classroom full of difficult children would have been preferable to standing here feeling like a total imbecile. He was, he told himself sternly, a free man. Yet no, no, there were ties that bound him to . . .

'She says she's going on the stage.' Amy mopped at her eyes

with a handkerchief. 'She thinks that's going to be easy. Tell her, please. She might listen to you.'

'She won't.'

Amy looked at him. He was so ill-at-ease, embarrassed. 'For God's sake, don't regress,' she implored. 'We can't have you battening down the hatches again. It was months before you spoke a single word to any of us.'

He lifted a broad shoulder. 'If I thought it would do any good, I would speak to your sister.' He paused, stared down at his shoes. 'But I shall offer to take her to London. The journey can be done in a day. Then, at least, you will know that she is safe.'

Amy's blood boiled anew. Was there nothing this silly man would not do for Eliza? Like a callow youth, he was willing to go to the ends of the earth for a woman whose value had suddenly plummeted in the opinion of her older sister. 'Do as you wish,' she snapped. 'As head of this family, I resign. From now on, I shall serve myself.'

'No, you won't.' His tone was soft, gentle. 'Because you are not capable of that.' He turned and left the room.

Amy powdered stained cheeks and applied a little pink lip colour. The man was right. She would always maintain appearances. After all, she had her pride . . .

EIGHTEEN

Peter Wilkinson could not remember a time when he had been more angry. Yes, he could, but he didn't want to think about Mam with her big red hands, cold, all-seeing eyes, voice that pierced the air, screaming, fury, locked in the dark, dressed as a girl, no food, no water . . . *Stop, stop, don't let her hurt you any more; she is dead, gone, but not into any kind of light save the furnace below. Let her burn beyond time.*

He looked at himself in the mirror, saw ugliness and hopelessness combined to make a lost, lonely creature, often hated even by himself. All he had was the Light, the living flame, that brave flicker of hope around which he had wrapped his heart, his whole life. 'The Lord has His plan for me,' he told the uncomely reflection. 'Soon He will give me the power to be a real man, so that I can go to Makersfield and take my place among the guardians.'

Doris came in. 'Talking to yourself again?'

'Praying,' he replied.

She pursed mean lips, so like Mam's, went into her scullery and clattered pots. He waited, listened to the ritual, teeth in a jam jar, quick splash of water on her face, towel pulled off a rail on the back door, scrub face and hands dry. She emerged, toothless, heartless, frowned at him, stamped off to bed. Every day, every night, she did the same things, made the same remarks, looked at him with a mixture of contempt and pity.

243

His own mother had hated him, and Doris didn't like him, either. Stephen, his brother, saw the best in everyone, so his approval didn't count. Stephen did not discriminate between ugly and beautiful, between good and bad. Stephen took little interest in salvation, was too busy baking bread and cakes, selling stamps, issuing postal orders, listening to the village gossips as they queued for his wares. 'I am not alone, because I have the Light,' mumbled Peter.

Inside themselves, inside the crematorium, they had all been laughing at him. Tilly Walsh's Light had blown out, and he had seen people trying not to let the sniggers escape. They were at a funeral, yet Guardian Wilkinson was so grotesque that they could scarcely contain their mirth. A figure of fun. A hideous man who collected insurance pennies. A misguided fool with his lamps and wicks and candles, with his bald head, crooked teeth, poor skin, bulging eyes.

Damn them all into the bottomless pit of Hades, every last man and woman. Mona Walsh, sister of the deceased, had decried and abused him. She would not set foot in the temple again; if she ever needed him, he would not be available. Those who acted against him must remain in darkness; never again would Mona Walsh receive help.

How little they knew, how stupid they were not to fear and respect him. He had seen the miracle first-hand, had sat with the Light until it absorbed its surroundings and became one with him. He had seen pictures dancing in the flames, because the Light was his vision, his future, the destiny of the planet and all who laboured blindly on its surface. How little they knew, those who had not witnessed.

Let them neither mock nor anger me, for I have a strength beyond their understanding. I am one with the Eternal Light, one with the world, and in my sight I behold their destiny, the fate of the unbelievers.

He dimmed the gas, brought a lantern to the table, stared into its flame. Focused solely on the Light, he allowed the room to disappear, to melt, to cease to exist within his new dimension. As he entered the hypnotic state, he felt an all-enveloping warmth, so deep that it took the December chill from his bones. This was the truth, the beginning, the end,

244

both the same. Where he existed, there was no time, breadth, length, weight: all was immeasurable.

Their faces came, one by one, each mouth smirking, decrying him. Methodists, Seth Dobson, James Mulligan, all seeing him as a fool. He was not a fool! One day, he would show the infidels. It was his to know, his alone, for he carried the certainty that he would be Supreme Guardian, since he had seen that vision within the Light's core.

Then, as he relaxed, the three girls visited him. The oldest was not his target; the other two spoilt him, spoilt him for choice. Either was surely a worthy wife of a guardian, a fit mate who would bring forth the next generation. She would sail the ocean by his side, would travel to the holy site, the place from which the miraculous Light had sprung.

Eliza, so lovely, sang in the woods. He heard her now as clearly as ever, watched her turning, dancing in the Light. Margot on horseback, a fine strong woman, able for a new life in the New World. Which to choose? In a moment, the answer would come. The flame grew, spread, shaped itself, gave the answer. So, she was the one. He smiled, placed his hands flat on the table and prayed. The miracle had happened. He was awake, aware, and he owned the pure truth.

On the first day of 1922, Eliza Burton-Massey packed her belongings into two cases. With no regrets, she placed clothes, shoes and trinkets on the bed, assessing what she would need, what she could manage without. A smile played across her lips as she remembered him pleading, begging her not to go. James Mulligan was not without his charms, but he could not keep her here.

Or could he? Placing herself at the dressing-table, she leaned her elbows on its surface, rested her chin in her hands. If he offered marriage, promised to make her sole mistress of Pendleton Grange, might she stay? Oh, he could wait. First she must live, enjoy herself, see London, meet people of influence. Yes, Mulligan could rest on a back burner for now. He adored her – she had seen that in his eyes. He was hers for the taking. When she was ready.

Amy knocked, entered. 'So, you are still bent on going?'

'Of course.'

'I thought James might have persuaded you otherwise this morning.'

'He tried.'

It would be so easy to hate a woman like Eliza, thought Amy. Everywhere she went, men stared, smiled, wanted her. She was talented, beautiful, serene, infuriating. But Eliza was her sister, and hatred was ugly. 'I'm sorry about yesterday,' she said.

Eliza smiled. 'It's no matter. We both said things in anger.'

'Are you capable of anger?'

'Yes, I am. I just hide it well – usually, that is.'

Amy sat on the bed and talked to Eliza's reflection. 'I just hope you will be safe. It's a big bad world out there.'

'As James Mulligan reminded me earlier.'

He would, thought Amy. Like every other man for miles around, he had gone hook, line and sinker for Eliza's undeniable loveliness. Why could no one see what Eliza had become? Perhaps Eliza had always been the same, her true self hidden until she allowed it to come out. 'Would you have gone if Mother had lived?'

'She didn't live, Amy.'

The older sister remembered how Eliza had almost fainted in A Cut Above when Mother had collapsed. She wondered now whether that had been genuine or just another facet of this consummate actress's repertoire. Was there a real possibility that Eliza had been born empty, that she could fill her shell with whichever manufactured emotion fitted the bill at any given time? What a frightening thought that was.

'I don't mind you not liking me,' said Eliza, 'but I do hope that you love me. I love you, but I'm not able to . . . connect all the time. Love for you and the rest of my family was born with me. Yet I have a mind that separates me from almost everybody. It works all the time, you know, even when I'm asleep. There's something in me that drives me on in spite of everyone's attitudes and feelings. This is what I am, how I am made.'

Eliza had never before attempted to explain herself. That she had insight into her own make-up was good – or was it? Even

246

though she knew her own devastating coldness, she seemed unprepared to do anything about it. Then all the answers hit Amy like a fork of lightning. Eliza could not mend herself: Eliza's flaw went beyond the limits of human understanding.

'You shivered then,' said the reflection.

Reflection. Poor Eliza was as two-dimensional as that. It was not wickedness, then, not in the true sense, because nothing could be done about it. Did Eliza live beyond the bounds of moral law, beyond nature? If so, how far might she go before being pulled up? If she didn't know right from wrong, was that quality a part of her essential self, or had family and teachers failed her?

'I shall write to you,' Eliza promised.

'Be sure to do that.'

'And get Margot to see a doctor. She won't talk to me any more, silly girl. I think she may be anaemic.'

So Eliza did care. She cared, but was not prepared, not able to be involved. Amy stood up and placed her arms round Eliza's shoulders. 'I'll miss you.'

'I'm not going just yet, and I shall be back to visit. Take care.'

Amy went downstairs to help Elspeth, whose old knees were giving trouble. As she peeled carrots, the oldest surviving Burton-Massey found herself worrying and wondering anew about the future. There was something wrong with Margot, something wrong with Eliza. 'I wonder what's wrong with me?' she said quietly.

Elspeth was preparing meat. 'Nothing,' she replied. 'Well, nowt that the love of a good man wouldn't cure.'

Amy glared at the housekeeper. 'Shut up,' she said, with mock severity. 'Life's complicated enough as it is.'

The banging and hammering from above was terrible. 'It'll be good,' Diane told Joe. 'Like sailors living on a ship – they sleep on shelves. We'll be in the same room again, 'cos Miss Walsh is having my room.' She'd been invited to call Mona by her Christian name but, ever mindful of her own sinful past, Diane did not want to sound too familiar. Auntie Mona? Not long ago the same woman had been one of Diane's targets.

Ida was holding on to her head as if it might burst wide open at any minute. Upstairs, James Mulligan seemed to be knocking the house to bits. Still, it would be worth it, she told her doubting soul. She'd have some decent company, and Mona would not be forced to go back to Bolton. Since the discovery of the girl in the kitchen of 13 John Street, Mona had not been keen on moving into the house. As for the Walsh family home – she definitely did not want to return there, so both places would return to the landlord for re-letting.

Mona entered with a tray of tea things, plonked them on the table. 'Why does he have to do it today?' she asked. 'He must be keen to get me out of Pendleton Grange.'

'Well, he were going to London, only he's not now. Must be short of summat to do. Tell you what, he's easy suited. Give him a hammer and he's like a pig in muck.'

Mona sat. 'London? What for?'

Ida glanced up at the ceiling, a pained expression distorting her features. 'He'll be through the floorboards in a minute. He's not got what you might call the gentle touch, has he?' These words were all screamed at top note, as the cacophony from above was truly deafening.

Diane mouthed a message to her grandmother, got coats and scarves, took herself and her brother into the blessed peace of outdoors.

The two women sipped tea, dipped biscuits, warmed themselves by the fire. 'London?' Mona repeated.

'No,' replied Ida, 'he's only taking her as far as the station. He was going to drive her down today, but she said no. He's putting her on a train in a few days, as far as I know. So he's decided to knock our house down instead of driving to London.'

'Bit of a bombshell that must have been for Amy,' said Mona.

'Aye, it would be. Tell the truth, though, nowt'd surprise me from that Eliza one. She's refused a lift because he'd be mithering her to come back, so she'll have decided to go by train.' Ida sniffed. 'She's been packing for days, or so I'm told. Oh, let her go and be done. I don't know why folk bother about her, 'cos Amy's worth ten of her.'

248

Mona refilled the cups, raised her eyes to heaven when the noise stopped. 'It's Margot I'm worried about.'

'Aye. Her little face is pale, isn't it?'

A voice from above called, 'Mona? Can you ever come up and hold this piece? It's not going on straight.'

Mona placed her cup in its saucer. 'I'm putting you to a right lot of trouble, Ida.'

'Nay.' Ida shook her grey head. 'The only trouble will be him upstairs. Go and see to him, Mona. If he makes them beds on a slope, our little Joe'll be through the window in his nightshirt before we can say knife. While you're there, ask his lordship does he want a cuppa and has he not got a muffler for that blinking hammer.'

Ida settled in her chair, watched the grandchildren playing outside. They'd made many new friends and were even talking about changing schools. Aye, this was a grand life and no mistake. Every weekday, Ida went to help at the big house. She got wages, vegetables, bits of bread and meat. Kate Kenny was forever miscalculating – 'See, I've made too much again. Carry it home, or it'll go in the swill.'

As for him, the Catholic, the Irish swine, he was the finest gentleman Ida had ever come across. It all went to show that prejudice was a waste of energy. Everyone was different, everyone had good and bad points. She grinned. Kate Kenny had his bad points on a list in her head. She was always teasing him, laughing at him, making fun of him. And he took it so well.

The only trouble was that this life could come to an end when James Mulligan returned to Ireland. No, surely Amy would let them stay in the tied cottage? Ida could not imagine being back in John Street, lying in her bed, knowing in her heart of hearts that their Diane was stealing just to feed the family.

She noticed him then. He was walking up the other side of the lane, away from his brother's shop. Even from this distance, Ida could tell that he was talking to himself under his breath. How she had used to admire him, the giver of parcels to the poor, champion of the underdog, forever in the local press for his acts of charity. Mona had wiped him out yesterday, had

249

called him all the names under the sun. Ida's heart lurched. He was approaching the children.

Thankful for her much-improved legs, Ida stood up, dragged a shawl across her upper body, walked to the door. 'Hello, Mr Wilkinson,' she said, suddenly keen to get on his right side. 'Cold enough for you, is it?'

'Certainly chilly, Mrs Hewitt. But you are looking well. The Light seems to have done its job.'

'Oh, aye, I'm a lot better, thanks.'

'We should hold a special service of thanksgiving.'

Ida swallowed. She'd been rude to him in the past, had even caused him to fall in the ice, but she was suddenly anxious not to insult him again. Not that she could work out why, but he seemed ... well, different. Angry, perhaps, or out of sorts. 'When the weather's better, eh?' she suggested.

'Good idea.' He smiled, doffed his hat, giving her the dubious double benefit of woven hair and dreadful teeth.

'Come in, now,' she told the children.

Once safely inside, Ida realized that she was shaking. She was afraid of him. Why? Why now, all of a sudden? Perhaps ideas had been put into her head after the discovery of that girl in the scullery at number 13. Oh, surely not. Yet deep inside her soul, she harboured a feeling, a sense that the guardian might just have been guilty, that he was building up to ... something.

The cleansings. She told herself to stop trembling in case she frightened the children—

'Gran?' Joe's face was screwed into quizzical mode. 'You're shaking all over.'

'It's the cold, love.' It wasn't the weather. The gooseflesh on her arms was caused by something primeval, an animal reaction to terror.

James clattered downstairs. 'It all looked very easy on paper,' he said, to no one in particular. 'Bunks, like sailors have, eh, Joe? It's just getting them straight ... Ida?'

'I'm all right.'

He turned to the children. 'I need tea,' he ordered. 'A huge amount of tea, and some bread and butter with a little jam, a bit of cake for Mona, who is, at this moment, wedged into the

250

corner of the room. You'll have to take hers in, because I can't get her out. So, your lodger is in residence.'

Ida sat in her rocking-chair. 'Wilkinson was out there.' She swallowed. 'I can't stand him going near Diane. Oh, I'm just a foolish woman, but he fair made my hair stand on end this time.'

'Calm yourself.'

'He was never out of my house. He was always good to us. What's changed?'

James squatted down in front of her. 'You are stronger, you are no longer dependent upon him. It's all about power. Not only have you left Bolton and the Temple, you are befriended by me, a Catholic. See how much you have changed. Now, I've told you how twisted that cult is. You already know what a difficult life the man has had. He is deformed in the head. But you and yours are safe, please believe that.'

She sniffed back a tear. 'I'll feel safer when Mona moves in.'

James stroked her face. 'She has moved in. She is stuck as fast as the sun in the sky, no shifting her.'

Ida looked hard at him. 'I thought you were joking.'

'I never joke about a wedged woman, Ida.'

She didn't know whether to laugh or cry. Oh, he was good at cheering folk up, was James Mulligan. 'What'll we do?' she asked.

He stood up. 'There's always goose grease. Or we could just leave her there while she loses a few more pounds.'

The cry came then. 'Is nobody doing owt about this? I can't move. Will somebody come?'

James and Ida dissolved into laughter. But if they had stopped long enough to look and listen, each might have noticed a hollow quality in the other's merriment.

Mona was freed eventually and life continued apace. But Ida felt uneasy for the rest of the day, and she could not fully account for that.

The news of Eliza Burton-Massey's planned departure filtered through to the villages of Pendleton and Pendleton Clough in a matter of hours. Opinions were expressed, theories propounded, then most folk went back to the business of

251

celebrating the arrival of a brand new year. What them up yonder did was interesting, but not all-consuming. They could get on with it – there were meals to cook and eat.

But Peter Wilkinson was not most folk. He was dismayed, confused because the Light had shown him that Eliza was the one for him. The Light did not make mistakes, so the fault was his; he had simply misinterpreted the message. So, he had to move his sights across to Margot, the youngest. She would be useful; she could ride a horse, and horses were plentiful in Makersfield.

Now, there remained just one hurdle: he had to prove to himself that he was a full man, one who was capable of reproducing himself. At this juncture, his feelings and plans became rather blurred about the edges. He knew that he had to find Margot, trap her, put her to sleep and mate with her. Once he had claimed her, she could be told about how she had been chosen, about America and the rich life she would enjoy within the compound.

He always got a headache when he reached this uncertain point. Faith was the answer. As long as he claimed her, the Light would guide her the rest of the way. Of course, everything had to be done stealthily, as non-believers would not accept his way of working. How sad they were, those who had not met the Light.

Preparations began straight away: he stored the chloroform, the rag and his dark clothing in a shed at the back of his brother's house-cum-shop. There might be a lot of waiting involved, as he would need to cover his tracks. It was complicated, but he was gladdened by the knowledge that the Light would guide him. Margot, not Eliza, he must remember that. He made a chant of it to remind himself. Margot, not Eliza. Margot was to be the companion of his future life.

James Mulligan made his way up the cellar stairs. He doused the lamp, placed it on the top step, emerged into the kitchen. For a few moments, he stood still, his head lowered as if deep in thought, then taking a large iron key from a pocket, he locked the heavy door, rattling its handle to ensure security.

Kate, who was trimming the pastry edges from an apple pie, noticed how old and weary he looked. Every time he came up from the cellar, he was as miserable as a wet washday. 'Away now till I make you a cup of tea,' she ordered. 'And I've a new batch of soda bread, still warm, it is, just as you've always liked it. Or would you like one of my famous potato cakes?' She knew that she was gabbling, but how she longed to comfort him, distract him, make his life easier and happier.

'Oh, Kate.' He groaned his way into a chair. 'It's getting to me. I feel like a bone torn at each end by a big dog.' He sniffed, picked up a spoon and played with it absently.

'Ah, well.' She placed the pie in the range oven. 'I suppose one would be an Irish wolfhound, the other an English retriever. The retriever is the prettier of the two, I don't doubt.' With her arms akimbo and an oven cloth dangling from each hand, she looked hard at him. 'A man with two mistresses is a country at war.'

'It's not funny.'

'Love is seldom amusing,' she replied quickly. 'And being dragged two ways can make a person a deal less than comfortable. Life has a way of sorting itself out, but.'

'It's agony.' He placed his elbows on the table, cupped his chin, watched her bustling about in her quick, sure way. Kate was a born organizer. She had built a good life with a husband she had adored, had watched him fade and die, had delivered a stillborn boy. And look at her now, he thought, agile, cheerful, acidic, amusing. 'Did I tell you recently that I love you?' he asked. He did love her. She was mother, friend, companion. She was also his little bit of Ireland in this foreign place.

She considered the question, bread-knife in one hand, a small loaf in the other. 'Yesterday,' she answered. 'Just after breakfast.' He was wrenching the heart from her; she could almost reach out and touch the pain that surrounded him. 'God knows, you can't go on like this. You'll end up in one of those funny hospitals with padded walls and scruffy, bespectacled doctors.'

'You know I'm too strong for that, Auntie Kate.'

She froze for a few seconds, saw him running down the lane, no laces in his boots, ragged shirt flapping in the breeze. 'He's

253

hitting Mammy again, Auntie Kate.' And she would go back with him, because she was the only one who could tackle Thomas Mulligan without fear of death. How many times had the child come for her? How many grains of salt in the dish?

'Don't think about it.' His voice was low. 'She can suffer no more, and he is where he belongs.'

'We've always been in tune, you and I,' she said. 'Sure, we can each read the other like a book.' She gazed at him, her expression an improbable mix of hope and despair. 'If I'd a hundred pounds just now, I'd back the English retriever to win the race.'

'Would you?' They both laughed, because their dislike for gambling and gamblers was another of many shared emotions. 'Ah, well, there's only time will put me straight. Talking of straight, it took me two hours to fit those beds.'

Kate nodded proudly. This was her lad now. His daddy, her brother, was dead, as was his poor mammy. She loved him as dearly as she would have loved her own child. 'You're more of a head man, James. Look how you came top of everything at the university. Now, anyone can build a bed.'

'I can't. The whole thing is balanced on bricks. I'm getting a carpenter to fix it.'

'Horses for courses,' she pronounced, before getting on with her chores.

Sally struggled in with a wicker basket of washing. She dumped it on the floor and shook a finger at it. 'If you don't dry yourself, how can I iron you?' she asked, before spreading it on maidens in front of the fire.

James looked upon the scene of domesticity, remarking inwardly how normal it seemed. Sulky Mary Whitworth entered, but even she didn't spoil the atmosphere, since many families contained a difficult teenage son or daughter. She had put back most of the stolen items, at least. Little Sally had not said a word, but James, a seasoned handler of children, always knew the score.

Kate shooed him out so that she and the maids could serve up a nice New Year meal of pork with all the trimmings. He stood in the hall and thought of the Burton-Masseys, whose house this had been through three generations. It seemed bare

254

out here, cold and uncared for. There were patches on the walls where paintings had hung, their liquid value converted now into racehorses. He had sold half a dozen horses at a hundred per cent profit. Now, he could start the hydro and get this place on its feet again.

But there was a deep unease in James Mulligan's bones, a sense of foreboding, almost. It was as if he stood in quicksand, forever mobile, unpredictable. Was this discomfort caused by the imminent departure of Eliza? Or were his suspicions about Margot making him fidgety? He had seen Wilkinson today, had looked insanity in the eye.

But no. The main reason for his malaise was just below his feet, in the darkness of the cellar. He was, he concluded, a fool and his own worst enemy.

NINETEEN

The second opening of A Cut Above, whilst a great deal quieter than the first, was a resounding success. This was due in no small way to the editor of the *Bolton Evening News*, a man who had decided to throw his weight behind the tragic Burton-Masseys by giving them cut-price advertising, plus several inches of editorial space.

The first thing Amy noticed on entering the shop was a huge mass of flowers sent by other tradespeople on Deansgate. As this was January, most blooms had been cultivated in hot-houses so the generous gifts must have cost a pretty penny. Camilla was already installed, coffee pots and cups to the left, teapots to the right, a smile on her homely, generous face. She was wearing a superb suit designed by the dead Louisa, sewn by the absent Eliza. Her hair, shiny after careful brushing, was pinned attractively to the top of her head, while the subtle application of makeup made her less horselike.

Later, Amy watched her potential customers as they milled about oohing and ahhing over fine materials, good handbags and shoes. But the main attraction came from a totally unexpected source. Ida Hewitt, she of the lost heart and uncertain legs, had produced three evening shawls in crochet so fine that it floated like gossamer. Two were earmarked immediately, while Amy had to fight to keep the third as a sample for display. What talents people had, she mused. Ida had also knitted a Fair Isle cardigan so beautiful that several orders were placed there and then. No more vegetable peeling for Ida, it seemed. Though the good woman would probably sit in the Grange kitchen to knit alongside her good friend, Kate Kenny.

There was excitement in the air as Amy made her little speech of welcome. She explained that informality would be the order of today and every day, that she intended to ensure that each customer would be treated as an individual with needs to be met and that total slavery to fashion fads would never occur. 'We may be small,' she told them, 'and therein may lie our potential success. All I ask is that you try us and make your comments openly to us.'

She went on to describe the future as clearly as she could manage. 'I envisage an extended family whose members will meet at the start of each season – perhaps at the inn, perhaps here in our parlour, with every one of you having a say, bringing ideas, pictures, even your own drawings. We shall not dictate to you. Our intention is to look at fashionable trends and incorporate them into design without becoming total victims to the suggestions of the big houses. This is an adventure. Come with us on this new journey; help us to create our own distinctive designs. There will be fashion shows, informal meetings here, a staff who will always listen and learn from you, the customer.'

Amy cast her eyes over the gathering, counted twelve people, saw excitement in their faces. 'Feel free to drop in any time for a chat, for a cup of coffee, or both. During opening hours, we shall be here for you.'

They liked the idea. Already friendships were forming as women turned to their neighbours to nod or to whisper words of approval. It was plain that Louisa had been possessed of a natural business sense, since the fashion shows and informal sessions had been her inventions. Amy continued, 'Attention will be paid to good fitting. Women do not come in sizes dictated by the fashion industry. Take me as an example – where ready-made clothes are concerned, I have to choose between a good fit on the hips, or a good fit across the bust. For the larger female, particular heed will be paid to this

257

problem.' She looked around the room: Mona had not yet arrived. Nor had Margot.

'Now, we have Mrs Jessie Evans who spent five years as a designer at Marshall and Brooke in Manchester. Yes, I can see that you have heard of them, so I know that you will appreciate their high standards and the prices to match. Mrs Evans is pure magic in the field of fashion – yes, she's the blushing one over there.' Amy twinkled at the shy, clever woman. 'She will do you all proud, ladies. And we shall be a great deal less expensive than Marshall's.'

Jessie Evans giggled, hid behind her handkerchief. Having fallen on her feet within a job that allowed her to cater for her children outside school hours, she was as happy as a deserted wife could manage.

Amy, more relaxed now that she had the audience's approval, went on to describe the services offered. Miss Mona Walsh, who was not available this morning, had run the laundry for many years. She would be on hand to give advice regarding the treatment of different materials – how to wash silk crêpe, how to iron fine worsted, how to sponge stains. As a larger lady, she would also be happy to assist those of a similar build to choose suitable fabrics and styles.

'I am in charge,' Amy said. 'For anything that goes wrong, for help, for complaints, come to me.'

'We will,' called the wife of an alderman. 'Don't you be worrying about that, love. A Lancashire lass is born complaining and dies complaining.'

As she listened to the resulting laughter, Amy realized that she was actually enjoying herself. She was optimistic. Already ideas buzzed about her brain like a cauldron of tangled colour – Ida's knitting and crochet, Mona's concept about hairdressing, her own thoughts regarding makeup and manicures. The hydro, too, might well become an extension of A Cut Above, a place where women would gather to talk about fashion and so forth. James was currently supervising the installation of a generator for electricity at the Grange. It was all happening, and Amy was glad to be a part of it.

*

Mona Walsh, having sworn that she would never enter a building that contained her past, found herself sitting in the room where she had cooked that last meal, the Christmas dinner that had never been eaten. All signs of the festive season had disappeared, cleared away by the good wife of Seth Dobson. 'Furniture's all going into storage,' she said quietly. 'Though I might as well sell it, I suppose.' She looked at the girl in Tilly's rocking-chair. 'Eeh, lass, this is a bugger and no mistake. Pardon my language.'

'That's all right. It is a bugger.' She was carrying the child of Rupert Smythe. Having put two and two together, Margot also suspected that her sister had run off to be with Rupert. What a mess. 'I shall have to tell Amy.'

'Aye, you will. No use trying to hide it for much longer, 'cos you're starting to show. A few more weeks and she'll guess for herself.' Mona's heart was stretched to breaking point. She was supposed to be at A Cut Above, but having offered this girl the choice between blue murder and visiting a doctor, she had felt obliged to accompany her to the surgery. 'I told Amy I was going to the doctor's for myself, like. But she'll be expecting me. Aren't you expected, too?'

Margot nodded.

'We'd best get going down to Mulligan's Yard, then.'

'No.'

Mona sat at the table, remembered the chicken and the gravy and Tilly's stuffing. 'You're not the first, and you'll not be the last.' She wished that she'd had a baby, married or not. If she'd had a child, there would have been somebody of her own in the world. 'We weren't close, me and our Tilly,' she said eventually.

'Oh.'

'But something like this will bring you and your sisters together.'

Margot sniffed. 'Well, Eliza is two hundred miles away, while Amy's busy with her shop. There'll be no time for me and my little problem.' She tossed her head. 'Eliza couldn't care less, anyway.'

'Amy'll care, though.'

'About the disgrace,' insisted Margot. 'About what people think and what they'll say.'

The girl was in no state to listen to sense. Mona felt that she might as well spit in the wind, because Margot had to talk to her family before listening to anyone at all. 'So what do we do now?' she asked. 'Shall we go back to Pendleton or what?'

Margot couldn't have cared less. 'I don't think I could hold up at the shop,' she said, after a long pause. 'But you might want to go along.'

Mona thought about that. She wanted to make a good impression, needed to make sure that Amy Burton-Massey took her seriously, yet she could not bring herself to abandon this poor young woman. 'We'll go home,' she announced. 'You can come to Ida's and wind some wool – she'll be at the Grange, anyway. I'm keeping my eye on you, young madam. Then, come tea-time, you and I are off to Caldwell Farm and I'll let you explain why I never turned up for my first day at work.'

Margot, too wrung-out for tears, was trying hard to come to terms with what could scarcely be described as a shock. She had known the answer all along, yet the pronouncement made this morning by a medical man had shaken her. Had she hoped, deep down, that the symptoms might indicate something easier? Oh, God. People would whisper in her presence, would point at her as she walked down the street – 'See her? Pregnant and not married. And she's supposed to have come from a good family . . .'

'It's not the end of the world,' offered Mona.

'It's the end of mine,' came the answer. 'I said Amy would be worried about what people might say – I'm doing exactly that myself.'

'Nine-day wonder,' said Mona.

'Nine-month wonder, you mean.'

The two women sat in gloomy silence for a minute or two, then Mona went to put the kettle on a gas ring in the scullery. She could offer no real help, nothing tangible. She had even considered keeping one of her two houses, allowing Margot to live away from Pendleton, but the family was known all over Bolton, and Margot was not used to being alone. 'She probably couldn't even light a fire,' Mona said, under her breath, 'let alone cook a proper meal.' It was too late, anyway. Both

260

houses were up for rent, the landlord had reimbursed Mona for improvements in John Street, so other tenants were to be installed as soon as Mona's possessions had been removed. 'Aye, it's a bugger,' she repeated, while brewing tea.

At the table, she asked the big question. 'Right, so what do you want to do?'

'About what?' Margot took a sip of hot tea, grateful for some warmth in this chilly, unloved room.

'About the baby. I mean, will you give it up for adoption?' Mona wished that she could cut out her tongue – hadn't she decided to shut up until Margot had discussed the situation with her sister?

Margot raised a shoulder. 'There are places, homes for mothers and babies. I could go to one of those and we could all pretend I'd caught TB . . .'

Mona waited for the sentence to end. It remained unfinished, so Mona spoke again. 'The baby would be taken away and given to some woman who can't have children.'

'Someone who'll want it,' Margot said.

'Aye. There's loads who'd give their right arms for a babby.'

Margot gulped down another mouthful of tea. Something had happened to her in recent days. 'I think it's moved a few times,' she said now. 'It felt as if I'd been eating greedily – as I used to – but without the pain. It's a part of my body, yet it's a separate thing, and I don't know what I'm saying.' She paused. 'I don't want it, but . . . But I still don't know what I'm saying.'

The girl was a battlefield. Although Mona had not experienced pregnancy, she had seen many a mother-to-be in the laundry, had noticed changing moods, tears, laughter that sometimes verged on the hysterical. All the women at the washhouse had been married. Even those as poor as church mice had been half of a pair. Margot had no partner . . .

'It's Rupert's,' said Margot now.

'Well, I'd gathered that for myself.'

'And he's in London, probably with my sister.' She pondered for a moment. 'Eliza is very strange,' she announced thoughtfully. 'She's like something connected to James Mulligan's new generator – switch on, switch off, no real

261

feelings. She fooled me, Mother and Amy for years, such a good egg, dutiful daughter, wonderful pianist, sugar and spice, all things nice.' She looked directly at Mona. 'There's no soul in her playing, you know.'

Mona, unsure of what to say, nodded encouragingly.

'She's cold,' Margot concluded.

'Eliza might be on the cool side,' said Mona, 'but your Amy isn't. She's a fine girl with a big heart and a good head on her shoulders.' The world on her shoulders, too, thought Mona sadly.

A faint smile paid a short visit to Margot's face. 'You make her sound like a pint of beer – a good head on it. Oh, Mona, what a mess. Why should Amy have an illegitimate nephew or niece? Who's going to want to marry me after this?'

Mona sighed heavily. 'Like you said just now, you can always give it away, love.'

The cup clattered as Margot placed it in its saucer. 'Can I?'

'I don't know, lass. Nobody does. Even you have to work hard getting an answer to that one.'

Mona stood up and pulled on her gloves. 'We'd best get out of here. It's colder in this house than it is outside.' She gazed round the walls at her mother's pictures, Victorian prints fading away, an embroidered sampler, a Home Sweet Home, a *When Did You Last See Your Father?*. 'I don't need any of it,' she said absently, 'though I suppose I'll hang on to the sewing-box and a few other bits.'

Margot's gaze followed Mona's, taking in the small trinkets and trappings that had accumulated over a lifetime or two. 'Amy says we've always to look forward. It's no use glancing over my shoulder and remembering what a fool I was with Rupert Smythe. It's like you, Mona, walking away from all your furniture. You need new things for a new start, leave regret behind.'

Mona smiled determinedly. 'You and me is in this together, lass. Come hell, high water, world war – God forbid – it's thee and me, Margot.'

'Thanks. I appreciate that.' And she did.

Our Jack and our Harry, those burly thirteen-year-old twins, were on the scene again, chopping wood, cleaning stables, trying to wash windows in temperatures that almost removed the ends of wet fingers.

Sally Hayes watched them. These brothers of Mary Whitworth were not her idea of decent people. Also, Mary had displayed for some weeks a deepening resentment for Kate Kenny and, most particularly, for Mr Mulligan. Mary was up to something again. The stealing had stopped, but there were still ongoings, plans that showed on the girl's face whenever she dropped a tightening guard.

'Sally?'

'Yes, Mrs Kenny?'

'Is this you daydreaming?'

Sally turned and smiled at a dragon who was really an angel in disguise. 'I don't like those boys,' she said. 'Couldn't we get some from the village?'

The housekeeper pondered. 'Well, we could, yes, but the Whitworths are poor and those two trek all the way from Bolton, so they must be keen.'

Sally looked over her shoulder. Both of them were grinning at her, their faces hard and set in lines etched deep by poverty and deprivation. 'I don't trust them,' she said.

'Neither do I.' Kate placed a batch of scones on the table. 'Here, lift these on to the cooling rack, Sally. No good'll come of you staring at them – it'll only worsen matters altogether.'

Mary Whitworth sauntered in, a feather duster in one hand, a letter in the other. She poked the envelope towards Kate Kenny. 'It's for you,' she said sweetly.

Kate took the letter, her eyes never leaving Mary Whitworth's face as she used a sharp knife to slice open the item of mail. 'Go and tell those two brothers of yours to stop mullarking about and get on with the jobs, or there'll be no money today.'

Mary, still brandishing the duster, left the room. Sally, who was placing the last of the scones on a cooling rack, froze when Kate dropped into her fireside rocker. 'Mrs Kenny?'

'Jesus, Mary and holy St Joseph,' breathed Kate. 'I've to get to Chester today, right away. A friend – a good friend.'

Sally waited.

'I think the weather delayed the post – the funeral's tomorrow.'

263

'I'm sorry.' Sally, not knowing what to say next, held her tongue.

'She came over to England at the turn of the century, worked for a rich family, then for another. Always well treated was Bridget, for she toiled like a horse and prayed like a saint.' She paused. 'Should have taken the veil, but she'd money to earn and send home. Aye, a prisoner of conscience, she was.'

'I'm sorry.'

Kate looked at the young maid. 'Pack me a bag, there's a good girl. Just the basics, just for one night, perhaps two. And I leave you in charge.'

Sally blanched. The two boys would be sleeping on the kitchen floor tonight. Mary was up to no good, so, if Mr Mulligan were to go out – oh, she should not be bothering about such things: Mrs Kenny's friend was dead, that was what mattered.

But, as she raced upstairs to pack Mrs Kenny's case, Sally's heart went into overdrive. There was badness in the air, a wickedness that was almost tangible. Should she speak to the master later on, ask him to get rid of Mary's brothers?

The coal cart arrived. Even from upstairs, Sally could hear the fuel clattering down its chute and into the cellar. She chose Mrs Kenny's garments and placed them in a small valise. Poor Mrs Kenny. An old friend dead, a funeral to attend. Concentrating on the task in hand, Sally placed the Whitworth family where they belonged – in the myriad bits of nonsense at the back of her mind.

TWENTY

The trouble with Jack and Harry Whitworth was that they displayed very few symptoms of common sense. If they wanted to do something they did it, never stopping for one moment to consider the possible outcome of their action. So, when they saw the coal flaps hanging open in the rear yard of Pendleton Grange, they slid down the gritty chute on to a black and jagged mountain in the cellar below. There would no longer be a need for their Mary to search for spare keys to the cellar door in the kitchen above. The fact that they needed a key to get out again simply did not occur to them – the future could take care of itself.

They were in. When the coal doors closed, when chain and padlock rattled, when all light was lost, they felt no fear, simply because they had not the imagination required to suffer that emotion. 'Dark,' mumbled Jack. 'And that slide were all covered in slack.'

'I've hurt me leg,' came the reply, 'bits of coal stuck in it where me trousers split.'

They sat in the gloomy pit for several minutes, pupils widening hungrily in the automatic search for light. 'Can't see a door.'

'Can't see any bloody thing.'

'What shall we do, then?'

'I dunno, do I? We should have waited for our Mary to find

265

a key.' Too late, a glimmer of common sense visited them – how were they going to escape? Mary had been sent out to the yard only minutes earlier with a message from Mrs Kenny. Mrs Kenny's messages were always the same, work harder, work faster, you're doing it wrong. Mary had still found no key.

'I'm hungry.'

'You're always flaming hungry.'

Silence hung heavy in the dusty air.

Then Jack was visited by a thought. 'Some bugger'll come for coal in a bit. I mean, they have to get coal, don't they?'

Another pause dragged its weary self into the arena.

'Harry?'

'What?'

'There's only him comes for coal. The housekeeper never gets it and he won't let Mary or the other one carry owt on the heavy side, like. He never lets nobody down here and that means he must have plenty to hide.' Jack sniffed. 'Her from th' orphanage thinks she's somebody. Her'd likely be too grand for coal-carrying.'

'Nobody'll be nobody when we find whoever he's got down here,' answered Harry. 'That bad Irish bugger's keeping some poor swine locked in one of these cellars. Brings food down, he does. They'll all go to jail except for our Mary.'

'Right,' announced Jack. 'Let's find the door out of this cellar into the next. If we go through all the rooms, we can save him what's been shoved down here.'

Harry considered the next move. 'I can see a bit now.'

'Aye, me and all.'

'Jack? It might not be a him, might be a her. And we could get in the papers, heroes, happen a reward.'

'Get a grip of my arm, Harry. We make our way round the walls till we find that door.'

'Have to find the bloody wall first.'

'Shurrup,' snapped Jack. 'It's got to be done.'

'Heroes,' smiled Harry. 'That's what we'll be. Flaming heroes.'

The magic had happened. Quite by accident, Peter Wilkinson had stumbled upon a small hut in the woods, a dilapidated

266

construction whose original purpose had been to shelter game-keepers while they spied on poachers. As this was winter, Wilkinson needed cover, somewhere to hide from the sight of others and from the cold during his solitary retreat. Within these boarded walls, he would commune with the Lord, would find his own salvation and, with the help of the Light, he might even find a path for Margot Burton-Massey, whose destiny surely lay in Texas.

The greatest miracle of all was a paraffin heater, a rusted item last used by an employee of the Burton-Masseys, he guessed. This treasure had responded to cleaning and was now ready for use. He could make tea and he could fry and boil, while his body would be kept above freezing point.

It hadn't been easy, not with just a bike, but the hut now contained fuel for the stove, two blankets and enough food for a week, mostly tinned and bottled stuff. Outside, in the frost, he had placed a box of bread and scones, allowing them to freeze so that their freshness could be maintained for as long as possible. His family, his customers and his fellows in the Light all believed that he had travelled to Birmingham on Temple business. But no, he was in Sniggery Woods with the Light, a Bible and ample sustenance for several days.

Because the trees were naked, he could see, with the help of binoculars, the back of Ida Hewitt's house, the edge of Caldwell Farm's garden, and a worn track that led between the two. Pendleton Grange was out of view, but that was no matter. Wilkinson concentrated on the lane, which was straight ahead when he stood in line with the shack's doorway, occasionally twisting his attention to the left in order to pick up any movement from the direction of Ida's house.

As evening dropped its shades, he watched two figures making their way from Pendleton village towards Caldwell Farm. He walked out of the hut, creeping stealthily towards this pair of companions. One was Mona Walsh, the second the girl of his dreams. Their progress was slow, while it was plain from the position of their heads that they were engaged in conversation. A dart of pure hatred struck his heart, making him gasp. Margot Burton-Massey had made a companion of Mona Walsh, who was no more than a washerwoman. He, Peter

Wilkinson, guardian of the Eternal Light, had been granted no space in the diary of Miss Margot. Mona Walsh, a one-time worshipper of the Light, had inveigled her way into the life of Wilkinson's dearly beloved.

He breathed away his anger and stepped back into the hut, closing the door in his wake. There were no windows, but three slits, each some eighteen inches wide and six inches deep, had been cut into three of the walls. Over these gamekeeper's spy-holes, Wilkinson had placed sacking, as he did not want even the palest glimmer of light to escape from his hide. Now, he would eat bread and cheese, would drink tea, would rest. She still walked in the woods, even in winter, and he had a week in which to claim her.

The sound of a motor cut into the guardian's thoughts, and he stepped outside once more. James Mulligan's car was rolling along the lane towards Caldwell Farm. He would be taking Amy Burton-Massey home after the second opening of that shop. Wilkinson had read about the shop in the *Bolton Evening News*. Any minute now, James Mulligan would be sharing space with Margot. Pores opened along Wilkinson's arms – he could feel every hair as it rose up and stood to attention.

She will never be yours, for you are the spawn of Hades. I shall take her from this place to a new life.

He blinked. How? How might he convince her? No, he must not question, must not worry. She would see the Light, would come to her senses after the cleansing, as she was truly worthy and good.

The Light is in my heart and in my soul. The Light will guide, and I must ask no questions. The flame will burn and cleanse. I am a messenger, a vessel. Praise the Lord in glory and gratitude, for He will show the way.

James pulled the car into a side track, turning off the lights and allowing the engine to idle. In spite of multiple reservations, he was going to talk to Amy. The journey from Bolton up to Pendleton had offered no opportunities for conversation, as Diane and Joe had been sitting in the back seat.

Amy bit her lip. The man had said not one word of warning before pulling off the lane, yet she had no fear of him, no sense of imminent danger. He would not hurt her; she could imagine no situation in which James Mulligan might become predatory. With her hands curled together in her lap, Amy waited.

James clasped the steering-wheel as if it were a lifebelt. Having decided to speak up, he was suddenly bereft of words. Had there been a dictionary to hand, that would have been no help, because the problem lay not within his mind but deep inside his heart. 'Amy.' He dragged the two syllables from the pit of nowhere.

'Yes?'

James cleared his tightening throat. 'Margot did not arrive at the shop, then?'

'No. Nor did Mona.'

He might be wrong, prayed to be wrong, yet he was almost certain that Margot had been trying to abort her child by riding recklessly all over the estate. 'Margot seems ill-at-ease these days.'

Amy's heart lurched.

'Have you questioned her?'

'No. No, I haven't.'

'And she has volunteered no information at all? Has she not said that she feels ill?'

'No.'

James's grip on the wheel was causing pain, so he tried to relax. 'Your sister is, I think, carrying Rupert Smythe's baby.' There, it was said. A motor taxi passed the end of the track, though neither passenger in James Mulligan's car truly noticed the vehicle.

'Amy?'

She shook herself out of her sudden stillness. 'I think I already knew that, James. Knew it and rejected it at the same time.'

He allowed a deep sigh of tension to leave his chest. 'I may be misleading myself and you, but I suspect that the absence of Margot and Mona was no coincidence. They were together today, I am sure of it.'

Amy swallowed, did not know what to say.

'I ... er ... I know of places where young mothers

269

go to give birth, then adoption is arranged . . .' The words died.

'And now Eliza is with him,' said Amy. 'I know it. She is in London with that dreadful man.'

'He'll get nowhere with her,' replied James. 'Eliza guards herself extremely well.'

'Yes . . . yes, she does.' Amy removed a glove, ran the freed hand through her hair. 'James?'

'What?'

'I cannot manage all this. It's not just Margot and . . . the baby. It's not just Eliza and her coldness towards the family, her recklessness. There's the business, the house, trying to keep track of money, balancing investment in the business with the needs at Caldwell Farm. I feel too young for all of it.'

'Let me help you,' he pleaded.

'Mother would not—'

'Louisa is dead. Even were she alive, she would have come to me, Amy. Louisa and I were becoming good friends, you know. Look,' he turned slightly in his seat, managing not to moan when the gear lever tried to bite his thigh, 'I rent a great deal of land from you at a price that is almost peppercorn. Double your charges, Amy. It will all be yours in the end, whatever.'

'Whatever,' she repeated, the consonants softened by an attempt to imitate his accent. 'Very well, you may pay double. And thank you so much.'

Words trembled on the tip of his tongue. He ached to hold her, to stroke the lines from her forehead, to . . . No. He could never do any of that, must not give in to such urges. But, oh, it was becoming so difficult . . .

'I shall speak to Margot,' she announced. 'And her wishes will be my guide. I am not surprised, you know. Margot needed love and thought she had found it. She is not a murderer, not a thief. I hope she will hold up her head— Was that Camilla's van on the lane?'

'I think so,' he replied.

'Poor little Margot,' whispered Amy.

'She will feel better when everything is out in the open.'

'Perhaps.' Amy began to cry. She leaned her head on the man's shoulder and allowed the tears to fall on his coat. 'It's too much,' she moaned, 'and I must be strong.'

'I'll be here.' This short sentence arrived after pushing its way past some powerful emotions. He wanted to be brother, father and friend to this woman. And more, so much more.

'Strong,' she repeated.

'You are stronger than you know.'

'I hope so, James.' She placed a hand on his chest and looked up at his face. 'You are such a good man.'

'An Irish upstart,' he answered.

'That, too.' Amy managed a smile.

His disobedient body craved to love her, but he could not allow any further contact. This was hardly the time for romance, anyway. He pushed her gently back into the passenger seat. 'Be calm,' he said. 'I shall come with you into the house in case . . . well, in case you need me.'

Amy dabbed at her eyes with a handkerchief. 'Wait a few minutes,' she begged. 'I don't want to arrive tear-stained.'

James Mulligan agreed. For Amy and because of Amy, he would sit in torment next to the woman he loved.

Mona was a wreck. She had spent the day with Margot and Ida, the latter knitting, the former existing in deathly silence. Ida's day off had coincided with Margot's visit to the doctor, so the three had been pushed together by this collision of circumstances.

Now Mona sat with Margot in the parlour of Caldwell Farm. Margot's eyes strayed repeatedly towards the mantel clock, while every chime of the grandmother in the corner had the girl on the edge of her seat.

'Not long now,' said Mona wearily.

'I can't do it. I can't tell her.'

'Then if you won't, I must,' was Mona's answer. 'You can't carry on this road, love. Putting it off's only making it worse for yourself and everybody else.'

Margot closed her eyes.

'I'd forgot Ida's day off.' The hours spent in Ida's cottage had been difficult for Margot. 'I thought it would have been just the two of us. See, I'm only the lodger.'

'Yes. It's no matter,' replied the younger woman.

'Still, at least the kiddies are back at school.' Mona bit her tongue. She should not have mentioned children, not while . . . yet why not? Margot needed to face up to the fact that the planet would continue to turn in spite of her own troubles.

'I suppose Rupert will have to be told,' mumbled Margot.

'Aye, well, I reckon Camilla will batter him when this all comes out. She can't stand the sight of him as it is.'

Margot's eyes opened. 'You see, it's not just the shame,' she said, 'it's him. I don't want him. I don't want to marry him.'

The older woman held her tongue.

'I can't be forced to marry, can I?'

'No, you can't.'

Margot studied her chewed nails. She had got herself out of what Mother had always termed 'that disgusting habit', yet here she was again, working her way down to the quicks. 'Marriage would give the child proper status. Yet I could never be happy with a man whose backbone is clearly made of treacle.'

Mona hid a smile. In spite of her situation, Margot remained spontaneously funny and very perceptive.

'I was a fool and I got caught out. Must I pay for the rest of my life for that stupidity? And should this baby pay?' She patted her belly. 'I know this much, Mona. Rupert would make a very poor father.'

Mona nodded thoughtfully. 'I never married, as you know. But, oh, Margot, I'd give a lot to have a son or a daughter now. Bugger the disgrace – pardon my language again, dear – aye, bugger the shame. To have someone of my own, happen a couple of grandchildren.' She paused. 'But I was never pretty, so I'd no chance of marriage – few chances of even courting. So I wasn't in the same boat as you. You could get any man, but I suppose . . . well, a baby could get in the road of any . . . any other . . .'

'I know,' sighed Margot. 'I have no chance of achieving a decent marriage, not now.'

Seconds dragged. 'If you have the child adopted,' Mona began.

'Yes,' replied Margot.

The fire belched and delivered a stream of smoke into the room. 'Mother hated that fire,' said Margot absently.

272

'I bet she did. We've got . . . we had one the same at home.'

'And now you're starting a new life, Mona.'

'I am that. Stopping with Ida till I decide where to go, working at the shop, dressing up nice. Aye, it's a fresh start.'

'You're brave,' said Margot.

'So are you,' came the reply.

A car arrived, pulled up near the front door. 'Now we'll get the measure of my backbone,' Margot said.

'Aye, and it's not treacle.'

'Jelly,' Margot answered. 'Jelly, but not quite set.'

Eliza stepped out of the car, brushing the front of her coat before walking towards the door. She paid the driver and stood watching him vaguely as he turned to go back the way he had come. She was safe now, safe for a while, at least. There would, of course, be more questions, but she was on her own little patch of England now.

Elspeth Moorhead opened the door. 'Well, you didn't stop down yon long.' The housekeeper pulled herself together. 'Sorry, Miss Eliza, but I were that surprised to see you—' The words were cut off as Eliza pushed her way into the house. 'The luggage is on the drive.' This sentence she threw over her shoulder.

Elspeth went to fetch her husband. In her opinion, Miss Blinking Eliza Burton-Massey wanted her bum smacking. Hard. With a horsewhip or some such thing.

Eliza strode into the parlour, grinding to a sudden halt when she found herself in the company of Mona Walsh. Margot, white as a sheet, was clinging to the arms of a chair and, it seemed, to the edge of sanity. 'Where's Amy?' Eliza demanded.

'Er . . . we thought you were her,' said Mona weakly.

'But I am not.' Eliza removed gloves and scarf.

'She's at the shop.' Mona felt very uncomfortable with the new arrival, yet she could not abandon Margot. 'First day today,' Mona added. 'Mr Mulligan will be fetching her home.'

'I see.' Eliza sat down. 'Ring for some tea, Margot,' she commanded.

Margot made no move.

'I'll see to it.' Mona left the room for the safer atmosphere of the kitchen.

273

The two sisters sat in silence. Margot chewed avidly at a thumbnail, while Eliza leaned back and closed her eyes. She was in something of a mess, but she had no intention of talking to Margot, who was young, silly and clearly distraught.

Minutes dragged by. Mona brought in the tea, poured, handed out cups and saucers. 'Course, he'll be taking Diane and little Joe home, too. Before coming up here, like.'

'What?' Eliza raised a perfectly arched eyebrow.

'Mr Mulligan.' Mona sat down. 'Before he brings Amy here, he'll take the kiddies home to Ida.'

Eliza sipped her tea. 'So why are you here?'

Mona almost choked. 'I . . . er . . . I should have started at the shop today, like, only I had to go to the doctor's, so I never got to the shop and—'

'Margot and I will pass on your apologies.'

Mona glanced at the younger girl. She could not leave poor Margot to the tender mercies of this cold-blooded creature. 'I'd sooner see Amy myself, ta.'

'As you wish.' Clearly annoyed, Eliza left the room, cup and saucer in one hand, a leather bag in the other.

Margot swallowed audibly. 'I can't say anything while Eliza's here. She'll just mock me, I'm sure.'

Things were becoming rather complicated for Mona. She wasn't keen on the dark, so the idea of walking back to the village was not a pleasant one. Also, the unexpected return of Eliza threw a spanner in the works. 'We have to get Amy on her own.'

'But—'

'Never mind but, Margot. Eliza might well be here tomorrow, then the day after that. It's got to be done. We've spent all day working our way up to it, so . . .'

Another vehicle arrived. They heard Elspeth opening the door, waited for Amy's voice, heard a different one. Mona reached over and touched Margot's hand. 'She'll not be long, love. This is her first day and she'll have been busy.'

'Where is she?'

Mona shivered involuntarily. 'That's Camilla, isn't it?'

Margot nodded.

What the hell now? wondered Mona. The house was

becoming as crowded as Trinity Street station during the Bolton holiday fortnight. 'It'll be all right,' she told Margot, without conviction.

Margot shrank into the chair. It would definitely not be all right.

'Me foot's stuck,' Jack moaned. 'Hang on.' He dragged himself out of a pile of coal. 'And we've come in circles,' he complained. 'Back in the bloody coal-hole again.'

'Enough here for fires all year round in our house,' grumbled Harry. 'There's nowt else for it, Jack, we have to find the kitchen door and bang on it till we get let out.'

Jack agreed wholeheartedly. 'Far as I can tell, the one locked down here must be gagged or summat, it's that quiet. Mind, we can't have been in all the rooms.' They had found a locked door, had clattered their fists against it. Whoever was shut inside must have been bound and gagged.

A thought wandered through Harry's skull and he caught it as it passed. 'We don't know where the kitchen door is, 'cos we never found no stairs. I'd kill for a cup of water.'

They slid down a wall and sat side by side. 'Jack?'

'What?'

'Kitchen door has to be near the coal-hole. You wouldn't keep coal in a cellar miles away from the kitchen.' Harry congratulated himself on his brilliance. 'Stairs must be in here, then. At the other side of this pile.' He waved a hand towards the coal. 'We have to get past the coal to the other side. So we'll stick to the edge, like, go round instead of up.'

'Right.' Jack, too, was astounded by his brother's cleverness.

They shuffled along, hit the end of a wall. 'It's a wall inside the walls,' said Harry. 'Come this way.' They walked around a structure built to keep the coal within its designated space, turning with the wall into a clean walkway. Except for a couple of holes from which coal could be taken, the area was free of clutter. 'And her up there'll bloody kill us, too,' concluded Harry, as they placed themselves side by side on the bottom stone step.

They sat in gloomy silence for several minutes. Then Jack spoke up. 'Right, you go and bang on the door.'

'Why me?'

'Why not?' asked Jack. 'You're the brains.'

Harry pondered. 'Let's hang on a bit, see what happens.'

'You're the one what's thirsty,' said Jack.

'Aye, and we're stopping here for a bit, so shut your cake'ole.'

They sat, shivering on icy stone, a mountain of fuel in front of them. 'We could happen light a fire,' suggested Jack.

'Shurrup,' snapped Harry.

Jack shut up.

Camilla Smythe, red-faced and breathless, threw open Eliza's bedroom door. For several seconds, she steadied herself on the jamb, her eyes riveted to the figure inside the room. So beautiful, so rotten, this woman was. Like the Bible's whited sepulchre, Eliza Burton-Massey was all shell and no living innards.

The lovely woman, prone on the bed, lifted herself into a sitting position. 'Camilla?' Her voice was clear, showed no sign of surprise. She propped herself against pillows, folded her arms, arranged her face in what was meant to be a sympathetic expression.

The unexpected visitor strode into the room, stopping only when her knees hit the side of the bed. 'I want the truth. No nonsense, do you hear?'

'You should not rush about so, dear,' came the reply. 'Your colour is very high and—'

'Shut up!' screamed Camilla.

Eliza almost smiled. 'If I shut up, as you so elegantly advocate, then I can tell neither truth nor lies.'

'You killed him,' whispered Camilla.

Eliza shrugged. 'There then is still no reason for me to speak, since your mind is clearly settled on its own version of the event. I was in the house when Rupert had his unfortunate accident, but I played no part in what happened.' She paused fractionally. 'I am very sorry for your loss.'

Camilla's hands tightened themselves into twin balls of fury. 'The event? My version of the event? My mother is devastated and my father is permanently drunk. Rupert was not a particularly good man, but he was still my brother and their son.'

'He fell,' Eliza pronounced.

'He fell from the steps just outside your room.'

'That is the assumption,' drawled Eliza. 'The stairs in those narrow London houses are difficult. They have many turns and twists. Rupert was drunk – the police said so. He was probably coming up to tell me something.'

'And you ran away. After the police interviewed you, you rushed back here.'

'The police know where I am.' Eliza closed her eyes for a moment. He was tearing at her, spoiling her clothes, forcing his hard mouth on to her lips, grabbing, squeezing flesh, pressing himself against her body.

'Eliza?'

'What?'

Camilla swallowed. 'Did he . . . assault you?'

'Did he assault me? Oh, no, of course not.' The door had burst inward, forced open by the weight of their bodies. The catch on that door had never been good. No other tenants lived up in the roof. She had been alone. She was alone now. No, he was with her. 'Please,' he begged.

'Never,' she spat into his face.

He was strong, so strong for a thin man. They fell on to the bed. She could not win, could not defeat his object. Object. She lifted a candlestick from her bedside table and crashed it into his temple. Heavy, he was so heavy, breathing, alive, asleep. There was very little blood, just a few flecks on her pillow case, and she had changed that later.

'Eliza?' demanded Camilla.

Carefully, she pulled herself free of him, washed the candlestick, washed herself, arranged her clothes. She covered his head with the pillowcase to avoid further staining, dragged him inch by inch from the bed and on to the landing, using her foot to launch him down the stairs. As quick as a flash, she ran back into her room, picked up a book, sat by the window for a few seconds.

Emerging almost immediately from her refuge, Eliza stood, book in hand, a scream forced from her throat. Someone

277

announced that he had broken his neck, the landlady had hysterics, Eliza descended the stairs and cried prettily.

'Eliza?' Camilla was almost screaming.

Elspeth Moorhead dashed in. 'Whatever's the matter?'

Camilla turned. 'He's dead,' she said clearly. 'She killed him.' Her voice rose until it filled the house. 'Eliza murdered Rupert,' Camilla shouted.

Elspeth placed an arm around Camilla's shoulders. 'Come with me, love.'

Sobbing, Camilla was led from the room.

As she closed the door, Elspeth looked into the beautiful face of Eliza Burton-Massey. The lovely eyes were wide open and, for once, they revealed an expression. Elspeth could not be sure, would possibly never be sure that what she saw was a gleam of absolute triumph.

She guided poor Camilla down the stairs and into the kitchen. It was time to produce the cup that sometimes failed to cheer.

Upstairs, Eliza lay back on her bed. The few days spent in London had taught her two things: she must never trust a man and she was not made for theatre. Rejection hurt more than any physical wound. Her singing voice, clear but too thin to travel, had failed to impress at auditions. Her playing, too, had been judged nondescript, and she had been left with one asset – her perfect body.

Eliza had been offered a position on the day of Rupert's death. For three pounds a week, she was invited to sit naked and motionless behind a thin layer of voile while men stared at her. Which brought her back to the first point, the one about never trusting men.

She absolved herself of the sin of murder. No man would ever use her until she agreed to be used. That his intention had been rape was very clear, though he might not have achieved his goal after drinking so much. But he had annoyed her beyond endurance. She had left him, the theatre and London behind.

What now? Her brain, never still, burrowed its way towards the future. Bolton, grey and particularly dull at this time of year, held little promise for Eliza. A cotton town was not the

278

place for her. Up here, on the fringe of Pendleton, there was land and more land, but—

But. There was also James Mulligan. He was the sort who could make things happen, a man with plans. If she could capture him, persuade him to hang on to Pendleton Grange, then she would be the wife of a very rich man. Amy and Margot could keep Caldwell Farm, of course, but the lion's share should belong with Mulligan and his wife.

Mulligan's wife. Eliza closed her eyes and, with her problems solved, drifted into restful sleep.

TWENTY-ONE

I love you. An arrangement of eight letters in a form that could change lives for ever, a short statement, such a long stride. He could never tell her how he felt, how the pain was becoming unendurable. 'Mona was not at the cottage,' he said, the words limping from a tongue that ached to say so much more. 'She is at the farm with Margot, I am sure of that.'

'Yes.' Amy's mind buzzed, while her heart lurched about like an ill-controlled marionette. Trouble, more trouble. It was as if she sat somewhere near the electricity that was being generated at Pendleton Grange, as though she were being penetrated, invaded by a power that was invisible and, therefore, unavoidable. Margot. Poor, stupid little girl. 'Camilla's there, too,' she mumbled. 'That was her van earlier.'

'Yes.'

She turned and looked at him; his profile was clearly delineated even in this poor light. 'Your face has softened,' she whispered, surprised as soon as the words were out.

'Perhaps I have softened.'

Amy produced a hollow laugh. 'Still a tough businessman, Mr Mulligan.'

'I try.'

This was nothing to do with Margot, Amy realized with a jolt. She was in a small metal world, a wheeled container that took people from place to place, and the electricity was in here,

280

in the car. She turned her face, rubbed a hole in mists of breath and stared out through glass that merely reflected herself. Then she saw him there too, watched as his head moved slowly until he was watching her. No.

'We must go, Amy,' he told her.

Away from, or towards? she wondered fleetingly. Then Margot crashed into her mind once more and she pulled herself up. How could she daydream while Margot was in trouble?

'Amy?'

Although she owned a short name that lived for just a split second before falling from his lips, she heard the caress. She was not in love. She had no intention of being in love. 'Let's go, then.' Her voice shook, moved air in the car until it shivered, reminding her of Sunday mornings when church bells rattled the atmosphere. 'I am walking into hell,' she said quietly.

'There is supposed to be no hell on earth,' he answered.

'Oh, yes, there is.' Hell was a father wounded in body and mind, a man who gave away the security of his family at the turn of a card. Hell was a mother dying young, a heartless sister, another who was probably pregnant. It was a shop that would not care for itself, a household run by a woman too young to be in charge. Hell was sitting beside a man who might comfort her, a man she began to fear. No, no, she had no fear of James Mulligan. Her terror had been formed within herself, because some kind of magnetism was luring her in his direction. 'Yes, hell is here,' she insisted.

'It will be all right,' he promised.

'Will it?' Tears pricked, threatened to tumble again.

'Believe me, Amy.'

'I shall try.'

He moved the car to the lane, turned left and carried on towards Caldwell Farm. Camilla's van was slewed at a crazy angle, wheels turned as if she had stopped while taking a sharp bend. Immediately James's mind was on red alert. What had happened here? Had Margot lost the child? Was Rupert back from London and on the prowl? Had something terrible taken place?

'Perhaps she wants to talk about A Cut Above.' Amy

referred to the shop's planned meeting at the Pack Horse Inn, an occasion for which Camilla Smythe would be catering. 'We're having a fashion evening,' Amy concluded hopefully. No, no, that had already been discussed. So what had brought Camilla out in the dark and in weather that was uninviting?

'Perhaps Camilla simply needs to visit a friend,' he suggested.

'I don't know why,' Amy said quietly, 'but I don't want to go inside.'

She was a woman of instinct, he told himself. All females suffered from instinct, but this one was brighter than most, alert, antennae always at the ready. 'It must be done,' he said.

'Yes, I do realize that. After all, we cannot set up house in a car, can we?'

Set up house. James felt sure that he could never set up house at all, let alone with a woman as precious as this one. 'Come along now,' he said brusquely. 'Whatever, it must be faced.'

Knowing this to be true, she stepped out of the car and gazed upon a world that seemed peaceful snuggled beneath its light blanket of snow. After taking a last look at sanity, Amy Burton-Massey stepped into the future. By her side, a dark-clad tower of strength walked with her. Because of his presence, she found the ability to compose herself. And, in spite of everything, she found herself hoping that he might always be there.

Camilla pulled herself away from Elspeth's restraining arms. 'I have to go back up there,' she shouted. 'Please, I beg you not to stand in my way.'

Elspeth, frailer than she had been, now almost in her seventies, released her hold. 'Don't,' she begged, freeing Camilla suddenly. 'There's trouble enough in this house . . .' The words died. She had not the strength to argue.

Camilla, having banged herself against a wall, rubbed her shoulder. 'I have to get there before she does. I am trying to prevent further problems by getting Eliza out of here. Yes, I must arrive first and make an effort to—'

'What?' Elspeth, breathless after her exertions, sank

into a ladder-backed chair. 'Get where before what happens?'

Camilla inhaled to steady herself. 'I have to reach Eliza before Mother does.'

Elspeth closed her eyes, placed elbows on the table and cupped her chin with her hands. She had had more than enough. Mona and Margot were in the parlour, sitting as still as stones, plainly expecting the roof to fall in. Miss Eliza was upstairs in a huff, while Camilla, face as red as her hair, was storming about the kitchen like a lioness hunting prey.

'She killed my brother,' announced Camilla, with certainty, as she paced the floor. 'I know she did, I know it, I know it.' To emphasize her words, she punched the air with balled fists.

Elspeth shook her head. It was all beyond her and she could contain the situation no more. 'Do what you want,' she said wearily. 'To be honest, I'm getting to the stage where I couldn't care less.'

'I know he was a rotter but—'

'Please,' begged the housekeeper, 'just don't tell me any more, because my head's fit to bust.'

'Sorry, but—'

'Be sorry somewhere else. I don't mean to be rude, miss, only . . . well, I can't take no more and that's the top and bottom.'

'Sorry,' repeated Camilla. 'She, of course, doesn't seem to care about anything.'

Elspeth, who knew that Camilla referred to Eliza, kept her counsel. It had been her experience on this particular day that the least said was the soonest mended – well, the soonest avoided. Elspeth did not like Eliza, but murder? Was she capable of that? She probably was, thought Elspeth. There was a mean streak in the middle Burton-Massey girl, a downright nastiness that seemed not to have visited Margot or Amy. Such an angel, too, such a gentle, sweet person on the surface . . . 'We share a name, you know,' whispered Elspeth. 'Eliza and Elspeth are both Elizabeth.'

Camilla looked at Elspeth and felt like holding on to her, felt like clinging to anyone human, but she knew that she would find no comfort today. 'Rupert's dead,' she mumbled. 'My brother is dead, Elspeth. And my mother is convinced that Eliza was involved.' She paused. 'So am I.'

Elspeth felt the same, though she made no effort to speak. When it came to the madam upstairs, nothing would surprise Elspeth, nothing at all.

Margot looked at Mona. 'So he's dead,' she whispered. The whole house had been shaken by Camilla's loud declarations. 'Well, at least I won't have to worry about being forced to marry.'

Mona noticed that there was little sorrow in the girl, no apparent feeling for the man who had fathered the unborn child. 'Don't you care about him being dead, then?'

Margot studied her bitten nails. 'Yes. Yes, I feel sorry for his parents and for Camilla.' She looked up. 'And very worried about Eliza. If what Camilla shouted is true, then Eliza might go to prison – or worse.'

'No regrets for him, love?'

The younger woman nodded slowly. She placed both hands on her stomach and stared through the window. 'He might have improved, you know, might have settled down and become decent. But I have my doubts.' After a few seconds, she rose and paced the floor. 'I miss my father. But, then, I knew him, you see. This little one will not miss Rupert, as he will never have known him.'

'Might be a lass.'

Margot smiled sadly. 'No, it's a boy. I know it's a boy, Mona.'

'Really?'

'Oh, yes.'

They heard the car, waited, listened as Amy entered the house. She was talking, and the answering voice belonged to James Mulligan. 'I'll take him on one side,' whispered Mona. 'Give you two a chance to be alone.'

'No need,' replied Margot. 'He knows about the baby. He saw me riding and knew I was trying to . . .' Her voice died. 'This child has survived so much, Mona. I cannot give him away.'

'No. I've known that since this morning, love.'

Another car arrived. 'Who's that?' asked Margot.

'We seem to have a houseful,' said Mona. She hoped that

284

this was not the police, prayed that Eliza would not be arrested.

A door slammed, then another voice arrived, loud, hysterical. 'Where is she?' screamed a female.

'Mrs Smythe,' Margot mouthed.

'Where are you going?' Amy's voice from the hallway was cut off by the sound of Helen Smythe's screams.

The woman pushed her head into the parlour, scanned Mona and Margot, retreated. 'Where is your other sister?' she demanded.

'In London,' answered Amy.

'She's here.' Helen Smythe's voice took on a hysterical edge. 'The police in London said she had returned home. My son is dead. He was pushed down a staircase by your sister. She may have fooled the police, but she can't pull the wool over my eyes.'

James Mulligan entered the parlour, nodded at the two occupants before stepping out again and closing the door. Mona did not know what to say, what to do. The situation was changing by the minute, and the chances of Margot getting to talk to Amy were looking slim.

The door opened once more and Amy stepped inside. Her hands, shaking with nervousness, clutched each other in an effort to stop the tremors. 'There is going to be merry hell,' she told the parlour's occupants, 'so tell me and be done with it, Margot.'

Margot gulped down a lump of panic.

'Come on, love,' begged Mona.

Amy crossed the room and knelt before her sister. 'Margot, I love you. Many people love you.'

The tears began to flood silently down the younger girl's face. Mona, suddenly experiencing a choking sensation, got up quickly and stood by the window where her own eyes began to leak away the tensions of the day.

'Pregnant,' wept Margot.

'I know, dear,' soothed her sister.

'Rupert.' The name was fractured by a sob into two separate syllables.

'Yes, I know that, too.' Amy kept herself outwardly calm.

James had shot upstairs to deal with whatever was happening with Camilla and Mrs Smythe, and Amy's first duty, as head of the clan, was to minister to the youngest of the wounded.

Margot's weeping subsided. 'Eliza came home.' She drew in a shuddering breath. 'And she's in her bedroom and Camilla went up earlier and we all heard her shouting that Rupert is dead and Eliza killed him.'

Amy placed her head in Margot's lap, felt the little bulge, wished that she had paid closer attention to this beloved sister. 'Sweetheart, I am so sorry about Rupert. I know you loved him a great deal.'

Margot laid a hand on Amy's head. 'No, I thought I loved him. And, you know, I am sorry he is dead because he won't get the chance to redeem himself in this world.'

The older sister sat back on her heels, each quivering hand clutching one of Margot's. What a way for this to happen, what a terrible, lonely route Margot had taken to merit the words about to be spoken. 'Margot.' Amy squeezed the nail-bitten fingers. 'You have grown up, sweetheart.' Yes, Margot was a woman now.

James held on to Helen Smythe's flailing arms, pulled her against the door. 'If you try to attack Eliza one more time, I shall fetch a policeman.'

Camilla, who was shielding Eliza against the opposite wall, was witnessing a scene she could not have imagined in the worst of nightmares. Her mother had gone wild. Helen Smythe's hair, which, apart from the odd trim, had not seen scissors in years, had escaped from bondage and was spreading in fine wisps all over her face. Between the fronds, mad eyes darted from side to side, narrowing malevolently each time they alighted on her proposed victim. Camilla, shocked to the core, pressed her weight against Eliza Burton-Massey.

'A policeman?' screamed Helen. 'Bring one, bring 'em all, because I want this creature arrested for murder.'

'She has already been questioned,' said James, his tone as reasonable as possible given the circumstances. 'You heard her, Mrs Smythe. The death of Rupert is being treated as an accident.'

Helen bared her teeth. 'She followed him down to London secretly. She was probably trying to force him into marriage.'

Eliza, who was not in the least frightened by the scene, decided to put the woman straight. 'I had no interest in your son as a potential husband, Mrs Smythe. The room in the attic was cheap; I rented it while I looked for work.'

'So,' spat Helen, 'he took an interest in you, tried to kiss you, I suppose? And you killed him.'

You are getting warm, Eliza mused, since your darling son was trying to rape me. Well, this woman would never believe that. Who would believe it? She was her own sole witness. 'I was reading,' she said clearly. 'Someone tapped on my door. The landing outside the room was very shallow. I imagine that he stepped back and stumbled.'

'Imagine all you like,' yelled Helen. 'You saw our money and you chased after him.'

Eliza smiled. 'Had Rupert been the last man on the planet, I would not have married him, Mrs Smythe.'

James shivered. The involuntary movement passed right through his body and trembled along the arms of the woman he held. Staring into the lovely eyes of Eliza Burton-Massey sent fear right into the depths of his soul. No matter what the police believed, James realized that he was almost certainly in the presence of a killer.

Eliza returned his gaze steadily. She intended to lay claim to him at the earliest opportunity. In fact, had she thought things through before leaving Lancashire, she might have missed out London altogether. James was the one for her.

'How dare you?' cried Helen. 'When your family is brought so low, you are in no position to make choices. We managed to put a stop to the business between Rupert and your sister for the same reason. Not good enough.'

'Your son was the lowest life-form in England,' said Eliza, the words undecorated by any emotion. 'He probably took the virginity of my younger sister.'

Helen renewed her struggles. 'Let me go, let me go!' she called repeatedly.

James hung on for as long as possible, releasing his hold only when Helen managed to turn and rake nails down both sides of his face, catching a corner of his left eye in the process. She then leaped across the room and drove a fist into her own daughter's stomach, causing Camilla to drop like a felled ox. Immediately, Helen laid into Eliza, pummelling and scratching, taking handfuls of hair, then throwing the girl on to the bed.

Eliza rolled and dropped to the floor, grabbing Helen's legs and pulling until the woman fell heavily. 'Touch me again,' she whispered, 'and I shall do murder.' She rose to her feet. 'No one touches me,' she said, her breathing still easy and even. 'Remember that, Mrs Smythe.'

As all this happened within a matter of seconds, James and Camilla had been powerless. James wiped blood from his face, dabbed at the sore eye, while Camilla, winded, struggled back to her feet. 'Mother?' she screamed.

'Get her out of here,' snapped Eliza.

Camilla turned on the girl. 'I know you did it. I know you killed my brother.'

'You know nothing,' Eliza replied, her eyes fixed to the woman on the floor.

'You may have had reason to strike out,' continued Camilla. 'Did he attack you? Did he?'

James helped Helen Smythe to her feet, placing her in a small nursing chair just inside the door. Helen, winded and shaken, made no attempt to speak.

'This is my bedroom,' said Eliza clearly. 'A bedroom is a sanctuary, a private place. No one should ever enter another person's room without invitation.' She turned to Camilla. 'So take that woman you call Mother away from here, please. And do not come back, ever.'

Camilla, afraid and hurt, gathered up her mother and led her from the room.

Eliza sat at the dressing-table and rearranged her disordered hair. 'It's a good thing that I can spare some of this,' she remarked, tossing her head, 'because that dreadful woman took enough to make a wig, I'm sure.'

James sank into the chair recently vacated by Helen Smythe. He could not believe his eyes. Here sat Eliza, probably a murderess, certainly a cool customer, preening, applying powder, a dab of rouge, some lip colour. Her hands were steady as she stroked a pencil across beautifully arched eye-brows, while she coloured in her lips. She was a fascinating piece of work.

She turned and awarded him a brilliant smile. 'There,' she said, 'no lasting damage.'

His tongue seemed to have stuck. What might he say to a creature such as this? How dutiful a daughter she had been, how pretty a pianist, how lovely a sister. 'What have you done?' he achieved, after some seconds.

'What have I done?' She raised shoulders and hands. 'Nothing. It was an accident, James. You do believe me, don't you?' She fastened an alluring smile to her lips. 'James, apart from Amy, you know me better than anyone.' She sidled up to him. 'We have always been good friends, you and I.'

His feet felt as if they had been riveted to the floor by steel bolts. She looked like a very beautiful film star, one whose act-ing went into every slow step. 'You were a good friend to Sally, if you remember,' he said. His feet still refused to budge a fraction. 'But you dropped her when it suited you. The girl was devastated; she worshipped you.'

She stopped moving for a moment. Ah, yes, she had tried to persuade the girl to travel to London with her. 'Sally is a servant,' she said now. 'I tried to help her, but one can only do so much for the under-educated.'

James inhaled in an effort to keep his fury contained. 'Sally Hayes is one of the cleverest people I know,' he said softly. 'She is an avid reader and not just of fiction.'

Eliza laughed. 'Such a philanthropist, James. You even lifted the Hewitts out of the slums.'

'A worthy trio,' he replied. How could Eliza remain so cool when, only moments earlier, she had been engaged in a physical fight with a woman at least twice her age? He found his feet and backed away from her, his hands guiding him through the door and towards the landing. 'Are you going to push me, too, Eliza?'

She stopped moving, blinked slowly. 'What?'

'You pushed Rupert. Will you do the same to me?'

'Of course not, James. I love you, have loved you for the longest time and,' she pulled herself up, straightening visibly, 'I did not kill Rupert Smythe,' she said emphatically.

'Ah.'

'And what do you mean by "ah"? Am I to take it that you, along with those dreadful Smythe women, believe that I could deliberately take a human life?'

'Did he attack you?' James asked.

She inclined her head to one side. 'He tried several times to kiss me, but I would not allow it. Who knows what his intentions were when he came up to the attic?'

'If it was self-defence, Eliza, you must inform the police.'

This was incredible. She stood now within a stride of the man of her dreams, and she was losing him. She was gorgeous and she knew it. For as long as she could remember, men had almost fallen at her feet. Fallen. She blinked again, saw the man's body tumbling, rolling, crashing. 'I thought you liked me.' The words emerged in a childlike tone. 'You listened to my playing – I played for you, only for you.'

He watched her closely, saw that her expression changed only slightly as she spoke. 'What are you, Eliza? For your mother, you were perfect. Then, when she died, you became manipulative, cold, unfeeling. Or were you like that all the time? Is life a play, a stage where you strut and act out scenes to suit yourself?'

She shook her head slowly. 'All I wanted was to get out, to go and see the world.'

'And the world does not want you – is that it?'

Eliza raised her shoulders. 'I came back because Rupert Smythe died. I could not remain in a house where a friend had died, and I needed the comfort of my family, the safety of my home.'

'You need nothing, you need no one,' he said.

'I need you.'

He paused. 'You could have moved to another house in London.' Again, he waited. 'But offers of work did not come in – am I right?'

'It was early days,' she answered quickly.

'Yet you gave up and came home, to a place you despise.'

She blinked again, more quickly this time. 'I needed to come back to think,' she said. 'To think.'

290

He gazed on her as she retreated into herself, saw the light in her eyes dimming, noticed that the corners of her pretty mouth were now downturned. She had killed the father of her own niece or nephew, the lover of her younger sister. At this moment, she resided in a place where none of that had happened . . . No. Amy had been right after all. There was hell on earth and Eliza was a part of it, was possibly reliving the events that had taken place in London. 'Eliza?'

She frowned. 'James?'

'Yes?'

'Don't you love me?'

He breathed deeply. Standing at the top of a staircase within reach of Eliza Burton-Massey was not a good idea. 'No,' he replied, 'I do not love you.'

'Ah.' The syllable emerged slowly, as if she had to give great thought to the response. Everyone loved her. She was universally admired and desired. This man could surely be no exception to the rule? He was playing hard to get, she decided, was trying to make the seduction scenes more interesting.

Well, two could play that game. She brushed past him, failing to notice how he shrank back as she passed. 'I am going out for a walk,' she announced to the house in general when she reached the hallway. 'I need to clear my head.'

James slid down the wall and crouched at the top of the stairs. She had gone and the air was fresher.

TWENTY-TWO

Mary heard the banging just after seven o'clock. Sally was in another part of the house, busy being in charge while Mrs Kenny attended a funeral. With her feet up on the fireguard, Mary was taking advantage of a day without the sarcastic Irishwoman. She sipped at hot, sweet tea and meandered through a *Bolton Evening News*, her feet and legs warmed by glowing coals, head propped on a cushion normally reserved for Kate Kenny's brief spells of respite.

Mary was not best pleased. For a start, her younger brothers had disappeared from the face of the earth and Mam would need an explanation. Then, to add insult to injury, Sally Hayes had been appointed boss in the absence of the housekeeper. Mary had served months at the Grange before the arrival of madam. Ah, well, let her do it all; Mary had no intention of budging till the man of the house returned.

When the cellar door rattled, Mary almost shot out of her skin. The person trapped down there had finally managed to escape. It might be a mad creature, she thought, as she dropped the newspaper and placed a fist against her heart. Perhaps Mr Mulligan had some weird relative down in the cellar, a human who was not quite human, a thing with red eyes, long beard, black stumps for teeth.

For several seconds, she remained glued to her seat. Where was bloody Mulligan? He was the sort of man you could set

292

the clock by, usually home by six, dinner in the kitchen, long chats with Mrs Kenny, then down to the cellar, up to bed. Mary and Sally always left the two adults alone in the evenings, coming down into the kitchen only to clear up and make a bit of supper for themselves. Well, his dinner would be dried to nothing tonight . . . the door rattled noisily again.

The trouble with Pendleton Grange was the thickness of the doors. The doors upstairs were not as heavy, but eavesdropping on the ground floor was almost an impossibility. The cellar door was the most substantial of all, a great heavy thing, inches thick, four long black hinges required to keep it in position. And some poor beggar was trying to get out of the prison below this very kitchen.

A thought dawned. Harry and Jack had disappeared very suddenly this afternoon and the coal had been delivered. Oh, God. Had they slid down the chute? She stood up and crept across the floor, placing her ear against solid oak. Had they gone down there? And, if they had, was something torturing them?

Whatever, thought Mary, she was in trouble. Harry and Jack were her brothers, so she could well be blamed for their misadventures. As for whatever lived down there, Mary was afraid to death of it. She bent to the keyhole. 'Jack?' she shouted, in a tremulous whisper.

'Mary?'

Blood and stomach pills, they were locked in there. 'Have you found him?' she whispered again.

'Who?'

'The bloody prisoner.' Shouting in whispers was having a serious effect on Mary's vocal cords. 'The one what's being kept down there.' She coughed, then pressed her ear against the hole once more.

'Just a load of coal,' answered Jack. 'All the other rooms is empty and there's just one locked. We couldn't hear nobody, neither. We come down through the coal-hole because you didn't find no key. And we're thirsty.'

'Keep quiet while I think.'

Mary paced about the kitchen. If one of her brothers had fallen down the chute, that might have been accepted as an

293

accident. But both? No, hang on, she told herself. Perhaps the story might work if one had fallen down the chute and the other had gone to the rescue. Only why hadn't they shouted to the coalman? Oh, God, what was she going to say?

'Mary?' The stage whisper shot out of the keyhole and right across the room.

She returned to the cellar. 'Shurrup,' she snapped. 'Little Orphan Sally's about and if she hears you my job'll be took away. You have to wait.'

'We're thirsty.'

'I know. Keep quiet while I think.'

'Mary – we'll die!'

She filled a small watering-can at the sink, brought it to the cellar door. 'Put your mouth against the keyhole.' She poured. 'Did you get any?'

'A bit,' replied Harry.

Mary spent ten full minutes repeatedly emptying the watering-can through the keyhole and into her brothers' mouths. Then she ordered them to go away from the door while she had a long ponder. There had to be another key somewhere. But where? She had searched the kitchen from top to bottom, drawers, cupboards, pots and pans, bread-bins, potato baskets, tea-caddies, flour containers, fruit boxes, sacks, shopping-bags.

He would come home eventually, would go down the cellar to do whatever he did . . . Mary shot across the kitchen yet again. 'You there?'

Harry's voice answered. 'We're hungry.'

'Well, if you think I'm shoving bread and dripping through this here keyhole, you can bloody think again.' Her brain was in a whirl. 'Get back down with the coal,' she ordered. 'Mr Mulligan'll be here any minute.'

She waited for a response, ear flattened against wood. 'There's a gap,' said Harry. 'Only a little 'un, but you could shove summat under it.'

Mary looked up at the ceiling. 'Jaysus,' she muttered, in an almost perfect imitation of Kate Kenny. 'Not one more word,' she said to the keyhole. 'I'll do what I can, then bugger off away from this door.'

'Right,' came the answer.

There followed five or so minutes of frantic activity while Mary cut bread so thin as to be almost transparent. She covered the results with smears of plum jam and posted them beneath the cellar door. The boys grabbed and pulled, causing bits to break away, while Mary, frantic about the mess, used a dull ham-knife to push crumbs towards her starving siblings. When the two daft beggars got out of there, she would kill them, she really would.

'What are you doing?'

Mary swung round to face Sally. 'I were – I were scraping summat up off the floor,' she replied. 'I don't know where it come from, like.'

Sally was not amused. She was worried about Mr Mulligan, who was seldom as late as this. 'I might go down to the cottage,' she said, 'to see if he brought Diane and Joe back home.'

'Please yourself, Sally.' Mary spoke loudly, her mouth as near as possible to the keyhole.

'Stand up,' advised Sally. 'I hope you're not trying to get down there. It's nothing to do with us, whatever's in the cellar.'

'I'm cleaning – I told you.'

Sally looked at the clock, picked up the bread-knife. 'Have you been eating bread and jam?'

'Why? Is it a crime?' Mary sauntered towards the table.

'You've made enough mess.'

'I'll see to it.' The older girl could see that Sally was in a bit of a state. 'I don't know why you're worrying, he's big enough to look after himself.'

'It's just a feeling,' mused Sally out loud. 'As if there's something wrong. Have you ever had a feeling like that?'

Had she ever? Here stood Mary Whitworth, two daft thirteen-year-old lummox-headed brothers in the cellar with God alone knew what, jam all over her hands, job hanging by a thread. But she wanted Sally to go out. 'My mam always says you should follow them feelings,' she said. 'They're called sixth sense.'

'Yes, I've read about that.' Sally sat down at the table.

Oh, heck, thought Mary. Surely Little Orphan Sally wasn't going to start being friendly, didn't intend to kick off with a nice chat while Jack and Harry were just yards away?

'One of us should look for him,' Sally said.

'I'm frightened of the dark,' replied Mary quickly.

'You?' Sally almost laughed. 'Frightened of nowt, you. If your family were frightened of darkness, there'd be a lot less burglaries down in Bolton.'

Mary refused to be riled. What Sally had said was probably true, but Mary still didn't like it. People had to live and—

'I hope he hasn't had an accident,' said Sally now. 'I'm not that keen on motor cars. I mean, you can tell a horse what to do, but an engine's not the same.'

'No,' replied Mary. 'He could be in a ditch.'

That did the trick. Sally leaped from her chair, grabbed her outdoor things from a peg and dashed towards the door. She turned. 'Mary?'

'What?'

'If he comes back, tell him I'm looking for him.'

'Right. I'll tell him to go and look for you while you're out looking for him.'

Sally fixed a stern eye on her opponent. Mary didn't realize it, but she was picking up a lot of Mrs Kenny's words and mannerisms. The difference was that Kate Kenny, underneath the witty comments, was a decent person. 'You want to shut yourself in a drawer with all the other knives,' commented Sally, 'keep all the sharp edges in the one place.'

Mary offered a rather stiff smile. 'I were only trying to cheer you up,' she said, 'take the edge off things, like.' Even now, she could not resist goading Sally.

'You'll cut yourself, you will,' snapped Sally, before leaving the house.

Mary felt as if she might be sick. She leaned over the huge kitchen sink and retched fruitlessly. Where was the key to the padlocked outside coal doors? And, even if she found it, would Daft Harry and Dafter Jack be able to climb the steep chute?

She gave up the idea of vomiting and returned to the fireside. With no other options to choose from, she was going to have to sit this one out and deny all knowledge of her brothers' predicament. Except – oh, heck. There'd be all sorts of crumbs and bits of jam on the other side of the door. And once Mr Mulligan opened it . . .

Mary, like the rest of the Whitworth clan, had one saving grace to her credit. To a man, all the Whitworths were excellent sleepers. She nodded, leaned her head on Mrs Kenny's cushion, woke with a jolt, wondered what was going to become of her. But the fire was warm and the chair was comfortable.

Within five minutes of Sally's leaving, Mary Whitworth was fast asleep and dreaming of coal cellars, coal doors and keys.

'There was a light, Gran, honest.' Diane stood with arms akimbo in front of the fireplace. 'In the woods, I saw a light. It flickered a bit, then it went out.'

'Don't be daft,' replied Ida. She was working on a difficult pattern, lots of slipped-over stitches, four colours and very fine wool. 'I promised Amy this for tomorrow, Diane, so I have to get on with it.' She changed needles. 'Look, there's nobody in the woods this time of year and this time of night.'

'I saw it, too,' piped Joe.

'Aye, well, you always see everything our Diane sees.' Ida grinned at him. He was stronger, fitter and, at last, he was getting a bit cheeky. In Ida's book, lads were right to be on the cheeky side. 'Put that kettle on, Joe. Mona's been gone ages – I wonder where she's got to.'

'She'll be talking,' answered Diane. 'She's usually talking.'

'Aye,' replied Ida. 'She'll be gabbing away with Amy and Margot.' Mind, there hadn't been much gabbing today. Margot and Mona had sat there like a pair of dummies, and Ida had felt as if she had been in the way. 'In me own house, too,' she muttered to herself.

'Did you say something, Gran?' asked Diane.

'Just reading me pattern,' lied Ida. 'Make some toast, love, that fire's settled nice now.'

Diane skipped about as if walking on air. She was unbelievably happy. Every morning, she rode in a motor car to school, then, when school closed, she and Joe walked down to Mr Mulligan's office to do a few jobs, shopping, sweeping up, dusting. They also got lent out to other folk, the butcher, the laundry where Mona used to work, a grocery in Deansgate. She and Joe were always getting tips and extras like sausages, a pat of butter, bread. Life without stealing was wonderful.

297

She will come soon, will submit herself to me and to the Light, because all is ordained by a greater power, a plan devised before and beyond the scope of mere mortal flesh. I see the fields of Texas, dry as dust and waiting for the rain. We shall plant ourselves here in the desert; we shall fertilize the barren place, shall bring life where all is brown and bare. I see the wood as it begins to burn, bush of Moses resurrected from the word, from the Bible. Praise the Lord, for my moment is at hand.

Sally pushed the door inward. 'Mrs Hewitt?'

'Eeh, love.' Ida put down her knitting once more. She had almost finished the second sleeve and could sew the item together in the morning. 'It's cold out,' she chided, 'and black as hell. Whatever are you doing? Get sat down here now. Diane, pour her a cup of tea – she looks frozen to the bone.'

Sally sat and shivered.

'What on God's earth is Kate Kenny thinking of, letting you out on a winter night?' asked Ida.

'Gone to a funeral. There's only me and Mary, and she's up to something.'

'Whole family's up to something,' Ida mumbled. 'Who died?' she asked, in a clearer tone.

'A friend in Chester.' Sally blew into chilled hands. 'She said she'll try to be back tomorrow afternoon some time, but she couldn't promise.'

Diane pushed a cup into her friend's cold hands. One of the best things about living in Pendleton was that Diane had made a friend of Sally Hayes. Slightly older and wiser than Diane, Sally retained enough childishness to enjoy skipping, hopscotch, bowling a hoop and playing ball. 'What's happened?' Diane asked.

Sally took a few grateful sips of sweet tea. 'It's Mr Mulligan – he's gone missing.'

Ida pondered. 'Is he not . . . you know . . . ?'

'No, he's not in the cellar, Mrs Hewitt. His car's not at the house – he never came home.'

'Well, he brought these two back at about a quarter to six,' said Ida. 'He had Amy in the car, because he always takes her home, too. Well, usually. Sometimes Camilla Smythe does it if she happens to be in town.'

Sally took a larger draught of tea. 'I don't know what to do, I suppose I should go up to Caldwell Farm.'

'Not on your nellie,' replied Ida quickly. 'The big house is just about half-way between us and the farm – you can't go traipsing that far, Sally.'

'But I can't stop here,' Sally moaned. 'There's her up there on her own for a start. She was in the kitchen with her ear up to the cellar door, said she was cleaning. She never cleans when Mrs Kenny's out, she just dozes or gets up to mischief.'

Ida sighed and shook her head. 'I'd walk up with you to the farm, love, but it's twice as far as the Grange and I might not get there. Some use I'd be if you had to carry me.'

'I'll go,' offered Diane.

'No, you won't,' commanded Ida. 'You're stopping right where you are, lady, and that's an end to it.'

'But, Gran—'

'No!'

Ida walked about a bit while she had what she called a good cogitation. There was nothing else for it, she concluded after two circuits of the small room. Sally wanted to get to Caldwell, while Ida, too, was concerned about the whereabouts of Mona and Mr Mulligan. 'Diane, go across to the shop and ask Mr Wilkinson if he'll take me and Sally up to Caldwell Farm in his motor van. Tell him it's a bit of an emergency, like.'

Diane shot across the floor like a bullet from a gun.

'And, lady,' continued Ida, 'you make sure you stop in here till I come back, look after Joe and put him to bed.'

'Yes, Gran.'

'And no chasing lights what aren't there.'

'Yes, Gran. I mean, no, Gran.'

'I saw a light,' said Sally.

'Buckets of blood,' sighed Ida. 'Not you and all.'

'Oh, it were just a little one,' said Sally apologetically.

'Where?' asked Diane, her fingers clasped to the doorknob.

'In the woods,' answered Sally. 'When I was running down the lane to the village. A long way back, it was.'

'Hmmph,' muttered Ida. 'Better tell the army to come

out, then. I looked and I never saw nothing.'

The expression on Diane's face was little short of triumphant. 'See, Gran, it weren't just me.'

'Me and all,' called Joe.

'Aye, you and all, as ever,' replied Ida. 'Forget lights, all of you. Joe, get ready for bed. Sally, drink that tea afore it gets cold.' She turned to Diane. 'And, you, get going while the going's good.'

Diane got going.

There was movement out there; he could not see it, yet he was able to sense it through the Light. It burnt strong and true in a glass-sided lantern on top of an old fruit box. His strength was such now that he could create his own Light from a safety match, no need to carry it with him any more. His prayer was so powerful these days that he could breathe life into any flame.

Two vehicles had driven back down from the farm and off into the dead of night. The third, Mulligan's, he thought, had not made the return journey. So Mulligan was still up there with Amy and the young one, the woman who belonged to the Light.

The first car had moved slowly away from the farm, while the second, probably a van, had been driven away at a very fast speed. Where was the devil Mulligan? What was he doing at this very moment? Calm, Wilkinson ordered. He must remain calm while waiting for Margot. It might not happen tonight, but she would come soon, he knew that.

Grant me peace and quiet while I meditate, O Lord, while I prepare myself for the task to come. Bring your infinite peace into the space I occupy, allow me the power to follow my destiny. She will come and I shall bring her to you and to the miracle. With her I can be a man, for you will show me the way.

In the seat of guardians she and I will reside, open to the sky and to your glory. In that land I shall make children. In that land, under the everlasting stars and planets, she and I will live as one, guarded by your Eternal Light, the flame of Moses.

My task is plain, for you have shown me the path, Lord. The obstacles are clearing now, for it is time to stake my claim.

He praised the Lord once more, then carried on waiting.

TWENTY-THREE

Up at Caldwell Farm, things were still rather out of hand. Elspeth and her husband had gone to bed, the former upset by the scene in her kitchen, the latter after wearing himself out in a fruitless search for the errant Eliza. Eliza, like her sisters, had spent her life walking in the woods, but had seldom stayed out so long in weather like this. She had seemed odder than ever, and was possibly being pursued by police or by the bereaved family of Rupert Smythe.

James Mulligan was pacing about ceaselessly, Margot wept with relief in a corner, Mona tried to stay awake, while Amy, reeling from several shocks, simply stared through a window at nothing in particular.

Camilla's brother was dead; Margot had been made pregnant by the deceased, Eliza had seen him die, had possibly contributed to the event, Mrs Smythe was hovering on the brink of insanity, while Amy herself was not feeling too stable in that department. Could life become any worse than this?

The winter night was black, illuminated by a mere sliver of moon that skipped in and out of high cloud. She saw James striding about, his reflection clear in dark glass, so she pulled the curtains and swung round to face the room. 'She can't stay out all night,' she announced, to no one in particular. 'She knows she'd freeze to death.'

'I must go and find her,' he said. 'There could be a severe frost tonight.'

'No,' replied Amy, after a short rethink. 'She won't let herself get too cold, don't worry.' Her selfish sister was centre stage again, even when absent from the scene. 'I shall make some tea, then we can work out what is to be done.'

Margot got up. 'No, Amy, allow me. I need to do something to take my mind off ... things.' She left the room, a handkerchief dabbing at the last of her tears. For all her surface bravado, Margot was becoming upset by the thought of Rupert being dead, by the idea of her sister being involved in a killing.

In the kitchen, Margot set a kettle on the range, then sat at the large deal table. It was her fault. She had allowed Rupert to take liberties, and now he was dead. Perhaps he had told Eliza what had happened, perhaps she had been cross with him. If Eliza had killed Rupert, she might have done it for her younger sister's sake. Eliza had not known about the baby, though she might well have guessed the extent of the affair.

The younger sister thought for a few moments. Eliza seemed cold and distant, but she might well have had deep feelings on this particular subject. 'So now,' whispered Margot, 'if she dies out there in the cold, that will be my fault as well.' She walked to the kitchen window and stared out at a thin layer of snow, at clouds high enough to allow the earth to freeze solid. Something had to be done straight away, without cups of tea and conversations.

Very quietly, Margot took Elspeth's coat, hat and shawl from a peg on the back door. She wrapped herself carefully, glad that the housekeeper's girth warranted sufficient cloth to cover the bulges of a mother-to-be. Silently, Margot crept out into the night, her eyes widening in a search for light. She would find her sister even if she had to search until tomorrow.

After five minutes, the empty kitchen was visited by Amy. She stopped dead by the table, eyes darting about, took in the absence of Elspeth's outer garments, the furious kettle on the range. 'James?' she cried.

Immediately, he was by her side. 'She was making tea, so where has she—?'

'Look upstairs,' commanded Amy.

'But—'

'Just do it, please.'

When he had gone, Amy leaned heavily against a wall. What next? There were two of them out there now, one pregnant, the other a self-engrossed creature who would not have cared about Margot if the latter had been at death's door. Amy could only guess at Margot's feelings just now, because pregnancy made women different, or so she had been led to understand. So Margot was out looking for Eliza, who was possibly being stalked by the woman whose son she had been accused of murdering. Yes, Helen Smythe had been removed by her daughter, but she might have got away, was surely mad enough to run riot until she found Eliza. What a mess. Amy had to admit to herself that if she had to choose which sister to save, her vote would go to Margot. Panic bubbled in her throat. She took the kettle off the hob and placed it in the hearth.

To add to the confusion, someone was hammering at the front door. Amy ran to open it, found Ida Hewitt and Sally Hayes, with Stephen Wilkinson in the background.

Ida stalked into the house, straighter and stronger than she had been in years. 'I see Mr Mulligan's car's here,' she said, 'so is Mona about?'

Amy waved a hand in the direction of the parlour. 'Just go in there, both of you. We have a rather difficult situation here.' After making this understatement, Amy forgot all about Stephen Wilkinson and closed the front door.

James rattled down the stairs two at a time. 'No sign of anyone,' he said.

'Mr Mulligan?' Sally crossed the hallway. 'Where have you been? Your dinner's all dry and Mary's on her own because Mrs Kenny went to the funeral and—'

'Not now, Sally,' he said. 'Go into the parlour and— How did you get here?'

'Mr Wilkinson's van,' replied Sally. 'He drove us up from Mrs Hewitt's house – I went there to search for you.'

'Very good of him, I'm sure,' said James. He opened the front door and found Stephen Wilkinson standing on the step, cap in hand, plainly prepared to offer further help. 'Thank you

303

for waiting.' James placed a hand on the good man's arm. 'Would you take Ida, Mona and Sally home, please?'

'Certainly.' The brother of Guardian Wilkinson cleared his throat. 'Is there something wrong?'

This man was trustworthy, had been cast in a mould so different from his male sibling's.

'Why do you ask?'

'Young Sally Hayes was talking about the woods, said that she and Diane Hewitt had seen a light among the trees. Little Joe says he saw it, too.'

It appeared that Eliza had found the sense and the where-withal to light a fire. But Margot was chief priority for the moment. 'So there is a fire in the woods, Mr Wilkinson?'

The visitor shook his head. 'Well, if there is, I saw nowt on the way up here.'

'A fire would have been visible from the lane,' said James. 'Especially at this time of year with no foliage to hide flames. Unless it has been put out, of course.'

Stephen stepped into the house. 'I hope you don't mind, Mr Mulligan, but there's a chill wind blowing outside.' He fiddled with his cap. 'From what I heard, it wasn't like a fire, just a small light, you understand.'

'Not at all, don't apologize. I'm sorry, we should not have left you standing there. A small light. Not a fire,' James mused aloud.

'Is there trouble on?' asked Pendleton's baker and post-office keeper. 'You see, I'd offer more help, but I've a batch of small tins and oven-bottoms in and—'

'Thanks,' said James, 'but there are enough of us, I think.' He paused. Another man could be useful . . . No, let Stephen go off and see to his shop. 'Er . . . if you see Eliza or Margot Burton-Massey on your travels, will you let me know?'

'Certainly.' Stephen got back into his van, waited for the women, wondered about Eliza, Margot and his baking. Mr Mulligan looked in a right state, whites of his eyes a bit blood-shot, hair even more out of order than usual. Ah, well, this wasn't getting his bread rolls ready, was it?

James closed the door, leaned his head against it for a second. Was Amy right? Was there hell on earth? He felt as if he hadn't slept for three days, exhaustion dragging at his muscles, tension promising to give birth to a sizeable headache.

In the parlour, Amy, Mona, Ida and Sally sat in grim silence. 'I've told them,' said Amy eventually, 'that Margot and Eliza are both missing.'

James sighed, pushed his hands deep into pockets. 'Mr Wilkinson is outside – Mr Stephen Wilkinson, Ida. He will take Sally back to the Grange, you and Mona to Bramble Cottage.'

'I'm going nowhere,' declared Mona. 'Looked after that girl all day I did, and I shall see the job through.' She could stay awake, she could.

'Go home, Mona,' advised Amy.

'But I—'

'In the van, all three of you, this minute,' ordered James, a distinct edge to his tone. 'There is nothing you can do here. If necessary, I shall drive round and mobilize all farmers and land workers. Neither of you would be capable of joining a search party, so go home right now.'

'There speaks a schoolteacher,' mumbled Amy, as three docile lambs left the room.

He stopped in the doorway and glanced over his shoulder at the frightened, brave young woman. 'Never underestimate a teacher, Amy, for his is the hand that rules the world.'

Diane urged Joe through the garden. 'We can be back before she gets home.' His legs were not as strong as they needed to be, but exercise was good for him. This would be exercise, walking from here to the woods. 'Come on, stop messing about. It's a mystery, this light, and I want to get to the bottom of it. Gran won't be coming home for ages, I'm sure.'

Joe, not convinced by his sister's words, dragged his heels. 'She'll be back in a minute, she's in the baker's van. He'll have to come back to his cakes and I bet he'll fetch Gran home.'

Diane tutted impatiently. There definitely had been a light in the woods: she had seen it, Joe had seen it, Sally had seen it. This was a great opportunity for adventure, a factor that had disappeared from Diane's life when the stealing had stopped. She missed the sensation of living on the edge, that flow of life-blood through her veins when she had stood within a hair's breadth of discovery. He was still dragging his feet.

'Come on, Joe,' she begged for the umpteenth time.

Joe did not share his older sister's addiction to adrenaline. 'We'll get in trouble,' he moaned.

'She's at the farm,' whispered Diane, dropping her voice in case a neighbour might hear. 'You know what she's like, Joe – she could talk the four legs off a horse. Once she gets with Miss Amy, it'll be all mohair and three-ply. You know what Gran's like when she starts on about knitting and crocheting. She could be up yonder till gone midnight.'

'I'm scared,' he replied truthfully.

'So am I – that's what makes it fun.'

'Well, I don't reckon it's funny, our Diane.'

She stopped walking. 'Go back in, then. Get in bed, then put pillows in my bed, make it look as if I'm asleep.'

Joe swallowed. He hated being in the house alone, had never been alone at night. 'I can't.'

Diane emitted a long-drawn sigh of utter impatience. She loved her little brother, but he could be a right pain in the neck. 'Then we can blame it all on me if Gran comes home before we do. Say I made you do it.'

'All right.' With extreme reluctance and on legs that were still not quite up to scratch, Joe followed his sister into a darkness that promised only to thicken once the trees began. He was terrified, while Diane, used to anticipation, was merely excited.

'Diane?'

'What?'

'It might be a bogeyman.'

She clicked her tongue with all the expertise of her grandmother. 'Don't be so soft,' she chided. 'There's no such thing as the bogeyman, Joe. And there never was.'

He sniffed the air in the manner of an animal seeking prey. Emerging slowly from his trance, he rose, stretched, inhaled again. Although the wind shook branches nearby, he was alert to other movements, subtler shifts of space and air. Foxes? he wondered. Badgers, owls, bats? Or was humankind approaching?

306

Peering into a sliver of broken mirror, he smoothed his hair, dragging strands across the balding central track, glueing the pieces in place with macassar. Peter Wilkinson did not notice the sickly smell of this application, as he had used it for years. Meditation had revived him. He sipped at a cup of dandelion and burdock, wiped his mouth, lowered the stove's light, drew back the wicks of two lamps. Something told him that his time had come, that the moment of triumph was close at hand.

His heart lurched, but he commanded it to beat evenly, steadily. He must not make mistakes, as he might alter the course of existence for ever. This could just be his finest hour, the zenith of his life so far. Should he be proved wrong, should Margot not put in an appearance, there would be another chance tomorrow.

A twig snapped. In spite of enormous self-control, he shuddered momentarily. It could be anyone, might even be the papist from Pendleton Grange. No, Margot walked in the woods; this was likely to be his lady, his destiny.

He opened the door just a tiny crack, fastened an eye to the resulting small space. 'Ah, it's you.' His tone was conversational. 'You are the wrong one. Just a moment, please.' Confused for a split second, he hesitated before picking up the necessary equipment. He knew exactly what had to be done.

After emptying fluid on to a rag, he left the hut completely, took hold of his victim, held the cloth to mouth and nose. There would be no pain, no terror. With not the slightest compunction, Peter Wilkinson grabbed a stone and crashed it into the unconscious skull. He had made his decision, and no one must get in the way.

Ida and Mona entered the cottage, waved as Stephen Wilkinson parked his van across the lane. 'Nice chap, that,' said Mona. 'Bit different from yon brother of his.'

Ida eased off her coat, hung it behind the door. 'Brrr, it's cold out there. I'll make a brew.'

'Mr Mulligan had me watching the queer feller just before our Tilly died. We found that lass, you remember, that naked girl in my new house. Mr Mulligan reckons Peter Wilkinson were responsible.' Mona eased herself into a fireside chair. 'Where's the kiddies gone, Ida?'

'Bed,' came the reply from the kitchen.

'Best place,' Mona said. 'I'll not be stopping up long meself. Even the marrow in me bones is aching.'

They sat with their tea, each mulling over the day's happenings, Margot's confirmed pregnancy, Mrs Smythe's hysterical outbursts, the disappearance of Eliza, then Margot. 'Margot will have gone looking for that other one,' said Mona. 'And it's been a long day for somebody what's carrying a child. She were doing so well and all till Eliza decided to go for a wander.'

Ida agreed. 'Did you take her to the doctor's, then?'

'Aye, that's where we were when Amy opened the shop. Still, it wanted doing. That young one needs to know where she stands. Ooh, I hope nowt happens to Margot. She's a lovely young woman once you get to know her. Then there's the poor innocent little baby and all, I'm that worried about it, too.'

'Will she keep it?'

'I reckon she might.' Mona glanced around the room, a look of puzzlement on her face. 'Ida?'

'What?'

'Your Diane's nightie's still hanging on the clothes maiden.'

Ida looked at the item in question. 'She'll have her dirty one on, couldn't be bothered changing them over more than likely.'

The two women stared at one another. 'No,' said Ida. 'They won't have gone out. They can't have.'

Mona jumped up, almost spilling her tea in the process. 'Shall I go and look, Ida?'

Ida nodded. She sat perfectly still while Mona trod the staircase, the answer plain in her mind before Mona shouted. They weren't up there. Somewhere, outside on a bitter night, Diane and Joe were busy getting lost.

Mona re-entered the room. 'What must we do, Ida? This is getting daft now. Not daft funny, daft because there's no sense to it.'

'We mun get Stephen Wilkinson out again,' replied Ida. 'Long enough them two kiddies looked after theirselves while I lay there like a dead woman. There's summat going on in them woods, Mona. And my Diane is drawn to trouble.'

'She's a good lass.'

'I know that, Mona, but she craves excitement, needs to go

308

about acting like a flaming detective. Go on, love, fetch the baker back. He's got to go up to Caldwell again and tell Mr Mulligan what's happening.'

Mona pulled on her coat. 'Four missing now.'

'And Sally said something about Mary Whitworth's brothers doing a disappearing act as well. They're supposed to be sleeping in the laundry, but there's no sign according to Sally.'

'Six,' pronounced Mona, before leaving the house.

Ida sat bolt upright in her chair. A feeling of great unease played along her backbone, chilly fingers reaching up her neck until the hairs stirred. She thought about Charlie, her only son, just another private who had given his life in 1916. Her mind drifted to Brenda, wife to Charlie Hewitt, mother of Diane and Joe. She had never been a mother, that one. She was a prostitute, a dyed-in-the wool streetwoman with no thought for anyone but herself.

Oh, how Ida had missed Charlie. She could see him now, playing jacks and bobbers, bowling a hoop, having a game of football with an inflated pig's bladder, marching off to war, so proud in his uniform. 'And now I've lost your kids,' she told him. 'Mind, I will say that daughter of yours has a head on her. But I told her to stop in, I did. Watch over them, Charlie. Please make sure they come back to me tonight.'

She gazed into the dying embers, remembered how she, like Brenda Hewitt, had been of little use to Charlie's children. 'I just lay there,' she whispered, 'lay there praying for death so I could join Charlie. I never worried about them two poor kiddies. So I'm just as bad as blinking Brenda. Still, with a lot of help, I've done a sight better lately.'

The clock ticked its leaden way towards nine. Ida and Mona were seldom up this late, while the children usually went up at about eight o'clock in winter-time. Where were they? What was in the woods? And would whatever it was leave her grandchildren alone?

Mona came in. 'He's set off for the farm, Ida. Just got some loaves out, then off he went like a good 'un.'

'He is a good man,' Ida repeated. She watched her friend as she removed coat and gloves again. 'I'm glad you turned up here, Mona. You're a comfort.'

309

I'll be no comfort if them children don't come home, thought Mona. 'We're lucky to have one another, love. I know it's a bit cramped, but I can't imagine living on me own now.'

'We have to get them two back.' Ida's voice cracked. 'She's not a bad girl, our Diane. She's just a bit on the adventurous side.' The tears flowed. 'I could have done more. I should have pulled meself together years back, when they needed me.'

Mona crossed the room. 'Stop this now, Ida Hewitt. You're not hitting yourself with a big stick no more, not while I'm living here. Your Diane'll look after Joe and—'

'I shouldn't have left them, I should have let Sally go up to the farm on her own.'

'Aye, and the moon should be made of green cheese and all.'

Ida attempted a smile. 'They'll be all right, won't they, Mona?'

'Course they will.' Mona sat down and prayed. They would be all right, because the alternative was unthinkable.

He dragged the body along uneven ground, felt every bump as he forced the dead weight over stones, fallen branches and exposed roots. There was no fear in him: he was a chosen one, a decider, a maker of the future. This had been the wrong one, so he had eradicated the interloper and was now waiting for his destined partner to put in an appearance.

When Eliza Burton-Massey's still form lay behind the gamekeeper's hut, Peter Wilkinson covered her with a couple of sacks and some old newspapers. She would not smell: the weather was too cold for quick decay. Eliza, who had unwittingly become a part of the grand plan, would be with the angels, because she had played her part in the Light's plan.

He returned to the shack and prepared a pot of tea, using water drawn from a clear stream at the other side of Sniggery Woods. Soon, he would read passages from his Bible in order to absorb more strength into himself. Eventually Margot would come. Then everything could take shape. He was so near to the Lord, so secure in the Light Eternal – nothing could touch him now.

'So I went back in the shop and telephoned the police,' said Stephen Wilkinson, who was torturing his cap yet again, squashing and twisting it between thick, clean fingers. 'See, with there being two kiddies missing—'

'Four, possibly,' said Amy. 'Sally said that Mary Whitworth's younger brothers seem to have disappeared from the face of the earth.'

Stephen shook his head. 'Well, I've lived up here going on twenty year, Miss Amy, and I've never known such queer goings-on in all that while.'

Amy sat on the second stair. James had gone out to make one final search of the woods before calling out the farmers. But if the police were on their way, perhaps the landworkers would not be needed. 'Diane's a sensible girl,' she pondered aloud.

'Mrs Hewitt and Miss Walsh are worried past themselves,' replied the baker. 'It's all to do with a light in the woods.'

Amy nodded. 'Yes, there's the old gamekeeper's hut – hasn't been used since my father's time – so I directed Mr Mulligan towards that. In the dark, it won't be easy. But on the other hand, if there is the slightest glow coming from the hut, the darkness will become a help to the searchers.'

'Hasn't Mr Mulligan got a lamp?'

'Yes, he found a storm lamp in the stables.'

'Ah.' Stephen straightened his cap and placed it on his head. 'Then he could be seen by whoever's in there.' He sighed and lowered his chin. 'I must go back to the shop, miss. I've the post office to open in the morning, and cakes to ice. Might not be much of an excuse, but I can guarantee that village'll be wanting its breakfast tomorrow.'

'Yes, you go.'

He walked away, turned. 'Mind, if you need anything – the phone, my van – just let me know.'

'I shall, thank you.'

When he had gone, Amy placed her head against the wall and wept. She knew why Margot had run off, realized that guilt had driven the girl to dash off in pursuit of Eliza. Was Eliza worth the effort? Yes, Amy told herself determinedly. All humans warranted saving. But if anything happened to Margot, Amy would not be able to contain her feelings towards her other sister.

311

The house felt so empty. The Moorheads were in bed, blissfully unaware of more recent developments. James was now out in the cold, as were the two children from Bramble Cottage. It was a nightmare, and all Amy could do was to sit here and wait for someone – anyone – to return from those dark, thick woods.

The idea of someone hiding out in the gamekeeper's hut was bizarre – surely no one in his right mind would be in there while the weather was so bad? But what about a person in his wrong mind? She shuddered. Lights in the woods? Ridiculous. Eliza and Margot would be carrying no lamps. Margot in particular knew every inch of Sniggery, every branch, every leaf in summer-time. Eliza was a different matter: it was not like her to be outside so late and so long.

Sally Hayes was no liar. Diane Hewitt, for all her chequered past, was no longer given to uttering untruths. So there must have been somebody there earlier on, because lights did not create themselves without the intervention of thunderstorms. Margot, James and Eliza were out there. Even in her panic, Amy noticed how James, rather than Eliza, had come second on her list.

Four children missing, too. What on earth had happened to Jack and Harry Whitworth? By all accounts, they were stupid, shiftless creatures who came up to Pendleton Grange three or four times a year to do odd jobs. Kate Kenny complained about them, then paid them because she carried a soft heart beneath the brusque exterior. According to Sally, the two boys had not been paid – their money was still in a jam jar on the kitchen dresser.

Oh, if only Kate Kenny had been here. Kate had a way of driving through problems, head down, horns sharpened, wits on red alert.

'All I can do is wait,' sobbed Amy. Like the wife of a serving soldier, she had to sit and find her patience.

TWENTY-FOUR

A ray of pale moonlight settled on her hair. Wilkinson drew in a sharp breath, picked up the necessary implements, poured chloroform on to the cloth. She was staring right at the shack, so he lowered the lamps before stepping outside. 'You came,' he said.

'What?' Margot could not quite make him out, though the voice rang a bell. 'Have you seen my sister?' she asked. 'Eliza Burton-Massey – she was walking in the woods, I think.'

'Yes,' he replied, 'but she's gone now. Will you step into the hut? I can make you a warm drink.'

An extra chill visited Margot's body, causing her to shiver violently. This new coldness was not a result of frost: it was a reaction to the man. There was something odd about him, something odd about anyone who chose to spend a January night in a gamekeeper's hut during severe weather. 'Where did my sister go?'

'Home,' he answered firmly. 'She went to her home. Your sister is now where we all belong.'

The baby moved. Margot dragged Elspeth's winter coat across her body, tightened the grey shawl. 'Then I shall go home, too,' she said.

'It is not time yet,' he told her. 'Your destiny lies on a great plain in a new country, a dry land rich with oil. We shall go there, you and I, to begin the new dynasty.'

Margot's heart began to beat like a bass drum. She caught her breath. 'You are crazy,' she said, her voice thinned by terror. 'What have you done with Eliza? Where is she? And I shall go nowhere with you.'

He leaped across the small clearing, grabbed her as she turned, stuffed the rag over her mouth. In spite of her struggles, he managed to contain her until the chloroform hit home. She was limp now, limp and compliant. He dragged her by the feet into the hut and placed her on the floor, her head almost touching the outward-opening door. To close it, he had to step over her carefully. This one must not be marked: this one had to be saved intact and beautiful.

He removed her clothes, folding the items carefully and stacking them all on the upturned fruit box. She was heavier than he had expected, difficult to manipulate in so confined a space. But this was the right one, because his own body was responding, was preparing itself for the joining.

He picked up a lamp and looked at her face, so lovely, so calm. Her upper body was perfect: she had the breasts of a mother, a mother of many children yet to be born into the Light. The waist was slightly larger than he might have expected and . . . and . . .

And this was the wrong one. He should have chosen the other, she who had been in London, the unexpected arrival. Confused, he swung the lantern away from Margot and wondered about Eliza. Eliza was a truly beautiful woman, but she was . . . she was with the angels.

He knelt, placed the lamp next to Margot. This girl was with child. Tentatively, he placed a hand on the slight distension, felt a small movement from within. Here lay no virgin, no bride for a guardian. He did not know what to do.

Then he heard the words, words shouted by the devil's own henchman. 'Eliza, Margot, where are you?' It was the papist, the Irishman, disciple of Lucifer. Lucifer meant light, the wrong light, the wrong woman naked on the floor, the right one – where? Outside, covered, cold, beaten.

He strode over Margot, picked up a lantern, threw open the door and stepped outside. He had to save himself, because he was a guardian, a chosen one. There would be another for him,

314

perhaps the oldest of these three well-bred girls. Women were disposable, replaceable, but he, who would become Supreme Guardian one day, was too valuable to be lost.

Dropping his lamp, he ran off as fast as short legs would carry him, bumping into trees, feeling the small, skeletal branches as they reached to scratch his face. He fell head first into a field at the woods' edge, forced himself upright, carried on and on until he completely lost track of where he might be.

Then he saw a lighted window, moved towards it, slower this time, careful not to make a sound. The third one was in there, so this was Caldwell Farm. She was standing at the window, was waiting for her sisters to return. Waiting for Mulligan, too, he supposed. She and the Irishman were often seen together.

Confusion reigned in his head once more. Without the Light, without frequent bouts of meditation, he was virtually powerless. Where to go? He crept round the back of the house, found a barn, covered himself in hay. Tomorrow, he would think again.

Diane left her brother where he had fallen. Winded but unhurt, Joseph Hewitt sat on cold earth, leaned against the bole of a large tree and waited for Diane to return. He rubbed his shin, shivered and drew thin legs into his body. It was cold enough to freeze the eyes in your head, as Gran was often heard to say.

Diane moved stealthily. She heard a dragging sound, saw light shining dully through covered slats in the hut. Two or three minutes passed in silence. Then someone shouted, called for Eliza and Margot. The door crashed outward and more light poured out, this time illuminating the figure of a man. He ran down the side of the shack, and just before discarding his lamp, held it for a split second so that it shone upward on an ugly, familiar face. It was Guardian Wilkinson.

The girl shivered. She did not want to see any more, had no wish to share space with Peter Wilkinson. Anyway, there was Joe to attend to. Diane turned and went back to Joe. He had probably heard and seen nothing, which was just as well. In Diane's book, Guardian Wilkinson was an item to be avoided. Gran would be back by now. A tale had to be invented.

All the way home, Diane instructed her brother in the art of deception. 'Why did we go out, Joe?' she asked repeatedly.

315

'We heard a kitten crying, Di,' he replied, twenty or more times.

'And what did we do, Joe?'

'Followed the crying till we couldn't hear it any more,' he said, through chattering teeth.

'Well, mind you stick to that story, Joe Hewitt, else we'll be in very hot water.'

Hot water sounded great to Joe, but he remained compliant. Where their Diane was concerned, the line of least resistance was the best option.

James stopped running. He had lost the storm lamp several seconds earlier and was unable to see where the man had gone. Turning back, he stumbled in the direction of a hut, the game-keeper's hide to which Amy had sent him. There was a slight glow coming from two slats, one at the rear, the other on one side. The door and the other wall of the shack were invisible from James's current vantage point.

As he passed the rear end of the structure, he heard a small groaning sound. There would be few young animals about at this time of year, he thought. There it was again, a groan of pain, muffled in some way, as if it struggled through cloth. He bent, used his hands to feel his way around the rear of the shed.

'Good God,' he exclaimed, as he made contact with cold human fingers. 'Who's that?'

'It hurts,' replied that same small voice.

He found the head, knew that his hand was covered in blood. 'Eliza?' he asked. 'Margot?'

'Eliza.' The word, forced through bubbles, sounded like a death rattle and James had heard many of those.

'What happened?' He knelt and supported what was left of Eliza Burton-Massey, cradling the weight of her against his breast. 'Oh, Eliza, who did this to you?'

'Man,' she answered. 'Bad man.'

Be strong, he urged himself. You are strong, you have done all this before. But before had been a battlefield, a place where men went to win or lose, to live or die. 'Eliza?'

'I did it,' she whispered. 'I killed.'

She was making a dying statement. 'Rupert?' he asked.

'Ye–yes.'

'He was going to hurt you, Eliza?'

'Yes.'

'Then God will have mercy on you.'

He held her close to his chest till she died, his eyes closed as he concentrated on listening, waiting for that final, long-drawn sigh. He placed what remained of her head on sacking and what felt like newspaper, closed her eyes, sat back on his heels. 'He forgave a crucified thief. I pray that He will also take you to His right hand.'

His heart burned in his chest, his head ached, his hands were so frozen that he could scarcely feel the tips of his fingers. Eliza, so lovely, so cold now in more way than one. God was good, God had a forgiving nature. 'Into Thy hands I commend this spirit,' he mouthed.

He left her where she was, stood up, walked around the shed until he reached the door. There, spread out before him, lay a familiar sight. He remembered Mona Walsh's 'new' house, the place she had taken to get away from Tilly. This was exactly the same – clothes folded precisely and set on a box, the girl naked, sedated, completely vulnerable.

Reaching for a wrist, he felt for and registered a pulse, then strode over her body towards a stove. He turned up the heat, found a blanket and was just about to cover Margot when a cry interrupted him. 'Stop,' commanded the voice. 'This is the police and you are surrounded.'

They were here. Relief flooded James's veins as he saw a dozen lights around him. 'There's another behind the shed,' he called. 'Eliza Burton-Massey. I think she's dead.'

Some of the lights moved, but most stayed. James stood up and placed the blanket on Margot's body. She would be fine, he told himself, everything would be dealt with by the law. No one approached him: they were commanding him to stay still, to raise both hands, to stay inside the hut for now. Puzzled, he waited for something to happen. 'She's freezing to death,' he shouted.

'Hands in the air,' came the barked reply.

He lifted his arms, lowered his chin. Unthinkable as it might be, he realized that he was being treated as a criminal. He was on the spot, was bloodstained and very shaken. James Mulligan was the prime suspect.

'Step outside the shed,' was the next order.

He walked past the open door, hands stretched above his head, feet dragging along frozen earth. It dawned on James then that he might well go to prison, could even be hanged. 'I did not do any of this,' he explained calmly. 'I came to search for these girls – ask their sister.'

A police sergeant approached. 'I remember you,' he said. 'You were in a house in John Street when that other young woman was attacked not long back.'

'But . . . but Mona Walsh was with me when I found that girl.'

'And you might well have put her there earlier on. I'm sorry, Mr Mulligan, I know you're well thought of, but here you are, covered in blood, a young girl stretched out on that floor – what do you expect us to think?' He walked into the shed, uncovered Margot, found no obvious cuts, no wounds. 'And where's the blood from?' he called over his shoulder.

James turned, fixed his eyes to the sergeant's face. 'The blood is from Eliza, older sister to Margot. Margot is the naked one. Eliza died in my arms.' He held out his hands, raised his shoulders in a gesture of despair. 'You ask me what I expect. What I expect is that you get that young woman out of the shed and into hospital right away.'

A constable staggered on to the scene, gagging as the contents of his stomach fought to escape. 'She's . . . she's dead. The other one, round the back – she's . . . a right mess.'

Another policeman arrived. 'Back of her head's been caved in,' he said, 'and, yes, she's dead.'

'Arrest me,' advised James. 'Then get Margot into a hospital as quickly as possible. The man you want is Peter Wilkinson. He ran away when I approached.'

'You said that last time and all.'

'Yes, I believe I did.'

Two officers led James away to a police van while others ministered to the unconscious Margot. James sat silently on a wooden bench in the rear of the vehicle, wrists cuffed, an officer at each side of him. He felt little fear now that reason had crept into his head, because he knew that he had done

318

nothing wrong. Amy would vouch for him, as would Mona, Ida, Sally and Kate. When he thought of Kate, he almost smiled, almost pitied Bolton's constabulary. Kate, when she returned from the funeral, would be mortallious troublesome. He closed his eyes, prayed for Eliza, for Margot and the unborn child.

They took him into the central station, read him his rights, asked him if he had anything to say. 'Not much,' he replied. 'Except that I expect a full apology tomorrow.'

The police did not know what to make of him. He made no trouble, refused to enter into conversation, would not be interviewed. He simply sat and stared at the officers, drank tea when it arrived, ate toast, changed into clean clothes, would not be drawn out.

Placed in a cell, he made the best of things, lying down on the thin mattress, pulling a single blanket over his head. But he could not chase Eliza from his thoughts, could not forget the sight of Margot stripped of clothes and dignity, an article, an item, a piece of Wilkinson's twisted plot.

At last, he fell into a fitful doze, only to be awakened by a female voice that did not belong to his aunt. He sat up, raked a hand through his hair, listened.

'How dare you?' she asked loudly. 'How dare you arrest that man?' Ah, it was Amy, God bless her. In spite of the condition of her sisters, she had come to plead for him. 'You will let him go this instant,' he heard her demand.

The response was muffled.

Then she began again. 'James Mulligan is a person of excellent morals.'

He rose from the lumpy mattress, walked to the metal door.

'My sister is dead,' he heard. 'My other sister is in hospital. You have brought in the very man who saved Margot. Well, let me tell you this, I will have your badges – do you hear? I will have you all sacked.'

A mumble of voices interrupted her flow.

'I don't care what his father was.'

They would have needed to be extremely deaf not to hear, James mused. Amy had no need to shout as she had one of those voices that travel even when reduced to a whisper – and she was not whispering now.

319

'Damned fools,' was her next offering.

There followed some further incomprehensible conversation, then all was quiet.

Back in his bed, James thought hard about Amy. She had lost a father, a mother, a sister. Her other sister was pregnant, while Eliza, who would be in the morgue by now, had committed murder. God bless Amy, he begged.

An hour or two later, the door opened. 'You can go now,' said a male voice. 'We have another suspect to find.'

James closed his eyes. 'I am exhausted,' he replied, 'so I would rather sleep – if you don't mind.' Much as he would have liked to comfort Amy, James was finished for the moment and he knew it.

The officer shook his head. Sometimes, folk were very strange.

What Kate called the 'divil' in James came to the fore at that moment. He would leave when he was ready, not when the police dictated. He had done nothing wrong. 'Two eggs for my breakfast,' he said. 'Runny yolks, if you can manage that.'

Bravado gone, James had to swallow hard when the policeman had left. What was he doing? Amy needed him. But he wanted a rest, some thinking time, a few hours to get over the shocks. And, yes, let the police be his servants this once, let them make the breakfast. Yet his heart ached when he thought about Amy. Perhaps he should have gone to her ... No, he was truly finished, depleted, all but vanquished. Using his fingers as a rosary, he did what all good Catholics did, praying earnestly for Eliza, for Margot, for the unborn.

Mostly he ached for Amy, the woman he loved, she who would be for ever beyond his reach. Oh, God, that Eliza should have died in such a way ... His fists curled while temper bubbled inside his chest. And Margot, how was she? It was no use. Much as he would have loved to stay and impose upon these inept guardians of the law, he had to get out. Furiously, he rubbed the water from his eyes before banging on the door of his cell. 'I want a car now,' he demanded quietly. 'And a driver, of course. There are several calls I need to make. You may cancel my eggs – I shall be breakfasting elsewhere.'

The constable peered through the flap in cell number eight. 'We don't run a taxi service, Mr Mulligan.'

320

'You didn't,' replied James, his tone still controlled, 'until tonight, that is. Now, unless you and your colleagues want to see your faces plastered across the front of daily newspapers, you will respond to my demands with untypical alacrity.'

The young man, who had not the slightest acquaintance with alacrity, crept away to face the wrath of his duty sergeant.

James sat down, elbows on knees, his face in his hands. He was not too tired to help Amy, would never be too tired to go to her assistance. Perhaps she would be with Margot at the infirmary, at the morgue identifying Eliza. He would find her.

The sergeant stepped in, a false smile illuminating irregular features. 'We'll take you wherever you want to go,' he said, the words forced between gritted teeth. 'But there's just one thing before you leave.'

'Yes?'

A notebook was removed from a top pocket. 'I won't bore you with all of this, sir. Instead, I shall begin with the trouble at Pendleton Grange.'

'Trouble?'

'Oh, yes, sir.' The man cleared his throat. ' "I entered the kitchen and found a Miss Sally Hayes and a Miss Mary Whitworth. They were involved in a loud argument, which was becoming physical. Miss Whitworth pulled Miss Hayes by the hair and dragged her across the room.

' "When the two girls saw us, the fighting stopped. It was then, at two minutes to ten, that I heard a banging noise. This noise was coming from the cellar door. There being no key available I, Sergeant Ian Proctor, together with Constables Eric Thornton and Arthur Mallet, proceeded to remove hinges from said door in order to reach whoever was doing the banging.

' "When the door had been removed, we found two young boys named Jack and Harry Whitworth, brothers of the above-mentioned Mary Whitworth. Miss Mary Whitworth said, 'The master is the only one with a key. He must have locked them down there.' We were then advised by Miss Whitworth to search the cellar as Mr James Mulligan visited it regularly and took food and drink with him. Miss Whitworth expressed the belief that someone other than her brothers had been imprisoned in the cellars of Pendleton Grange for some considerable time.

321

' "Miss Sally Hayes was of the opinion that the two boys had entered the cellar via the coal chute and, going on the state of their clothes, we judged this to be a possibility. The lads agreed that they had slid down the chute and that the coal merchant had unwittingly locked them in. We then searched the cellars and—" ' He closed the notebook with a snap. 'We searched your cellar, Mr Mulligan, and found . . . you know what we found, sir.'

'Yes.' James remained unshaken.

'You must have your reasons, Mr Mulligan.'

'I do.'

'And you wouldn't want that on a front page, I take it?'

James tutted. 'Are you blackmailing me, Sergeant Proctor?'

'Not at all, sir. And, by the way, we fixed the cellar door back on.'

'Thank you.' At last, James managed a slight smile of gratitude. 'But please give me a car and a driver and we shall hear no more about any of this.'

James was led to the desk where his belongings were returned to him. He signed the book, then waited on a bench for his 'taxi'. Seated next to him, a tramp snored and muttered in his sleep, a thin stream of saliva drooling from bluish lips.

'Sir?'

James stood up.

'Yes, constable?'

'I am your driver,' the young man said.

'Well, then, take me to Caldwell Farm – it is on the outskirts of Pendleton village.'

'You don't live there, sir.'

James sighed in an exaggerated fashion. 'I may have reached the dizzying heights of my thirties, but I do know where I live.'

'It's gone two in the morning, sir.'

'And I can tell the time.'

'They'll all be in bed, Mr Mulligan.'

James leaned an elbow on the counter. 'Constable . . . er?'

'Thornton.'

'Yes, well. If one of your sisters had been murdered, if another had been attacked and put in hospital, would you be asleep?'

322

Eric Thornton considered the question. 'No, I don't think I would, sir.'

James thought for a moment. 'Right, you take me to Pendleton Grange, constable. If my car will start in this frost, I shall deliver myself to Caldwell Farm. But if my car refuses then you must take me to the Burton-Massey farm.'

They sat in the police car and set off northwards. James stared straight ahead, not even flinching when the car lost its grip on slicks of dark ice.

'Mr Mulligan?'

'Yes?'

'The cellar – nobody'll say nowt.'

'Good.' At last James turned his head and looked at the sturdy young man at his side. 'Perhaps you should not give me this information, but I am forced to ask . . .'

'Nothing wrong with asking,' replied the constable.

'How is Margot? Have you heard?'

'Fine, sir. Her sister sat with her till about midnight, after she'd identified . . . you know . . .'

'Eliza's body.'

'Aye. Terrible business, that.'

'And you are looking for the killer?'

The driver nodded. 'Evidence in the hut proves who it is, sir.'

'And that it wasn't me.'

'Aye.'

They drove the rest of the way in silence. James worrying and wondering about Amy, remembering the words he had heard her speak at the police station. Margot was going to be well. Eliza, who had killed Margot's lover, was cold in the morgue. After identifying her sister, Amy must have come straight to the station to plead for his release. She had backbone, but every human had a breaking point.

His car started. The police vehicle followed it down the driveway, then turned right towards town. James steered left in the direction of Caldwell Farm. Amy should not be alone at a time such as this.

His hands were sticky with Eliza's lifeblood. He tried to wipe them on hay, but the blood had crusted and was stuck firmly

323

to his skin. The weather cut through him, ice burning deep into flesh and bone. Caldwell Farm was so near. There were only two resident staff, or so he had been told, an old couple who had been with the Burton-Masseys for many years.

Stealthily, he crept towards the back of the house. She was in the kitchen, head in hands at the table. She was alone. Amy Burton-Massey was a remarkable woman, not as pretty as Eliza, more handsome than Margot. His teeth chattered. The servants would be asleep, no doubt. According to Stephen, his brother, the Moorheads were more of a liability than a help these days. Uncontrollable molars bit into his tongue; if he stayed out here much longer, he would most certainly freeze to death.

The door was unlocked and it opened without complaint. Well-oiled hinges gave no warning as Peter Wilkinson admitted himself into the presence of the one remaining Burton-Massey girl. 'Don't scream,' he advised quietly, when she raised her head. 'It will have to be you now.'

Amy had no idea what this peculiar man was talking about. Then she noticed the blood, the state of his clothing, tatters caused by . . . by tree-branches? 'Wilkinson,' she said, 'brother of our baker, the post-office man.'

'Yes.'

She was too exhausted to experience real fear. The full range of human emotions had visited her in recent hours, from terror to relief and now, back to . . . what? This ridiculous figure would have been laughable had circumstances been different. His hair hung down at each side of his head, long strings that were usually plastered across the naked pate. He owned terrible teeth and dough-coloured skin, while his eyes were . . . They were nasty. 'What do you want?' she asked, as if visitors at two thirty in the morning were not out of the ordinary. 'Cup of tea?'

He nodded, then sat down by the fire, grateful for a little warmth. His eyes never left her as she filled a kettle and set it to boil. 'A biscuit?' she asked. Why was he here? And the blood on him – whose was that?

'I would be grateful for something to eat, yes.'

She bustled about, made him a sandwich, poured two cups

of tea, placed herself at the table. 'Have you been involved in an accident?' she asked.

Glad of this suggestion, he leaped in. 'Yes, yes, I have. Some fool knocked me off my bicycle.' A bright idea slipped into his mind and fell immediately from his tongue. 'I think it was that Mulligan chap throwing his weight about again.'

Amy nodded thoughtfully. 'When did this happen, Mr Wilkinson?'

The man blinked. 'Oh, an hour or so ago. I was . . . I was studying winter wildlife.'

'In the woods?'

'Yes, yes, and along the lanes, too. A car drove right into me. It must have been him, since Pendleton Grange is the only house on that particular stretch.'

'No.'

'I beg your pardon?' He made an effort to lift the hair from his neck, tried to place it back where it ought to have been.

'Mr Mulligan was arrested.'

He forced a smile to stay away from his face. 'Arrested?' he managed, after a pause of several seconds. 'But why?'

Amy raised a shoulder. 'My words exactly. I went to the hospital to visit my sisters . . .' She paused. 'Margot has been attacked and Eliza . . . is dead. She was murdered.'

Wilkinson swallowed a noisy gulp of hot tea. This was marvellous. How many birds with one stone? A rock, the crunching of bone, a limp and lifeless body. 'She was the wrong one,' he mumbled.

'What?'

'Nothing.' He waited for further information, received none. 'Was he arrested for murder?'

'Yes.'

'That's terrible.'

'I told the police about that,' she replied. 'There is no man less likely to commit murder than James Mulligan. He is not the type.' A feeling of unease crept along the many paths of Amy's shocked nervous system. 'And he could not have been driving the car that knocked you down. He has been locked up for several hours. As I was trying to say a moment ago, after visiting the hospital, I called in at the police station and told the sergeant in no uncertain terms that Mr Mulligan is not the killer.'

'How can you be so sure?' asked Wilkinson. 'Many people are capable of terrible sins.'

'Yes.' Her tone was thoughtful. 'But not James Mulligan. I feel confident that he will be released very soon.'

He stared at her. 'Do you know who I am?'

Amy shrugged. 'You are Stephen Wilkinson's brother and, I understand, a member of some sect or other.'

'I am the Guardian of the Light Eternal.'

'Ah.'

Clearly, the woman was not impressed. He told her the story of the burning bush in Makersfield, Texas, of the people who had been drawn to the miracle, of the word being spread throughout the world. 'That is where I shall go to begin the new life,' he concluded.

'And you say that you are searching for young women?'

He inclined his head gravely. 'Of course, the common-or-garden type of girl is very much in demand. But for myself, as a guardian, I require someone from a more elevated background.'

The mantel clock ticked. It was a cheap thing belonging to Elspeth, rather tinny and inclined to slowness. Amy studied the table, not wanting to look at the plainly unstable visitor, not wanting to think about Eliza, about Margot. But it was no use. 'You killed my sister,' she said suddenly. The clock stopped.

'The wrong one,' he said.

'Wrong?'

He stood up in front of the fire. 'You must excuse me,' he said, 'but I became very cold while I was outside.'

'Eliza is cold,' Amy replied. 'She is on a slab in the morgue. You crushed her skull.' With his legs spread and one hand resting on a fireguard behind his back, the man looked like a very poor music-hall parody of Napoleon, all self-importance and bigotry. 'Why did you murder my sister?'

'She was the wrong one.'

Terror struck at that moment. It was as if Amy's body had been on hold, in retreat, unavailable for comment. But now she realized that she could well be fighting for her own life. 'And

326

Margot?' In spite of all the effort, these words emerged shakily.

'When Eliza went away to London, I gave up all hope of her.'

'Hope? How could you have hope of securing the affections of either of them?'

Undeterred, he continued, 'So I chose Margot.'

'You chose her?'

'One day, I shall be Supreme Guardian.'

Amy could scarcely believe her ears.

'It is my destiny.'

A new feeling visited Amy's consciousness. She was suddenly angry, coldly furious. 'Must your destiny involve members of my family? Does your religion allow you – encourage you – to kill one girl and to strip the other naked in the snow?'

He lowered his eyelids, raised them after a second or two. 'It is all foretold,' he informed her. 'When the first bush ignited, we knew that, like Moses, we had to lead our people to a Promised Land, a New World. This is our preparation for the end.'

The end. 'But why did you remove my sister's clothing?'

'To make sure that she was the one.'

Amy made to rise from her chair, decided to stay as small as possible, sat down again. 'And you would have taken her kicking and screaming to America?'

'Oh, no.' He used a sleeve to dry up a drop of mucus that hung from his ugly nose. 'The Lord would have spoken to her after our coupling.'

The term 'daft as a bedful of fleas' flashed through Amy's mind. Elspeth Moorhead was the mother of many such bald statements. Should Amy scream and wake the Moorheads? No. They, too, might become victims. 'Coupling, Mr Wilkinson?'

'Oh, yes. I meant to claim her.'

Amy prayed silently, begging the true God to help her.

'But she was already with child,' said Wilkinson. 'Early days, but pregnant, dirtied.'

'She is in hospital,' replied Amy, 'being treated for hypothermia. They are having to warm her up because you left her to die.'

Wilkinson's eyes began to mist over, and he stumbled back

327

against the fireguard. 'When we reach America, you will understand,' he said. 'The Lord will give you strength.'

So, the creature who had killed Eliza, who had exposed Margot and her child to the elements, had come for Amy now. She shivered, wondered how she would get through until morning. Why had she forgotten to lock the doors? 'I am to come with you to America, then?'

'Yes.'

She glanced down at her little fob watch, a gift from Mother. It was almost three o'clock and the Moorheads would not rise before seven. Four hours. Four hours to kill, four hours during which she might be killed. 'Shall I pack a bag?' she asked.

'I must look at you first.' His tone was thick.

'You put Margot to sleep – or so she told the nurses – a cloth over her nose and mouth.'

'Yes, I did.'

There was no guilt, Amy realized with a jolt. This man truly believed in all this dangerous nonsense. And had she not heard Mona say that he was probably impotent? 'How do you propose putting me to sleep?' As soon as this loaded question hit the air, Amy kicked herself inwardly. She should not goad him into action, should keep herself safe for as long as possible.

'I hope that you will come to me voluntarily.'

Amy swallowed, almost gagged. 'How shall I persuade myself to do that?' There she was again, forcing him to take action.

'We shall pray together,' he answered.

'And if I refuse?' The anger was heating up, was beginning to rise to the surface. She longed to pick up a weapon, to finish him off. He had committed one murder, had tried to commit a further two by exposing Margot and her child to cruel elements. 'You will get nowhere with me,' she said. 'You are quite the ugliest creature I have ever seen. The word ugly attaches not just to your physical appearance – which is quite bizarre, as I am sure you know – but also to your inner self. How can you speak of God when you are a cold-blooded murderer? That is the worst crime, as it offends all laws, social, criminal and moral.'

328

His mouth opened, closed again.

'You will not dare to touch me,' Amy continued. 'The girls you practised on were all unconscious, were they not? And not one of them was touched.' She decided to apply once more for an explanation. 'Why did you kill Eliza? Why was she the wrong one?'

'She went away to a city of sin.'

'Yes,' agreed Amy readily.

'Then she came back and . . . and she was the wrong one.'

'Margot was the wrong one, also,' said Amy.

'Margot is with child,' he answered.

Amy got up from her seat. 'I am asking you now to leave my house.'

He made no move.

'I am ordering you to leave,' she insisted.

He grinned. 'I intend to stay.'

'Then I shall go,' said Amy.

He crossed the room and hit her cheek with the flat of his hand, sending her reeling towards the back door. She righted herself, turned the handle and drew the door inward. 'Oh, thank God,' she muttered, blood streaming from the corner of her mouth.

James entered the house. 'Good morning, Mr Wilkinson,' he said smoothly. 'All three? In one night, all three Burton-Masseys? My goodness, you have been busy.'

Amy leaned against a wall, heart thumping wildly, face stinging, mouth bleeding. She watched in dumb fascination while James Mulligan balled a fist and crashed it into Wilkinson's jaw. 'Damn you,' he spat, 'you murderous bastard.'

Felled like a slaughtered ox, Wilkinson folded on the floor. Amy, too, slid down the wall, her legs refusing to take her weight. 'Thank you,' she managed to repeat, the words bubbling through split flesh.

'Not at all,' replied James. 'I've been waiting for ages to do that. Now, let's take a look at your face . . .'

TWENTY-FIVE

'Here, get up off the floor. My mammy believed that many ills come from a person sitting on stone flags.' Only a slight quickening in his breathing betrayed the fact that James Mulligan had just laid a man out cold.

She allowed him to lift her. 'Thank you,' she said again. 'But I thought you were locked up.' He lifted her as though she were a tiny, weightless thing.

He peered at her lip, could feel her agitated breath on his face. 'And I was so, but a woman came in and played merry hell, terrified the life out of the whole lot of them, she did. So thank you, Miss Amy Burton-Massey.'

She closed her eyes for an instant, saw Eliza on the slab, Margot in her hospital bed. She could not bear any of it. 'Did she die quickly, James?'

He would not tell Amy about Eliza's dying statement, not yet, at least. Perhaps this young woman would never need to know that Eliza had killed Rupert Smythe. 'She died almost instantly,' he lied. 'In seconds, I imagine.' No, poor Eliza had lingered, long enough for the creature here on the floor to have captured Margot, too. He prayed that the brain damage might have removed all pain.

Amy allowed him to clean her mouth with a handkerchief. He was gentle for so tall and broad a man.

'Your lip is swollen,' he informed her, 'but there's no

permanent damage. Now, I'll make sure that Mona gets to the shop tomorrow. You will stay at home for a day or so, no work, just visit Margot and rest yourself.'

'Yes, sir.' She moved her head. 'What about him?'

'Ah, yes, him.' James, too, fixed his eyes on the bundle on the floor, looked at his handiwork. He put himself in mind of his own father, a father who had been cruel and dangerous, a drinker, a gambler, a man who had indulged himself and only himself. 'You see what I am capable of, Amy?' Thomas Mulligan had won many a brawl in Dublin's public houses.

'Yes.'

'And you don't fear me?'

'Not at all. Had there been a knife to hand, I would have finished him off, James. This was a terrifying situation.'

'So it was.' He nodded sagely. 'Yes, this was an unusual occasion.'

'Thank God.'

He placed her in a chair near the fire, his hands achingly lonely once contact with her was lost. Even Eliza's death, the attack on Margot and, now, the threats to Amy, could not take away the longing, the sheer agony of loving this woman. He must attend now to matters practical, must get himself into sensible mode. 'Gun cupboard?' he asked.

'Under the stairs – why, James?'

'I'll stay with him. You go and fetch me a loaded shotgun. Extra bullets, too.'

'But, James, I—'

'Do it. Remember that the insane can be possessed of great strength once driven to the edge.'

Amy looked at the man on the floor. He was still breathing, but he looked as if he might well spend the rest of his life where he was, motionless, so deeply unconscious. 'I can't see him giving us any trouble, really, so—'

'Amy?'

'Right.' Like a child obeying the male parent, Amy went to do his bidding. The guns had not been used for years; Alex Burton-Massey had finished off many a fox with this little arsenal. Father had not approved of foxes, especially when they had killed masses of poultry only to make off with just

331

one chicken. Yet he had refused to join the hunt, because hunting was obnoxious. 'Starved dogs sent out to find a dinner that would not appease a couple of them, damned fool hobby.' As she picked out the best-looking of the guns, Amy heard his voice echoing down the years and into her head.

She sat on the second stair, gun between her knees, bullets in a cardboard box by her side. Father, Mother, now Eliza. 'Just Margot and I now,' she whispered into near-darkness. 'And whatever Rupert left in Margot's womb.'

What next? she wondered. Another funeral, once the doctors had finished poring over Eliza's remains. Strange how she had managed to look beautiful even when dead, the head wrapped in a piece of linen, curls breaking free to occupy that alabaster forehead. Then, once the burial was over, another wait, Margot and a birth, an unwanted child.

Amy checked herself. The baby would be a piece of tomorrow, a step towards the future. 'We shall love him or her, no matter what,' she mumbled. But first, this other business, the matter of the lunatic intruder. She stood up and carried the gun into the kitchen. God forbid that James should use it.

'Wake Moorhead,' James said.

'Now?'

'Yes.' He picked up the weapon, examined it, loaded it, left it broken. 'He must take my car and fetch the police.'

Amy turned to leave the room once more, then stopped in her tracks. 'He has never driven a car. Mind, he did work the land for many years, so he has used a tractor.'

'There you go, then, problem solved.'

'But what if . . .?'

'What if gets nothing done,' replied James. 'What if is a hide into nowhere – another of Mammy's sayings.'

She obeyed, returned to the kitchen and sat in silence with two men, a gun and a bubbling kettle. James made tea, flinched in unison with her when he saw the pain caused by hot liquid against a cut mouth. 'Will I cool that down for you with more milk?'

She shook her head, allowed her eyes to rest once again on the guardian. 'No, thanks. The police will be looking for him, no doubt.' Her gaze lingered on the hideous, now snoring figure on the flags.

'Yes, there'll be enough evidence in the shed and on his clothes to arrest him. I was thinking, I wonder where people get these strange ideas regarding religion.'

She didn't know, couldn't have cared less.

'Taking little bits of the Bible, usually Old Testament, then blowing them up out of all proportion.'

'He spoke of wise virgins,' replied Amy eventually. 'Killed Eliza because she had been to London, the city of sin, then dismissed Margot because of her . . . well . . . she is swollen.'

'And so he turned to you.'

Amy placed the cup in its saucer on the fireguard. 'There was no reason, no sense. How would he have managed to drag any of us to Texas?'

James thought for a few moments. 'They are preparing for the end of the world,' he told her at last. 'The end of the world will be dictated by the Supreme Guardian, who may very well instigate mass murder and suicide before changing his identity and running away with the profits.'

Amy sighed, picked up her cup. 'Mass hysteria, mass suicide – why do they listen?'

He lifted a shoulder. 'Who knows?'

A sleep-bewildered Eric Moorhead wandered in. 'Has summat gone on?' he enquired, one hand brushing over snow-white hair. 'Bloody hell – pardon me, miss – what the heck's happened in here?'

James and Amy were both too tired to relate the full story. 'Go to Bolton,' said James, 'to the police station. Tell them that Peter Wilkinson is here, at Caldwell Farm.'

'Aye, right.' He moved towards the body on the floor. 'Snoring like a pig,' he commented.

Amy looked at James. 'Tell Moorhead what he needs to know, please.' She went out to wash her face and comb her hair. Chill water bit into her cut lip, but she continued to splash her face. Anything touched by that evil man must be cleaned as vigorously as possible.

The reflection in the mirror showed a white face, a drained skin. She lit a second lamp, watched the light as it danced over furniture and gave life to inanimate objects, shifting the shadows, turning, twisting. The dresser had more life in it than

333

Eliza did. And Margot, poor little Margot, alive and in shock.

She wept softly into a towel, fighting the sobs as best she could. Through the window, a black sky was peppered with stars, each a tiny hole punched into navy velvet. Was heaven up there? Was it anywhere? Would Father, Mother and Eliza live on? Oh, God, please keep them, she prayed inwardly.

When she came down again, Moorhead had gone, while Wilkinson, muted by that single blow from a massive fist, remained blissfully unaware of his surroundings.

'I gave Moorhead tea and toast,' said James, 'then told him the rudiments. He knows that Eliza is dead and that this man killed her. You should go to bed.'

'No.'

'Amy . . .'

'No.' This was her house; she could go to bed, stay up, dance a jig if she so chose. He made her feel like a child in the presence of her father, because some instinct kept telling her to obey him without question. 'I don't mean to be rude, James, but I want to see this through.'

'Of course. Shall we make more tea?'

She drew a hand across her forehead. 'I suppose so. Anything that will keep us awake until the police arrive.'

A groaning sound emerged from Wilkinson's throat. In a flash, James snapped the gun into active mode and pointed it at the intruder. 'Don't move,' he warned.

'James, don't—' begged Amy.

'Give me some credit,' came the reply. 'Right.' He addressed Wilkinson now. 'Sit up with your back against that wall.'

Slowly, the man eased himself into a sitting position. His jaw, probably broken, hung out of line with the rest of his face. When he managed to focus fully on James, his eyes burned bright with undiluted hatred.

'The police are on their way,' James informed him.

Wilkinson tried to speak, but damaged bone prevented him.

'You will be behind bars within the hour.'

Do they not know who I am and why I am on this earth? Why can they not understand that my future lies with an educated female who will bring good breeding stock into the Light? The people of Makersfield need intelligent women to care for their

334

*children, women who could teach whole generations to honour the
Eternal Light, to praise the Lord and—*

*It is the devil's creature. There he sits with a gun directed at my
head, his face hardened against me. The Burton-Massey girl frowns,
too. And I can say nothing because the brute has broken my jaw.
It was all meant to be, all dictated to me as I sat within the circle
of Light, while I meditated. The papist knows nothing; he is steeped
in mistakes made by Rome, errors passed down the years as if they
were edicts from God Himself.*

*Prison? They cannot imprison me, have not the ability to con-
tain my righteousness and my wrath. Does this Irishman believe
that I shall hang? The Light will intervene, will show me what I
must do to break the chains of humankind, for I am beyond and
above the judgement of mere mortals. I have done no wrong: I
merely removed obstacles.*

'I think he's clinically insane,' said James. 'He may well finish
the rest of his days in an asylum.'

Amy had nothing to say.

'You must beg forgiveness,' James added. 'Pray for yourself,
Wilkinson.'

The guardian could feel his eyes bulging even further than
normal, as if they sought to escape their sockets. What did this
man know of penitence, prayer, forgiveness? Catholics were all
the same, drunken louts who produced too many ragged children
and huge profits for distilleries and breweries.

James lowered the gun. 'You understand that you have
murdered Eliza? That you placed Margot in danger? Can you not
grasp that you have done wrong and that you will be punished
by the law of this land? The Light is not true, Peter.'

At the sound of his given name, the man snarled, causing pain
to shoot right through his head. He was Guardian Wilkinson and
no one should use his first name unless specifically invited.

'I know people in America, good men who have investigated
claims from Texas. A dry land, as you know, where desiccated
vegetation burns quite frequently. From accidents of nature and
from men with matches, your Light has grown. As we speak, the
Supreme Guardian is on the verge of arrest for fraud.'

'Liar,' managed Wilkinson, though the effort almost killed
him.

'No, Peter. I tell the truth and only the truth.'

Wilkinson blinked. There was something in James Mulligan's voice that was almost hypnotic. He felt much as he had when contemplating the Light, when meditating. So this was one of Mulligan's gifts from the devil.

'Hear me, Peter. Look at me, look at Amy. She is not a bad person. You cannot believe in your heart of hearts that it is right to drag unwilling young women across the Atlantic ocean; nor can you truly believe that any such person would go voluntarily. You are in a dream, Peter. You are the one out of step. The rest of us walk different paths, but the rhythm is much the same. Peter, the Temple of Eternal Light in Texas is under siege by the police who are trying to get people out before it is too late.'

Wilkinson emitted a single sob. Lies, lies, more lies.

'It is true,' James insisted. 'It's all over for you and for the rest of those poor, misguided souls.'

A sliver of doubt insinuated its way into Wilkinson's brain. Was the true temple under siege? No, this was all part of a plot drawn up by men such as this, the unchosen. He moved his head, winced as pain shot through his jaw once more.

A car drew up outside, then another. Four policemen entered the kitchen, truncheons on alert, feet battering the floor as the beefy men took away James's gun and dragged Wilkinson to his feet. He was arrested there and then, his rights read aloud before handcuffs were employed.

Moorhead waited until the back door had closed. 'Well, there's nowt as queer nor folk,' he announced, before plodding up the stairs and back to the warmth of his bed.

Alone, Amy and James drew breath as if for the first time in over an hour. 'I should not wish to repeat that experience,' said James.

Amy rose and placed her hands in the small of her back, where a stiffness had been born as a result of sitting in such tension. 'Will he hang?' she asked.

'Probably not. He may well be judged too insane to plead one way or the other.'

There was an awkwardness between them now, as if the sudden disappearance of Peter Wilkinson had forced them to

336

face life all over again. 'I'll do all I can,' he said softly. 'Funeral and so forth.'

'Thank you.'

'And you were brave there, Amy.'

'So were you.'

He lowered his chin and his voice. 'No. Nothing brave about a big man hitting a little man. Broke his jaw, too.'

'He was better off asleep,' replied Amy. 'Will you go home now?' she asked.

'No. You will not sleep. Neither shall I.'

They repaired to the parlour and set the fire, each busy with kindling, coal and paper. Huddled in coats, they sat each side of the fireplace, oblivious to puffs of smoke and crackles of wood. 'It'll warm up in a minute,' James announced hopefully.

'This room never gets warm,' she answered.

'Then I shall send someone to look at the flue.'

'Not today, James, not today.'

'All right, so.'

They slept fitfully, both uncomfortable in a chair, each uneasy in the other's company. It occurred to Amy in one semi-conscious moment that this was the first time she had spent a night with a man, and that she felt no fear of him. What she did feel was inexplicable, a sort of dependence that she objected to, a sense of belonging with him, almost needing him.

For his part, James watched, watched while she slept, pretended not to be awake when she looked at him. It was the sort of game a twelve-year-old might play, peeping at a girl, acting silly, imagining a kiss, an embrace.

At about six o'clock, they gave up and made breakfast. Amy managed a slice of toast and three cups of tea, while James, plainly a country man, ate bacon and eggs. When his plate was cleaned, he spoke. 'Moorhead can take Mona to the shop and the children to school,' he said.

'But—'

'But we shall see what the day brings, Amy. I have to go to the Grange to see the workmen, but apart from that I intend to be here with you.'

'Thank you.' The words sounded hollow, unsure.

The house got to its feet eventually, Moorhead concealing

337

yawns as he fetched wood and coal, Elspeth looking covertly at the young mistress and Mr Mulligan, her head filled to the brim with tales her husband had uttered on rising.

At eight o'clock, Elspeth answered the door and allowed Gordon Jones into the parlour. Dr Jones had cared for the Burton-Masseys for many years, and his heart almost broke when he saw Amy, so pale, so tired and so alone. Ah, no, here was Mulligan, a fine chap, a rock of a man. 'Mr Mulligan.'

'Dr Jones. We have had quite a night of it.'

'So I understand,' replied the doctor. 'Rumour has it that you were arrested.'

'I was.' James told the tale while Amy, her face whiter than bleached linen, sat close to the fire.

When he had heard the full story, Dr Jones squatted low on his heels in front of Amy. 'There has been a development,' he said softly. 'Something I think you should know.'

Oh, God, not more bad news? She tried to smile at the visitor, failed completely. 'Is Margot worse?' she asked tremulously.

'Margot is very well,' answered Gordon Jones. 'I was with her an hour ago and she is in fine fettle, eating everyone's breakfast.'

'Good.'

Dr Jones glanced at James. 'Amy, this is about Eliza.'

'Eliza? But Eliza is dead.'

'Yes.' The doctor took hold of Amy's hands. 'The staff at the morgue examined your sister's body. There will be more detailed investigations, but they did not have to look hard to find out that Eliza was . . . Amy, your sister was already dying.'

Amy frowned. 'I don't understand. He killed her – that man, the one who was here.'

'Yes, yes, he did.' The doctor cleared a lump of agony from his throat. 'Your sister's skull was damaged. There was a growth, Amy, a cancer on her brain. It was large enough to be visible.'

She inhaled suddenly, a hand to her mouth.

'Eliza might well have been dead within months.'

'No,' she insisted. 'There was nothing wrong with – with her.'

James turned and looked through the window. How much more could this poor woman take?

'Oh, my God,' she breathed. 'Oh, God . . .'

'Amy?' The doctor rose and stepped back.

338

She stared into the grate, watched the flames dancing and darting as if they believed this to be just another day. An awareness was creeping over her, pushing its face into her mind, making her think, remember. Eliza. So beautiful, so creative, so . . . cold. Cold now, certainly, but cold in her heart for some time . . .

'Can I get you something?' asked the doctor.

'No.' It was all becoming clear, beginning to make sense. But first, there was a question to be asked. 'Dr Jones?'

'Yes?'

'Something in her head?'

'A brain tumour, Amy.'

She nodded slowly. 'Might such a growth have affected her behaviour? She changed so much after Mother died – oh, poor Eliza. We all thought—'

'Calm yourself.' Dr Jones placed a hand on her head. 'I brought the three of you into this world. You were all lovely girls, clever, gifted and beautiful.' He blinked away a mist over his eyes. 'She changed, yes. There is a theory that severe shock can activate a tumour. Your mother's death might have made Eliza's condition worse. That is not to say that the tumour was caused by Mrs Burton-Massey's sudden death – it was probably there already – but shock may have been a factor in the tumour's accelerated development.'

Amy smiled. 'Thank you.'

'Not at all. Would you like a sedative?' he asked.

'No. I must visit Margot and arrange the funeral. Although we have to wait for . . . for whatever must be done with Eliza's body, I shall talk to the undertaker.' She stood up and shook his hand. 'Thank you,' she repeated. 'You have answered so many questions. But I have one more, one you failed to answer earlier.'

'Fire away,' invited the doctor.

She inhaled deeply as if arming herself. 'The thing on her brain, the tumour. You have said that it might have been made worse by Mother's death, but could it have altered Eliza's behaviour, turned her into someone different?'

'The short answer is yes, Amy. The longer version is that we don't know enough yet about the human brain, though patients with problems like Eliza's have altered beyond recognition. Their movements, speech and hearing can be affected, as can memory and behaviour.'

'She stopped caring,' whispered Amy.

'No,' replied the doctor. 'Parts of her brain ceased to function. Her soul remained much the same, I'm sure.'

'I thought she was bad,' explained Amy. 'The things she did, the icy attitude to me and to Margot. It was all a part of her illness, wasn't it?'

'Yes.'

Amy's shoulders relaxed. Perhaps the wicked Wilkinson had done poor Eliza a favour, because she would not have to linger now in pain and confusion. How easily and readily we judge one another, thought Amy, as James saw the doctor to the door. I believed that my sister was evil, even told her that she was a nasty piece of work. But I was ill-informed and cannot blame myself, as that would be negative and stupid. All the same, I shall direct my prayers to Mother and ask her to keep Eliza with her.

Had Eliza killed Rupert Smythe? Had she pushed him down those tortuous stairs? Well, Mrs Smythe could not expect an answer now. The blue-eyed boy was gone and . . . and Margot was expecting his child. How simple life had been before all of this.

James came in. 'More tea, Amy? I am just about to send Moorhead to take the children to school.'

'Yes, a cup of tea, please. And . . .' She looked at him, saw a face made dingy by stubble, a creased coat, tired eyes, limp cuffs on a shirt loaned to him by a policeman. James's own shirt, stained with Eliza's blood, had been removed as evidence. 'I don't know how I would have managed without you.'

His eyes met hers. 'You would have managed, Amy.'

'I think not.' She was uneasy, yet the discomfort was not a bad feeling. 'I might not have overcome him, James.'

'Oh, you would have stopped him. You are a strong girl, Amy.'

What was he really saying? And was this the appropriate time to be finding a man attractive, effective and kind? 'Not as strong as you seem to think, James.'

He felt a heat in his face, stepped back and went off to brew yet more tea. Brushing aside Elspeth Moorhead's offer to

340

help, he warmed the pot, set a tray, found spoons, cups, saucers.

Elspeth carried on peeling carrots. In her almost seventy years on God's earth, she had learned a thing or two. Even at this unbearably sad time, Elspeth Moorhead recognized a man in love, so the tears that tumbled into vegetable peelings were not all sad. Mr Mulligan would do very well for Amy, very well indeed.

TWENTY-SIX

Sally woke at about seven o'clock. The great house was always quiet in the mornings, yet today's silence was particularly empty, causing her to feel that she was the last creature alive on earth. Ah, she remembered now. The police had been here, then Mary and her two brothers had run away into the night, leaving Sally all alone in a place with fourteen bedrooms.

She jumped up, splashed her face, dressed quickly. Mr Mulligan was under arrest. The police had reported that Eliza Burton-Massey had been found dead. On the stairs outside her attic room, Sally paused, remembering how kind Miss Eliza had been for a while. Then she had changed, had become sullen and dismissive, almost cruel. Perhaps Eliza had upset some ill-tempered man, but that man was not Mr Mulligan. Poor Eliza. Whatever she had done or been, she had not deserved to die so young.

Sally knocked, then opened Mary's door. The bed had not been slept in, so Mary had probably gone for good. Mary Whitworth had accused Mr Mulligan of locking those two brothers of hers in the cellar. Rubbish. And once the cellars had been searched by police everyone knew that there was nothing else down there. So much for the prisoner under the kitchen, mused Sally, as she reached the main landing.

He had not been home. She looked around the neat room: just a bed, a table, a chest of drawers and a small wardrobe. The man

342

lived so sparsely, as if he meant to leave no mark here. Having sold the inn in town and some paintings from the house, he was now investing in a hydro so that the Burton-Masseys would have a good living once he had returned to Ireland. But would he ever get home? Would he be out of prison? God forbid that he should hang . . .

What could she do? She cut and buttered a slice of bread, poured herself a cup of milk, carried her makeshift breakfast through to the hallway. When she opened the front door, she saw that his car had gone. So, as well as being under wrongful arrest, Mr Mulligan had lost his car. She glanced sideways in the direction of the larger of Pendleton Grange's two conservatories, but no one had arrived yet. A swimming-pool was under construction inside the building, while tennis courts and some extra stables would be built when spring came. Would the builders bother to turn up when they found out that their employer had been put behind bars? 'Ooh, hurry up back, Mrs Kenny,' Sally pleaded softly. 'This all wants sorting out.'

On a whim, she ran back to the kitchen and dragged her outdoor clothing from a peg. She could not work, could not sit and wait while one of the nicest men on earth languished in jail. Something had to be done. Sally wasn't quite sure how or why, but this all needed to be put right. Mrs Kenny was going to be home this afternoon, but that was hours away. And who had stolen the car?

The tram terminus was over three miles away by road, so she decided to cut through fields to save time and feet. Sally was on her way to Bolton; Sally would give the police a piece of her not inconsiderable intellect.

The trouble with grown-ups, Diane decided, was that they kept too many secrets. They knew a lot but, whenever pressed, they said things like 'You'll find out when you're older', then went off in whispering huddles, thereby making the whole thing even more interesting than it might have been.

But Diane had her ways, and these ways were aided by the fact that three bedrooms had been created with partitions so thin that everyone could hear snores, coughs, sneezes and even shifts of a quilt on a bed. So she sat upstairs and listened. Within the

343

space of three minutes, she learned that Eliza Burton-Massey had been killed and that Mr Mulligan had been put in prison.

She indulged in a few quiet tears, then decided to ration the weeping, save it until later. Because Diane Hewitt was suddenly very angry. Mr Mulligan hadn't killed anyone. The child's first instinct was to tell her grandmother about the guardian in the woods, but she could not. Last night's expedition had been explained away by lies, and Ida Hewitt was not fond of untruths these days. Also, Diane could not say how she had found out just now about the murder, or she would be chastised for eaves-dropping again.

Mona was speaking now. 'Aye, the milkman told me – it's all over the village, he says. But Mr Mulligan could never kill any-body. And Margot were there and all, stripped down to nowt. Well, he'd not do a thing like that.'

'No, no, you're right there, Mona.'

'In prison and all,' continued Mona, 'for summat he's definitely not done. I mean, I'm sure many an innocent man dangles on the end of a rope. Police is only interested in tidying up, not bothered who they hang. Courts is the same.'

'Well, the kiddies'll have to stop at home today,' said Ida. 'He always takes them to school – what shall I tell our Diane?'

'Eeh, don't ask me, love. That granddaughter of yours is as old as the hills any road.'

Ida coughed. 'This cold's hanging on a bit.' Diane heard the sound of Gran blowing her nose. 'I'd decided to shift them over to the village school and all, but will we still be living here?'

'Course we will,' replied Mona immediately. 'I've enough to buy the house if needs must. But it won't come to that, will it? He's innocent. And any road, he says he's going to give the estate back once he's mended his dad's doings. So whatever happens, Amy'll have a say in it.'

'I hope so,' answered Ida. There followed a sizeable pause. 'How will you get to work, Mona? That shop's had enough set-backs, and I can't see Amy being up to much now that her poor sister's been murdered.'

'Oh, I can't think,' said Mona. 'Let's make a bit of breakfast, then decide what's to be done. But I'll tell you one thing for nothing, Ida.'

344

'What's that?'

'I'd like to know where Peter Wilkinson were last night. Supposed to be in Birmingham by all accounts. He's no more in bloody Birmingham than thee and me. Remember that lass me and James Mulligan found in your old house? That were Wilkinson's doing. I get a funny feeling yon man's at the back of this lot and all.'

Diane tiptoed out of the room and down the stairs, the truth fizzing about in her head and tempting her to speak up. No, she must say nothing yet. She tried to keep her face normal as Gran and Mona entered the kitchen. 'I've put the kettle on,' she said.

Joe came in from the front garden. He set four places, found butter, knives and cups. Diane brewed the tea while Ida brought bread and porridge to the table. The child could not look at the adults, could not say anything about what she had seen. But she would – oh, yes, she would.

The car pulled up at the front gate.

'Here's Mr Mulligan,' cried Joe.

Diane pretended not to notice hope dawning on the faces of the two women. After all, Diane knew nothing. She drank her tea, put on hat and coat, made sure that little Joe was warmly clad.

Mona was first at the car. 'Oh, it's you,' she said to Eric Moorhead.

He nodded. His instructions were that he must not say a word about what had happened, especially in front of the children. 'Mr Mulligan's busy,' he said, 'so I've to do the driving today.' He smiled at the children. 'Come on, then, let's be getting you to school.'

The drive was conducted in total silence. Moorhead, who was used only to farm machinery, simply ploughed ahead, ignoring most crossroads, hitting the verge a few times, blissfully unaware of his passengers' misgivings. He dropped a shaky Mona at the shop, then deposited the children outside their school. 'Er ... don't go to Mr Mulligan's yard after your lessons,' he said. 'I'll pick you up here. Stand where I can see you.'

He drove off.

Joe looked at his sister, an expression of bemusement on his face. 'Well, we're alive,' he said, his eyes fixed on the

345

disappearing car. 'That was frightening, it's a wonder we're still in one piece.'

'Only just.' What was going on at all? Why hadn't the man said about Mr Mulligan being away at least? She bent down. 'Joe?'

'What?'

'You know how Gran's had that cough for a week or two?'

He nodded.

'Tell them I've caught Gran's bad cold. Say I'm in bed, too ill for school.' She squeezed his arm, fixed him with a gimlet stare. 'Please, Joe?'

'Why?'

'Because I've got to go and do something.' Her thoughts remained disordered, but something had to be resolved.

'What have you got to . . .?' Joe's words trailed off. Their Diane had a face on her like a clog bottom when she was determined. 'You've got Gran's cold,' he said resignedly.

'Good lad.' She planted a kiss on his cheek, then skipped off down the road. She was going to be a heroine, like somebody in a book who just turns up and puts things right. Plans were vague, but anger sustained her.

Then the spring went out of her step when she thought about Eliza and Margot and Amy. But she was hell bent on making the police let Mr Mulligan go. So, instead of skipping, she adopted a slow march and said a little prayer for Eliza.

For over an hour, Diane walked the streets of Bolton, her whole being concentrating on what must be achieved. Whatever the method, she would get Mr Mulligan out of jail today. Halfway through her third tour of Deansgate, she bumped into Sally Hayes, her greatest friend in the whole world. 'What are you doing here?' she cried.

'You should be at school,' answered Sally.

'And you should be at the Grange.' They both stopped outside a chemist's shop, each pretending to be interested in great bottles of coloured fluid and advertisements for liver pills.

'He's in prison,' said Sally, 'and somebody's pinched his car and all. I don't know what's going on.'

'Well, the milkman says Miss Eliza's been murdered. Is that right?'

346

Sally nodded. 'And Mr Mulligan's been arrested. I . . . I didn't know what to do. Like it didn't seem proper to carry on as normal, cleaning up and all that. So I came here to . . . I don't even know why I'm here. I've a feeling I might be on my way to the police station, though.'

'Well, I know why I'm here, Sally, and my reason's the same as yours. And I'm glad to have some company and all. Come on, we've something important to do.'

'But – but what?' Sally had to run to keep up with the younger girl's determined pace. 'What, Diane?'

'We're getting him out of prison, that's what.'

'Eh?'

'Trust me.' Diane sounded very much the adult. After crossing the road, she stopped in her tracks, almost causing her companion to shunt right into her. 'The car's not been pinched,' she announced. 'Mr Moorhead brought us down in it this morning.'

'That's something, I suppose,' said Sally. Then she began to wonder about how Moorhead had got the car, why he had it, how Mr Mulligan had contacted Moorhead and . . . and it was all beyond her.

There was a small crowd outside the police station, some with cameras, many with notebooks. Diane's stomach rose into her gullet: she was not keen on trying to fight her way through this lot. They were all waiting for Mr Mulligan to be dragged out and pushed into the courtroom, she mused. 'Excuse me.' She prodded the nearest journalist on the back. 'I have to get inside.'

The man looked over his shoulder. 'You'll not get in, love,' he told her. 'It's like bedlam, is this.'

She pushed, pummelled and fought her way through to the front where a pair of constables stood in the doorway. 'And what do you want?' one asked.

Diane blew a string of hair from her face, then made some attempt to smooth her clothing.

'Shouldn't you be at school?' asked the other.

'I've got . . .' Diane turned and looked at a man who had just pushed her from behind. While giving him her famous hard stare, she searched her mind, determined to find what she wanted. She knew the word, had read it in newspapers, but she couldn't lay

347

her tongue across it. 'Evidence,' she screamed in triumph, swinging round to face the guardians of the law. 'I've got evidence.'

'Aye,' drawled the nearest policeman, 'and I've got a pain in my backside.'

The crowd laughed uncertainly.

This was a desperate situation and Diane Hewitt would deal with it. She was becoming inured to the ploys of adults, to the 'go away till you're older' faction. Grown-ups were just tall children. They did right and wrong, were not perfect and were often very ill-informed. 'You've got the wrong man,' she announced clearly.

The congregation was suddenly silent.

'And how do you know that?' asked the younger of the two policemen.

'Because I was a – a what-you-call-it . . . I was a witness.'

At this point, the sentries decided to err on the side of caution. If this little nuisance had been a witness, she needed to be taken away from all the hungry pressmen before her evidence got spoilt. The constables made a gap between them large enough for Diane to squeeze her slender frame into the station. 'I want me friend with me,' she insisted. 'Sally Hayes – she's one of the maids from Pendleton Grange.'

While one went off to disentangle Sally from the knot of journalists, the other took Diane into a small room. 'When your friend gets here, I'll fetch the sergeant,' he said.

Diane waited. Eventually, a bedraggled Sally was brought into the arena. 'Are you all right?' Diane asked.

'Apart from being nearly trampled underfoot,' replied Sally.

Diane glared at the newly arrived sergeant. 'You want to shift that lot before they do damage,' she advised. 'I am a witness and I very nearly didn't get in.'

The sergeant looked up at the ceiling, plainly annoyed to have been dragged away from his elevenses or some other important part of the daily routine.

'I'm not messing,' Diane told him.

'She never messes,' piped Sally.

'Well, I've heard different,' pronounced the tall man. 'She's Diane Hewitt and she's had her fingers in a fair few pies.'

'Yes,' Diane agreed smartly. 'But, like me Gran says, the pies was too hot so I've give over doing all that.' She felt very pleased with the way she was handling these so-called mature folk.

He sat down opposite the two girls. 'Right,' he said, a false smile stretching the fresh face. 'Fire away.'

Diane inhaled. 'You've got the wrong man.'

'The wrong man,' echoed Sally.

Large fingers tapped on the table.

'He never did it,' added Diane.

'Couldn't do anything like that,' said Sally.

He stopped drumming on the table. 'You two a double act?'

Sally and Diane glanced at each other. 'No,' they chorused.

He fixed his eyes on Diane. 'You tell me,' he said, 'by yourself.'

Diane took as deep a breath as she could manage. 'Our Joe fell and he was behind a tree, then I carried on, see, till I got near the little hut. And the guardian were there. I saw Mr Mulligan with me own eyes and—'

'Slow down, please,' interrupted the sergeant. 'And what was Mr Mulligan doing?'

'Nothing,' replied Diane smartly. 'But, you see, he got arrested even though it wasn't him what did it. Please, please, listen to me.'

'I'm listening,' he replied, suddenly aware that the occasional flash of steel in the girl's eyes was a symptom of intelligence and determination.

'I was a laudator in the Light,' the child continued. 'That was how I met Mr Wilkinson – that's Mr Peter Wilkinson, not Mr Stephen.'

The man nodded encouragingly.

'You're right, I have to slow down, like,' said Diane, 'get it all in order. My head's too busy.'

'Just tell me everything you remember,' asked the sergeant.

And she did. She went through the cleansings, the attempts to get young women to cross the Atlantic. 'Have you never known that somebody's bad, even though you can't prove it?' she asked the man.

He nodded. 'All the time, love.'

'Well, I can prove this,' she said. 'I saw that man running away. He'd been in the hut thing, that shed where gamekeepers

349

spied on folk pinching birds and rabbits. Mr Wilkinson did the killing, he must have. I heard Mr Mulligan shouting. He were running, I think. But he weren't running away, he were running towards, trying to help. The one running away were Mr Peter Wilkinson.'

The sergeant opened his mouth, was ready to explain the altered situation, but the girl carried on regardless.

'Like I said about knowing bad folk, you can tell a good one and all. Mr Mulligan is one of the best men on this earth.' She paused for a split second. 'He must be good, because Gran likes him even though he's a Catholic. Well, he picked us up, me, our Joe and me gran. He got me reading all kinds, proper books, poems. He sends fruit for our Joe – that's me little brother with the rickets. Let him go. You have to let him go. I were there, you see.' She inhaled against a tide of hysteria. 'Mr Mulligan is an excellent man.' She had done her best, had even remembered a good word. 'Excellent' described James Mulligan to a T.

'Have you done?' Bushy eyebrows were raised.

'I suppose so.' Diane's shoulders sagged. She felt as if she had just run a very long race.

The sergeant faced the constable in the doorway. 'Fetch us all some tea,' he said wearily, 'while I get to the bottom of this lot.'

Diane glanced at Sally. 'She knows him,' she informed the sergeant. 'She knows Mr Mulligan.'

'Mr Mulligan's my boss,' said Sally. 'He is so kind. Got me from the Chiverton Children's Home and gave me a proper job.'

'Aye, I've heard,' said the sergeant.

Diane took a breath, continued to labour her point. 'Mr Mulligan chased him. He chased the guardian away. There were a light in the woods, see. It were him in that there hut.' She shut her eyes tight, pictured the scene she had witnessed.

'Guardian Wilkinson?' the man asked.

'Yes.' She opened her eyes. 'So you've got the wrong man.'

The sergeant blinked slowly. 'Who have we got?' he asked.

Diane looked at Sally. Happy enough to have discovered that grown-ups were daft, she still knew that there was only so much idiocy she could take. The sergeant, the boss of the whole police station, didn't know who he had in the cells. A saying of Gran's popped out of Diane's mouth before she could apply

350

the brakes. 'If you don't know, then you don't deserve telling.'

The man's mouth twitched. 'No, I know who we've got. But do you know who we've got locked up?'

Diane and Sally both nodded furiously. 'Course we know who you've got,' said Sally. 'That's why we're here. You have got my boss in the cell. He's a fine man.'

The man's red hands tightened until the knuckles gleamed white. 'Who do you work for?' he barked, the words directed at Sally. 'Go on, tell me again. Then I'll have my say.'

'For Mr Mulligan, of course,' Sally answered.

'And who are you here to speak up for?' he asked Diane.

Seconds marked their own death on the face of a wall clock, a thin, black hand moving stickily across at least ten marks. The sergeant wiped a hand along his brow. 'In the cells,' he said slowly, 'there is a Mr Peter Wilkinson.'

The girls glanced at each other. 'The guardian?' asked Sally.

'Yes.'

Diane opened her mouth to speak, found no words, shut it immediately.

'Then where is Mr Mulligan?' Sally's voice was shrill.

'I have no idea,' replied the weary man.

'You've gone and lost him,' Sally accused. 'He never came home last night.'

'Lost him?' boomed the sergeant. 'Is he a dog? I'll answer that one for you, no, he isn't. He's a grown man and he walked out of here middle of last night. As far as we know, he's at home holding himself in readiness for giving a full statement. He's a witness.'

'So am I,' said Diane.

'I know.' These two words were squeezed past the sergeant's clenched teeth. 'And you have to tell me everything you heard and saw, and you do not talk to that lot outside, the newspaper people.'

'Oh, right.' Diane felt important now. She was a witness and she had evidence and Mr Mulligan would not dangle at the end of a rope. 'He must have murdered Miss Eliza,' she said very softly.

'That's as may be,' answered the policeman. 'Only it's got to be proved.'

351

Diane was suddenly angry once more. 'Why didn't you tell us before?' she asked. 'Why did you let me rattle on when you knew Mr Mulligan wasn't here?'

The sergeant straightened his spine. For the life of him, he could not remember how the conversation had gone, whether he had listened properly, whether the child had been talking non-sense. 'We've got to write it all down,' he said now. It wasn't going to be easy. He had no detailed idea what she had seen, where she had seen it, when—

'Sally, you go home,' said Diane.

'But what if—?'

'Just go and find him. He's got no right messing about while there's murder going on. See if he's at work or at Caldwell Farm.' She emitted a heavy sigh. 'It's time a few people got a bit of sense,' she grumbled to herself. Then, in her usual clear tone, she spoke to Sally. 'Search high and low, please. Tell him he's got us all in a right state.'

Sergeant Cooper looked at the clock. The child who needed interviewing was not an easy customer. He blew out his cheeks, opened a drawer and took out a form. If recent experience could be taken as a guideline, he might be here till well past his shift's end. 'Right,' he began. 'Name?'

Diane looked up to heaven, waved goodbye to Sally, then gave her full attention to the man in charge. 'You know my name,' she replied.

'I still have to ask it,' he said.

Diane Hewitt folded her arms and leaned them on the table. It seemed there would be no end to the stupidity, then. She was the child, he was the adult. How would he feel if she acted her age? 'Do you know you have hairs growing out of your nose?' she asked.

The man licked the end of an indelible pencil.

'And your tongue'll go blue if you keep doing that.'

He placed the pencil on the table. 'Fish and chips do you?' he asked.

She awarded him a brilliant smile. 'Yes, please,' she said. 'Food'll help me to remember.'

He stood up and walked to the door. Tonight, he would trim those nose-hairs. But tonight was a long, long way away.

352

TWENTY-SEVEN

' "The perimeter walls of Makersfield's Eternal Light Settlement were scaled by Federal officers at dawn yesterday. There was little or no resistance, since the leader of the cult, Elijah Freeman, had absconded days earlier. Members of the sect were hungry, thirsty and disoriented, many having been starved of food and water for several days.

' "The condition of most people was so poor that some officers, even those who have served for over twenty years, were overcome by the distressing sight of children whose limbs were scarcely strong enough to support them. Medical teams are working round the clock to feed and tend inhabitants before evacuating the site.

' "It appears that members of the Temple of Eternal Light were required to starve as part of a penance, though the Supreme Guardian is said to have enjoyed a wholesome diet and unlimited privileges. As far as our correspondent can evaluate at the present time, Elijah Freeman has forty-seven children within the campus, most born of girls who were no more than thirteen or fourteen years of age when first 'offered' to him.

' "Survivors will be taken eventually to hospitals where their physical and mental health will be assessed. The bodies of two babies and two adults were removed this morning. Three wells had been sealed and there was no other source of water, so we conclude that Freeman and his closest allies were responsible for the potential deaths from starvation of over two hundred and fifty residents of the complex.

'"Rumour has it that those who tried to escape were shot and buried within the walls; it will therefore be necessary to dig over the whole area once the people have been removed. Decent citizens of surrounding towns and settlements were shocked by these revelations. One, an oil prospector named Hubert Collinge, had been trying to alert communities for some months, but to no avail. 'I guess people were scared,' he told our reporter. 'I sure as God knew there was something wrong in there, but no one would listen to me. The temple is so remote that Freeman got away with real murder.' Collinge, a six-foot tall man, was sobbing as he expressed feelings of real grief, guilt and anguish.

'"Temples of Eternal Light throughout the western world are gripped by shock at this terrible time. Most are expected to disband in the wake of recent revelations. We understand that many in Europe have sent young girls to Makersfield, Texas, in the vain hope of offering their female children a better life."'

James folded the newspaper.

Kate, who had been listening wide-eyed and open-mouthed, sat down suddenly in her fireside chair. 'The devil's work,' she pronounced. 'And what's to happen down yonder, now, with the guardian in prison on a murder charge? Does the temple close?' She jerked her head in the direction of Bolton.

'God knows.'

Kate eyed him speculatively. Because of her friend's funeral, she had missed all the action. Now, three weeks later and with the tale told many times, she still remained in deep shock. James had been arrested. Had the whole thing not been so tragic, it might have been laughable. But there was something else, another layer to her nephew's unease. 'It's Amy, so,' she pronounced, with the air of one who would brook no argument. She had watched him at Eliza's funeral, his eyes fixed on Amy, sadness etched deep into his features.

He turned his head and looked at her. 'What was that?'

'Plain as the proverbial pikestaff,' she said. 'You are a man in love, James Mulligan.'

It was no use. She knew him, could see right into his mind, heart and soul. 'No comment,' he replied.

354

Kate Kenny sauntered to the table, took a sip of tea and picked up the newspaper. She placed her cup in its saucer, pretended a sudden interest in headlines. 'And how's your business in the cellar?'

'Don't,' he replied. 'Stop it, Kate.'

'And why should I?' she asked, spreading the paper on the table. 'For I am just about your only living family and there is nowhere else for you to turn. You cannot expect me to sit here without expressing some concern.'

He stood up.

'That's right,' she cried, 'run away from me, then. Howandever, you cannot run from yourself.'

'But I can go home,' he replied. 'I've sold every horse to a Cheshire stables, so the money's there – I might appoint a site manager for this place. The businesses in town can easily be made over to Amy and Margot. Yes, I may well go home.'

There followed a lengthy silence. James stood at the window and gazed at the almost empty stable block. Kate fiddled with a brooch at her throat. 'James?' she said eventually.

'Yes?'

'Don't leave her, not yet. Sure, the poor girl has lost her mother and one of her sisters – and isn't Margot only just out of the hospital? And that Smythe woman is still raving on about her son, St Rupert. Can you imagine Amy coping without you? This new publicity has made her shop so popular that the orders are a mile high and—'

'Kate, be quiet, please.'

'But I am only—'

'Shush,' he commanded. Kate was right. He would have to be here while the hydro got built, while it opened, while all the places in town got passed over to the Burton-Massey girls. And A Cut Above was doing rather too well ... 'It's killing me, Kate,' he said.

'I know.'

'I want to run before it gets any worse,' he continued. 'She is so alone. Margot will become wrapped up in her baby, I've no doubt. For all her flightiness, she is going to make a good mother.'

'Yes. Oh, James, how I worry for you.'

355

Swivelling on a heel, he faced her. 'I'm not ready for this,' he murmured. 'This was not meant to happen. And I can't conquer it, Kate. It's as if she is a part of me, of what I have become over these past months.'

She waited.

'God, I wish I'd never come here. But with my father leaving such a mess, I was duty-bound, Kate. Nothing at all on God's good earth would have persuaded me not to come over. The mess I found – the inn on its last legs, the house mortgaged to the hilt, a woman and three daughters cast out ... What else might I have done?'

Kate raised her shoulders. 'I don't know, son, and that's the truth of it.'

He smiled wanly. 'God's good,' he said quietly.

'He is so. And with His blessing, the path might just become clearer, James.' She tried to inject some hope into the words, failed miserably. Ah, well, there were chores to be done. This was Sally's day off, and the other madam, Mary, the Light-fingered, had disappeared back into the bosom of her family. With a heavy heart, Kate set about the business of the day.

'Miss Eliza had what they call a brain tumour,' Diane explained to Sally. They were hiding in a deserted corner of the Bolton Central Library, both of them on pins, as Diane should have been at school.

'I know.' Sally glanced at the clock. 'We'll have to shift if we're going to get there before dinner-time. Your teachers might do their shopping during the dinner hour.'

'That'd be why she stopped liking you, Sal.'

'I know,' repeated the older girl. It was plain that Diane was not in a listening mood.

But Diane decided to shut up for a minute. She was closer to Sally than to any of her school friends. She didn't want to lose Sal, because Sal played out like a younger girl, still liked hop-scotch, skipping ropes and, when teams could be scraped together, a game of rounders. 'I don't mean to get on your nerves,' she explained eventually.

'Sisters get on one another's nerves,' replied Sally, 'and we're like sisters.'

356

Diane smiled. 'You see, the congregation's all stuck in a rut,' she declared.

Sally, used by now to Diane's butterfly mind, agreed. 'They won't know what to do. I mean, how many years have they prayed to that light, Diane? It's what Mrs Kenny would call a vocal point.'

'She does that on purpose,' Diane murmured. 'She knows it should be focal point.'

They stared at a blank wall for several minutes, each deep in thought. Had they bitten off more than they could chew? Would today's actions cause further disasters? After all, they were just a couple of kids, so what did they know?

'"The Emperor's New Clothes",' Diane declared eventually. 'That lad were the only one who dared to tell the truth. Everybody else was, "Ooh, you do look nice, Your Majesty" – blinking liars the lot of them. He saw the Emperor was naked and he said so. We have to be like him, like the boy who told the truth.' Her voice raised itself in excitement. She had better keep quiet.

'How are we going to do it?' Sally asked.

Diane raised a thin shoulder. 'I'll make it up as I go along.'

A librarian came towards them, thin lips clamped together, iron-grey hair scraped back into a severe bun. She pointed at the word SILENCE on the wall, then strode away, fat buttocks stretching the tweed skirt. 'Like two pigs fighting in a little tent,' remarked Diane loudly. Her keeping quiet had lasted all of thirty seconds.

The woman stopped in her tracks, turned, looked at Diane. 'Out,' she said, in a stage whisper.

Sally elbowed Diane in the ribs. 'Come on,' she urged.

But Diane was quite enjoying herself. Adults could be dealt with. 'If we can't talk, how do we ask questions?'

The librarian blinked. 'You aren't even reading,' she said.

Diane took a step nearer to the irate custodian of literature. 'We might have been whispering about which books we need.'

'But you weren't.'

'No, we weren't.'

'So get out.'

'But we might have been. Can you see what I mean?'

Sally pushed Diane from behind, steering her out into the street. 'You're getting to be more trouble than you're worth,' complained the older girl.

'My gran says that,' came the reply, 'but she says I'm lovable with it.'

Lovable with it? Sally was beginning to wonder how on earth she had managed to get herself involved in these latest and rashest of plans. It had all sounded all right at the time, job to be done, someone must do it and so forth. But Sally's enthusiasm for the project was diminishing with every step she took.

Diane stopped. 'A lid,' she pronounced, as she ground to a halt.

'A lid?' Sally failed to follow this new train of thought. In fact, she might have stood a better chance of keeping up with another type of train, the ten thirty for Manchester out of Trinity Street. 'Diane?'

'I'm thinking.'

'Yes, I can tell.' When Diane was thinking, wheels turned. Her face always screwed up against the dimmest of lights, while her forehead seemed to become one huge frown. A lid. A lid for what?

'There's loads,' continued Diane now.

'Right,' said a bemused Sally.

'Can't breathe,' mumbled the thoughtful child. 'Without air, a fire can't breathe.' There was an important job to be done, a task that needed to be performed by a brave, fearless person. The only folk with guts in this world were children. Adults seemed to collect more uncertainties as they matured, so children had to take the lead.

She opened the back door very quietly. There would only be elders here, she supposed, as she insinuated her way into the inner sanctum. The blessing table was there, a thin, lumpy mattress stretched across a trestle. She remembered a service during which a fat girl called Maria Hough had been cleansed, and this very couch had collapsed beneath her weight. Everyone in the temple had heard it.

On a side table stood the ewer and bowl that had been used

358

for the ceremony, white towels folded immaculately at one side. From snatches of conversations overheard by Diane, she had gathered that Mr Wilkinson had been a meticulous folder of cloth.

The lamps were on a shelf, each one dead and cold, so there was nothing to be done in this room. But just to make sure that today's gestures would be understood, the child picked up towels and flannels and threw them to the floor. Nothing here was clean; everything was filthy, contaminated by Guardian Wilkinson.

She walked to the outer door. 'All right, let's be having you and it,' she told Sally.

The two girls carried a heavy object into the room. 'Glad the mill's got them new bins,' Diane said. 'Nice big lid, this is.'

Sally blew a tress of hair from her cheek. 'They'll stop us,' she said breathlessly.

'They'll help us,' replied Diane with certainty.

'But—' Sally closed her mouth firmly when she saw the expression on her friend's face. Diane believed in herself. Diane had a certain undeniable power. 'All right,' Sally breathed. 'We do it your road.'

Leaving Sally in the sanctum, Diane opened the door and stepped into the old mill shed that was now a temple. Rough floors had been sanded down by members of the cult, while the walls, brown and green, were decorated by pictures portraying the life of Moses. These gave the hall a distinctly Catholic air, as if they imitated the Stations of the Cross.

Benches and chairs were placed in a rough circle at the centre of which the Light still survived. Approximately half of the seats were occupied, mostly by elders who were retired from work, then a few jobless men, some women, no children. Diane caught her breath as she looked at these people. They were lost, bewildered, as confused as those who had followed Moses out of Egypt. It has to be done, her inner voice repeated. They are waiting for help, and there is none, not since they read the newspapers.

Diane remained on the stairs leading to the inner sanctum until every head was turned in her direction. Without the slightest glimmer of stage fright, she hopped down two steps and began to speak the words that needed saying.

'It's all over,' she announced, noticing how round their shoulders were. 'We can't pretend and carry on as if nowt's happened.'

The congregation shuffled feet, coughed, looked at each other. Their planned meeting was over, and they remained in great distress. It was plain to Diane that they needed help and that she would have to become a maker of decisions. She felt so much pity in that moment that she was forced to sniff back a tear.

'It has to be done,' she continued, 'and you all know what I'm talking about.'

Sally appeared in the doorway, placing the heavy, circular lid against the jamb. She watched in near awe while Diane Hewitt preached to her elders and betters.

'See, we were all took in by it,' Diane said next. Well, that was a lie for a start, because she hadn't been taken in by any of it. 'You all know what's happened in Texas and here as well.' She inhaled deeply. 'Mr Wilkinson did things in there.' She jerked a thumb over her shoulder. 'He did things to girls and some of them girls have spoke to the bobbies now. It was all wrong. The fire they found, the first one, was likely caused by the hot sun on dry twigs and leaves. Other fires was lit deliberate – it's all been proved.'

They were motionless now. Each soul in the room possessed its own hope, its own despair. The temple had been their meeting-place, their solidarity. Shockwaves had already travelled through the community, though some diehards clung fiercely to their faith in the initial flame.

'We can keep the temple,' Diane said now. 'We've had some money given us.' She stopped for a moment, brought to mind what Mr Mulligan had said: 'I can give this money, but I cannot do any more than that.'

The child shook herself back into the here and now. 'We can make our own preaching,' she said. 'You don't have to be anything in particular, just a Bible-reader. We don't need a guardian, we can look after one another.'

At last they began to mumble around their circles, stopping only when Diane's voice was raised again. 'In the week, this shed can be used for different things – them of us who can read must teach them as can't read. You could have mothers' meetings, stuff like that, buy some toys for children to play with. Then, on Sunday, do your own service.' She paused. 'But that thing's got to be put out.' She pointed to the flames. 'And me and Sally have come here to do it.'

Again, they were still. An old man rose to his feet, cracking knee joints echoing in the silence. 'I've nobbut months to live,' he said, 'and this here temple were my strength. But it's nowt to do with yon flame.' He waved a stick towards the Light on which so many had come to depend. 'It's us what matters. It's us being here like this, all together, like, that's where we come up trumps. The lass is reet. She's said all as wanted saying.' He sat down.

Three men left the ranks and walked to the steps. Diane stood to one side and allowed them to pick up the heavy lid. Between them, they carried the item to the middle of the room. A woman gasped, placed a hand to her mouth. Another wept quietly, while two old couples left the temple quietly, heads bowed.

Diane approached the pivotal point of so many lives. Standing by the flames, she raised her hand and placed it on her heart. Mr Mulligan had told her what to say. 'We all believe in God,' she said solemnly, 'and in His Light in Heaven. This is no longer a holy light, so we will extinguish it.' She'd had a bit of trouble with 'extinguish' and was glad when it came out all in one piece. During practice, the word had seemed to catch on her teeth, falling into fragments before hitting the air.

The men, aided by Diane, placed the lid on top of the Light's metal bowl. A corporate gasp emerged from onlookers, while small puffs of smoke leaked to announce the struggle as fire sought oxygen. 'Leave it to cool,' Diane suggested. 'Then pour water on it just to make sure.'

Blindly, she left by the front entrance, Sally in hot pursuit.
'Diane?'
'I'm not skriking.' Fiercely, Diane rubbed at her nose.
'Aw, love.' Sally put her arms around trembling shoulders. 'We did right,' she said. 'Well, you did.'
'It felt . . . it felt like I was . . . killing them, Sally.'
'You were saving them.'
The unlikely saviour sobbed.

'It weren't right, Di. None of it. You are the first right thing to happen in there.'

'I know, I know, but it still hurts in my stomach. They're so poor and lonely, some lonelier than others.'

'They were paying with daughters and granddaughters.' Sally dabbed at Diane's wet cheeks. 'There were nothing free, Di. They'd have started shipping them out to Texas for breeding – thank God none of them's already gone. You did right, love. For the rest of your life, you'll know you did right.'

The girl who had done right walked with her supporter through the streets of Bolton, tears drying as she feasted her eyes on familiar sights. Lumbering trams overtook lumbering horses, market folk shouted about their wares, women with turbaned heads gossiped on corners. The dummy outside Bowes clothiers sported new overalls; two of John Willie's men carried a sideboard out of the shop. 'I love Bolton,' Diane announced.

'Better than Pendleton?' asked Sally.

'No, different.'

'I know what you mean.' Sally breathed in smoke-tainted air, caught the scent of fish and chips, coffee newly ground, a whiff of smoky bacon. 'It's like an exciting story, then a peaceful one.'

Diane laughed out loud. 'There's been nowt peaceful up at Pendleton just lately.' Then her laugh faded. 'It's been terrible, Sally. And he did it all. Guardian Wilkinson did murder.'

'Aye, he did.' Sally looked over her shoulder. 'There's our tram.'

Diane's mischief surfaced once more. 'Nay, Sally. We report to Mr Mulligan, get him to buy us some dinner, then we hang about till he's going home.' The chin rose in mock defiance. 'We are going to travel in style again, Sal. I think we've earned it.'

TWENTY-EIGHT

By ten o'clock in the morning, the sun was already in a threatening mood. A flawless sky seemed to shrink away from such violence, paling as if in fear of it, while clouds simply took the day off, refusing to put in an appearance in the face of strong opposition.

Ida Hewitt blew a strand of hair from her face. 'We shall all cook,' she declared. 'Come three this afternoon, we'll be like a few hundred Sunday joints, roasted, basted and ready for gravy.' She mopped her brow with a handkerchief. 'Never mind,' she added, 'soon be Christmas.'

Kate Kenny laughed. 'You know poor Elspeth's doing fortunes in that little tent? Well, she used gravy browning to make herself look a bit more exotic. The browning has all trickled down on to her blouse, so she's decided to wash her hands – and her face – of the whole business. She's doing the fortunes, only she's going to be herself and she's taken her vest off.'

Ida did not approve of vestlessness. 'Catch her death,' she muttered, waving at Amy who was moving two ponies to a shaded pen. 'There's not many women looks good in jodhpurs, but Amy manages to.'

Kate's eyes slid across to where James stood, his own gaze fixed firmly on Amy. Things had got no better for him. He was passionately in love and there was not a thing could be done to

363

alter that fact. Kate turned away and offered up a quick prayer. Nothing was impossible, she informed her Maker. God had to help James now, because he was beyond the reach of his aunt's guiding hand.

'You all right?' asked Ida, as she arranged a row of baby clothes.

'I'm fine.'

'You're not.'

'Then I'm not, so. Come on, I've all the jams and pickles to arrange on my own stall.'

The grounds of Pendleton Grange were beautifully prepared, grass manicured, hedges trimmed, flowers burgeoning in the beds. To the left of the house, a single-storey building housed a brand new swimming-pool; tennis courts, still virginal, awaited the arrival of villagers from Pendleton and Pendleton Clough. 'They'll ruin all his gardens,' moaned Ida.

Kate said nothing. The place was so happy today, bunting stretched across the lawns, stalls selling everything from cakes to white elephants, a greasy pole placed above the pond, animals awaiting judgement by a local vet, a place where photographs would be taken, adults dashing about laying a treasure trail for the younger element.

Camilla Smythe's van crawled up the drive. The friendship between her and the two remaining Burton-Masseys had been too deep to perish; Camilla knew now that Eliza had been suffering from a brain tumour, so she had forgiven the murdered girl for whatever she might have done in London seven months earlier. Helen Smythe, on the other hand, was a different kettle of fish altogether ...

Amy, having deposited her ponies, went to help Camilla unload the van in preparation for the setting up of a tea and sandwich stall. James Mulligan, shirtsleeves rolled, struggled to maintain order among prize-seeking cows, pigs and sheep. The local vet was currently carrying water to another area where domestic animals endured a last-minute grooming from keen owners.

'It's going to be lovely, so it is,' sighed Kate, 'and any profits straight to the orphanage, just as it should be.'

Ida laid out a set of embroidered traycloths. 'Why won't he

get married?' she asked, out of the blue. 'Is it just because of that bad-tempered dad of his?'

'That's for him to know and us to wonder about,' answered Kate, rather quickly.

'Sorry,' muttered Ida, 'don't like stepping on folk's toes.'

Kate inhaled deeply. 'Nothing to be sorry for, but. He's all I have left and he's a sore worry to me, has me desperate.'

Ida pondered for a few seconds. 'She must be able to see it, Kate. You'd have to be six feet under not to notice what's going on. Not that I mean . . . well . . . that there's something . . .'

'I know, I know.' Kate watched the band as its members spilled from a charabanc, caught sight of a few colourfully dressed children who were preparing to dance. 'You're right, Ida. He loves her right through to the bone. Amy must be aware, for his heart is dripping down his sleeve.'

'Happen she's too busy with her shop – did you see the write-up in the paper? Gone from strength to strength, she has.'

Kate was of the opinion that James was receiving signals from Amy, messages that were clear but unspoken. 'No, it's not that at all, Ida. She's had a lot of changes and a deal of suffering to cope with. The shop is her distraction. Her love for my nephew is buried beneath grief and suffering, yet it's there.'

Ida nodded her agreement. 'She won't sit near him.'

'I know.'

'And they don't have them long conflabs what they used to have.'

'I know.'

'Even bought her own van so as she doesn't have to come home with him.'

'I know.'

They knew. Yet there was little or nothing they could do with that knowledge. With the hydro almost finished, it would soon be time for James to return to Ireland. The two old ladies, versed in life, hopeful for the future, were unable to perform miracles. They prepared their stalls, all the time glancing up to watch Amy and James avoiding each other.

Mona, who was to help Camilla with teas, sandwiches and

cool drinks, dropped by to visit her friends. 'Right, not long now, girls. We open at eleven,' she said. 'Are you two ready? Because if you are, come and give me and Camilla a hand covering everything up, keep flies off.'

Kate froze. They were walking towards each other. Then James veered to the left, Amy to the right, and they all but collided. Say something, Kate urged within her mind. The great galloping fool needed to speak to Amy, had to speak to her. Go on, she almost shouted. Go on, get it done with.

'Kate?' Mona was puzzled.

'We'll be there in a minute,' replied Kate at last.

Mona marched off towards the tea tables.

'They're talking,' whispered Ida.

'Yes,' answered Kate. 'For a minute, they're talking.'

Amy looked up at him, dazzled by rays of sun that jumped over his shoulder and into her eyes. She manoeuvred herself into a less painful position. 'Going well,' she said lamely.

'Nearly ready,' he replied.

Amy glanced down at her stained clothing. 'No point in me getting changed as I am in charge of pony rides.'

He looked past her, trying not to breathe in her scent, her essence. 'Perhaps I should help with – with the gate,' he managed, 'you know, the tickets of admission.'

She cleared her throat. 'Yes. But aren't you the boss of that motley crew?' Amy waved a hand in the direction of prize heifers and sows. 'Some of them look rather splendid,' she added, after a pause.

'Amy?'

Her throat was suddenly dry. 'That's a rather fine-looking Aberdeen Angus over there.'

'Amy?'

'What?'

'Oh, God.' He drew a hand through tangled black hair. 'I want to . . . I have to talk to you.'

Amy felt her fists curling, suppressed a shiver that snaked up her spine. Here stood a man who had become her friend, who was no longer a friend. Nothing had happened: there had been

366

no quarrel, no disagreement. 'Why?' The single syllable emerged high, as if dropping from the lips of a child.

'Things,' he replied quietly. 'Things I need to say.'

'Er . . . about the hydro?' she asked.

'Among other topics, yes.'

She stepped further away, knowing that she was running inside, trying to escape from the sheer confusion of – of what? Why was she bewildered? 'Are you going back to Ireland?' When seconds had passed without an answer, she finally looked him in the eye. What was going on in that fine brain? And what was happening inside herself? Her heart skipped, causing her to inhale sharply. No. Oh, no. He must not return to Ireland. He must not . . . leave her.

'Amy?'

Unable to speak, she nodded.

'This isn't the time or the place,' he said, 'and it's going to be so hot. Would you meet me tonight by the lake? Surely the heat will disperse by midnight?'

She inclined her head again. 'Midnight,' she promised. And her heart was lighter.

Diane was in the thick of it again. Having discovered that adults were malleable, she had gone into the business of sorting them out. She had solved a problem between quarrelling neighbours in Pendleton by suggesting that the trimming of a hedge was a small price to pay. 'If you cut that down, she'll get more sun in her garden.' It had worked. Like a detective, she made notes, plotted solutions, got herself into all kinds of scrapes. 'Diane,' her grandmother had said, 'what are you up to at all?'

'Training,' the child had replied darkly.

'What for?'

'The police.'

Ida's answer to that had been a glance at the ceiling followed by a few words of concern for the constabulary. It looked as if their Diane had set her sights on becoming the first ever female chief inspector. 'God love them,' Ida had been heard to mutter, 'because they don't deserve what's coming their way.'

At the summer fair, Diane was on the gate with Sally.

367

Neither had paid, so each was expected to contribute her time and effort to the proceedings by being helpful. The younger girl, in possession of a new florin, decided to hang on to her money: she would help Sally with the hoop-la, and she would have a good look at all the free stuff. She could drink water, which cost nothing, then the band and the dancing were available for everyone at no extra cost. 'Two bob,' she kept muttering. 'I've got two bob, Sal.'

Sally had little to say. It was too hot, there were people trying to sneak in without paying, and she had had enough last time. The last time to which she referred inwardly was the episode at the police station. Now Diane was on what she called a special mission. Sally, the older by more than three years, had been dragged into the mire once more.

'It'll be all right,' Diane said, several times. 'It just wants doing, Sal.'

'But why does it have to be us?'

Diane took a ticket from Stephen Wilkinson. 'Enjoy yourself,' she advised, awarding him a brilliant smile. His brother might be awaiting trial for murder, but the village postmaster was a fine, decent soul.

'Diane?' pleaded Sally.

'What?'

'I mean ... what I mean, Di, is that we shouldn't be interfering. Things like this have a road of sorting themselves out. It's not like an ordinary problem. This is love, so they have to fall in love on their own or fall out on their own.'

'Rubbish.' Diane held her defiant head so high that it almost tilted backwards. 'Listen,' she said, with forced patience and after collecting a few more tickets, 'they're daft. They get their heads that full of stuff like work and things as they can't see what's in front of them. Mr Mulligan loves Amy and she loves him. I've heard it all at home, me gran and Mona. See, the old folk won't do anything about it, so it has to be us again. We have a chance of growing up with a bit of sense because we've started young.'

In her heart, Sally could not help agreeing with the younger girl. The grown-ups within Sally's sphere did not always function correctly. They needed a little shove now and then, a slight push in the right direction. In Diane's much stronger opinion, they needed a kick up the backside. But . . . but what? Things were going to change anyway, so why not make an effort to steer life towards the better option?

'Sal?'

'What?'

'You with me?'

'Course I am. You know I am.'

'Good.' Diane grinned at Mr Mulligan. 'Hello,' she said, 'are you taking over here now?' He might be taking over the gate, but Diane was about to attend to the rest of his life without even consulting him.

'I am. Go and watch the dancing, then do the hoop-la. Have a lovely day.'

It was wonderful. The two girls dashed round the treasure trail, each finding sweets and home-made biscuits along the way. They watched an Irish piper filling his instrument, not by blowing but by pumping the instrument with his arm. Children performed reels, their elaborate costumes in green and gold glittering with shiny beads.

At twelve, knitters began their furious race, needles and wool moving in masses of colour. Then there was the greasy-pole, the tug-of-war, the races. Pendleton won hands down in most categories. Pendleton Clough would have to supply several kegs of beer as payment for their second-class status.

Orphans came, whooping and leaping about the tennis courts, using the new pool, a lifeguard at hand in case of mishaps. Ponies trundled about in the cruel heat, children on their backs, until Amy decided that the beasts had had enough. A band marched, youngsters skipping behind the parade; refreshments ran out twice, most people were photographed.

By three o'clock, the party had ground to a halt. As if reacting to a signal, everyone suddenly sought shade, some near hedges, many under trees. The old slept; the young, disappointed by their own lethargy, made daisy chains and chatted in small groups.

Diane nudged Sally. 'Now's as good a time as any,' she said, 'and the longer we put it off, the harder it'll be. Come on, we have to shape, get them two daft beggars together on their own.'

369

'Oh, heck,' gulped the maid-of-all-work. 'They'll kill us.'

Diane nodded her cheerful agreement. 'Yes, but you only die once – me gran says.'

'Me gran says, me gran says,' mimicked Sally. 'And you take no notice of her.'

'I'm lovable with it,' grinned the smaller girl. Her expression changed. 'Oh, heck. Oh, heck, Sal. Forget Amy and Mr Mulligan for a minute.' She swallowed audibly. Her own plans were laid aside as she prepared to be upstaged. What she saw, what everyone saw, made the air even heavier than before. There were no clouds in the sky, yet a storm gathered on a hot July day during a summer fair at Pendleton Grange. Even the ponies seemed to hold their breath . . .

Margot had made up her mind. William was not going to be hidden from sight just because he had no father, or because the father he might have had was a dead rake. The baby was a fortnight old now, a pretty blond child with no visible flaw, and he was ready to make his début.

Margot had decided to get it all over in one fell swoop. 'You see,' she told her son, as she leaned over the pram to straighten his matinée jacket, 'the mountain has come to us.' There were hundreds of them, it seemed. But she held her head high against a judgemental world. Why take her punishment in small portions eked out over a period of months? And what had she done? The real sinner, a man who had tormented young girls, who had killed William's aunt, was languishing in jail awaiting trial. 'I killed no one,' Margot muttered, under her breath. 'I hurt nobody except myself and you, little one.'

When she thought about the riding, the attempts she had made to be rid of the baby, she tensed into a state where the major nerves of her body became like steel: Margot had never suspected that a child could bring so much love as he screamed his way into the world. William was fast becoming the centre of her universe, the reason for her continuing existence.

Her steps slowed as she reached the driveway of Pendleton Grange. All eyes would be on her, gossip would ripple through ranks like a summer wind across fields of corn. It had to be done. It had to be done now, before she lost the strength.

Most people were seated, probably overcome by the day's powerful heat. Margot pushed her pram towards the edge of the field, waiting with unaccustomed patience for the world to inspect her son. 'Your first parade,' she told him. 'Best behaviour now, no dribbling or crying.'

Then a car pulled up on the drive, tyres slewing and displacing gravel. A few chippings caught the pram, and Margot turned her newly acquired maternal anger on the driver. 'What on earth . . .' she began. But when she saw the occupant of the parked car, she took a step away. Oh, no, not here, not now.

Helen Smythe leaped from the vehicle. Her usually coiffed hair fell in ragged strings around her face; her clothing, always pristine, was creased and dirty. She dashed from car to field in a matter of seconds. 'Slut!' she screamed. 'You thought you would trick him, but he tricked you by dying courtesy of your sister.'

Several people rose carefully to their feet – it was plain that the paternal grandmother of Margot's son was in no mood for negotiation.

'Give him to me,' continued the distraught female.

Margot positioned herself between the pram and Helen Smythe.

'That farm is damp,' cried the latter. 'I can give him everything he needs, an education, a decent home.'

Margot tossed a few curls from her face. 'Your son had everything he wanted, and look how he behaved. Go home, Mrs Smythe.'

At the back of the audience, Amy found herself next to James. 'No sudden moves,' she muttered. 'The woman is clearly crazed.'

He inclined his head in agreement. 'Rupert's death has knocked the lady out of her, I'm afraid. And she must be stopped now or Margot will become a bundle of nerves.'

'No, she won't,' Amy promised. 'She has developed a passion for my nephew. There is no chance of anyone getting a look-in. So far, she has proved herself an excellent mother.'

They noticed movement in the far hedge. 'Oh, God,' said Amy. 'Diane Hewitt's secret society is on the march again.'

'Only two members so far,' he replied. 'It's when she starts with dogs, boot polish and laundry that we have to worry.'

'What?'

'Never mind, Amy.'

Margot faced her tormentor. 'William is my son – I have rights. Aren't you an expert on the rights of women, Mrs Smythe? Now, go home and behave yourself.'

Diane popped up from behind the hedge. 'Oh, hello,' she said graciously. 'Can I get you a cup of tea?'

'No,' snapped Mrs Smythe. She did not notice the second girl, since Sally had crossed the lane lower down and was now behind the dishevelled interloper. Moving with all the grace and cunning of a panther, Sally Hayes, orphan, good girl and maid-of-all-work, removed the keys from the ignition. Even if Mrs Smythe did manage to grab the baby, she wouldn't get far in a dead vehicle.

While Sally ran off, Diane remained, her hard gaze fixed on Mrs Smythe's face. 'If you touch that baby of hers,' she jerked a thumb in Margot's direction, 'I'll get the police. Then this lot behind me in the field will be all over you like measles, Mrs Smythe.'

Members of this lot in the field were moving anyway, galvanized by the sight of Sally running off with the keys. A solid mass of people surrounded Margot, some pulling at the pram, others making sure that Mrs Smythe stayed away from her target.

Camilla arrived, beetroot cheeks at odds with burnished red hair. 'Mother!'

Helen Smythe turned. 'They killed him. This woman's sister killed Rupert – I know it. Surely I deserve to have a hand in the rearing of Rupert's son?'

Ida, dragging Mona in her wake, pushed herself to the front. 'See?' she gasped. 'There's loads of us, so you don't stand a chance. If you don't beggar off, I'll hit you – do you hear me?'

Camilla stepped in front of her mother. 'No one will hit her,' she declared firmly. 'She's ill, driven out of her mind by my brother's death. How many of you lost men and boys during the war?'

Ida backed off. She understood. Loss could send people

372

mad, could put them in bed for months on end. 'Take her home, lass,' she advised Camilla, 'and keep her there.'

The fuss died after Helen had been driven off in her daughter's motor van. Little William was cooed over. A star to the core, he did not cry as he was passed from hand to hand. Margot, her heart still working double time after her close encounter with Helen Smythe, began to relax. She had done the right thing, had chosen to face the future head on. He would be loved. No matter what happened after today, William Burton-Massey would be protected by these villagers.

Amy dried a tear. She suddenly felt fiercely proud of her sister, whose backbone remained rigid despite the child's illegitimacy. No, she told herself. It was because of William's status. Margot had gambled her last card, had turned up the ace of hearts. 'We all gamble,' said Amy aloud.

'We do,' replied the man at her side.

'Ah, James,' she murmured.

He smiled. 'Ah, Amy. I shall see you later.'

The day drifted idly towards evening, the heat refusing to remove itself even when its source began to drop towards the Pennines. Stragglers and tidiers wandered about the grounds, while several groups of people continued to chat beneath trees.

At a denuded hoop-la stall, Sally and Diane watched the scene, both on pins while they awaited their chance. Sally, after running off with Mrs Smythe's keys, was not looking forward to the next piece of trouble, though she agreed with Diane – something had to be done before the end of this day.

'Sal?'

'I know, I know.'

'I do him, you do her.'

'Right.' Sally dragged a length of damp hair from her face, pushed it behind her ear. 'They'll kill us.'

'Stop saying that,' answered Diane.

The two girls hugged, separated, then formed the pincer movement on which they had agreed. Little Saul Dobson from Pendleton Clough had lost his guinea pig. This remarkably stupid animal, whose name was Squidge, had insinuated himself under the door of a stable, had refused to come out, while poor Saul, distraught with worry, had been dragged home for a bath. That was the fairy-tale to which Diane and Sally intended to cling.

Thus it was that Amy Burton-Massey and James Mulligan found themselves locked up together in a stable as hot as an oven. Too late, they noticed the door closing, heard bolts shooting home in the door's top half, the bar slamming into position on the lower part.

'You've twenty minutes,' yelled Diane. 'Get it sorted out before we all go mad. There's iced water in that enamel bucket and there's two cups and all.'

'And no guinea pig,' added Sally, for good measure. 'So don't bother looking for it because we made it up.'

The girls stared at each other. 'We've been and gone and done it now,' smiled Diane. 'Come on, let's see if there's any food left.'

'We should leave all this until midnight,' said James, 'because it's too hot for thinking and talking.' He filled a cup, passed it to her, filled another. Instead of drinking, he poured the contents over his head.

Amy made no reply. She had stumbled quite by accident over her feelings for this man, though she realized already that he had owned her heart for some time. This was embarrassing. Two children had forced them in here, so how many had noticed the non-courtship that had not been going on? 'The whole village must know,' she whispered.

'And Pendleton Clough,' he replied.

Amy sighed, took a draught of water. 'I don't even know what we're talking about.'

'Yes, you do.'

She felt the heat in her face as it registered beyond any calculable scale. 'Explain it to me, then.'

No, he would not do that, not in this cruel weather. But he could begin to trim the edges off, he supposed. 'How do you feel about Pendleton Grange?' he asked.

'It's a house,' she replied, knowing the response to be foolish.

'In which you and your family used to live.'

374

'Yes.'

A fly buzzed by his face and he waved it away. 'It's a beautiful place,' he said now, 'and the hydro will keep you for ever.'

No sensible words entered her mind, so she remained silent.

'Amy?'

'What?'

'The shop and the rents – they will give you and Margot an income. And the house will still be yours, but . . .'

What was he up to? Was this an older version of Diane Hewitt, a plotter, a planner, one who kept everything secret until the very last minute? 'Spit it out,' she demanded.

James smiled ruefully. She had probably been as open as this all her life – never mind the niceties, the truth will do. 'Have you seen Joe Hewitt's legs?' he asked. 'Crooked, thin, better now than they used to be.'

Amy fished about in her drink, pulled out a piece of ice and rubbed it all over her face and neck. 'I wish I had the energy to horse-whip his sister once we get out of here.' She glanced at him. 'Go on, then, play the cards.'

'Nothing up my sleeve.'

'Your sleeves are rolled,' she reminded him, urging herself not to look at brown skin and firm muscle.

'I want to open a school,' he announced.

'I see.' She didn't, but the need for peace made her utter the white lie. 'In Ireland?'

'No.'

Her heart leaped joyfully, and she fought to keep her facial expression neutral. He was intending to stay. Had the atmosphere not been so oppressive, she might even have kissed him. No. No, she wouldn't. Amy was a lady; ladies waited. I am a lady in waiting, she giggled inwardly.

'It's not just the orphans,' James said now. 'There are children in the towns who need a special sort of school, one that cares for mind and body. They need a swimming-pool and we have one. We have tennis courts, ponies, woods and trees. If we open up the attics we could get another twelve boarders – we can sleep thirty children, plus staff, very easily. Nurses on hand, Amy. Windows wide open, airy dormitories, lessons outside in the summer.'

'Deprived children?' asked Amy.

'Exactly – non-boarders, too. Think of the lives we could change. And you'd still have the shop, so you wouldn't need to be involved full time. But imagine introducing a child from the slums to horses, pigs, cows. Imagine him collecting eggs, learning to milk, picking mushrooms for his own breakfast.'

'Yes.' She fanned her face with a handkerchief.

He waited. 'Well?' he asked eventually.

'Just do it,' she answered. 'The house is yours.'

He was not going to travel that particular route again, had no intention of arguing about who owned what, because the path had been trodden so many times that it bore signs of erosion. 'Look, Amy, what I need to know is this. Would you mind if the house were used for the betterment of young lives?'

'I have no particular attachment to it,' she answered. 'I have always believed in looking forward.' She smiled at him. 'If you keep looking over your shoulder, the future is fraught with accidents. Rather than bumping into lamp-posts, I keep my eyes front.'

'Could your future contain two or three dozen needy children?'

Was this the proposal? she wondered briefly. No, he would not propose in this way, would not be so impersonal – might not propose at all. 'I think it's an excellent idea, provided you can get funding.'

'I can. We would also be a charity.'

'And you are a qualified teacher.'

'Yes.' Following Amy's example, he rubbed a sliver of ice over his face. He had sorted out the deprived, was leaving himself on one side for now, would speak tonight when the air was lighter, when . . . when his face might be in shadow. 'Do you mind where you live?' he asked.

'No, I don't.'

'So Caldwell Farm is just another place for you?'

She nodded her reply.

'Mona loves that house,' he continued. 'I mind the time she first saw it – not long after her sister's death. "That's a proper house," she said several times. Ida and the children are cramped

– they'd be better at the farm. The Moorheads could have the cottage . . . So . . . you wouldn't mind a move?'

'As long as Margot and William are safe, I have no preferences for myself.' Another lie. She wanted to live close to him. That was nearer the truth, though the reality was that she wanted to be closer than close . . .

'I have made some tentative plans,' he said.

Tentative? The man was intending to up-end everyone's life, had probably studied blueprints for days on end. This was not a person who worked in generalizations: like the captain of a ship, he knew his course. 'May we finish this at midnight?' she asked. 'Because my brain is as sluggish as the rest of me.'

'A day to remind us of hell's heat,' he answered.

'Indeed.' She sighed.

Then they waited in silence for release from prison.

TWENTY-NINE

Kate Kenny was a woman whose clock changed with the seasons, her body either lingering in bed during winter mornings, or leaping up with the lark each summer's dawn. She had to be busy while the day gave light, resting when the sun dipped, going into her hibernatory phase with the start of autumn. The day after the fair, she was on early shift, as the sun rose before five o'clock and she was too concerned about James to lie still and do nothing.

She had much to think about, as her nephew was teetering on the brink of a recklessness he had never displayed before. She welcomed his courage, praised his newborn strength, feared for him, too. The fear shot into her hands, making them busy as they punished silver till it shone its way towards blinding brightness. He had stayed out all night. He had spent the night in the company of Amy Burton-Massey.

'I can't carry on,' he had told his aunt.

'I know,' had been her reply. 'Whatever, go with God.'

'With God?' His eyebrows had been raised half-way up his forehead.

'Yes, with God,' Kate had insisted.

And he had gone. The bed had not been slept in. James Mulligan, confirmed-for-ever bachelor, had spent more than six hours in the company of a woman. Or had he? Was he wandering alone out there, rejected, isolated in this cruel, bitter world?

'Mrs Kenny?'

Kate jumped. 'Holy St Joseph,' she breathed, a hand to her chest. 'You scalded the heart out of me, Sally Hayes. Whatever are you doing up at this time?'

Sally was always up early, though she usually took her time getting ready, nice clean frock and apron every day, hair smooth, nails scrubbed, face shiny and fresh. 'They're outside,' she ventured now.

'Who's outside?'

Sally looked over her shoulder. 'In a stable,' she whispered.

'Some good people come out of stables,' answered Kate, 'Jesus Christ among them. I take it you mean my nephew and Amy Burton-Massey?'

'Yes.' Sally filled the kettle and set it to boil before turning to face the housekeeper. 'Holding hands, they were.'

Kate managed not to react. 'Make tea enough for four in case they decide to come in, Sally.'

The young maid smiled at the housekeeper. With Diane Hewitt's help, Sally had achieved so much. She was beginning to agree with Diane – adults did need a push from time to time. 'Mrs Kenny?'

'Yes?'

'Will they get married?'

Kate kept her expression neutral. 'Make that tea,' she pretended to snap, 'and keep the nose on your face. Don't go sticking it into other people's ongoings.'

'Yes, Mrs Kenny.'

'Stop grinning, Sally. Should the wind change, you'll have a split face the rest of your life.'

'Yes, Mrs Kenny.'

'And stop saying "Yes, Mrs Kenny."'

'Yes, Mrs Kenny.'

Kate looked up at the ceiling. 'Dear God,' she implored, 'is it not enough that I am stranded here in England? Did You have to send me all these pure eejits?' She addressed Sally once more. 'Make that tea then go ... somewhere – anywhere. Take the morning off. And if you say those three words, I'll stretch you from here to Christmas by putting you through them squeezers.' She pointed to the mangle. 'You would not want that, Sally.'

'No, Mrs Kenny.' A wild happiness had entered Sally's veins, and she could not help being naughty. She wanted to dance and scream, to throw a few pots at the wall, to celebrate. Instead, she brewed tea, fetched cups, saucers, milk and sugar to the table. There would be a wedding and she would be able to wear the gloves given to her as a leaving gift by the staff at Chiverton Children's Home.

'Is this you still here, Sally Hayes?'

Having developed an immunity to Kate's sarcasm, Sally answered in the affirmative, simply nodding.

'Go.'

'But me and Diane . . . I mean yesterday . . . I just want to see them together, Mrs Kenny. They are made for each other. Diane heard her gran and Miss Mona saying that. I won't stare, I promise.'

'Aye, keep your promise, Sally, by putting as much space as possible between your excellent self and this house.'

Sally blinked away some happy-but-sad tears. 'You know what, Mrs Kenny?'

'Go.'

'You know what? If I had a granny, I'd want her to be just like you.'

The older woman's heart melted like wax beneath a wick. She adored little Sal, that conscientious, kind, beautiful child who wore her feelings in her eyes. 'You're a good girl altogether, but a desperate pain to me. Finish that tea, pick up your soda bread and let me see the back of you.'

'Yes, Mrs . . . Granny.'

Kate picked up her polishing cloth and set it flying with alarming accuracy at Sally's face. 'Out,' she screamed, laughter a mere inch from the surface. 'Take yourself and your cheek to the other side of Pendleton Clough, Miss Clever, or you'll be mangled.'

Choosing not to be mangled, Sally set off to find her partner in crime, that famous amateur sleuth, Miss Diane Hewitt. She and Diane had done it again – they had made the grown-ups see sense.

They had talked all night. For Amy, it had been a home-coming, a sense of remembering this man from her future. It

380

had been an encounter with destiny, she supposed, something meant to happen, a gift straight from God.

As morning approached, James became less calm. He had not proposed, not yet, though his plans had been expressed in a way that clearly involved her. If she would have him, that was. It was now or never, because she had to know, had to be in possession of the whole truth before making her decision. 'We'll go in now,' he said.

She looked up at him. This was a face she could trust, yet there was trouble in it. Did he intend to make her into just a business partner? No, the kisses had been warm, urgent. Why had he not mentioned marriage? Why had he skated lightly over certain parts of his plan? She knew more than she had sought to learn about dormitories, children's playthings, the benefits of swimming and how much fruit a five-year-old should eat in a week. As to the arrangements for her own future, all she knew was that she had agreed to give Caldwell Farm to two old women and two children.

'Where . . . ?' she began.

'Yes?' He offered her a broad smile.

'Nothing,' she answered. 'I shall ask later.'

They entered the house, just catching sight of an inner door while it closed in Kate's wake. 'She has left us in peace,' said James, as he placed two tartan rugs on a chair. 'And look – a feast of toast and jam. We, Amy, are the richest pair of people on earth.'

She sat down, remembering how glad she had been to wrap herself in one of those rugs: even in a heatwave, the air grew chill towards morning. She poured tea, munched on a slice of toast. 'James?' she said thoughtfully, when he sat opposite her. 'What is going on?' A lady in waiting? No, she had arrived, wanted the answers, needed a future.

'I love you,' he replied.

'But—'

'I have dealt with my buts. In a moment, you must face yours.'

'You love me, I love you. Show me the buts.'

He stood up and scraped back his chair. 'Come with me.'

Amy allowed herself to be led to the cellar door. She

stood in shocked silence as he turned a huge key in the lock.

'Let's go down,' he urged.

She watched as he lit a lamp, showed no resistance when he led her into a blackness lit only by a spill of light from his lantern. 'We used to play hide and seek down here,' she said. Her words bounced from walls and back into her ears. This was his secret. He was about to show her his true self, whatever that was.

They travelled past the wall that restrained coals, Amy holding fast to his hand while he made his practised way through several small cellars. At last, he stopped and placed the lantern on an upturned crate.

She breathed in the cellar's dankness, a scent given only to places never visited by sunlight. As her eyes adjusted, they lit upon a rocking horse, a dolls' house, a case from which spilled assorted small toys. Closing her eyes, she sent herself back to childhood, saw three little girls playing and squabbling over the better doll, a father acting like a bear, chasing, catching, causing shrieks and squeals of delight. Amy swallowed. Yes, this had been her home.

James unlocked another door, led her into one of the very tiny rooms. She stopped abruptly in her tracks, saw a slice of light piercing a grating, followed its path until her gaze rested on a figure of the crucified Christ. The table on which it stood was clothed in a pristine white cloth on which rested a makeshift tabernacle and a pair of tall candlesticks.

From behind a little curtain at the centre of this altar, James took a chalice, a paten, a stole.

Her throat was suddenly dry and tight. The food, the bread. He had been – no! Surely not? 'This is no more,' he whispered across two yards of semi-darkness. 'But I don't want you to think I sacrificed it for you. It is finished.'

'Finished?'

'I was released from my vows a month ago.'

There was nothing she could say, so she kept silent.

'Being ordained seemed a good idea at the time, Amy. I was raised a Catholic, was educated by monks. And my temper – my father's temper – kept me from living the ordinary life.' He stopped, pondered. 'As a priest, I felt safe. Then, coming here to mop up after my father, I began to feel differently, became a man who had made a mistake.'

This was a mistake of giant proportions, thought Amy, as she absorbed the shock. 'You said you were a teacher.'

'I told no lie, Amy, for many priests teach as well as ministering. And, yes, I did see your father's war, as I was a chaplain for two years.'

Amy stood rigidly still. 'I don't know what to say,' she mumbled at last. 'You gave this up, but not because of me?'

'You are a part of it, but not the whole,' he said.

She nodded thoughtfully. 'You were a chaplain in the Great War. Then you went home to run a church and a school.' She felt forced to repeat everything in order to take in the magnitude of the moment.

'Yes.'

She paused for thought. 'What do you want from me, James Mulligan?'

'A wife,' he answered, 'a soulmate, one who cares for and about others.'

Amy bowed her head. This promised to be complicated, though anything worth having usually arrived with baggage. This handsome philanthropist was to share her life. The concept of refusing him did not enter her consciousness, because she had loved him since . . . since for ever, since before meeting him. 'I will marry you,' she said, noticing that he was completely motionless. 'Did you think I would say no?'

He waved a hand through light and shadow, the move sweeping across all the tools of his calling – candlesticks, vestments, the paraphernalia of Mass and Communion. 'I am, to say the least of it, a Catholic, and my children must be reared as such.'

'I don't mind,' she replied.

'And you will live here with me?'

'Yes.'

'And the yard?' he asked.

'The yard will continue,' she answered. Mona still had the wash-house, there was A Cut Above, there were people who had worked there for donkey's years. 'We shall rename it Mulligan's Yard officially,' she said, 'because Margot will not

383

mind and I am to become Mrs Mulligan. You deserve recognition for what you have done in this town.'

He crossed the space and knelt before her.

'Get up,' she chided. 'I shall only laugh.'

'Marry me,' he ordered.

'I will,' she returned, 'but get off your knees.' She smiled up at him after he had risen. 'Why didn't you come as a priest? Why did you pretend to be a layman?'

He laughed softly. 'Would you have done business with a priest? A raving Roman?'

'I don't know,' she answered.

'Then never mind, for we are agreed, are we not?' He spat on his hand, shook hers. 'That's a good bit of business we just did, my love, and we have shaken on it, too.'

'Yes, James, you played a good hand there.'

They left the cellar, left the past behind and climbed stone steps into the kitchen.

In the hallway of Pendleton Grange, an elderly Irishwoman wept into her apron. With the turn of an ace, her brother had brought together this wonderful couple. She dried her eyes and spoke into the soft silence of morning. 'For once, you played well,' she told Thomas Mulligan. 'May God forgive me for saying so.'

Boo